The House of Brides

The House of Brides

A Novel

Jane Cockram

An Imprint of HarperCollinsPublishers

THE HOUSE OF BRIDES. Copyright © 2019 by Jane Cockram. All rights reserved. Printed in the United States of America. No part of this book may be used or reproduced in any manner whatsoever without written permission except in the case of brief quotations embodied in critical articles and reviews. For information, address HarperCollins Publishers, 195 Broadway, New York, NY 10007.

HarperCollins books may be purchased for educational, business, or sales promotional use. For information, please e-mail the Special Markets Department at SPsales@harpercollins.com.

FIRST HARPERLUXE EDITION

ISBN: 978-0-06-294479-5

HarperLuxe™ is a trademark of HarperCollins Publishers.

Library of Congress Cataloging-in-Publication Data is available upon request.

19 20 21 22 23   LSC   10 9 8 7 6 5 4 3 2 1

For Alice and Edward

The family—
that dear octopus from whose tentacles
we never quite escape, nor, in our
most inmost hearts, ever quite wish to.

—DODIE SMITH

The House
of Brides

Prologue

Yesterday I found an article about Barnsley House in an old magazine. It took me a moment to recognize it; I was unprepared to stumble upon it and had only known it in winter, anyway. It was a shock to see the place captured in the full glory of sunshine, and before I knew what I was doing I had ripped out the pages to savor later, away from the prying eyes of the others.

In one photograph, the blue curve of the harbor is filled with sailboats and fishing trawlers. It's likely they took the photos years ago, when the hotel first opened. In the spring perhaps, when the weather was starting to warm up, the fields around not yet burned in the summer heat. Max says at that time of the year the sky is full of drones taking photos for country houses about to come on the market, and pictures of the famous coastline for lifestyle television programs.

I see that view every time I close my eyes, but it's better to have it here in front of me: the grass sloping away so that the cliffs and the village beyond lie hidden, the line of sea concealing sandbars beneath deceitful waves. From Barnsley you can't see the cobbled harbor or the pier from which the little ferry departs every hour, tide permitting, to tour the coastline. You can't see the fish and chip shops and the galleries with their blown glass or the tucked-away cafés and terraces of bed and breakfasts, and yet here they all are in the photographs, as if they were a part of the hotel itself.

It's easy to remember what it felt like to see Barnsley for the first time. Not in a photograph but in the flesh, the grand house appearing in front of me. The beauty of the limestone is hard to see in a photograph, and harder to explain. The stone is different from that of other houses in the area, softer somehow, and in the summer, Max said, it felt warm to touch for weeks on end. Some days, when the sun was not strong enough to warm Daphne's cold antipodean bones, she would lean up against the wall and hope that the warmth would penetrate through her summer dress and cardigan. That was before my time. It has only been cold, bitterly cold, since I have known it.

Will the hotel be successful again? Or is the article pointless, directing wealthy American tourists towards a house of ghosts? A hotel that has lost its way, and the woman who ran it, and not in that order. I have to hope we can turn Barnsley around, because it has somehow gotten in my blood, just like it got in the blood of the women who came before me.

1

"A toast to Miranda," my father said as he raised his glass to the air, then collided it heavily with the similarly upheld glass of my stepmother. "May your career at Grant and Farmer be long and successful!"

It wasn't the first time he had toasted a new direction in my career—god knows there had been a few twists and turns before this last crash and burn—but it was the first time he had been involved in getting me the job. After everything that had happened, I didn't really have a choice not to take it.

My father had had to call in a few favours. And when that didn't work, I think he had to start making promises. Compromises. I don't think it got to actual exchanges of money, but I'm not sure. I didn't think I was imagining things when I detected a slight threat in his voice. A more than slight emphasis on the word *long*.

"Yes, darling Miranda. Good luck at Grace and Favour!" my stepmother Fleur said, joining in the toast even though she had already finished her second glass of champagne.

I laughed despite myself. Fleur was really only funny for a small portion of the day, somewhere between her second and fourth drink. And that window was much shorter than you might expect, given her expertise at consuming champagne and dry white wine.

Plus, I wanted to enjoy this celebration while it lasted; it was the first time we had had anything to celebrate for a while. Judging by the look in my two younger stepsisters' eyes as they sat quietly and poked the ice cubes in their lemonade while the merriment continued around them, they also knew just how quickly things could change. *Just wait*, their faces were saying, *she'll muck this up as well.*

"What's someone with a degree in creative writing going to do at a PR company?" my godmother Denise asked, turning towards me after the toast had settled down. As usual, my family had chosen to forget about my postgrad studies in nutrition and diet. Around us, the waiters set down trays of antipasti: glossy grilled red sweet peppers, fat rolls of prosciutto, and plump

Sicilian olives. My favourite Italian restaurant, this was always the location for any family celebration, and as far as family celebrations go, me finally getting another job was fairly significant. At least that's what it seemed my father was trying to tell me by inviting everyone in the family, including my godparents, along to the celebratory dinner.

"What's someone with a degree in creative writing going to do anywhere?" my father boomed from his end of the table, laughing loudly at his own joke and looking around to make sure some of the surrounding patrons were laughing as well. So much for me trying to go unnoticed.

"Isn't all PR creative writing?" Fleur interjected. "Or am I getting confused with fake news?"

I was worried all the talk about creative writing might veer into a discussion about the creative writing that had landed me in hot water, so I concentrated on Denise when I answered. "I think I'm just going to be more like an EA to begin with—I won't have anything to do with actual clients. Maybe eventually I'll be able to work on some copy, things like that, I guess."

I didn't sound any more enthusiastic than I felt. Working on copy was so far away from what I had been doing. Running my own business. A successful blog. A book deal. The media said I was an influencer.

"What's an EA?" one of my half sisters piped up. Ophelia, that time, but it could have just as easily been Juliet, given that their general knowledge was equally nonexistent. And yes, we all have names from Shakespeare. My mother started the tradition, and my stepmother continued it. My name meant something to my mother, whereas I suspect my stepmother had to use Google. Math brain, she says. Pea brain, I think.

"They book flights, arrange meeting rooms, that kind of thing," my stepmother cooed, stroking Ophelia's hair soothingly due to the potentially upsetting nature of this disclosure. "And that's why you don't want to do an arts degree." Ophelia and Juliet nodded solemnly, even though they were years away from making any decisions about their tertiary educations.

I concentrated on loading my plate with a selection of the antipasti, paying more attention than I really needed to on getting the placement of the food just so, trying to blink away the tears that were threatening to spill down on the terra-cotta side plates.

"I think it sounds lovely," said Denise and squeezed my hand, but the sympathy in her voice made it worse. She would be thinking of my mother, her best friend, and wondering how I could have turned out so mediocre when my mother had been so extraordinary. I wished she would go back to London with her perfect little family and leave me here with people who didn't expect too much of me. It was easier that way.

Conversation turned to a skiing trip Denise and Terence had planned. I felt myself zoning out, thinking instead about the *casarecce* with eggplant and Italian sausage that would soon be coming my way, and the tiramisu to follow if I was willing to risk Fleur's disapproving comments.

"And this is why she can't hold down a real job," I heard my father saying just as I realized the waiter was trying to place my dinner in front of me. "Daydreaming all the time." It was true, I was a daydreamer. My dad used to think it was funny, charming even, but lately he had been making all sorts of pointed comments. *You can't be this vague all your life, Miranda. You're twenty-six now—isn't it time you faced reality?*

I could see why he was worried. I couldn't imagine myself sitting at a desk all day, paying attention in long meetings, remembering numbers, names, dates—but that's what I'd be doing when I started at Grant and Farmer.

There was laughter all around: shrill from Fleur, polite from Denise. I could see her watching me again, and I smiled weakly to show I was okay.

The noise of the restaurant was gathering in volume as the night progressed. Chairs were scraped back as patrons rose to greet each other, the sommelier squeezed corks out of prosecco bottles, and waiters carried endless bowls of steaming pasta out of the kitchen. The mood was light, the smells heavenly, and at tables all around us people were smiling, laughing, sipping on Chianti and pinot grigio, leaning in to hear each other properly above the buzz.

All the tables except for ours. If it wasn't for the food and the conversation arising from it, we would have been almost completely silent. *What did you order? Spaghetti* alle vongole. *Looks delicious, don't you have mature tastes? This Barolo is delicious, Bruce. Yes, it's a favourite of ours. This place never changes, does it? That's why we like it, Terence.*

It had been a bad idea to invite the O'Hallorans: somehow the presence of outsiders highlighted the unease that I had somehow grown accustomed to over the years, and now I could see what our cobbled-together family must look like through their eyes. If my mother were here, our table would look just like the others and I'm sure I wasn't the only one thinking that. The tiramisu would have to wait for another time. I needed to get out of there.

"Girls? Do you want me to take you home? Haven't you got some homework or oboe practice to do?"

The relief on Juliet's and Ophelia's faces was immediate. The evening opened up in front of them: a frenzy of social media, Netflix, and phone calls while their parents were out of the house. It wasn't easy growing up with my father and all his rules.

No phone calls after 9:00 p.m.
No phones in the bedroom.
No television during the week.
No sleepovers with the opposite sex.
No phones at the table.
No piercings.
No tattoos.
No alcohol.
No drugs.
No. No. No.

I know, I lived with him for a long time. Too long, if you ask me. And him. And Fleur.

And now I'm back at home again.

Juliet and Ophelia, though, they still seem to think I'm cool, if only because I can drive them around and go on my phone whenever I like. They even think it's cool I now work at an activewear store and can get them discounts on the compression tights they and their friends wear at all times. Unfortunately, my father is not so easily impressed.

"Take my car, poppet." My dad made a big fuss of pulling his car key out, closing his hand around mine. "We'll get an Uber." Like he was doing me a favour.

Juliet and Ophelia chatted all the way home in the car about school, boys, their friends, *The Voice*.

"Why didn't you guys pipe up at dinner?" I said after ten minutes had gone by and I was finally able to get a word in. "You seem to have a bit to say now."

"Denise is weird. She always looks at us funny when we talk. She hates us," Juliet offered.

"And she hates Mum." So Ophelia felt the same.

"That's not true." I hadn't thought of it that way before. I just thought of Denise and Terence as part of the family.

"It is. And she's always staring at you with this weird look on her face. Have you noticed?"

I turned the corner into my old street, barely paying attention to the road. Even though I had lived away from home for a few years, I could still drive here on autopilot.

I still thought of it as home: the fixer-upper Federation my parents had bought when they were first married and thought they had all the time in the world together. Turned out they didn't have that long, and the house didn't get fixed up until years later, when Fleur and her retinue of expensive architects and builders came on the scene.

"No," I lied.

Denise *had* spent a lot of time on this visit staring at me. People had always told me I looked nothing like my mother, that I totally resembled my father. Your mother was beautiful, they would say in the same breath, as if I couldn't understand the implication.

But maybe Denise could see something in me? Maybe I was becoming more like my mother as I aged? I tried to check my reflection in the rearview mirror as I pulled up by the house, but I couldn't see anything in the dim twilight. There was a loud scrape as the wheels hit the gutter. I cursed under my breath as I realized the rubbish collectors had left our empty bins across the driveway.

"Oh, Dad's going to kill you," Juliet whispered. Glee, there was definitely glee in her voice. "How many champagnes did you have, anyway? Alky!" They laughed together, high on freedom, lemonade, and schadenfreude.

"I barely finished one." It was true, I wasn't much of a drinker. I probably would have ordered a Diet Coke if Denise and Terence hadn't been there. "Can you please move the bins?"

The request was met with the sound of slamming doors. The pair of them raced up the stone steps.

I pressed the button for the window. "Ophelia? Juliet? Can one of you please move the rubbish bins?"

"Come on, Miranda, I'm busting." Ophelia made a show of hopping from one foot to the other, a movement that owed more to years of speech and drama lessons than any actually pressing bladder needs. "Just leave the car there. Dad won't mind."

I looked up at the tree above the car, its sap the subject of numerous family arguments over the years. The tyre was pushed right up against the kerb—any damage would only be visible once it was moved.

"Okay." I sighed. "Next time don't drink so much lemonade." It was only for a moment, I told myself; I'd come back and move the bins and the car once I got the girls sorted. I climbed the stairs to join them, admiring the garden as I went.

For all Fleur's faults, she did have a talent for gardening. Or landscape architecture, as she always corrected me. At this time of the year the garden looked amazing, and a well-placed light highlighted the blooming jacaranda in all its glory. My mum would have loved it. One of the few things I had been able to deduce from her writing was her love for the natural world, her affinity with the outdoors.

The scent of the house hit me as I opened the door. Closed up all day, it seemed to have manifested its fragrance: the remains of Fleur's ever-present fig candles, gardenia blossoms floating in a bowl on the hall table, and the unmistakable scent of a pine Christmas tree. Underneath it all, the smell of home. Some things hadn't changed, despite everything.

"Christmas tree already?" I asked Ophelia as she pushed past me, her desperate need for the toilet seemingly forgotten, while I idly riffled through some mail on the hall table.

For a long time, there hadn't been any for me. School magazines from time to time. Catalogues. Nothing interesting.

And then the thick envelopes from lawyers' offices had started coming in. Some days there were bundles of them. Other days just one or two. But for a few months, it was relentless.

I breathed a sigh of relief that there was nothing for me today.

"You know Mum," Ophelia called back. I heard her collapse on the sofa, the noise of the TV swelling into life. She was home, and could switch off. From where I stood, I could see Juliet through the bank of glass windows at the back of the house.

I nearly flicked past the envelope. Brown paper with

one corner completely covered in jewel-colored stamps, all imprinted with the Queen's tiny little head in profile. The exact sort of envelope I had spent my whole childhood looking out for.

The address had been crossed out and rewritten, crossed out and rewritten again. It looked as if it had been in the postal system for some time, and had obviously come halfway around the world. That wasn't the odd part, though. The odd part was who it was addressed to.

My mother.

2

The letter had been opened. The flap, once diligently stuck down with layers of thick tape, now
floundered adrift from the main body of the thing, the
tape dried up and useless. The return address was familiar to me: more symbolic than anything, a beacon
from the past rather than an actual place. Barnsley
House. It was like receiving a letter from the North
Pole or heaven.

Of course, I had looked for that return address in
my youth. On the backs of birthday cards and envelopes. Every time a letter arrived with the regal stamp
in the corner, every time I saw the Queen's head on the
blue, purple, and teal backgrounds, I had hoped that
this time, the letter would be from Barnsley.

In the end, my father bought me a stamp album. He

had misinterpreted my interest in the post for a keen interest in philately. For years I diligently tore out the stamps and soaked them off the paper in a saucer filled with water, even though I had no interest in them at all. My only interest was in finding a letter from the address written on the envelope in front of me now.

It was enough for a moment just to stare at the mystical formation of those letters.

I took a deep breath, trying to dull my anticipation slightly. After twenty years, I had come up with more than enough scenarios for this moment. A small but meaningful outreach. A Christmas message. An offer of full-scale adoption.

This was different, though. The letter was addressed to my mother. Did they not know she was dead?

Listening carefully for the movements of my half sisters, I moved across into my father's study, the door barely making a sound as it closed over the plush carpet. Dusk had moved quickly through the room, making it harder to read the words, so I took the letter to the window seat, forcing myself to sit down and breathe despite the rush of blood in my ears.

I slowly unfolded the paper, paying close attention to the thick cream stock of it and then bringing it close to my nose. Musty, yes. But a slight smell of damp. Smoke, even. I had expected a Proustian moment—a waft of my mother's tea rose perfume or a healthy masculine cologne—but I was disappointed; it didn't remind me of anything apart from the fireplace in the damp beach shack we used to rent at Wilsons Prom over Easter.

I read the letter, the first time quickly and the second time slowly, trying to find details that weren't there.

Dear Tessa,

I found your photo by accident. I shouldn't have been looking. Dad always said I'm too curious for my own good, but that's what comes from no one ever telling me anything.

The trouble in this place is, you go looking for answers to one question and you end up finding an entirely separate batch of secrets.

Anyway. I found a photo of you, and you looked friendly, normal. Not like people in old photos normally look, with weird hairdos and funny jumpers.

When I turned over the photo, it said, "Tessa, 19," in spidery old writing, like whoever wrote it was afraid to press too hard with their Biro.

For some reason, I had never thought of you as a real person. I mean, I knew you wrote The Book. I knew you had been gone for a long time. But I had never thought you might have been able to help us. We hadn't really needed help before.

Something bad has happened. There's something wrong with my mum. Dad says someone needs to look after us, but he says we need to keep it in the family. He is going to send us to boarding school after Christmas. Even Agatha. Despite what's happened.

Will you come and help us? Please.
Love, Sophia Summer (your niece)

It was a shock to hear a young, contemporary voice from Barnsley. A voice that could belong to any of the young girls I knew—a voice that sounded like Ophelia, or Juliet. I had read *The House of Brides* hundreds of times. My mother's book was a best seller when it was published and went on to sell hundreds of thousands of copies before it went out of print in the late 1990s. But I hadn't before thought what the book might mean to the people who lived at Barnsley today. That they might refer to it as The Book in the same reverential and singular way I did.

The House of Brides was my only connection to my mother and her past, and even then, it wasn't the most personal connection. What I knew about Barnsley House was what all the readers knew about it. And what I remembered about my mother was pretty much what they knew as well. It was more than that: my mother *was* the book, and the book was the reason I studied creative writing at university.

The House of Brides went deeply into the history of Barnsley House; the women who had married into the family and brought more fame and prestige with them. They were writers and architects and socialites, women who, unusually for their time, had pushed the boundaries and found success, notoriety. Sarah Summer. Beatrice Summer. Their names were more familiar to me than those of some of my father's living relatives. Between those women and my mother, I had a lot of pressure on me to do something special with my life.

Most of the time I had been scouring the book for clues about my mother, fruitlessly. Counter to the modern trend of writers inserting themselves into the nonfiction narrative, she was curiously absent. I could feel her attention to detail, her swift turn of phrase, but there was nothing else of her in it, nothing apart from the familiar head shot: her hair fair and fluffy, her smile wide and nonthreatening.

Her book was a straightforward history of Barnsley House and the women who had lived there over several generations. There were scandals, yes: suicides and secret liaisons and the obligatory gothic tropes—secret rooms, ghosts, and unexplained fires—but it was a book of history. A past typical of a country house of that era but I had always imagined Barnsley as a benign place now. Perhaps I was wrong.

All this time I had been wanting someone from Barnsley to come looking for me. But now that someone had, I wasn't so sure it was what I wanted after all.

3

Barnsley House. I typed the name in and then looked at it, listening to the sounds of the house around me, waiting for some sort of sign that it was safe to proceed. Outside, the street was quiet, apart from the occasional car door or the slam of a basketball against a backboard in our neighbour's driveway. There was a limited amount of time before my father and Fleur came back from dinner, and I didn't want to answer their questions about what I was doing just yet. I didn't really know what I was doing just yet.

Wikipedia, Great Houses of England, TripAdvisor; a raft of entries came up. I clicked on the Wikipedia link, thinking an overview would be the best place to start.

Barnsley House

Barnsley House, also known as Barnsley House Hotel, is situated in a unique geographical location at the tip of two coves on the rugged coast of England's West Country. Continuously the family seat of the Summer family for over two hundred years, it passed to the ownership of Maximilian Summer in 1987 and is run as a country house hotel with the Michelin-starred restaurant The Summer Room. The garden is supposed to have been designed by Hugo Bostock, but there is no known documentation of this, and it is considered by most historians to be too far south of Bostock's usual area and thus most likely derivative.

The house, then known as Barnslaigh, first appears on maps in the seventeenth century. By the eighteenth century it was the site of a small ferry point in a line that ran in the summer months between the villages dotted along that coastline. The water was notoriously rough, and the ferry service now runs only in the warmest months. Consequently, the land and the small manor house were sold off to a local farmer, Montgomery Summer, who was expanding his already substantial landholdings. Summer built the house that stands there today.

Unusually for the time, Barnsley was built in stone brought in from the Cotswolds, and as a consequence the house is striking, and unique in the area. The gardens, which in their heyday were overseen by eighteen full-time gardeners and ground staff, have been restored and updated in recent years to their former glory by the current incumbent.

Barnsley House has a long and colourful history and is known locally as "The House of Brides," in reference to the best-selling book by the same name, written by Tessa Summer. The book's title refers to the distinctive character of Barnsley's chatelaines over the years. Although the house has come close to sale a number of times, it has always been these enterprising and resourceful women who have saved the estate from passing from family hands.

The first and most notable "bride" was Elspeth Summer, who convinced her husband to build her the aptly named Summer House on an island just offshore from the main house. Elspeth was a complete hermit, and refused to accompany her husband on his travels abroad. He brought her back a collection of unusual plants from all over the world and she had great success in establishing an almost tropical garden on the site. Her love of white wine from France was well known, and she attempted to start a vineyard on the island to grow the grapes to make her own. This project failed in the adverse conditions, but the island was renamed Minerva Island by the family after a rare grape varietal from France (*minervae*). Still known by that name, it is private but open to tour groups during the summer months.

Elspeth's daughter-in-law, Sarah Summer, unusually for the time, accompanied her husband on many of his travels, and developed a keen interest in architecture. Inspired by their grand tours, she controversially oversaw the transformation of the nearby Anglican chapel of St. John's in Minton to an almost exact replica of a tiny Italian church she had visited in Tuscany.

Much later, in the early twentieth century, Barnsley House was the home of the famous writer Gertrude Summer, one of the last American heiresses—who married the then owner and brought with her an American fortune. She used the house as a backdrop for her crime fiction, lampooning the British upper class who refused to accept her into their inner circle. In the process Barnsley House became almost as well known as her books, the sales from which, along with her inheritance, propped up the estate for years. The marriage ended amid claims of infidelity, and Gertrude moved farther along the coast, where she would live for the rest of her life.

The house fell into disrepair after the Second World War, in which it had gained some notoriety as a training ground for intelligence officers. It had a brief resurgence under the ownership of Maximilian Summer (senior) and his wife Beatrice, who became known for their wild house parties during a time when most other country houses were being sold and entertaining as a whole was being scaled back. The notorious and short-lived Barnsley Festival was both founded and then folded under their watch.

By the time the current owner, Max Summer, inherited from his father Maximilian, the house was decrepit and the debts were piling up. Together with

his wife, Daphne Summer, Max Summer has rein-
vigorated Barnsley House as a luxury country house
hotel.

Most of this I already knew, or had a vague knowledge of. There was no mention of anything untoward
happening lately, despite what Sophia mentioned in her
letter.

I assumed Sophia was Max and Daphne's daughter.
There was no mention of any children on the Wikipedia page, so I quickly clicked on the link for Daphne
Summer. It directed me towards an article from the
Daily Telegraph from July, and I read it hungrily, eager
to find something written about Daphne from an outsider's point of view.

For the longest time, I had cared about nothing except myself. Or to be more specific, what other people
thought of me. My entire existence was based around
projecting an image of my lifestyle, and if something
wasn't on Instagram, then in my mind it hadn't happened. I had missed a lot. The real world. Friends.
Family. Common decency.

It felt good to be thinking about something else.

4

THE SUMMER SUNSHINE

BY KELLY O'HARA

Somehow you get the feeling that Daphne Summer—celebrity chef, newspaper columnist, and cookbook author—doesn't like the spotlight. In fact, she seems to positively hate it. If she could let the food speak for itself, she would, she says.

Unlike other chefs of our time, she doesn't have an urgent need to reinvent the wheel, or change the way our nation eats; she just wants to make good food, and she wants to make it using ingredients from close to home. Oh, and she wants the rest of us to do that too.

Even this desire is punctuated by her characteristic self-deprecating cackle, and as we sit in the garden outside her eponymously named restaurant Summer House, she blows her fringe out of her eyes and says, "Well, maybe I do want to change the way people eat after all." She is on a break between a hectic lunch service packed with day-trippers and local diners, who she says are her mainstay, and a full house expecting dinner that evening. On the lawn in front of us, her three children frolic, the picture of health and happiness, only calling to their mother to watch the occasional handstand or cartwheel.

Her Australian accent, barely recognizable on her television program, is stronger in real life, and she says if not for Max Summer, who she romantically met and married within a week in the late nineties, she would be back in the Sydney she still misses. Lucky for us she did meet him, because the food I've just eaten in the Summer House was like nothing else I've experienced in this part of the world.

The flavours are delicate without being fussy, and it seems as if the ingredients have had very little done to them, which usually means a very great deal has been done. The provenance of each dish is listed on the handwritten menu: the seafood comes from local fishermen, whose tiny vessels I could watch bobbing in the cove as I ate; the lamb from the farm attached to Barnsley House, and also run by the Summer family for generations; and the herbs which enliven every dish are picked the same morning from the extensive kitchen gardens bordering the house, where Daphne has invited us to wander as we chat.

Not formally trained, Daphne learned her skills at the high-end restaurants that used to be attached to every five-star hotel in London. At first, as a young and poor Aussie backpacker, she washed dishes, and then she worked her way up through the kitchen, finally cooking under some of the more well-known enfants terribles of the nineties restaurant scene. It was outside one of these kitchens that she met her husband.

Sneaking out for a post-shift cigarette, she ran into Max, who was doing the same, trying to escape from an unsuccessful date in the dining room.

As we talk, Daphne frequently interrupts to point out things in her garden. "It's a far cry from the old veggie patch I grew up with," she says, gathering broad beans into an enamel colander along the way. "My dad worked at the bank, but he loved his garden, and he had a small plot for vegetables.

Nothing like this, though: half the time we had enormous gluts of silverbeet and rhubarb and the rest of the time the snails got to things before we could. It made me realize, though, just how much work goes into growing one carrot, so now, as a cook, I make certain I treat that carrot with some respect."

Daphne seems to make a point of never calling herself a chef, instead referring to herself as a cook. Despite the awards she has received, she says she still feels more comfortable with it that way. "I'm not a chef. I'm just someone who loves food, and wants to share it with as many people as possible. There's only so much my family can eat, so it became a job. That's all." It's a typical remark from this humble woman, whose cookbook *My Summer House* was one of the best selling of the last year.

Still striking in her mid-forties, I imagine she must have been quite a stunner when she met Max. When I mention this, the cackle comes again, before she fixes me with a beady eye. "Max likes signs of great character, and deplores weakness. Too often a pretty face can be misinterpreted as either." She refuses to elaborate, instead refilling my glass of rosé as we arrive back on the terrace.

And what of the rumours that a problem with alcohol shut down production of her first series last year? She only occasionally sips wine, and she chooses her words carefully. "It's a common thing in this industry. The stress of service, combined with the blissful relief of a drink afterwards, and one can trigger the other. There was an incident, and it was blown completely out of proportion. I've cut back since then, but for me, as a cook, a meal without wine is no meal at all."

The remote location of Barnsley House, set on a spectacular coastline above a series of rocky beaches, is greatly appealing to the people who come here to escape the world. Its end-of-the-earth charm is nice to visit, but living here must be lonely. Daphne doesn't think so, though. "I could stay here forever. People are always asking me to come up to London, to consult on this one or cook at this thing, but I'm happy here. I have everything I need."

With that, she bites the end off a broad bean and spits it out in the garden, squeezing out the glorious green buds within for me to examine. "You see? What else could I want?" She's right: Barnsley House is as close to paradise as you can get.

For more information, visit barnsleyhousehotel. co.uk. The author was a guest of the West Country Tourist Board.

I was sitting thinking about what I had just read when I heard a car pull up out front. Hurriedly, I erased my search history and closed down the tabs. From the window I could see my father getting out of the Uber, smiling at the driver, and then holding the door open for Fleur. His smile quickly disappeared as he caught sight of his car parked under the tree. Even from the house, I could see that the sticky sap he so despised had already made a mess of his roof, and I immediately regretted my impulsive decision to leave the car there.

My father, who had helped me through the last year. He had supported me when everyone else in the world was calling me a liar, and rightfully so. He had moved heaven and earth to get me a job with some old friends, a job in which, if I was really honest, I'd be lucky to see out the three-month probation.

Something told me that tonight was not the time to bring up the letter; in fact, my deepest instinct was not to mention it at all.

On an impulse—what else?—I dashed back to my father's desk and opened the small safe underneath the chair. The code, despite everything, was my mother's birthday. It always had been. I just hadn't had to use it before.

Nineteen sixty-eight. The Summer of Love. Student protests in Paris. And my mother, landing on the earth, in the middle of nowhere. Barnsley House. I wondered if her life might have turned out differently had she been born somewhere else.

It was dark inside the safe, and I was in too much of a rush to turn the light on. My father and Fleur were on the front steps now.

"How hard is it to put the car in the garage?"

"She was probably distracted." Fleur must be tired of sticking up for me.

"She does it on purpose. So bloody ungrateful."

" 'After all I've done for her,' " I said to myself, thrusting my hand deep inside the safe, just as my father said those exact words outside the window.

The doorbell rang loudly. Dad's keys were on the table in the hall. Unsurprisingly, there were no sounds of my stepsisters. Ophelia was probably asleep on the sofa by now, Juliet still outside on her phone. My fingers finally wrapped around the small blue book, almost new and hard around the edges from lack of use. I slammed the safe shut and pushed the chair back into position.

"Miranda!" He sounded angry now. Racing towards the door, I half tripped over the side of his rug, at the same time as my phone started to buzz on the desk where I had left it.

My father had hidden my passport from me in the depths of my misery. He thought I was a flight risk. I'd known where it was all along, I just didn't have anywhere to go. I jammed it down the front of my leggings as I unlatched the front door. Just in case. At the last moment, I tucked the letter in there as well.

5

My father didn't come inside straightaway. Instead, he and Fleur had a quiet discussion I could not discern even though I was standing quietly on the other side of the door, my breath held, trying to work out if I had time to retrieve my phone. They had years of practice at this, having raised three daughters together. I too had years of practice at listening, unsuccessfully, the function of my ears having turned out to be only slightly better than my eyesight, despite years of consuming excess bananas. #potassium #hearhear #wellness

This was bad. If my father was moderately upset, he would call the name of the offending daughter as soon as he opened the front door. Summoned in this way, the daughter would appear, slightly cautious but unfazed, knowing that for the greatest infractions a conference would first be held with Fleur. Motivations would be discussed and character assessments made, and eventually a punishment would be agreed upon, all inaudibly. An immediate summons is in itself a sort of reprieve.

I am a grown woman, and even now, I know this is how it works. I should have put the car away. I should have moved the bins. I shouldn't have been lazy or listened to teenagers. Listening to teenagers had gotten me in trouble before.

I decided to risk it. Experience told me these conversations could go on for some time. I dashed back into the office and grabbed my phone.

"Miranda!"

I jumped. I had been so carefully listening for the small sounds, I was not at all ready for the big ones. The passport slipped ever so slightly from my waistband. Surprising, as my waistband had been quite tight of late.

"Dad?"

The door pushed open wider. I stood frozen in the middle of the room. It was too late to pretend to be doing anything. My hand went instinctively to the rose gold fob chain necklace—a family heirloom passed down from my mother—at my neck. I never take it off, even though it hangs low and annoys me while I run. Or used to annoy me when I still ran.

"What are you doing in here?" my father barked.

This question was like an impulse from him, the words out before he knew it. One of his many rules: no loitering in his office.

"Just . . . just looking up something on your computer."

I was hoping that Dad's command of computers remained as rudimentary as ever. The year before he'd surprised me by hiring an expert to bury negative search engine results with a series of more recent and more positive stories—which didn't work, by the way. There's an old saying, "The cream rises to the top," which might have made sense in the days when people used to keep a cow in the backyard, but in cyberspace it's just not true. The pale watery stuff, the part without any flavour or substance, that's what sticks around these days.

Anyway, I didn't want him to know I'd been looking up Barnsley House on his computer.

"I want to talk to you about something else." I looked out the window; the car was already covered in the sticky sap he hated so much. Fleur had disappeared, deep into the house. Even she didn't want to be around for my latest disappointment.

"The car. I'm sorry."

Dad looked out the window, his face changing. His shoulders dropped slightly, like the battle he was preparing for had suddenly been called off. Breath visibly left his body.

When he spoke, his voice was almost weary. I didn't know if it was the carb overload or the Barolo, but he was tired.

"I've asked you to put the car in the garage before, Miranda. The sap does irreparable damage to the paint if left for more than a few hours."

I wanted to say that it was Ophelia's fault, that she was desperate to use the bathroom, that I meant to go back and move it, but even in my head those sounded like more petty excuses. By the sound of Dad's voice, he'd had enough of my excuses.

"Sorry. I'll take it down to the car wash in the morning."

Fifty dollars. That's how much the car wash cost, the only one my dad let near his car. Fifty dollars left a big dent in my paycheck these days.

"What did you do with the letter?"

I was so busy thinking about the car wash that I didn't see his question coming. "What letter? I didn't see any letter . . ." This was not convincing. Not by anyone's standards. Certainly not by mine.

"Don't lie to me, Miranda! I've had enough of the lies." Dad moved towards me, and for a moment, just a moment, I thought I had finally pushed him too far. Despite everything that we'd been through together, he had never reacted like this.

I stepped back, hitting the desk. He had me cornered. The impact of the desk on my body brought him back to himself, and he breathed out. A long, frustrated sigh.

"Miranda." He held his hand out towards me, expecting me to give in.

So I did. I fished the letter out from the waistband of my leggings. As soon as it was clear of my body, he snatched it from me and thrust it deep into his own pocket, without checking the contents. "I know what you're thinking, Miranda."

This was impressive because even I had no idea what I was thinking. All I knew was that I had found a letter with a plea for help from a relative I had never met. That I had been waiting to hear from someone, anyone, from Barnsley for as long as I could remember. That at this point it would be nice to be useful. To have a fresh start. I wouldn't call it thinking, though. *Thinking* was too precise a word for the giant maelstrom of emotion I was experiencing.

"What am I thinking?"

"You're thinking this might be a way to escape all your problems."

I pictured myself at the airport. Carry-on luggage only. Waving my father and Fleur off at the gate. Tears in their eyes. Even better, I pictured my arrival at Heathrow. A large family greeting me. An old uncle, a gaggle of friendly teenagers. An overgrown and shaggy wolfhound. In an airport? It was a fantasy, after all.

"I'm starting a new job next week." I hoped it sounded more convincing than it felt.

"Yes."

"I haven't got any money."

"No."

"I've never met this girl."

"No."

"I've no obligation to her. She sent this letter to my mother. She doesn't even know I exist."

Dad looked shifty. "Does she know I exist?"

The house around me was quiet, as if it was holding its breath alongside me. Outside, the boy next door bounced a basketball in a steady rhythm only punctuated by irregular thuds against the backboard. Usually my father sighed in exasperation at this constant sound track to our evening, but tonight he didn't seem to notice. He did, however, step back and softly close the study door, as if he hadn't realized how utterly self-absorbed Ophelia and Juliet were and how little interest they would have in this conversation.

"Your mother and I tried to keep in touch with them. We sent them photos when you were born. When your mother died, I contacted her brother. Do you know what I got back? A solicitor's letter."

Oh. I was familiar with that feeling. My father rubbed his eyes. The buzz from the wine at dinner had faded, leaving him tired and crumpled.

"What did it say?" I tried to ignore the crushing disappointment building inside me. Tried to forget about the years of thinking there might be a letter from my mother's family. That there must have been some reason they didn't get in touch. From the look on my father's face, it didn't seem like that letter was the one I had been waiting for all these years either.

"It didn't say much at all. Just the usual solicitor-speak. That neither your mother nor any of her descendants had any claim on the Barnsley estate."

"Nothing else?"

"I assumed it was because of what happened with your mother when she left. But now I don't know if he even knew at all."

"What happened?"

He shook his head. Clammed up again, like all the other times in my childhood when I asked questions about my mother and her family. He wandered over to the sideboard and poured himself a whisky into one of the crystal tumblers Fleur had arranged just so.

"Is that safe to drink?" In all the years the whisky had been there, I had assumed it was just for show. Another Fleur touch. In fact, up until that moment I hadn't been 100 percent certain it wasn't cleaning fluid. By the look of the grimace on my father's face, he wasn't either.

"So, what I'm trying to say to you is: there is nothing there for you, whatever harebrained scheme you're cooking up. And I know you better than you know yourself—even if it hasn't occurred to you yet, at some time in the next day or so your mind will come back to this letter in my pocket, and you'll think maybe, just maybe, you should get involved."

"I wasn't . . ."

My father put his hand—the one holding the whisky—up vigorously. The tiniest amount of whisky splashed out on his hand. I watched the droplet sit there, anything rather than make eye contact. I wasn't sure I could disguise the emotion in my eyes.

"Some things—some people—are better left in the past. You might think it's a good idea to head over there and see what you can do to help. That you can make up for—" He hesitated. "That you can fix things for everyone. That you can do something extraordinary. But Miranda"—and he looked at me this time, square in the eye, and I couldn't do anything but look back—"it's time for you to grow up. It's time for you to accept that life is ordinary."

I knew he was wrong then. I knew that I was destined to do something great. Sure, I'd had a false start or two. Sure, I'd made a few mistakes. But if my mother had shown me one thing, it was that life didn't need to be ordinary. I didn't need to be ordinary.

I had been young, the day of our conversation, but my mother had been insistent. The fob chain—removed from her neck as she lay in the bath, warm water dripping down my neck and under my school tunic as I bent down to receive it—was a piece of my mother, the essence of my mother. I didn't know it was a farewell gift, that the words she spoke that day were a calculated bequest. That she must have known then how sick she was.

"This belonged to my mother. And now I'm giving it to you. It's a reminder of where I come from. Of where *you* come from." She stopped to draw breath—whether due to her illness or because she had always been inclined towards dramatic pauses. "Barnsley House."

I waited again, taking a moment to inspect the necklace closely. Even though it had always hung around my mother's neck, it was mine now, and every curvature of gold and precious link belonged to me. My fingers traced the initials etched into the shield:

P.G.

It didn't make sense. My grandmother's name had been Beatrice, the name my mother had chosen for me as a middle name. Miranda Beatrice Courtenay.

"The most beautiful place on earth," my mother said, her eyes roaming around her current situation in disdain. The bathroom had not yet been renovated. My mother had tried her best with a secondhand claw-footed bathtub, but the floorboards were bare and the wallpaper hung down in places. Many places. "One day maybe you will go there."

She closed her eyes. "Barnsley is so beautiful. So beautiful. It's magnetic. People are drawn to the place. Special people." Her eyes snapped open, fixed on mine. "People like you and me."

"Who's P.G.?" I asked, glad to have her attention. I showed her the shield, but she wouldn't look at it.

"The House of Brides."

I was too young then to know or understand the my-thology of the place. All I knew was that *The House of*

Brides was my mother's book. *The* book. She *was The House of Brides.*

"Sarah . . . Gertrude . . . Elspeth . . . there's been some amazing women in this family." My mother sat up, bathwater sloshing and cascading. I looked away, protecting my mother's privacy, but she grabbed my hand, forcing me to look at her. I tried not to notice how bony her fingers were, how her once strong body looked so frail. "Promise me, Miranda. Promise me not to be ordinary." Her lip curled slightly at the word. "Promise me you'll be an amazing woman too."

My skin prickled at the memory. There was a shout from next door. A basketball bounced heavily down the road. A dull thud as it landed on the bonnet of my father's car, and then the slightest pause before the car alarm pierced the still night air. We stood looking at each other for a moment longer, as if a few seconds more might clear the air between us and somehow magic away the disappointment and regrets of the last year. Finally my father sighed and turned to leave. I heard him grab the car keys from the dish outside in the hallway, and then suddenly his head reappeared in the doorway.

"Grant and Farmer, Miranda. Next Monday. No excuses." And then the front door slammed.

6

It was the shame that got me in the end. People say you can't run away from your problems, but you can. You just need to find somewhere like Barnsley with a dodgy internet connection and people so self-occupied that they couldn't care less about what everyone else in the world is doing. It was a shock to find people who didn't know or care what was happening on Instagram or social media. It was just what I needed.

It wasn't the letter that finally pushed me over the ledge, though. Despite what my father said that night in the study. I didn't have a plan at that point. But maybe the seed was planted, and all it took was for someone to nurture it along. In the end, it was some woman I didn't even know who made me hit rock bottom. A stranger. She was one of the few people who said something to my face. Most people hid behind their Twitter profiles or tried to soften the blow of what they were writing with endless hashtags. #authentic #wellness #phony

A normal day at work, a couple of days after I found the letter. It was my last week at the activewear store; I was due to start at Grant and Farmer the following Monday. Despite the building summer heat, I felt cold all the time. It was either the guilt or the air conditioning they ramped up in the shop to make customers feel more like trying on compression pants and man-made fibres.

The woman who tipped me over the edge seemed innocuous at first. Early forties, reasonably fit; good legs but self-conscious about her midsection. Standard weekday customer. We were getting along well. After everything that had happened, my most meaningful connections were with strangers. She played cardio tennis twice a week, did Pilates. Drank more than she should, but doesn't everyone? Tried the 5:2 and the blood type diet without much success.

I was on change-room duties that day. We took it in turns to rotate around the store. An hour by the change room, an hour on the floor merchandising and chatting to customers, an hour at the register. Perhaps if I had been on the register, she might not have said anything. It's less of an emotional exchange at that point. Customers are starting to worry. The logical brain kicks back in.

Have I made the right decision?

Should I put this on the Visa or use the grocery money?

Do I really need this crop top/yoga mat/waterproof shell jacket in both colours? Is that the parking inspector?

The real world edges closer.

But we were back in the cocoon of the change rooms: all soft lighting and well-angled mirrors. The world is a good place back there.

I had her on the ropes: three-quarter tights in the new barely-there fabric, two extra-long tank tops with racer backs, which in turn necessitated the purchase of a particular bra. It would be a good start towards hitting my total for the day. She had just made the obligatory turn and stretch in the mirror when she said it. One minute I was assuring her that no, I definitely couldn't see her underwear through her leggings, and yes, she should feel 100 percent confident during her Pilates squat sessions; the next minute I was left reeling, bent over and backing from the change room. My safe place? Not so safe anymore.

"You're that girl, aren't you?" she said, her head

bobbing between her knees as she tried to catch a glimpse of her rear view in the mirror.

At that stage I was a shell: I went through the motions of day-to-day life but I found no joy. Apart from my family and my work colleagues, I didn't see anyone. I was too scared to contact my old friends, and my followers, well, they were following someone else by then. The store manager knew my story, but no one else knew who I was. The extra ten kilograms I had gained through comfort food and house arrest had something to do with it, but I had stopped highlighting my hair and avoided eye contact. Besides, most of my posts had been of food and what I used to call #fitspo. I mostly kept my face out of it.

The hanger I was holding clattered to the ground. I hastily pulled the door to the change room closed so she couldn't see me.

So she couldn't be sure.

"Who?" I said, trying to keep the wobble out of my voice.

"That girl? The one with the app? The one who made the claims about fertility and cancer and whatnot." She laughed, as if she found the whole thing ludicrous. As if she couldn't quite believe she was even talking about me, let alone to me.

"Her?" My voice sounded high. Unhinged. "What would she be doing working here? I'm sure she's tucked away somewhere with plenty of money and is waiting for the whole thing to blow over." Because that's what they were saying about me online, and I didn't have another credible option.

"You look like her, don't you? I suppose you hear that all the time! Hardly an ideal person to be compared to! Everyone hates her! After what she told that woman! And with no medical background. It's criminal."

It wasn't. My lawyers, after much deliberation and even more billable hours, had decided that the complainants didn't have a case. If I refunded the money from sales of the app and suspended my social media accounts, then that would be the end of it. Except it wasn't. I was kidding myself if I thought it was.

"I don't think she ever made any claims about cancer," I said, desperately. "That was that other girl." I hadn't. In my darkest hour, that had been some consolation to me. That others had been worse. That others had done more damage.

It had started on Instagram. Sharing photos of healthy food. Rainbow salads, açai bowls, bliss balls. It was just a hobby to begin with, while I was at uni, but my timing was right. My followers grew and grew. I did a photo course, a digital media course.

People started to invite me to wellness seminars. There were enormous rooms of women who wanted to hear what I was saying, who took photos of me. They cheered when I spoke and reposted my photos, commented on posts. Companies paid me for product placement. I started to believe I was special. That this was the extraordinary life I was destined for.

Some people my dad knew in the media approached me to put together an app. It was an instant success. The seven-day detox and the clean-eating month were the biggest sellers. They paid for my car, and I was able to move out of home.

Maybe if I'd just stuck with that, it would have been fine. But one day a woman contacted me and told me she had been trying to have a baby, struggling to conceive. And then she had followed my diet and gotten pregnant. It put an idea in my head. A new app, a diet to enable and encourage fertility. Mother Miranda.

"Mother Miranda! That's it. It is you." The telltale glow from her smartphone screen shone out from above the door. Her voice became certain and accusatory, just like they all were online. "You've got a bloody nerve. My sister bought your app—"

"Most people say I look like a young Julianne Moore." I tried to keep the anger out of my voice, but for the first time in days, my body temperature rose. The woman wouldn't stop talking. Even Rosie on the register was listening.

Blocking the door with my body, I twisted the lock, leaving the woman trapped inside, still talking about what a horrible person I was. Am. I slipped out the door to the stock room, fumbled in my locker for my bag and my keys and my phone. I took off my lanyard and swung it from an overhanging rack.

I was almost out the back door when something gold caught my eye. Somehow my fob chain had become tangled up with my lanyard and was hanging, still swaying slightly from the motion of its speedy removal. Snatching it back, I held it tight in my hand. It was still warm from my skin and seemed to transmit a sense of calm. Like it somehow connected me across the years and the oceans to my mother's family. Like maybe it offered me a chance to be a different person.

There was nothing for me here. The banging from the change room made that almost certain. I opened the heavy back door, ignoring the alarm triggered by my exit, and felt the heat of the midday sun warming me. A deep breath. The blank screen of my phone was less of a shock to me these days. Once it was a deluge of messages and notifications; now it simply showed the date, the time. An innocuous background with a standard-issue screensaver.

I brought up the Qantas home page, convinced that if I did it quickly, it wouldn't feel so bad. That I wouldn't have a chance to change my mind. It took longer to calculate the flight times and prices than I expected. At any time, I could have closed the browser, written it off as a bad job, and gone back into the store with my tail between my legs. But I didn't. The price, when it came up, took my breath away. Christmas was coming, and there were only business-class fares available. They were way more than I had in my bank account, way more than I would have spent at the height of my success.

There was only one option. He answered on the first ring, but he always did for his daughters. Whatever our differences, he was always available to me. He didn't talk straightaway, finishing off his conversation before acknowledging me. I hoped he had forgotten about our conversation the other night.

"What's up?"

Each phone call was a reminder of the one I had made to him months before, in tears and overwhelmed. The panic in his voice hadn't quite gone, but it was less now.

"Dad?"

"Yes, poppet." Frustration mixed with the relief that it wasn't urgent. That I wasn't sobbing like that other time.

"I just saw an amazing book for Fleur. For Christmas. I'd love to get it for her, but . . ." I let my voice trail off.

"But what?" Definitely more frustration than relief now. He muttered something to someone, away from the phone.

"It's expensive."

A sigh.

"It's about the gardens around Lake Como." It was a low blow. Dad had taken Fleur to Italy for their honeymoon, and they often talked about how they might return once the girls finished school. I tried not to think how this little jaunt of mine could set them back a couple of years.

"Can't this wait?"

"It's the last one. They're from an overseas supplier, and they can't get any more before Christmas. I just want to get her something nice to say thanks. For everything."

Shame rose up like bile in my throat, and I swallowed it down. It was getting easier to deal with over time, like I'd had exposure therapy to bad behaviour.

Still, this was as bad as it had gotten for me. Despite what people said about me, everything I had done was done with good intention. I genuinely thought I was helping people. This time I was under no such illusion. I forced myself to remember my father's face in the study the other night. The way he clammed up and wouldn't tell me any more about my mother. The way he kept secrets. The way he was lying to me.

"I'll put you on to Susie." His PA. She ran his life. And his finances. She would give me his credit card details. I'd ask for the American Express, as I knew that had no limit, and well, at least he'd get some points out of it.

"Thanks, Dad."

"And, Miranda?"

"Yes?" I had him on speakerphone by that point, hastily refreshing the screen so that the ticket wasn't lost.

"I know I don't need to say this." I felt him hesitate. "Just the book, okay?" Shame again. Hot and acid. But by that stage I could barely taste it.

"Okay." He put me on to Susie, and she gave me the details. The transaction went through without a hitch. I was on the next flight to Heathrow, courtesy of my dad.

As I said: rock bottom.

7

"Have you been in this part of the country before?" the taxi driver asked as we approached Barnsley for the first time. The entire countryside was bathed in tepid light, the day not quite sure if it had arrived or not.

"No."

"You're in for a treat." The car eased off the motorway and onto a smaller carriage road.

The land around began to open into fields, and beyond them, wild hills covered in bracken for which I had no reference point. The never-ending plane ride followed by a long wait at Heathrow for the bus and now a taxi from the nearest town: I had no idea whether it was day or night, let alone where on earth I was or what the local fauna was called. It was a far cry from the warm and fuzzy scene I had envisaged for my arrival at Barnsley. I knew it had been a fantasy, but in my jet-lagged and disoriented state I was beginning to rethink my plan to show up unannounced.

In the distance, an unfamiliar animal stood frozen on a rocky outcrop.

The driver seemed to sense my confusion. "The edge of the moor," he said. "We follow it all the way around to Barnsley now."

"What's that creature?"

"A stag. They're rampant around here. There's talk of culling them, especially after the accident, but you know, animal rights groups and the like . . ." He left the sentence unfinished and shifted in his seat.

The accident?

After a moment more, he added, "Do you have sensible clothes?"

"Yes, I think so. I have a proper jacket, and boots—is that what you mean?"

His eyes scanned my travelling outfit in the mirror. The cotton pullover and jeans that had seemed appropriate in the rising heat of an Australian summer were barely enough in the whipping cold that had confronted me when I left the bus. I saw his eyes glance over my mother's fob chain around my neck. It shimmered in the last of the afternoon light, and I attempted to tuck it into my clothing.

"You'll need practical clothes down here. Wellingtons. Wet weather gear." He looked at me in the rearview mirror, sizing me up. "I don't suppose you'll fit into Daphne's things."

My skin, below its layers of impractical clothing, prickled slightly. We sat in silence as the day resolved itself into evening, darkness settling quickly. Finally, a long way down a twisting lane covered on either side by scraggly hedgerows, the driver stopped the car in a small turnout.

Alongside, I could make out the shape of an enormous pair of iron gates unequivocally fastened with a sturdy chain and lock. There was a sign, with gold letters announcing Barnsley House, but the light above was dark.

"They don't know you're coming." It was a statement, not a question.

My confusion must have shown on my face. The driver didn't look as if he believed me when I assured him otherwise. I hadn't expected it to be so dark when I arrived. I hadn't expected it to look so . . . abandoned. "Why don't you give them a ring, love?"

Yes—why don't I?

I thought quickly.

"My phone doesn't work over here. Is there another way of getting in?"

"The family use the private entrance down the road."

"Yes." Trying to sound more confident this time, I added, "That's what they said, I remember now."

I waited. The driver hesitated, and then sighed. He pushed the hand brake down and eased the car back out onto the road.

"Who did you say you were again?"

"A friend. Of the family." It had been a split-second decision to lie. Not sure why. Reverting to form. I hadn't wanted this man to ask questions.

"They don't get many friends calling in these days."

He watched me carefully in the rearview mirror. I could only hope the surrounding darkness was disguising some of my nerves. The last thing I needed was questions. I had reclaimed Sophia's letter from my father's study; it burned in my jacket pocket. It was surely my imagination, but it seemed to radiate heat as we drove slowly along the tree-lined road, like it was picking up some kind of signal from the landscape.

"Here it is. Barnsley House," he said as we pulled in again, only slightly farther down the road.

The gates were open. The driver hesitated before he decided to press on, an ever so subtle lurch that brought me against the tension of my seat belt.

The driveway, now we were off the main road, was winding, and in some places it dropped right down to meet the rough grey sea. "You look familiar," the taxi driver said, eyeing me in the mirror. "Have you been in the news?"

I had, but it seemed unlikely that news of my misfortunes would have spread this far. Before everything that happened, I used to get a little frisson when people recognized me. I used to feel special. Even though it was rare, I liked it. It was one of the things I missed about my old life. "I don't really follow the news," I said, and it was true. Much to my father's despair, I had never had the thirst for news he did. Like many people, I only found the news interesting when it had some bearing on my own life, and then in the last year, suddenly, my life became the news, and I lost all taste for it. I knew from experience just how destructive the news could be to a person.

Or a family.

Which is why I had stopped googling Barnsley and the Summer family soon after I started. Certainly, I had enjoyed an initial frenzy of gorging myself on the history of the house and reading about the restaurant, but there were some links I couldn't click on. Some publications I couldn't read. After what they had written about me, I had sworn never to read anything written on their pages again.

"You look like that actress, that's it. Thought I knew you for a second."

I breathed a sigh of relief.

There were gaping holes in my knowledge, but I preferred it that way. I was going to find out firsthand or not at all. I wasn't interested in someone else's trial by media.

As if he read my mind, the driver said, "The internet down this way isn't terrific."

"It's okay, I can find somewhere in town if I need to go online," I said, not really sure which town I was referring to, hoping that somewhere in this isolation lurked a town, preferably one with a cozy café and free Wi-Fi. As much as I was enjoying being offline, it was still somehow comforting to know it was there.

Just call me Patty Hearst.

"Which town is that, love?"

"The one where I got off the bus, South Bolton."

"Did you get a look at the place?" He laughed. "That's it, a bus stop on the main street. There's no internet cafés tucked away, you know."

"Is there a library?"

"No. Not the sort you mean. Jean Laidlaw runs a library, but it's more of a historical society. And it's in Minton, not South Bolton. It'll be Minton you're after, not South Bolton."

"Right." That might come in handy down the track. I made a note to keep an eye out for Minton. And Jean Laidlaw.

Low clouds, barely visible in the dark, moved towards us, and the first drops of rain landed on the windscreen. "Right on cue," the driver said from the front seat, giving me yet another curious look in the mirror. There was something else in the look this time as well. A warning.

I chose to ignore it as we rounded the last bend and emerged from under a canopy of trees, and I saw the house for the first time. The magic of Barnsley entered my bones from that very moment.

It was not what I was expecting. It looked different from the back. Smaller, more like a house than the colossal fortress I had conjured up in my mind. I didn't know the darkness was concealing the vast bulk of the house, and that light shone only from the windows in the part of the house the family used, and that was a very small part. The house would reveal itself in increments, just like the family who lived inside it.

To me, the dark trails of bare ivy vines framing the

glowing windows and doors were beautiful, far lovelier than the sunlit images I had seen. But the place was deserted. We had stopped in a large gravel turning circle beside a small vestibule. There were no cars anywhere. I couldn't see any guests. The garden was in darkness.

If my intuition was right, I was the only person in the place. My plan of arriving as an anonymous hotel guest was on shaky ground.

A black Labrador came racing out from the side of the house, and the taxi driver gave a cry of delight. He leapt from the car and let the dog jump all over him, not bothered by the muddy paws or the slow-falling drizzle. The wrestling might have gone on indefinitely had I not gone to fetch my rucksack from the boot. He extricated himself and intercepted me.

The dog jumped around him, whipped into a frenzy and unable to calm down. His tail whacked into my leg, hard, and I cried out. The driver looked at me strangely and then patted the dog on the head reassuringly. "There you are, Thomas, there you are," he said, his voice soothing.

"Not a dog person, really," I mumbled, as if it wasn't self-evident. I paid the driver, carefully counting out the unfamiliar notes, uncertain whether I needed to tip him. I decided to give him five pounds, mostly for not asking too many questions. He seemed delighted with that and was about to go when he changed his mind and came up close.

"Are you sure you're all right, going in there?"

"Fine. They're expecting me." Still the dog circled. There was no movement inside the house, no light switching on in the vestibule. Surely someone would follow the dog out any moment now, or else what was the point of him?

In the small vestibule outside the back door was a rusty dog's bed and piles of discarded shoes. Gumboots and trainers, flip-flops and school shoes, they were all tossed together in an indiscriminate pile. Everything about it said domestic bliss: a happy family lives within.

"You don't have to worry about me," I said, my hand instinctively going to the necklace, touching it through the light cotton of my jumper.

The door in the vestibule opened, and a woman's head popped out. A cat slunk out behind her. The dog barked, and the driver ducked quickly back into his car. He started the engine, and the wheels turned so quickly that small pieces of stone flicked up and hit me in the shins.

It was only once the noise of the car had subsided that the woman spoke.

"Have you come about the nanny job?"

8

"You'll have to come and see Max," she said, whistling to the dog immediately after.

Thomas looked at the woman suspiciously and then barreled past, knocking her as he went. She blew her blond fringe out of her eyes, a gesture that seemed to convey both good-natured frustration and an ironic commentary on my arrival. "I'm Mrs. Mins. I hope I'm pleased to meet you."

She had gold hoops in her ears—larger than I would have thought appropriate for the countryside—and was wearing a wrap dress in a clingy jersey fabric. Brown was not a colour I would wear, but it suited Mrs. Mins very well. She was much older than I, perhaps in her early fifties, but she looked very good for her age. I felt dowdy despite being at least twenty years younger.

The nanny job. I had *not* come about the nanny job. I'd babysat as a teenager—hadn't everyone?—and I had no intention of doing it again. The tantrums, the messy meal times, and the minutes crawling past. No, thank you.

But as the minutes ticked by, it felt harder to say so. Why else was I there? I didn't really have a reason to have come; at least, not one that I could announce immediately. I hadn't expected to be put on the spot like that. My father's warnings were echoing in my ear: some things—some people—are better left in the past.

My plans of simply turning up and talking to Sophia seemed flimsy now I was standing here in the kitchen. She was a teenager. I couldn't just turn up and ask to speak to her without setting off all sorts of alarm bells. I should have stayed in town for a night, gotten my bearings. I should have had more of a plan. It was too late for that now.

The kitchen was warm, and much smaller than I had expected from the size of the outside, bathed in a soft light from the fairy lights strung above the antique dresser. There were no children in sight, and yet there were signs of them everywhere. It was rustic compared to the commercial kitchen I used to hire to test my recipes, and without any sign of the expensive equipment and technology I had once thought indispensable.

The signs of a happy home were everywhere—schoolbags chucked on the floor, a basket of wet washing shoved against the cupboard, homework books open on the kitchen table. A pot spluttered on the stove, the heat so high that red sauce was spraying unnoticed across the top of the Aga. Mrs. Mins was waiting for me to say something. "Yes, you too," I said, and put out my hand to shake hers.

"*Have* you come about the nanny job?" she asked, a small streak of colour rising on her exposed décolletage. Was there fear in her voice, or is it something I have imagined in hindsight? My father's voice again: *It's time for you to grow up.*

A job was growing up, wasn't it?

"Yes. Yes, I have," I said. The familiar relief of untruth spread through my body, the thrill of invention giving me audacity. It always had. I bent down, opened the front zipper on my rucksack. "I've got some references here somewhere, or did you get the ones I emailed?"

"Don't worry about that, I'm sure Max received them. Although between you and me, he's not great on the email. Plus, I don't know if he warned you, but the internet connection around here is a bit dodgy."

"Oh, yes, he said," I replied, thankful for the heads-up from the taxi driver. He had helped me in more ways than he would ever know.

"Come through then and see Max," she said. "You can leave your bag there."

I braced myself for the meeting with my uncle Max, wondering how much he knew about me, or if he even knew I existed. After what my father had told me, I doubted he had even read the letters.

The initial buzz of the lie had faded, and now came the second stage: the fear of exposure. The third stage could go either way: elation at the continuing deception or the crushing humiliation of Being Found Out. It was the first and the third stages I found so addictive.

What other choice did I have? Sophia's letter led me to believe the situation was quite delicate. She didn't have anyone to trust. Her only option was someone she had never met, on the other side of the world. Maybe it would be better to keep my identity to myself until I worked out my next step, until I worked out just why she had been so desperate. This was my only way in, for now. Besides, I had cared for Ophelia and Juliet since they were little. I could handle a few little English kids.

Mrs. Mins walked me down a corridor lined with

children's art in antique gold-leaf frames. Someone, once upon a time, had had the sense of humour to remove the original contents and replace them with finger-painted portraits, abstract splashes of water paints, and yet more family photographs. The result was a blurred mass of smug happiness.

And yet Sophia had sent me the letter. The hotel, once award-winning and famous, now seemed to be shuttered. There was no sign of Daphne. There was no sign of the happy children from the photographs. Alarm bells were ringing for me, and I consider myself an expert: there are lies everywhere if you know what to look out for.

Mrs. Mins tapped softly on a closed door. A voice came from within and she opened the door. The familiar head of the Labrador emerged and then disappeared again.

"We've just taken a wedding booking for September," Mrs. Mins was saying as I stood behind her in the dark corridor.

"How many rooms?" Max asked. I couldn't see him, so I envisaged him sitting by a fire, scratching the top of Thomas's head.

"The whole place."

"Good. That's something. What's happening with the winter grass?"

"Mr. Mins says it's going like wild through the front lawn. He's got a plan, though."

"Anything else?"

By this point I wasn't entirely sure Mrs. Mins was going to mention my presence at all. I imagined being stuck in the hallway, hovering by the photograph wall in nostalgic limbo, until someone besides the dog noticed my presence.

Mrs. Mins walked into the study and shut the door behind her. Now I really was in the dark. The minutes ticked by. I listened carefully, but the walls were thick, and only a low murmur was discernable. There was still no sign—audible or otherwise—of the children. I wondered where they were and then remembered where I was. In a house this big they could be anywhere. It might be days before I came across them. Or would they be paraded in front of me, Von Trapp style, in some as yet unseen entrance hall?

Just as I was smirking at the thought, the door cracked open again and Mrs. Mins summoned me into the room.

9

If there is one person in the world who understands the difference between a persona presented on the internet and the reality of that person, it should be me. I know all about filters, smokescreens, deliberate omissions, and strategic inclusions. I understand marketing, branding, image building, and public relations. I thought I was ready for Max because I had found his Instagram account.

I was ready for a pale imitation of the man from the images. They always are. The men are never as tan or as tall as they seem online, and the women are always more tanned and more skinny. Everyone always looks older in real life. Or IRL, as I used to call it. Max was an exception to these rules.

He hadn't posted images for over a month, but the

account was still active. It had been a treasure trove of information for me to begin with, until I reached the familiar sickly saturation point and forced myself to stop scrolling. The last image he posted was of Daphne by a roaring open fire with a glass of mulled wine.

The earlier photos presented a charmed life: sailboats at sunset, alpine holidays, and children running about on endless stretches of green lawn. In real life, I knew now that the lush grass of the pictures was invaded by winter weeds, and I was expecting the human equivalent. A man in his prime, cut down by the insidious creep of life.

I was wrong.

Despite Max's grey hair, he had a youthful aura, and there was a playful nature about his eyes when he smiled, as he was smiling now. He seemed younger than my father; I guessed his age to be late forties. If my mother was alive, she would have been forty-eight. I suspected he was only a year or so older. The familiarity of him flummoxed me for a moment, until I remembered I was meant to be the nanny. I shouldn't let my recognition show. *Cool, Miranda. Play it cool.* My eyes skittered around the room, anxious to find something else to look at.

I concentrated on his clothes. He was wearing a black turtleneck jumper that should have looked silly but, against all odds, didn't. It showed off his lean build and didn't make him look like he was carrying extra flesh around the jowls the way it did on some men.

"Hello," he said. "I'm Max Summer." He stood up and offered his hand for me to shake but stayed behind his desk, forcing me to approach and come out of the shadows where I had been attempting to stay for as long as possible.

"Miranda," I said, purposefully leaving off my surname, Courtenay, even though I was sure it would not distinguish me. I wasn't sure he would remember or even know my mother's husband's name, but it didn't seem worth the risk.

"Miranda," he said right away, and looked me up and down. I felt his eyes on every part of my body and felt relieved that they were, for the most part, covered by clothing. "Have you come to reclaim your kingdom?"

I kicked myself.

Max must have seen the fear in my eyes because he laughed then and said, "Not a Shakespeare lover, then?"

"My mother was—," I said, before stopping.

I was used to people commenting on my name in Australia. Or, more accurately, I was used to people screaming out my name in a high-pitched wail, in imitation of the last minutes of *Picnic at Hanging Rock*. I wasn't used to people making the Shakespeare connection, the connection my mother had intended.

If Max had not worked out who I was already, I needed to stop giving him clues. My motivations were so twisted and disingenuous I had let reality recede; I had forgotten what I might be employed to do and who, in Max's eyes, I was. For now, I did not want Max to know I was his niece. If I was going to make a good show of being the nanny, I needed to think like a nanny. "Where are the children?"

Max sighed in the manner of someone who has been unduly interrupted and then disappointed by the arrival. "The children," he said, the twinkle in his eye ever so slightly less twinkly.

"I can come back another time," I said, suddenly aware of the late hour and my unannounced appearance. Even to me, something seemed not quite right about my surprise arrival on a cold wintry evening right before Christmas.

Max ignored the offer. "Sophia is the eldest—she's twelve and doesn't feel she needs a nanny anymore, and she's right. You're not so much there for her as for the others. Mainly Agatha, but we will get to her. Sophia is like her mother, headstrong and passionate and able to do whatever she tries. She's sporty, but she's also clever, and she's an astute judge of character. She'll size you up pretty quickly, so be ready. After Christmas, she's enrolled to go to a boarding school nearby—she'll still come home at the weekends—and she can't wait. I've had enough of her telling me just how much she hates Barnsley, and I'm sure she'll change her tune once she spends a term at school. She doesn't know how good she has it."

This description told me nothing, really, and it didn't sound like the girl who had written to my mother. He could have been talking about any teenage girl I have ever known, Ophelia or Juliet or even myself at that age. Most twelve-year-olds I knew were coming into their own, and finding the rest of the population lacking. I wondered what really made Sophia tick. I already knew she had enough chutzpah to send a letter to someone on the other side of the world whom she had never even met, and that behaviour seemed to marry up with Max's description of her.

"Robbie is my boy, and he's a quiet one. Most of his friends are quick to wrestle and make rude jokes and cause trouble, but Robbie stands back and watches. He doesn't join in until he's entirely sure about the situation, and only then if he really wants to." Max paused, and I took the opportunity to ask how old Robbie was. He had just turned ten. "We didn't really celebrate it, not this time . . ."

I felt Mrs. Mins shuffle behind me. I had forgotten she was there, and it seemed Max had as well. "Thank you, Mrs. Mins, I can take care of this."

"Would you rather . . . ."

Max simply shook his head and sat back in his chair. Without being invited, I took a seat opposite. A hard spring had broken through the cracked leather and pressed into my backside. I hoped more care had been put into maintenance in other areas of the house.

"Robbie is really into old houses; forts, castles, anything with a slightly violent history. I think he fancies himself as a bit of a ghost catcher." Max chuckled. I didn't. Ghost chasing didn't seem too far-fetched a notion in this house.

"And then there's Agatha. Sweet little Agatha. You've never seen a more angelic-looking child." He went into raptures, describing Agatha and her white-blond curls, her blue eyes, and her rosebud mouth. I thought he must have been over-egging the pudding until I met Agatha and saw for myself he hadn't exaggerated. In fact, I think he had undersold her: Agatha Summer was the most divine child I had ever seen in my life. But what he left out of his description turned out to be far more important than the details he included.

"Can we come in now, and meet her?" a small voice called from behind me.

Expecting an indulgent smile from Max, I looked towards the door in anticipation. I was more than ready to meet the owners of all those shoes by the back door, to put faces to the names and descriptions, to meet my cousins. Mrs. Mins was standing by the door, pretending to peruse the bookshelves.

Even from where I was sitting, I could pick out the distinctive spine of *The House of Brides*. It was one of the special hardback editions, with the marbled dust jacket. That didn't surprise me. I imagined my mother carefully sending a copy, possibly inscribing a note inside. I hoped at some stage I would be alone in this room to check. What did surprise me was that Max had kept the book, despite what my father had told me. Not for the first time, I felt like I hadn't gotten the full story.

Ignoring the plea, Max said, belatedly and somewhat redundantly, "And this is Mrs. Mins."

Forced now to look at me properly, Mrs. Mins held out her hand like a paw. Uncertain whether to kiss it or shake it, I chose the latter. "I trust Max has told you all about the house."

"A little, yes." In truth, he had told me nothing,

about the house or, more alarmingly, about Daphne. There were signs of her presence everywhere and yet no one had mentioned her. "Ah, just the children, really."

Mrs. Mins took that as a sign to launch into a speech that sounded as if it had been rehearsed. "The Summer family have lived in Barnsley House for generations, but only in recent time did the need to diversify and generate more income become urgent. Between running this place and the island, the family money had all but dried up, and the inheritance taxes were making the situation worse. Mr. Summer had no choice."

"That's me," Max clarified.

"They're all called Summer, you see. It can get confusing."

"And we're often called Maximilian as well. I go by Max. My father went by Maximilian."

"Mr. Summer—this one—and his wife"—I noticed Mrs. Mins didn't call Daphne by name—"started the hotel. It was—is—very successful." She had taken on the boastful tones of a particularly conscientious National Trust guide. I half expected her to speak sideways into a walkie-talkie at any point.

"And it will be again. We've just taken a booking for September, haven't we, Meryl?" Max looked at Mrs. Mins, a vulnerability evident on his face.

She smiled at him reassuringly. The flush of color came back to her chest. I expected Max to intervene, to bring Mrs. Mins back to domestic matters, but he only nodded encouragingly, closing his eyes happily during some particularly sycophantic moments as she continued, telling me about the house during wartime and the contribution the family had made to the small fishing community, both in the past as large estate holders, and now as a massive tourism drawcard. It was clear Mrs. Mins took her job very seriously and had an emotional investment in the hotel, but it was less clear why she would be telling me in such detail.

I shifted in my seat. I wanted to ask about Daphne, but I didn't know how to ask without revealing how much I knew. "Is their . . ." I stumbled over the words. "Is their m-m-m . . . Could I meet the children?" I asked, losing my nerve at the final instant.

A scratching at the door was followed by another crash, metal hitting wood, a hiss. I wondered how long he was planning to ignore them.

"The children?" Max looked at me quizzically.

"Yes, I thought it might be nice to meet them?"

"Will you take the job?" Mrs. Mins asked in a rush, moving her body back in front of the door. I half expected her to throw herself against it.

If only my father had been there to see it: a job offer

within minutes. No uncomfortable excuses about missing referees. No awkward questions about the lawsuit.
No slimy references to the ill-judged swimwear photo
shoot I had done for a Sunday magazine. I should have
moved overseas earlier. I would have, had I known I
could make such a clean break from old life.

I didn't hesitate. I was here to help Sophia. I was
here to find out what had made her so desperate she felt
she had to contact a long-lost relative from the other
side of the world.

And, on a much more selfish level, I was here to
learn more about my mother. If I had to tell a few lies
in the process, well, so be it. I was the woman for the
job. "Yes. I'd love to. If you'll have me."

Max and Mrs. Mins looked at each other with relief.
Disbelief. Maybe even wonder.

"I'll bring the children in," Mrs. Mins said quickly,
as if I might change my mind and exit through one of
the French doors at any point. I imagined her leading
them in, single file, stepping out in military precision.

Her choice of words became clear a moment later, as
Sophia and Robbie filed in, followed by Mrs. Mins,
pushing Agatha in a wheelchair.

10

I slept badly, that first night at Barnsley. It felt like years since I'd slept well. Ever since the arrival of Sophia's letter I had struggled to fall asleep, and when I did, I was plagued by constant fragmented dreams. Most mornings I woke before dawn, and that first morning in Barnsley was the same. My head was buzzing. I wanted to know why Sophia had written the letter. I wanted to know why Agatha was in a wheelchair. I wanted to know where Daphne was. I wanted to know what it all had to do with my mother. I wanted to know what it had to do with me.

The combination of jet lag and so many questions going around in my head made getting back to sleep futile. Instead of trying to fight the insomnia, I decided to explore the grounds and get my bearings.

Late the night before, after we all ate, Mrs. Mins had taken me along a narrow corridor in the west wing of the house. Similar to a covered cloister, it was lined along one side with coat hooks and low lockers, and on the other looked out over what seemed to be a small rose garden. At the end of the corridor, a heavy door concealed another small foyer, with a meager utilitarian stairwell rising to the bedrooms above.

My room, a small but cozy lodging with a compact bathroom, was alongside the children's and the master bedroom. It was decorated in what I believed to be an early 1990s style, a Laura Ashley vibe that resulted in all flat surfaces being covered in matching flounces of fabric. The repeating pattern and the size of the room created a slightly claustrophobic effect, and I wondered if this was deliberate. Someone had put my bag down, and I rushed to check it as soon as Mrs. Mins had shut the door. The locks were intact.

My anxiety was still evident on my face the next morning as I checked out the bathroom. The jet lag had caught up with me the night before, and I hadn't even brushed my teeth before crashing into the small bed. A bath, too short to lie down in, and a small wall basin were crammed in beside a toilet. I checked behind the door in futile search of a shower, but there was none. My hair, in the tiny bathroom mirror, was in dire straits already; I wondered how it would look after being washed in a bath. My skin looked wan, as if it had already acclimatized to the pale European light, translucent enough to reveal the blue-black of sleeplessness under my eyes. I brushed my teeth quickly and tried to avoid the reflection.

Mauve light filtered through the galleried windows in the silent corridor. It sounded like the children were still sleeping. Max and Daphne seemed to have no qualms about placing someone they had barely met in such close proximity to their sleeping children, but now as I walked along the corridor, I saw that Thomas was nestled in his bed outside their bedrooms. He lifted his head as I passed and decided I was of no immediate threat.

Robbie was sprawled out facedown across his double bed, his covers thrown off, snoring softly. I took the chance to examine his room, in which every surface was covered with fastidiously labeled containers and boxes. The walls were plastered with posters of racehorses passing the post at the finish line, the type owners of racehorses might buy. I hadn't seen any stables as we came in, but I felt like there was plenty I had missed in the dark.

Sophia's room was next. It was a complete tip. Despite the piles of clothes heaped on her bedcovers, I could see immediately that her bed was empty. I found her in the next room, curled up tightly around her little sister. From the night before, I had observed that Sophia was fiercely protective of Agatha. She would be watching me closely around her little sister. I wondered if they slept together every night, or if it was just due to the arrival of a stranger in the house. It might mean it would be difficult to catch Sophia on her own. I would need to talk to her about the letter at some point.

Was that why no one had told me about Agatha? Protectiveness could be one excuse. As Mrs. Mins rolled Agatha into the kitchen, she had not taken her eyes off me for a second, and I in turn had not drawn mine from Agatha's face. If she thought something like a child in a wheelchair would rattle me, then she had underestimated me; what truly unnerved me was that Max had not told me. There had to be some reason.

Even more disconcerting was the absence of Daphne. It made sense she wasn't there for my unannounced arrival, but I would have expected her to appear for dinner.

The cold was a shock after the warmth of the kitchen. Zipping up my jacket and pulling the sleeves of my jumper over my hands, I headed around the edge of the house and found myself on a vast open expanse of lawn running down to the sea. From this angle, Barnsley House was truly spectacular.

My hand went to my pocket for my phone, reflexively. I was framing the shot, adjusting the filter, thinking how good it would look on my grid, already considering the caption, before I remembered.

Even if there was phone coverage, there was no point. No one cared.

My most popular post ever had been on the day I launched my app. I had thousands of likes. Other influencers reposted my photo. Direct messages flooded my in-box. It felt amazing. My picture of Barnsley, all sandstone and morning light, would disappear into a vacuum. The only person who would care would be Dad, and for all the wrong reasons. I put my phone away.

There were still no signs of any guests, and it seemed quiet, too quiet. Even at this hour of the morning there was usually activity at a hotel. Normally the gardeners would be out, and the housekeeping staff would be loading up their trolleys for the morning's work. Here, there was nothing. The place was deserted, silent apart from the ever-constant sound of the waves crashing on the stone wall behind me.

All the curtains were drawn in the upstairs windows

facing towards me, and I wondered if they were the guest rooms. I pressed my face up against the glass of the bay window. It was some sort of sitting room, decorated in a simple, tasteful way, a modern take on country house style. A large fireplace dominated the other end of the room, its grate empty. Either there hadn't been a fire in it for some time or someone had recently cleaned it out meticulously. There were magazines set out in formation on a central table but I couldn't see clearly enough to read the dates.

Hoping to find some signs of life somewhere, I stepped back, planning to look in another window. All the curtains were drawn, but one swayed ever so slightly with recent motion. I was sure they had been open only moments before. Hallucination? Imagination? Sleepless night?

I shook myself off. Told myself it was only an illusion or a draught. Or Daphne, finally. Or that there were guests, after all. Maybe someone had arrived late the night before, begging for a bed. It made sense, guests in a hotel. More sense than anything else my brain was imagining that morning.

There was plenty to see as I looked around the grounds, but I was more consumed in thought about the people at Barnsley House than the place itself. The gardens were in no way accessible for someone in a wheelchair; I wondered how Agatha managed. The paths were constantly interrupted by series of steps, and the lawns stretched away into the distance in steep declines. There was no fencing, nor any ramps.

Even the part of the house she lived in was cramped, the narrow corridors almost impassable. Max had carried her to bed last night, but he couldn't be around all the time. It seemed like everyone, including Barnsley House itself, was in denial about Agatha's immobility.

I wanted to know why Agatha was in a wheelchair and how long it had been that way, but I didn't know who to ask. Max was out of the question, and it seemed inappropriate to grill the children on such matters. More than anything, I wanted to know where Daphne was.

Mrs. Mins seemed the obvious person to ask, but she terrified me. At dinner, the night before, she had largely ignored me, only every now and then asking me searching questions that seemed designed to highlight my thinly concealed shortcomings.

Even then, I knew that to expose myself further to her would be foolish, and possibly even dangerous. Sophia hadn't mentioned her specifically in her letter, but I had no idea of how close she was to the family, and I intended to find out. Until then, I would keep her at a distance.

Unfortunately, in the way of that house, I kept being thrust back into her path. And that morning was to be no different. As I came around the westerly end of the lawn and into the kitchen garden, she was there, tending a patch that seemed, even to me, a nongardener, completely dormant. I wondered if she had been watching me, for there was no other reason for her to be out there in the cold, fully dressed and made up, at that hour of the morning, turning over the barren soil.

11

"Out getting your bearings, are you?" Mrs. Mins said, plucking away at invisible weeds. "The early bird gets the worm."

Mrs. Mins liked talking in well-worn aphorisms. I would learn that they were her way of protecting herself from thinking too deeply about anything, and one of the ways she had survived at Barnsley all these years.

That first time, I took her comments literally. It was early, and for all I knew, worms were something they served in the restaurant at Barnsley. Worms seemed the only likely thing she might be harvesting from that particular patch of barren dirt. "Are they for the restaurant?"

Mrs. Mins stopped her digging and leaned on the hoe. She looked at me carefully. "Have you not noticed?"

There was plenty I had noticed in my twelve or so hours at Barnsley. A creepy housekeeper. An absent mother. Overlooked children. A distinct lack of guests. Arctic draughts. None of these seemed appropriate to mention. "Noticed what?"

"The hotel is closed. So is the restaurant. It's been that way since the accident."

"But the website doesn't say anything about that," I stammered, shocked. It was true. I had spent a lot of time on that website: The image gallery. The suggestions for things to do in the local area. The history of the buildings. None of it had suggested that the hotel was actually closed down.

"It does if you try to make a booking. Max didn't want it to be too obvious. In fact, he never really made a decision. Just stopped answering the phones and bolted the main gates."

I thought of my mouse hovering over the "Book Now!" tab, and my decision to turn up unannounced. "Are you going to reopen?" I asked, still piecing things together in my mind.

"Well, he let me take that booking for the wedding, that's a start. But there's a lot of work to be done anyway." With a gloved hand she indicated the garden, the house beyond. That morning she was dressed in jeans and a navy fisherman's sweater, the type my father would wear when visiting friends' farms, but she still wore the golden hoops. In her work clothes, she looked even more at home than she had the night before, and once again more put together than I would ever be.

"How long has it been closed?" I asked, wondering how far to pursue my curiosity.

She didn't seem to mind. "It's almost a month now. I've had to turn away everyone who had booked for Christmas and New Year. All those bookings. Poof!"

"They'll come back."

"I'm not so sure. This place is starting to get a reputation."

"Sounds to me like it's had one for a while."

A small sound escaped from Mrs. Mins's throat. She looked down and kicked at a root in the ground. Conversation over, it seemed.

Growing up with Fleur had left me attuned to garden design, and someone with a trained eye had set this one out. In some ways, it was a nostalgic rendition of an Edwardian kitchen garden, with beds edged in basket fences and herbs surrounding every patch, but it had a more modern symmetry about it. It reminded me of gardens Fleur had taken me to at home. Stonefields.

The kitchen garden at Heide. It was bare now, but I imagined what it must be like in full flush. "You should see this garden in summer," Mrs. Mins said, as if reading my mind. "That whole bed along the wall is mint. Five or six different types. Did you know you could grow chocolate mint? If you could smell it . . . Over there—lettuces. At least four kinds. It's all herbs beyond the lettuce, every type you can imagine. I expect you're not too interested in that kind of thing, though."

"Oh, yes, I am," I said, before thinking better of it. I had been about to tell her my background. Herbology. Naturopathy. Wellness. Dietitian. "My stepmother is a gardener. Landscape architect, really."

Mrs. Mins looked at me properly, her eyes darting to my hands, looking for the signs that might give me away as a serious gardener. Finding none, she seemed to roll her eyes for an invisible observer. "What are you doing working in child care, then?" She looked suspicious.

"The children are still asleep," I said. Dodging the question.

She shook her head slightly, like she was trying to dislodge something from her ear. "Everyone sleeps late around here," she said, "except for me." Was it a threat? It felt like one, but despite my age, I have always been an early riser, and I didn't feel I needed to change. Mrs. Mins didn't have a monopoly on the early hours.

It seemed to me strange that Max should sleep late. My own father was always first up: making the coffee, reading the newspaper, watching the television news. I looked around again for signs of life. There was a hedge at the end of the kitchen garden, and beyond that green border was the car park, empty now except for a small vehicle, more like a golf buggy than a van. "Oh," I said. "Do you run the hotel for Mr. Summer?" What did she do all day, I wondered, while it was closed? Who was she?

It only took the slightest prodding to get her talking. "And everything else," she said, with the martyred sigh of the chronically overworked. "I wasn't meant to be taking over the children as well. That wasn't what I signed up for."

"And what did you sign up for?" I asked, leaning back to pick the heads of parsley so far gone to seed they came to my waist.

"I used to work on Capri—in Italy?"

I nodded as if I knew it.

"Max and Daphne came out to see me—they had heard about what I had done out there. I was working for a small hotel, a tiny little village on the side of the cliff that had been converted into a luxury resort. It had become very famous, and not just because of the setting. The luxury hotel industry is much smaller than you would think."

I had never really thought about it at all, but I nodded again anyway.

"We had an amazing chef—not a celebrity like Daphne, but he could cook very, very well. All the best staff used to come to work for me, and we had amazing reviews. People came for honeymoons, celebrations, but mostly it was people in the know, the sort of people who come every year, stay for a month, and don't even ask the price."

"It sounds amazing. How did Mr. Summer convince you to come here?"

"He offered me a lot of money, much more than I was making there. The owners didn't pay us much, but life was good. We had accommodation, and there were tiny restaurants in the back streets just for the people working in the hotels. But it wasn't the money."

It seemed she might talk forever, but she surprised me by turning around suddenly and walking off, leaving me in the middle of the stone path, forcing me to call out after her. "What was it?" I said. "How did he get you to come?"

She stopped, stood still for a moment. From behind,

she looked much younger, and I thought again how Max must be tempted by her. She looked up at the windows, and I could see that they were the windows along the children's corridor. Surely they must be close to waking. Mrs. Mins must have had the same thought, because it was only once she was satisfied there was no one there listening that she turned around again. "How did Mr. Summer get *you* to come?" she said, quietly.

Immediately, there was a sensation of blood rushing into my face. "The children . . . he needed someone for the children," I finally stammered in response. I had no real reason for my sudden appearance; I didn't even know if the job had been advertised. For all I knew, there had been a letter up a chimney, Mary Poppins style.

"The children," Mrs. Mins said thoughtfully. "That's certainly not how he got me here."

"Do you have children, Mrs. Mins?"

"Me? No. It's too late for that." It was an answer to another question, perhaps the one I should have asked. We stood awkwardly for a moment.

"And Mrs. Summer? Will she be having more children?" I was clutching at straws, but it was the only way I could think to bring her into the conversation. I was the nanny, after all.

"Daphne?" Mrs. Mins looked stricken. "Why? What did Max say?"

"Oh, nothing. I just thought maybe that's why she needs a nanny."

Mrs. Mins's eyes went to the upstairs windows. When she spoke, it was slow, as if she was assessing each word as she said it. "Daphne needs a nanny because she has been in bed since the accident. The doctors say she needs to rest. When she is better, she will be busy with the restaurant again."

"What accident?" I blurted out. Unlike Mrs. Mins, I didn't take my time.

"It's not my place to talk about the accident." *Nor yours*, she said with her eyes.

"I'll leave you to it," I said, when it became clear she would not be elaborating.

"Maybe you can help me out here when the weather improves. It's too much work for Mr. Mins and me, and we could use another set of hands. I could see if Max could pay you a little extra for it."

After the way she had been looking at Max the night before, I had been surprised to hear her talking about a Mr. Mins. Here was my chance to ask. "Does your husband work here as well?"

"You'll meet my brother soon enough." I nodded, confused and still unsure why she was calling her brother Mr. Mins. "Only if you know what you're doing, of course. I wouldn't want you out there if you weren't entirely certain about things."

It was a long time since I'd felt entirely certain about anything, and I couldn't imagine feeling certain about anything again anytime soon. Everything here seemed so ambiguous.

There was so much to learn.

There was one question I was desperate to ask, though, and Mrs. Mins's invitation to help her in the garden gave me the encouragement I needed to ask it.

"What happened to Agatha?" I said, so quickly the words ran together. I assumed it had something to do with the accident.

Mrs. Mins took a moment to process what I had asked. I suspected she knew I would ask sooner or later, and the timing of the question was the only part she found at all surprising. I expected she thought it would take me longer to work up the courage. "Curiosity killed the cat," she said, and left me waiting so long in silence that finally I had no choice but to walk away and find the children.

12

The children were awake. I rushed back through the small gate and into the house, expecting to find them in the kitchen, waiting for their breakfast. Robbie was sitting at the table, reading an old form guide. Sophia was there too, twirling her hair around one finger and leaning up against the counter. She looked much younger this morning, half asleep, and the short pyjamas she was wearing despite the cold revealed long legs she must have inherited from her father.

"Where's Agatha?" I asked.

"She's waiting for someone to bring her down?" Sophia replied, the intonation at the end of the sentence deliberately placed. I saw the wheelchair in the corner, remembered Max carrying her upstairs last night. The house was not suitable for someone in a wheelchair, and

Max had done nothing about it. Instead, he left Agatha in her bedroom—at the top of the tiny staircase and the end of a narrow corridor.

"Oh. Right." Sophia watched me as I headed towards the stairs. "Your dad didn't say anything."

It had been a long time since I had worked for someone else, which was one of the reasons I found it so easy to throw off my commitment to Grant and Farmer. I hadn't spoken to my father since I left. In a cowardly move, I had left him a note explaining that Denise and Terence had invited me to spend Christmas in London with them, and that I might spend some time looking for a job there after New Year's. There was no way he would believe that, but I felt it might buy me some time.

I had mostly quarantined the guilt about those lies, but I did feel sorry for Fleur and my stepsisters, who I am sure would have borne the brunt of his rage after my departure. This time, it felt like my lies were for a purpose, for the greater good, in a way they hadn't been before. That's how I justified it, at least.

What I did remember about starting a new job was that the people who already worked there usually gave you some sort of guidance. A job description. Some simple tasks to ease you into the environment. Maybe a tour of the facilities and a security pass. So far at

Barnsley I had received accommodation and a meal, and yet none of the other more traditional trappings of employment. It was an unusual setup.

I would have to work out a few things for myself. I made a mental list as I walked the now familiar path up the back stairwell. Bedtimes. Food preferences. Schedules. Car? School. Homework. Washing. Rules. None of my previous experience seemed relevant.

I walked past a closed door at the end of the hallway. Max and Daphne's room. It took on a different quality, now I knew Daphne was in there. I paused for a moment, hoping to hear something from within, but there was nothing. No sound at all.

Agatha was in her room, reading *Pippi Longstocking*. "I used to love that book," I said, sitting beside her. "The movie was too sad, though. I couldn't stop crying at the end."

"There's a movie?"

"Yes. We should watch it." I wasn't sure how I was going to manage that, given the internet black hole I had stumbled into, but possibly I could find it on DVD in the village. It seemed like the sort of place that would still have a shop where you could rent DVDs.

"You said it was too sad."

"Well, we'll watch something else. What other movies do you like?"

"*Annie. Anne of Green Gables.*"

Was it a coincidence that all these stories had dead or absent mothers? I didn't think so; I had been drawn to exactly the same stories at her age. The difference was, my mother was dead. Agatha's was just, well, absent. It wasn't my intention to reveal anything about myself so early in the piece, but I felt so sorry for Agatha, I wanted her to know I knew how she was feeling. "I lost my mother at your age," I said, and then, thinking perhaps that wasn't clear enough, I added, "She died. She was sick for a long time, and then she died when I was about your age."

As soon as the words left my mouth, I regretted their insensitivity. The poor child had a mother recuperating from a nasty accident, and I was talking about my mother's death.

Agatha looked up from her book, interested, but a little shocked at my forthrightness. She was wary of me. I didn't know then that she was wary of everyone, that she had good reason to be. I told her that my father remarried and our home became happy again, that my sisters had brought me a lot of happiness. That I could barely remember my mother at all, but I remembered loving her.

"Come on, let's get going," I said, hoisting her up in my arms. She was light as a feather, and I wondered if she ate anything at all. After my mother died, I stopped eating almost entirely; my appetite disappeared. I could only stomach carrot sticks and celery filled with peanut butter. It was the start of my journey to healthy eating and nutrition. Worst of all was the food my mother used to make: roast chicken, spaghetti Bolognese, French toast. I still can't eat any of those without thinking of her. If Agatha was used to Daphne's cooking, I wasn't surprised she'd stopped eating when she had to lower her culinary standards.

"What do you want for breakfast?" I asked, assuming breakfast was part of my duties. "Pancakes? Hot chocolate?"

"Toast," Agatha said. "With Marmite. No butter."

In the blur of my arrival the night before I hadn't paid too much attention, but Agatha had been eating toast then as well. With Marmite, no butter. It seemed even Michelin-starred chefs could produce fussy eaters. "And then what will we do?" I asked. I had no idea about the logistics of the wheelchair on that morning; how difficult it was to get around not only Barnsley House but also the village. I had visions of Famous Five–style shenanigans: the four of us rugging up against the cold and following the cliffside track into the village to explore. A thermos. Some sandwiches and a sponge cake. Not only did I desperately want to connect with the children, I was completely disoriented and eager to acquaint myself with the surrounding area.

"We've got to go to school," Agatha said, with great surprise. "The bus comes at eight o'clock." There was an element of delight in my ignorance.

No one had told me. Back in Australia, my stepsisters had been let out for the summer. For no logical reason, I assumed the English term ran to a similar schedule. "Are you still at school?" I asked. "It's nearly Christmas."

"We finish this week. We've got the concert."

There was no time to talk about the concert at that moment. The glittery clock next to Agatha's bed showed that it was already alarmingly close to the bus's arrival. We rushed about, getting Agatha dressed. I found myself getting more and more frustrated.

I wasn't used to worrying about other people. My instinct was to snap at Agatha, to tell her to hurry up. As I brushed her golden hair into an unruly ponytail, she wriggled, my hands tugging inexpertly at the ends making her protest and wriggle more. I was used to people pandering to me, not the other way around.

It could only be a matter of time before I was exposed as a fraud—a dreaded feeling with which I was already too familiar. All the signs were there. Lies. Complete lack of experience. Endangering other people's lives.

An ulterior motive. I cursed myself—and Sophia—for ending up in this position again.

Just as we were finally about to head out the door, Robbie disappeared upstairs.

I stuck my head into the stairwell. "Robbie? . . . Robbie!"

Agatha rolled up next to me. "He's gone up to say goodbye to Mum."

"Oh." I looked at her. Looked at the stairs. "Do you want me to take you up to say goodbye as well?"

"It's okay. She'll be asleep anyway," Agatha said, and rolled back towards the door, just as Sophia came down the stairs, fully dressed. I smiled at her, attempting to forge an alliance. Tried to show her I was someone she could trust. I offered to make lunch for her, and she sneered and said something I couldn't understand.

Robbie, who had just reappeared from upstairs, had to interpret for me. "She said we get lunch at school, miss," he clarified.

"You don't have to call me miss," I said, but they were racing out the door.

"Sophia?" I called out as she dashed past me. It was the first time I had been close to Sophia without Max or Mrs. Mins around. I wanted to give her a sign that I had received her letter. That I was on her side.

Sophia didn't even stop, just shook her head slightly, as if trying to dislodge water from her ear.

"I got the letter."

She looked at me blankly. "We're going to be late for the bus."

She was right. We only just made it.

13

As soon as I got back to the house, Max summoned me into his study. Once I was there he proceeded to ignore me, instead concentrating on numbers in what looked like an old-fashioned red ledger. While I was waiting, I took in my surroundings in a way I had not had a chance to do the night before.

The room was divided in two by a pair of sofas surrounding the fireplace. Behind each sofa was a desk; one for Max and, it appeared, one for Daphne. I sat on the sofa facing away from Max's desk, looking towards the area that Daphne had apparently only recently vacated. With my back towards Max, I could examine things properly. Tall stacks of bookshelves were filled with cookbooks, and old issues of cooking magazines ran into one long wall, hung with framed awards and articles.

It was easy to imagine the two of them sitting here in front of the fire on his-and-hers sofas and discussing their plans for the hotel and restaurant, their menu ideas, the children. Here, more than anywhere else so far, I felt her presence.

There was a smoky, intoxicating smell that at first I thought was coming from the ashy remains in the hearth, but my nose led me to the candle on the coffee table in front of me. Forgetting where I was, I picked it up and inhaled deeply: it smelled exactly like Max, yet distilled. "Put that down."

Max's voice jolted me back instantly, and I put the candle down, more out of embarrassment than fear. "My sister is coming today to meet you."

This was just like Max, to make two completely unrelated statements in close company and still expect the listener to follow his train of thought. "What about the children's mother?" Panic set in, and I had spoken without thinking.

Max looked at me sharply. "Elizabeth will be here shortly. She lives in one of the cottages."

"The cottages?"

"I'm sure you have seen them. Perhaps on your early-morning walk."

It seemed nothing happened at Barnsley House without Max being aware of it. Between Mrs. Mins and his own vigilance, he seemed to have every square inch of the vast estate covered at all times. Later I would find out about the cameras that did most of the work for him.

We sat quietly for a moment. I went over my morning walk in my mind. I had peered in a few windows, circled the house, but nothing untoward, I was sure of it. It was perfectly natural for someone in my position to be curious.

"Do you spy on all your staff?" I asked. Not waiting for him to answer, I got up from the sofa and headed towards the mantel.

There, among seashells, some old photographs, and invitations to Christmas drinks (last year's; it looked as if Max had been dropped off the invite lists this year), I found what I was looking for. I shook the box to see if it was full and then removed a match, striking it and lighting the candle before Max had a chance to stop me.

The door to the room burst open, and a handsome, bustling figure came rushing in. It was Elizabeth, Max's sister—my aunt. "Hello, dear, I'm Elizabeth," she said, barely looking at me but holding out her hand to shake mine immediately, even though she was still several paces away. She called everyone dear. She said it made life easier, and it did; she was the sort of person who could get away with not learning people's names. My heart rose into my mouth, and I didn't trust myself to speak. Luckily, she continued, not needing any encouragement from me.

"Max has probably already told you about me," she said, throwing herself on the opposite sofa. "A lot of promise, but never came to anything. Drinks all day. Husband's a shocking gambler, that kind of thing. Speaking of which—" She turned to the doorway and waited. "Here he is. This is Tom."

"Like the dog," Tom said, and nodded in greeting. He sat down next to Elizabeth and started to read the newspaper.

"The dog is called Thomas," Max said from behind me. He walked around and stood by the fire, keeping one cautious eye on the candle the whole time, as if afraid the flame would leap out of its own accord and engulf everything in flames.

"I used to be too, once," Tom said, and barely spoke again for the entire visit, burying himself in the racing pages.

"You've come to look after the children," Elizabeth said—a statement, not a question—keeping an eye on Max the entire time. She still hadn't looked at me properly, and I hoped she wouldn't.

"Yes." It was probably the only time in those first

few days when I might have admitted who I was, but I felt outnumbered. Max. Elizabeth. Tom. The house.

"Interesting choice. Can I smoke in here, Max?" She didn't wait for an answer, just produced a cigarette from somewhere about her person and leaned it to light it from the candle. "That smell," she pronounced, "reminds me of Daphne."

"I was hoping you would run through what was expected in the role," Max interrupted. "What the children need, etcetera."

"Have you met the children?" Elizabeth said, blowing smoke. I hadn't seen anyone smoking for years, let alone inside, and for a moment I was mesmerized. And then a slight feeling of rage crept in.

Mostly I had surrounded myself with people who followed the same lifestyle as me: no sugar, organic food, plant snacks. The smoke was suffocating, and I couldn't believe Max allowed it when there were children in the house. I couldn't believe he allowed it when lung cancer had killed my mother—his other sister. Or perhaps he didn't—Elizabeth didn't seem like the sort of person who asked permission for anything. I bit my tongue. Tried not to inhale the acrid smoky air.

"Yes," I said, at the same time as Max said "She arrived last night."

"Have you explained about Agatha?" Elizabeth asked, tapping the cigarette on the side of a ceramic dish. Ash fell in a perfectly placed pile.

"I'll leave you with Elizabeth," Max said to me. "I have things to do." He left the room, and Thomas followed. He never left Max's side, that dog.

14

"If you want to understand what happened to Agatha, you must start with Daphne," Elizabeth began, tucking her legs under her on the sofa, her stocking feet hidden underneath her dress. She had an old-fashioned way of dressing; woolen skirts and blouses, brooches and tights. On anyone else it would look fusty, but on her it seemed nonchalant and somehow timeless. Her sturdy boots and sensible garments matched the setting, but like all things at Barnsley, her style turned out to be carefully orchestrated. A clever costume. "I didn't like her to begin with, not at all," Elizabeth continued. "She was Australian, as you know."

I nodded. Everyone seemed to think Daphne's nationality was of interest to me. Was it just because I was also Australian, or had she spent her entire life in England being introduced in that way? "This is my wife, Daphne. She's Australian." It seemed to offer some elusive insight into her character that everyone else could decipher apart from me.

"Max met her in London. There were a lot of Australians in London then. Always a lot of Australians in London, I suppose. Max was floundering a bit under the responsibility of the house, and, well, everything. Even though we are twins, Max was born first. So they say. I've never been entirely convinced. Primogeniture and all of that. So Max inherited Barnsley. And that left Tom and me with a cottage. And the island."

She must have seen the curiosity on my face, because she placed her cigarette in the dish and carefully squeezed the ember out of it. I followed her over to the window behind Max's desk, trying to steal a look at the ledger on his desk as we passed. "Barnsley Accounts 2017," the cover read. Hardly riveting, I would have thought, and yet Max had been engrossed.

"Minerva Island."

Elizabeth pointed her tiny hand towards a landmass only metres off the coast. It was so close it seemed as if it must be connected to the mainland, yet, leaning forward, I could see a distinct and choppy patch of water separating the island from the land on which Barnsley stood.

"You live there?" There were no signs of life. Only a rudimentary-looking jetty on one side and then a thick mass of foliage partly concealing a deserted-looking stone building, a craggy stone fortress clinging bravely to the edge of the rising land. A flag stood strong against the buffeting wind, only its tattered ends giving any sign of the battle it fought daily against the elements.

"No. Don't be ridiculous. If you look closely you can see the remains of my great-great-grandmother Elspeth's attempt to grow grapevines. As you can see, it wasn't a success. Have you had a nice Barnsley Pinot Grigio lately?"

I looked at her blankly, I couldn't differentiate any one plant from that distance. "Didn't think so. The rest of that greenery is mostly a jungle. Elspeth's husband brought back ferns and bougainvillea, and some of them really took off." She returned to the sofas, so I did too. I waited while she lit up another cigarette.

Time moved slowly. The island had stirred up a strange excitement in me. It was partly the romance but also the mystery; in any case I felt the spark of a connection with the landscape, a deep familiarity.

Elizabeth spoke again. "There's no house out there. No power, no water, nothing. We used to camp out there in the summer. The garden was perfect for exploring and getting lost. Tom and I thought about trying to make a home out there at one point, but it would have cost too much."

Elizabeth crying poor seemed implausible to me. I had read *Pride and Prejudice*; I knew how it worked in English landed families, but I could hardly believe she couldn't have come up with the money to make it happen. With her expensive-looking clothes and her obvious intelligence, it just didn't add up. "Horses," she said, sensing the confusion on my face. I nodded, as if I was familiar with the problem.

"Even Max could see it was unfair, him with all this"—Elizabeth gestured around, cigarette ash flying about—"and us with not much at all. He promised me we would work something out, but none of us had much of an income, and country houses all around were being sold, converted into flats. Port Perry over the way hosts a festival in the summer; Concoppel has a farm shop, that sort of thing. My father was adamant before he died that Barnsley remain a family home." She paused. "He didn't leave us a lot of choice. Tom and I agreed to stay here while Max went up to London to meet with the banks. Lawyers. Those sorts of things. There was a family from Spain interested in leasing out the property as a whole, leaving us the cottages to live in. Both of us were dead against the idea, but Max thought it was a good idea to meet them and see what the offer was before writing it off entirely. We had a disagreement about it, and he left for London in a foul mood. A real stink, wasn't it, Tom?"

I had forgotten Tom was beside her.

"Terrible stink," he agreed, neither moving the paper aside nor elaborating.

Elizabeth paused to light yet another cigarette, giving the process an inordinate amount of time and attention. At least it gave me a moment to process what she had said so far. It was interesting to me, but how interesting would it be to anyone else? To, say, a newly arrived nanny from Australia who had no connection to Barnsley?

15

"Max was gone for one week, and when he came back, he had Daphne with him. One week. That was all it took. I hadn't even washed my hair, and here he was with the woman he said he was going to marry. She walked into this room—just here— and stood by the fire. It was a gloomy day, and I could barely make her out. I thought she was much younger at first, but as Max turned on the lamps, I could see her face more clearly, and she was at least Max's age. Just small. Very small."

It felt like hours since Elizabeth had started her story, and yet the silver clock on the mantel told me it was not yet lunchtime. Not even close. I felt sure that if Max had still been here, he would have told her to hurry up by now. I felt sure he would have stopped her from going into such a detailed account with the new nanny. "They pulled out paper napkins, covered with writing, sketches, sums, and I knew straightaway I was in trouble. A hotel, they said, not very many rooms, but a restaurant. An amazing restaurant, with food sourced from the gardens and local suppliers. People would travel from London, from overseas, just to eat here. Daphne would do the food, and Max would run the hotel. They were planning to start right away—Max even had a local builder coming in that afternoon to see about knocking down walls, putting in bathrooms. I thought: Where does that leave me?" She stopped. Looked around for something. "Tea?"

After my early morning and the warmth of the fire, refreshments seemed like a good idea. "Oh yes. Please." Something about Elizabeth made me mind my manners.

"Mrs. Mins will sort it out." She sat back. It took me a moment to realize she meant for me to communicate this to Mrs. Mins. I headed out of the room. Unable to find Mrs. Mins anywhere nearby, I undertook the task of making tea myself.

It took me longer than I anticipated to pull it together. The teapot was easy—it was on the counter and still warm from some unknown person's earlier brew—but I couldn't find any teabags. Eventually, just as I heard the phone ringing from the study, I found some tea leaves in an old tin from Fortnum & Mason. My nose told me they were definitely not herbal. It was proving hard to sustain my clean-living principles in this part of the world. That was my excuse, anyway.

Tom had put aside his newspaper and Elizabeth was sitting at Max's desk, talking on the telephone, when I came back in carrying the tray. I had found it on top of the fridge, and I suspected it had been made by one of the children. Wiping away the dust on it had revealed a portrait of a family: a mother, a father, and three children with stick legs and arms and big wide smiles. It was dated the year before. And Agatha was not in a wheelchair. "Thank you for your call. I'll be sure to let Mr. Summer know you phoned," she said, and promptly hung up.

"I'll be mother," Elizabeth said as I came in, standing up. It felt like she was looking at me properly for the first time. She'd left the ledger wide open, not attempting to conceal the fact she had been reading it. I made a note to close it before I left the room. I didn't want Max to think I'd been snooping.

"Mother?" I asked, my senses on high alert at the word.

"It means she'll pour," Tom finally said, when it was clear Elizabeth had no intention of answering.

Elizabeth poured out the tea carefully, raising her eyebrows slightly at the motley selection of mugs I had scavenged. I offered her a biscuit, and the corners of her mouth turned down slightly. I took that as a no. Tom took one and then another quickly, in the manner of someone who had not eaten for some time. He waited for Elizabeth to add milk and three sugars to his World's Greatest Mummy cup before retreating behind his paper again.

"I've lost my train of thought," Elizabeth said matter-of-factly.

"The hotel," I reminded her, though it was the last thing on my mind.

"I had never seen Max so happy, so energized, at least not since his school days. They worked hard, and got the hotel up and running by that summer. The restaurant was almost instantly successful. The newspapers came and did stories on the amazing Daphne and her kitchen garden: the kitchen garden that had been planted by my grandmother, and tended so carefully by my family, none of which was mentioned. Then came the children: one, two, three."

The tea was strong. The leaves had formed into a thick sludgy brew; I found it difficult to swallow. It had been a long time since I'd had cow's milk, but I added it now. And sugar. Elizabeth watched but left hers black. The milk and sugar made the drink more palatable; the unfamiliar buzz of caffeine was a bonus. "The press went crazy. Mother of three. Michelin-starred cook. Darling Daphne: the savior of the West Country, bringing in hordes of tourists and revitalizing the village and the harbour. She wrote a cookbook, and then they made a television series; Daphne cooked out on the lawn and the children ran around behind her, dressed in pinafores. It was all lovely, except that it wasn't, really."

My ears pricked. At last, I thought, I will get to the truth of the matter.

"Daphne wasn't the best mother. She never spent any time with her children, apart from when they were being used as props for her perfect life, and this caused endless fights between her and Max. She drank, and then she started taking prescription drugs. Her recipes were all about free-range pork, fair-trade chocolate, organic vegetables, and meanwhile she was out the back of the kitchen trying whatever the kitchen hands brought in. Cocaine, pills, speed."

A tear formed in Elizabeth's eye. She looked away from me, as if there was something on the mantel needing her careful attention, but it was too late, I'd seen it. "Max tried to protect her, and the children, but he couldn't be there all the time. On the morning of the

124 • JANE COCKRAM

accident, he was asleep. There had been another terrific argument the night before—the hotel was packed with guests, and there had been a scene. The police woke him up. Daphne and Agatha were badly hurt. It wasn't until much later that night that we found out what had happened. Max was heartbroken. He blamed himself, you see. Even though Daphne was driving, he took responsibility. He shouldn't have left the children alone, he said, and he hasn't forgiven himself. And that's why you're here. He doesn't believe it's safe for the children to be alone with Daphne anymore."

She placed her mug on the table. It was still full, her shaky hands threatening to spill the tea within.

"But what happened?" I was confused. Elizabeth turned back towards me. Now there was no doubt of the tears welling in her eyes.

"Sorry," I said quickly. "It's none of my business."

"No. You need to know."

I wasn't sure this was entirely accurate, given my ruse of being the nanny, but I was so desperate to hear what happened next that I didn't protest.

"From time to time Daphne threw herself back into her Catholicism as a sort of penance for everything else in her life—either that or to rile up Max, it was hard to tell. Whatever her reasons, she had decided that morning to take Agatha to Mass, even though the roads were wet and icy, and even though she had been drinking the night before. Max blamed himself, but the fault was all hers, and she knew it."

She stopped here suddenly and stood up, as if a bell had rung in another room that she alone could hear, summoning her to action. As with everything at Barnsley House, the supply of information had only left me more bewildered than when I began. Max had promised Elizabeth would provide me with practical details, but all she had done was confuse me further. I had come because Sophia had asked for help, and now that I was here, the situation was more delicate than I had expected.

"What is the nature of Agatha's injury?" I stammered, trying to take some authority and steer the conversation back to the children I was assuming responsibility for.

Elizabeth looked confused. "I think it's very clear she can't walk," she said, and gave her husband a little nudge to the ankle. He looked up blankly, and seemed surprised to find himself in the sitting room with the pair of us looking at him. "Tom, lunch."

Tom snapped into gear, folding his paper into a perfect rectangle.

"Wait!" I said, not meaning to raise my voice, but losing control. At the strident tones of my accent, her lip tightened ever so slightly in distaste. "Mr. Summer said you would tell me what I needed to do for the children?"

"Oh, yes. The children. Wait, Tom, while I think. There's Sophia, and Robbie, and of course Agatha," she started, listing them more for her own benefit than mine, I assumed. "They'll be at school most of the time. Feed them, I suppose. Get them ready for the bus. Homework. Supper. That sort of thing. When the hotel opens again, keep them from bothering the guests."

"Anything specific I need to know? Allergies? Medicines?" I had the sense that this would be my only opportunity to ask questions, that after this conversation Elizabeth would feel her duties concluded, and I would have to make my own way.

"No. Allergies? No. No. None of that kind of thing," Elizabeth muttered, herding her husband towards the door. She stopped. "There is one thing."

"Yes?" I said, anticipating a fear of the dark, an imminent piano recital.

"It would be best if Daphne doesn't know you're here."

"Oh?"

The only sound was the hiss of the logs in the fire-place and the steady tick of the clock on the mantel. I felt sure the racing beat of my heart could be heard above it all.

"It's for the best," Elizabeth said, turning to leave.

"Well, perhaps we'll see you soon," I called after her desperately, suddenly frightened at being left alone in the room. "Maybe we can take the children out to the island on the weekend for a picnic."

Elizabeth turned slowly around. At first I thought she was angry or shocked, but then her face broke into a radiant smile. Beside her, Tom also started to grin. The movement totally transformed their faces, making them seem years younger, almost young enough to be parents of young children.

"Would you?" she asked, breathlessly. "The children have never been to the island before. Daphne would never allow it. Would you?"

From where I was standing, I could see it. Despite its hostile appearance on that morning, I felt sure a sunny day and a picnic would transform it to a children's paradise. "Why not? I would love to come out and see the island. I'm sure the children would as well."

My heart raced as if I had achieved some great victory. I felt as if I was about to infiltrate the inner sanctum, as if going to the island would cement my position at Barnsley. Miranda, the first Australian to go to the island.

It was a thrilling feeling, the prospect of going against Daphne's wishes, even if it seemed she might never find out. Our farewells were spirited, and as Tom and Elizabeth left, I felt I had made important allies. There might be a future for me at Barnsley.

16

The first day ticked on.

I unpacked my bag. My activewear took up surprisingly little room in the enormous dresser. Three pairs of running shoes were lined up below, mocking me with their incongruity.

What had suited my old life in Melbourne was grossly out of place; I was grossly out of place. I left my copy of *The House of Brides* safely tucked away in my bag and stashed the bag under the armchair. The house remained silent. Elizabeth and Tom had disappeared, and Max had never returned from wherever it was he had escaped to earlier. I couldn't hear Daphne, even though I knew she was in her room. The children were gone. I was unsure of what to do next.

So I did what anyone would do in my situation. I snooped.

I headed downstairs to the solid door dividing the family living quarters from the main part of Barnsley House. Expecting it to be locked, I thumbed the latch and pushed heavily. It gave way immediately, and I fell into the corridor beyond.

It was freezing. The heating had obviously been off in this part of the house for a long time—maybe since the accident. It felt cold enough to be true. I closed the door behind me, and it disappeared into the paneling.

In the still corridor, *The House of Brides* came back to me. There was a bedroom somewhere upstairs in the east wing where Gertrude had done most of her writing. I knew there was a library somewhere as well. And then there were the rooms that would postdate the book. The restaurant, for example. A commercial kitchen. I was at the base of an enormous staircase, which seemed to be the T-intersection of the house itself. The house seemed to be built mostly along the top of the T, with all the rooms looking out to sea, while the utility section of the house was crammed into the stumpy base. Feeble sunlight filtered in through the stained-glass window of the landing but failed to disturb the gloom of the hallways on either side of me.

I headed to the left, past closed doors, until I reached

a larger set at the end. They were constructed from black steel, more modern than anything else in the building. I detected Daphne's touch. I pushed the door open, and a giant conservatory revealed itself. The Summer House. The restaurant had been aptly named; the walls were entirely glass, and inside was even colder than the corridor. I zipped up my vest and pulled my sleeves down over my hands, thumbs into the specially designed holes.

The tables were still set. Wineglasses stood in position, covered in a light coat of dust. Cutlery, only slightly tarnished, flanked starched napkins. The chairs were upholstered in the softest pink velvet. I stroked one, almost reflexively. Velvet always has that effect on me. "They were my idea." I jumped, knocking a wineglass over and upending a dish in the process. Sea salt and dust spread across the linen tablecloth. "Max wasn't mad on them."

Daphne.

Her Australian accent was more pronounced than I had expected, after all the years she had spent here. My vowels were already softening after only days.

I turned to look at her. She was moving slowly, quietly. Elizabeth was right. She was tiny. Her blond hair was slightly stringy, her once distinctive fringe longer and pushed to the side of her heart-shaped face.

"They're lovely," I said, for want of anything better to say.

"You're Australian," Daphne replied. My vowels weren't soft enough.

"Yes."

Daphne moved closer, her hand at her side, using the backs of the chairs for support as she moved through the room. Her frame was dwarfed by the clothes she was wearing: a faded oversize tea dress and a long cardigan. She cupped one hand under the lip of the table and in a cluster of capable movements used the other to sweep the salt into it. Looking for somewhere to deposit the dusty salt and finding nowhere, she smoothly deposited it back into its original dish. "Who are you?"

It was a reasonable question, but Elizabeth's warning ran through my head: *It would be best if Daphne doesn't know you're here.*

Before I had a chance to answer, Daphne spoke again. "You're a bloody nanny, aren't you?" She sighed and pulled back a chair, wrapped her long cardigan around her. Something clinked in her pocket. "I told them I was fine. They won't let me near the children, you know." Her words slurred slightly. It was only midmorning, and she was drunk. I was starting to see their concern. "Fetch a cloth from over there." She pointed in the direction of a sideboard. I followed her instructions and took a cloth from underneath. "And one for me too." For someone so small, she was quite adept at giving orders. I could imagine she would be formidable in a busy kitchen. "Now look busy."

I followed the direction of her head to the corner, where I could now see a small white camera, almost camouflaged in the paintwork. Daphne picked up a wineglass, so I did too, half-heartedly rubbing some dust about while she spoke. "I suppose they've told you about the accident. Max and Meryl." She said Meryl's name in much the same way a child would talk about a schoolyard bully. "I was driving. We hit a deer. Agatha was badly injured." Her voice had gone strangely monotone, and the glass shook in her hand.

"Were you injured as well?" I concentrated on my glass, playing it up for the camera, even though I could barely see what I was doing without my glasses. Whoever was watching would be impressed by my thoroughness. A familiar buzz went through me, the thrill of deception.

Daphne hesitated. I recognized the hesitation. Lie or tell the truth: it never gets any easier. But I couldn't tell *her* that. "Yes. Yes, I was. Quite badly."

"Why won't they let you near the children?" It was a dangerous question, and could be enough to set her off. Especially in her state.

She placed the glass down, used her fingers to stabilize the base. Despite her condition, her glass gleamed. "Would you like a tour of the house?" she asked brightly. As if she hadn't even heard my question from moments before.

"That would be lovely, thank you. I thought no one would ever ask."

"You seemed to be doing a pretty good job on your own."

We moved slowly. Daphne must have been light on her feet at the best of times, and that morning, with her feet clad only in hand-knitted socks, she barely made a sound. It would be easy for her to move undetected around Barnsley. "It's hard to picture it now, on a summer's day, in the full swing of lunch service," she said.

I nodded and tried to imagine. "The sun streams in the windows, and all you can see is green grass and the blue of the water. It's spectacular. There's nothing like it."

Daphne pushed through a concealed door. She reached out her hand, instinctive even in the dark, and rows of powerful fluorescent lights illuminated the room. Polished stainless-steel counters reflected in the brilliant light. State-of-the-art ovens and stovetops seemed to be waiting for the chef to return at any moment. For Daphne to return.

"Will you cook again?"

Daphne looked at me, frightened. I recognized the look in her eyes. Terror. Fear of failure. More than that, the fear of failure after great success. I saw it in the mirror myself, some days. "A woman from the village comes in to keep this area clean," she said before switching off the lights again and leaving me in complete darkness. "At my request."

The tour continued along the hallway.

"On this side"—Daphne gestured—"are the guest areas. A drawing room." She whipped the door open just long enough for me to see that it was the room I had peered into earlier. The curtains were closed and the room was in darkness, but the shape of the bay window was unmistakable. "It used to be the family's dining room once upon a time. They still use it on special occasions."

"I think I've read about the dining room in *The House*—" I stopped myself. Too late. Daphne looked at me suspiciously.

"Have you?" she asked, and then her face went blank. The thought had slipped away.

She continued walking, opening door after door just long enough for me to steal glimpses of dark and dusty rooms within. Her breathing grew labored, her steps ginger.

"Lounge. Bar. Morning room."

By this stage we had passed the stairwell and were at the other end of the building. "And above us are the family bedrooms?"

"Yes, that's right."

"We can leave it there, if you like."

"There's something upstairs I'd like you to see." She paused. "Seeing as though you're a *House of Brides* fan." It was hard to read her expression in the half dark.

"Upstairs? I don't know if that's a good idea. Maybe I can help you back to bed?"

Daphne started to climb the stairs. The rest of the house was silent, but I felt as if Max could reappear at any moment.

"You need to know what you're getting into." She was puffing, muttering more to herself than to me. I was beginning to wish I'd taken Elizabeth's advice, and stayed clear of Daphne.

"Why has Max . . . er, Mr. Summer . . . not made any adjustments to the house for Agatha?"

Silence, apart from the breathing. "Like a lift? Or some ramps around the place?"

"Yes. I know what you mean," Daphne snapped.

"Do the doctors think she will be in a wheelchair forever?"

Daphne produced some keys from the pocket of her cardigan and held them up in the light of the stained-glass window. The clinking—not a bottle after all. She seemed to be looking for one in particular. They all looked the same to me. "They thought so at first. But now, maybe there's a chance she won't be. It's the only thing that keeps me going."

We came to the top, and found ourselves at the cross passage of the house. It was mostly too dark to see much. In front of us was a solid wall with one doorway; to our left, a smaller passageway. I could see that this was the backside of our bedrooms, the upstairs slightly consumed by our modest quarters. There seemed to be some rooms in that direction, but the majority were to our right, along a large hallway that turned and disappeared beyond my vision. "The guest rooms," Daphne said, each word a struggle.

The combination of the poor light and my equally dismal vision made it hard to read the placards. One stood out, though; I remembered it from the book.

"The Yellow Room."

Daphne shook her head and passed by the Yellow Room. "The Island Room." She wrenched back the curtains with a strength I had not imagined, and the room was revealed. It was a corner room, more like a suite. The décor was classic but not twee: sturdy-looking antiques and a squishy armchair upholstered in tweed. A brass lamp on the bedside towered over a small pile of Penguin Classics.

"Named for its view of Minerva Island," I volunteered.

Daphne ignored me. She ran her hands under the mattress. Picked up the books and turned them over. Her manic behaviour was unsettling. She was unsettling. I could see why they needed someone to help with the children. She picked up a cushion from the chair, unzipped it. I was just about to leave her alone when her face relaxed and she withdrew her hand.

Something tiny and gold lay upon it. "I want you to take this for me."

"What is it?" I asked, disingenuously, for even in the gloomy light and with my terrible eyesight, I could tell it was a key.

"I want you to keep it safe for me. You have no ties to this place. No one will suspect you."

A sound escaped from my mouth, but Daphne didn't seem to notice. "If anything happens to me, I want you to use this." She pushed up against me, holding the key to me, her eyes darting. When I didn't make a move, she grabbed my hand and forced the key into it. Up close, the stench of alcohol I had been expecting was absent, but in its place was a strangely chemical smell. Something about her was not quite right.

"Have you ever been to the island?" I asked, desperate to return to normalcy. I tucked the key in my pocket, resolved to give it to Max later.

Daphne came and stood beside me, hugging the cushion to her chest. "No."

"Why not?"

"I don't think that's any concern of yours."

The voice took me by surprise. Thomas appeared first, and then, moments later, his owner. "I saw the curtains were open. What are you doing in here?"

"I was just showing this girl where you . . . ," Daphne stuttered.

"The school bus is due any minute," Max interrupted.

"Yes, Mr. Summer," I said, trying to draw his attention away from his wife, who was frozen in position by the window, her arms still wrapped around the cushion. She was trembling slightly, but a slight flush rose on her cheeks, and her eyes were defiant.

"Go on, then," Max said.

I looked back at Daphne, and she nodded slightly, as if giving me permission to leave. The terror I had noticed earlier, in the kitchen, had returned to her face. I had no choice but to leave her there with Max.

As I shuffled out into the dark hall, there was only the light from the Island Room to guide my way down the dark passage. Moments later they shut the door softly behind me, and I was completely in the dark.

17

Later, in bed, after I had fed the children a simple dinner of pasta (Marmite on toast for Agatha), helped with homework, and supervised bedtime, I couldn't sleep, despite my exhaustion. The details of the day circled around in my head, and wouldn't let me rest.

Everyone seemed to be hiding something. There were things that seemed not quite right, parts of the story that didn't quite ring true. Things only another storyteller would notice.

When I did get to sleep, I slept poorly. A dynamite combination of jet lag and anxiety. Would I have heard Daphne had I been in a deep sleep? I'm not sure. In the quiet hours after midnight, her cries seemed deafening, and as soon as I heard her, I leapt from my bed, certain she was hurt.

Thomas barred me from entering, his tail banging loudly against the doorframe, his mouth opening slightly with a low half-hearted growl. The shouting was fading and I could hear Max's voice, low and consoling, in response, so I returned down the corridor in my pyjamas, more awake than ever. I had run the chain of my mother's fob necklace through the key Daphne gave me, and it rested against my bare skin. Warm now, reminding me of its presence.

I switched on my bedside lamp, a small iron affair with a fluted bluebell-shaped shade. The room felt warmer straightaway, the shadows of the night pushed back into the chintzy corners. It was such a contrast to the refurbished rooms in the hotel. Clearly any money had been spent on the public areas of the house and not on the family's private area. My bag was under the faded-out armchair, where I had left it; the book called out temptingly from within.

My fingers located it by touch after only the slightest rummaging. It was not a fancy edition like Max's. The one I had brought with me was my treasured paperback, its absence less noticeable than the hardback first editions' would have been. I had smuggled it off to my room years earlier, pushing the other copies together to conceal the gap where it had been. My dad never said anything, but that doesn't mean he didn't notice. He never really said anything when it came to my mother.

Now I was starting to wonder why. Whether he knew something I didn't. It was only just now starting to seem off to me how little he had talked about her past and her family and how much I had missed out on. How little my father had talked about what she had achieved. It seemed amazing to me now that we had never talked about how different her life in Australia was from the one she had growing up at Barnsley. Or that she had ever left this place. No one else seemed to. Was it because there was no future for her here? Was it because there was no way she could ever become one of the famous brides?

The cover was soft, almost leathery to the touch, the cardboard creased at the corners, the edges of the pages as soft as the velvet of the chairs in the restaurant. *The House of Brides*. I hadn't dared get it out since I arrived, fearing it as though it were a talisman, not an inanimate object. As if parts of the book would jump into my head by osmosis, and I would unwittingly drop them into conversation. As if most of the book wasn't already steeped in my subconscious, a volatile bomb poised to implode at any moment.

Over the years, I had read it a number of times. I had read it from cover to cover, particularly in my late teens and university years, searching for clues about my mother. The acknowledgements pages were of the greatest interest to me then: the only personal pages in the whole book and littered with names that meant nothing to me, despite my constant hope that one would leap out in familiarity. The references to friends and places that had meant something to my mother made her seem like a real living person, but also left me feeling further adrift. She had a whole life before me, a life I knew nothing about.

I perched myself on the edge of the armchair and tucked my frozen feet under my bottom, hoping that some heat would transfer to them. Wanting to be alert, not too comfortable. A door slammed down the hallway, and I jumped. Thomas gave a short growl, and Max whistled to him softly.

Moments later, the sound of a door closing again. More gently this time. Thinking it was one of the children, I placed the book down and moved out to the hallway. Thomas was gone, but Daphne stood frozen at the door to her bedroom, her face agitated and streaked with silent tears. I moved towards her, and was about to speak when she shook her head slowly and raised her finger to her lips. Not sure what to do next, I held my hand out to her, but she shook her head again and gave me a tiny, wan smile. I had no choice but to return to my room and shut the door.

There was no chance of sleep, not after that.

Still listening for sounds from the hallway I turned over the first few pages of *House of Brides*. For the first time, I noticed that there was no dedication. Pausing a moment to think about this, I flicked through the whole book until I reached the index. This time, I wanted to know about Max.

I wanted to know why Daphne had become afraid of him. I wanted to know if it had anything to do with my mother's departure, all those years ago. There were only a few entries. The book was called *The House of Brides* for a reason. The men were sidelined, on the periphery and outshone by their more successful partners.

Maximilian Arthur Summer (1967–), 18–19, 32, 38, 42, 44, 225–29, 240

Max was a bit player in the narrative. My mother had stuck to her guns and robustly focused on the women in the story. It might have been revenge on Max for his sole inheritance of Barnsley, or it might go back even further to her relationship with her father. They were all *real* people, not just the ones who were still living, and I thought they held the clue to why she had fled to Australia.

The first few entries noted that Max was the current owner of Barnsley House, having taken it on after the death of his father. There was no mention of Daphne. My mother must never have met her, or perhaps she had, and deemed her not permanent enough to be included. I checked the date of publication at the front of the book: 1991. Just before I was born. Max hadn't even met Daphne. The book was written long before they married.

If my mother were alive, she could write a new chapter, add her in. I tried to imagine it; an updated edition, a party at Barnsley to celebrate, Max raising his glass in a toast, my father smiling proudly. The image refused to obey, shifting in my mind as if someone else was in control. I concentrated on the page in front of me instead.

There was nothing new about Max, nothing I had overlooked. At the times when she couldn't avoid mentioning him, her descriptions were dull, bereft of the colour and character she lavished on her female relatives. He came across as interesting solely by virtue of his inheritance, defined only by a set of dates and places. Born, schooled, inherited. My father's words echoed in my mind. *Some things—some people—are better left in the past.*

18

S till, despite my father's warning, I couldn't put the book down.

If there is one constant through the generations at Barnsley, it's their love of a party.

It has been much quieter in recent years, but in the time when my mother and father were in charge, the house was often packed to the gills at the weekend, even during the winter months. Of course in the summer the entire estate was full, even the outlying cottages, which for the rest of the year were deemed uninhabitable. But during the summer months, people would sleep anywhere to get a slice of the Barnsley Summer Festival.

The postwar years were famously rough on

country houses. Barnsley suffered as much as any and took longer to adapt than other estates in the area and change to suit the new world order. The situation at Barnsley had not improved by the time my father, Maximilian Summer, inherited in the 1960s. He brought his young bride Beatrice to his family home, and they had three children in quick succession—my older siblings, twins Max and Elizabeth, and then me, shortly after. They then set about turning around the fortunes of Barnsley House.

The Barnsley Summer Festival was the metamorphosis of a country house party into a ticketed event. It gathered popularity quickly, running for three years before the tragic death of Beatrice during the festival resulted in its cancellation.

But in its heyday it was a great success. A large stage was erected on the front lawn, and people lay around on blankets listening to music. It went on for days, with men and women sleeping wherever they lay, eating picnic food they had brought with them. By the end of the week everyone was tired, dirty, and in need of a proper meal, but the overall mood was still positive. One year, Ross Mackie came down with a record company executive and stayed in the main house; another time the Moderns jumped up from the grass and played an impromptu set. The model friends of Beatrice were only part of the temptation for the musicians. While the rest of the area was still shaking off social propriety, Barnsley House was a liberal hotspot, a beacon for creative types.

During the Barnsley Summer Festival of 1969, a balmy and oppressive night according to first-hand accounts, Beatrice and Maximilian returned to the house to host a small private dinner for an intimate circle. Some friends, some associates of the festival. Tension rose through the dinner. Rosamund West, who was present on that night and supposed to be a great friend of my mother, wrote in her diary:

Usual drama at Barnsley tonight. Beatrice arrived for dinner late and drunk. Visibly distracted. Smoked the whole time. Sniped at her husband all night. The music from the festival was too loud. There was no hot water for her bath. The room was stuffy.

It was like having a child at the table,

which in some senses she is, despite having three children of her own in the nursery. And twins to boot! I wouldn't have thought her capable. Maximilian wisely ignored her, but the air around them was fraught. Finally, at 10:00 p.m., she pushed back her chair and rushed out, leaving us all in peace. Unfortunately, that wasn't the end of the trouble.

I wondered who this Rosamund West was, and how much to trust her description of my grandmother. I doubted Max would have been happy with how my mother had portrayed their mother, but was it enough to completely destroy their relationship? I didn't think so.

The narrative resumed in my mother's voice:

The fireworks had just finished and the guests had sat back down when the night took a terrible turn. There were no smoke alarms in those days, so the first they knew of it was when the nanny came in, holding the infant Max and shouting.

Rosamund describes the scene:

She was sweating and distressed.
It was hard to understand her at first.
She was saying something about a
fire, but the music outside the dining
room had ramped up at that point,
and we were all a few sheets to the breeze.
We thought she was having an unusual
reaction to the fireworks; it had been
a particularly triumphant display.
Maximilian grabbed her by the shoulders,
embarrassed by the fuss. He pushed her
towards the door, a little too forcefully, I
thought. One of the other women there,
Hilda Le Page, spoke out. "Let her talk,
for god's sake, Mills."

I skipped forward, looking for the part about Max.

By the time the alarm was raised, it was too late.
Fire had consumed the east wing. In the confusion
of the festival and the fireworks, the firefighters
found it hard to get through; the best access was at

the front of the house, but that was filled with concertgoers, and in any case, the damage to the east wing was already immense.

Many of the patrons had passed out on the lawn or were simply too out of it to follow instructions. A good deal thought the firefighters were part of the entertainment and cheered loudly when they arrived. Women tried to dance with them, and men pushed drinks in their direction. It was a nightmare.

The nanny had saved the young Max's life. He had been in the room with Beatrice when the fire started. It took days for the fire department to piece together what had happened. Beatrice had indeed stormed out of the dinner that night.

In fact, she was known for her dramatic exits, and normally she would return to the party some time later, having settled herself with more alcohol and some restorative cigarettes.

This time, however, she had not come back. No one found this unusual either; the amount of alcohol they had all consumed made it seem only reasonable that some of them might pass out. In fact, Frederick Howard was asleep down one end of the table already, his face planted on the main course. It was that sort of night.

Beatrice had gone to the Yellow Room in the east wing. It was her room, as it had been for Gertrude and Sarah and, before them, Elspeth. Like her predecessors, Beatrice could look out over the lawn and across to sea. While Gertrude had sat there and formulated her fiction, Beatrice used the eyrie as a bird's-eye view over the estate. Perhaps she sat in the window awhile that evening, smoked a cigarette, thought about her behaviour at dinner. Did she care what the others thought of her? She would not have known that her antics that evening would be immortalized in Rosamund's diary. She considered Rosamund a close friend.

Whatever she did, for some reason, at around midnight she went out of her room and into the nursery. The nanny was asleep at the time, despite the continuing noise of the party outside. Did she hear the baby stir? It's doubtful. The walls at Barnsley are thick: the aftermath of the fire revealed them to be multilayered. Thick reeds, wooden paneling, and layers of bricks hidden beneath solid plaster. Besides, the nanny heard nothing.

Beatrice left behind two sleeping daughters—Max's twin Elizabeth and their one-year-old sister Therese—and instead took her two-year-old son.

The heir of Barnsley, the latest Maximilian Summer in an ever-growing line.

She took the young boy back into the Yellow Room and turned the bath on. There is no way of knowing why she thought Max might need a bath in the middle of the night. If he had been sick, there was no evidence of it in his bed afterwards. It was summer, and even though the infant had been unwell the previous winter with croup, at this time he was in fine health.

While the bath was running, she lit a cigarette and left it to burn in one of the numerous ashtrays in her room. Cut from glass and heavy, the ashtrays were a familiar sight around the house. Taking Max into the bathroom, she forgot about the cigarette and became engrossed in the task of undressing him, preparing him for his unexpected bath. The cigarette rolled from its teetering position, a slow smolder on the carpet quickly leaping to the voluptuous drapes. The noise from outside concealed any sounds from the fire.

The nanny woke to the smell of smoke. Rushing down the hallway, she found Beatrice slumped next to the bath, passed out from intoxication, smoke inhalation, or a combination of both. Max had rolled onto the floor, clad only in a nappy. The nanny quickly snatched the baby up, fetching the other children out of their beds on the way. She tried to raise the alarm, but her shouts were quickly swallowed up in the rowdy atmosphere of the night.

By the time she appeared in the dining room, it was too late. Maximilian and the others made it upstairs, but the air was thick with smoke and flames leapt out from the doorway of the Yellow Room. They couldn't pass. It was impossible to rescue Beatrice.

Even though I knew it was coming, the death of Beatrice—my grandmother—was a shock to me. I somehow expected things to turn out differently for her, now that I knew the house, now that I knew Max.

What shocked me the most, though, was the way my mother wrote about it. The impersonal use of her mother's name. The undeniable detachment. My mother was writing about the death of her mother with no more emotion than she would write about the death of someone she didn't know. She had been a baby at the time, only months old, on the night in question. She had never had a chance to know her mother, but even so, the sense of distance in her writing seemed odd. Cold. As if she was angry at her.

I sat back in the armchair. Thought it over a bit. The house was quiet now, settling into the long quiet hours between midnight and dawn. Wide awake, my mind ticked over quickly. For the first time since I arrived, I felt grateful for the jet lag that had dogged me. I'd been groggy and nauseated during the day, but now, in the middle of the night, I felt alert. Switched on. Like pieces of the puzzle were coming together.

The death of Beatrice.

Max in the room.

The book, published just after my mother came to Australia.

The estrangement between Max and my mother.

They were all connected.

I hadn't been able to read between the lines before, but I could see it clearly now. Beatrice had tried to kill her baby son that night, my mother had insinuated, and if not for the fire, she might have succeeded. Of all the events in *The House of Brides*—and there was plenty of infidelity and skullduggery—this was the most shocking. This was the most shameful. Not only did it set up her mother as a killer, but the victim was to be her own son.

Max.

My mother could have left the story out. She could have stopped the narrative at Gertrude, the bride before Beatrice. It would have made sense: compared to Gertrude and Sarah and Elspeth, Beatrice was a good-time girl, famous for her looks and her parties and not much else.

But instead, she put the story in, an unproven and veiled accusation. I was surprised there was a copy at Barnsley at all.

Seeking some reassurance, I turned back to the acknowledgements, this roll call of people who had been important to my mother and then disappeared. I read the names again now. Some of them were familiar because I had read the acknowledgements so many times, and others were just as foreign as they had always been. I waited for a sense of calm to descend. Sleep seemed like a good idea, if I could manage it, but something niggled.

One of the names. I went back, read them again.

Jean Laidlaw. I knew that name. The taxi driver. The historical society.

Perhaps I'd go and find Jean Laidlaw in the morning . . .

It didn't happen, though. Because the very next day, we discovered that Daphne was missing.

19

I didn't realize straightaway. Nobody did. The children went off to school as usual the next morning, and when Robbie went up to say goodbye, he came back down again without mentioning that Daphne wasn't in her bed.

I was attempting to make the children biscuits when the phone rang. My skill at baking is diminished somewhat by never having had a mother to teach me the basics, and despite my father's mother taking some interest in my development, she wasn't the type to hand down a cherished family recipe for scones or fruit loaf. The school I attended didn't offer domestic science, so I had taught myself how to cook, watching my friends' parents and gleaning some knowledge from cooking programs, including Daphne's, ironically.

And in the years in between, baking, especially the kind of sugar-laden treats I was at the moment producing, had not been on brand. Protein balls, packed with esoteric and expensive ingredients—those I could make with my eyes shut.

The dough was not behaving. It was sticky, and the misshapen lumps looked certain to become misshapen, unevenly cooked biscuits. The kitchen looked worse than it had on the night I arrived. Flour covered the bench top, and every knob of the oven was coated with the sticky dough.

The phone clicked over to the answering machine before I could wash my hands off properly. I was drying my hands when I realized that the voice on the recorded message belonged to Daphne. "Hello! You have called the Summer family. I'm probably busy in the restaurant, and I have no idea what Max is doing, but please leave a message, or call again in a couple of days if we forget to call you back."

Her voice was so different from the one I had heard the day before—confident and melodic, and containing a bubble of laughter, as if someone was standing beside her making faces. I wondered who, in this house full of serious and sad people, that might have been. The machine beeped, and Elizabeth's voice boomed out, forcing me to race across the room and snatch up the receiver with both hands. "Hello?" I said, not really sure how to answer a home phone and marveling at the novelty of it.

"I've got two things to talk to you about, and I need you to listen to me," she began, not pausing for pleasantries or to ensure she had the right person on the line. The connection was bad, and although I hadn't seen her cottage, I knew how close she was, and it made little sense that it should sound like she was calling from the other side of the world.

"It's a bad line," I said, shouting to make sure she heard me.

"It's always a bad line." I heard an intake of breath; she was smoking again. "You don't need to shout."

"I can't talk long, there's biscuits in the oven." Plus, I had plans to find Jean Laidlaw before the children came home from school.

"I'm not calling for a chat," she said, with another intake of breath.

"What are the two things, then?"

"I'm afraid I've had a talk with Tom, and the trip to the island is off the cards for now. It's too dangerous at this time of the year; the weather is unpredictable. It wouldn't be a good idea with all that's happened."

"Oh." I could barely disguise my disappointment. In a schedule that was completely empty, a trip to the island had been the one thing I was looking forward to with any sort of enthusiasm. "I was really looking forward to it. Are you sure there's no way we could come out? You and Tom seem to get to and fro quite easily."

"Agatha is in a wheelchair, dear," Elizabeth replied, as if I might have forgotten. "It is simply not safe. Don't even mention the idea to Max or the children. Or Daphne," she added as an afterthought.

"Could we do it when the weather is better? In the summer?" I asked hopefully, keeping an eye on both the clock and the oven.

Elizabeth laughed. "Do you really think you'll be around then?"

"I don't know . . . I like it here," I said truthfully, for it seemed the children were beginning to warm to me; the house and its secrets were drawing me in. I was beginning to forget the real reason I had come. I was beginning to think how nice it would be to simply be here as an employee, to start afresh where nobody knew my past. I didn't know how long I could get away with it. Surely it wouldn't be long before my father found me, or one of the Summers worked out my true identity.

Elizabeth's voice was more kind when she spoke again. "Well, we'll see. It all depends on Daphne. The summer is a long way off. We have to get through winter first." The buzzer on the stove rang out loudly, and even from the other side of the kitchen I could see that the biscuits were quickly changing from golden brown to burnt.

"Elizabeth? I have to go. The biscuits are burning. What was the other thing?"

"Biscuits. How gorgeous. Daphne makes these funny flat things called Anzacs. They looked unlikely but were delicious. Is that what you're up to?"

"No. Just ones with chocolate chips in them— they're more like cookies, I suppose."

"The recipe for those Anzac things is probably lying around somewhere, you should look around for it."

The smell of the burning biscuits was beginning to reach me now; it had turned from buttery to acrid in a matter of moments. "I'm sorry, Elizabeth, I'll have to call you back."

"There's no need to call me back, dear. When you asked me about the children, I knew there was something I was forgetting, but I was so thrown by the idea of a trip to the island that I completely forgot to mention it. Has anyone told you about the drawer?"

"The drawer?" I asked, inching towards the stove, wondering if I could possibly make the cord stretch far enough for me to reach the handle and whip the biscuits to safety.

"It's the drawer on the old dresser. You can't even tell it's there, that's the way they built them in those days, but if you feel along under the bottom shelf, there's a handle."

I let the cord slack in the opposite direction and headed instead towards the dresser, which I had only moments before been leaning against. There was no sign of any drawer, but sure enough, as I let my hand explore under the ridge, I could feel a small indentation. No matter how hard I pressed, though, the drawer resisted. "I've found it," I said. "It's locked." The key against my chest. Daphne's terrified face.

Some instinct told me not to mention it. Not yet. "Oh." Elizabeth's voice was unusually flat.

Giving up hope of salvaging any biscuits, I fished under the neck of my jumper and pulled the chain up and over my head. Trying not to make a sound, I set the key into the small brass lock on the side of the dresser. There was a little sigh, and the drawer released.

"Definitely locked," I repeated as I let my eyes scan over the contents. They at first seemed a useless collection of flotsam and jetsam: forms for school excursions; a small pot filled with loose change, some notes, and a credit card with Daphne's name on it; car keys and sunblock. Further back in the drawer there was a notebook, black leather and worn at the edges, and piles of paper, receipts, postcards, and letters. "I guess it's not much help to me, then," I said, trying to disguise the excitement in my voice.

"Daphne used to put everything in there," Elizabeth said. "Her diary, school forms, the like. She was always writing in a notebook. If we could just find the key, I'm sure you would find everything you need." The connection being as bad as it was, it took a moment for me to realize she had already hung up.

Elizabeth was wrong about a lot of things. The truth evaded her many times—whether by accident or by design—but she was right about that drawer. It had everything in it I needed.

20

It felt wrong, at first, reading the notebook. It was too personal, written for some purpose I had not yet gathered. It felt wrong, because I didn't know then that Daphne was missing. But even though it felt wrong, I saw it in the drawer and I seized upon it. Daphne was an enigma, yes, but more than that, she had trusted me when she was most vulnerable, both outside her bedroom the night before and the afternoon when she had pressed the key upon me with such urgency. I knew the contents of the drawer must be important.

The first few pages of the notebook were filled with day-to-day notes: recipes jotted down, shopping lists, reminders of things to do. It seemed Daphne had been preparing for Christmas—she had a full menu planned with initials next to dishes of which she seemed to have

uncharacteristically relinquished control. "MM"—
Meryl Mins, I assumed—was in charge of the pudding,
and "EC," the stuffing. It all seemed very cozy.

Robbie needed new school shoes, and Sophia was
booked for a checkup at the orthodontist on the sixth
of January. The minutiae of family life were of little
interest to me. Perhaps Daphne really was as mad as
she looked. I turned a couple more pages of notes and
reminders, and my idle thoughts about the orthodontist
appointment were completely forgotten.

Elizabeth,

This is for you. I don't know
if you'll find this note. I tried to
conceal it somewhere it might not
be found, but I also worry that it
might be too properly concealed and
never found. Both of these are a worry
to me, and you know how I worry!

You're always asking me why I
carry this book around, and I
always answer you truthfully: recipes,

shopping lists, things to remember.
Since I had the children, I can't
remember anything. Before you say
anything—it's not the drugs. It
came before that, but I guess those
years didn't help.

Sometimes I'll be out in the
garden, and I'll pick something:
fennel, or even just an herb, and by
the time I come to cook with it in
the evening, I will have forgotten
what I had planned. Even with
the fennel or the tarragon right there
in front of me! It's not great for
business, let me tell you. So I
started writing everything down. It
seems crazy, even writing this, but
this is my backup plan.

Just in case something happens

to me, I want someone to know
what I know. I think I'm in
danger. I know you think she's
harmless. She's not. She would
hurt me if she could work out a way
to do it without upsetting Max, and
I think she would hurt him too.
I know you'll think it's the drugs
talking, or the alcohol. Some sort
of aftereffect. But you know how long
I've been off that stuff, and I'm
more paranoid without it than I
ever was with it.

Here's the thing about Meryl—
and yes, I'm going to call her that
here, even if I don't have the guts
to use her name in real life—she
loves Max. Oh, Daphne, I can
already hear you saying. No shit! I

always love hearing you swear in your beautiful plummy accent. In fact, the first time I met you, you broke the ice with a well-placed swear word, and I knew that despite everything, all the odds against me, I was going to like it at Barnsley. Especially with you and Max by my side.

I love Max too, but it's a normal adult love. We fight sometimes (well, kind of a lot, especially since the accident), we test each other's patience, but we really do want the best out of each other. I know his weaknesses and he knows mine, and if one of those piles of weaknesses is stacked higher than the other, well, I completely accept it. I'm not *perfect. Max isn't perfect either. But in Meryl's eyes he is.*

Max says you don't know the full story about the Mins—

Here the writing stopped dead, and the last word was smudged slightly. Below it, Daphne had reverted to list-making.

Standing rib roast of beef. Duck fat. Clementines. Max present?????

It continued in that fashion, Daphne's handsome writing making even the most mundane collection of words attractive, and then over the page the writing changed again, slightly more slanted and less elaborate, as if written in a rush.

She bloody came in! Would you believe it? She came in while I was writing that last bit and I had to cover it up like I was back at school. That woman has eyes everywhere, and a sixth sense for mischief. It's probably why your mother employed her in the first place. I'll have to get this down quickly, in case she comes back again. I'm sure she was trying to see what I was writing.

"Your mother?" Beatrice had hired Mrs. Mins? I thought it was Max who brought her from Italy . . .

It was funny, even though I had met Daphne briefly, I hadn't got any sense of her as a person. It was hard to connect this strong, lively voice with the delicate shell of a woman I had encountered on my first day at Barnsley.

Max always said you don't need to know the full story about Mr. and Mrs. Mins. He has some protective vibe going on towards you. I tell him, Max, she may be your younger sister, but she could take you on any day of the week. It's true too, you're a good woman to have in your corner. Once you came on board about the restaurant and the hotel, I knew it was going to work. And it did. I'd fist-pump you if you were here, but I know how you hate affected gestures. Which kind of makes me want to do it more, ha ha.

It's an old-fashioned thing, I think, protecting the womenfolk. So here goes. Maybe despite what Max thinks, you know some of it or most of it. Women always know more than they let on. And in the end, I think it will be us—you and me— protecting Max.

Max told me all of this in the first flush of confidences, in the *nights just after we met. We were still in London, and at this point, we didn't know what was in our future; that only days later we would be engaged. But on that night, we laid everything on the table. I don't know if he would have been so forthcoming if he had known I would end up at Barnsley with him, as his wife. I was just a ready ear then, and Max needed a ready ear.*

I had to force myself to return the notebook to the drawer. There was the problem of the biscuits and the imminent arrival of the school bus to deal with. But mostly, I didn't want Daphne to catch me reading it. I didn't know then that I needn't have worried about that. I locked the drawer, carefully tucked away the key on my fob chain, and vowed to return to it as soon as possible.

21

The afternoon was closing into evening; darkness arrived at Barnsley more prematurely than anywhere else I had been. As we returned from the bus stop, I kept an eye out for Thomas—who was almost indiscernible in the dark—along the long and twisty driveway. I had learned that Thomas never ventured far from Max's side.

And Max had been nowhere to be seen since that morning.

It had been only days since I arrived, but already the children were feeling comfortable enough with me to unload their school-day miseries on the way back to the house. Agatha was quiet; school tired her out easily. Sophia was having problems with another girl at school who wanted to be her best friend and undermine her at the same time. Robbie was nagging me about an old haunted abbey nearby that he wanted to visit on the weekend. "I met your aunt yesterday," I said when the older two had finished, the phone call and the notebook having jogged my memory. I wanted to get their take on Elizabeth.

"Elizabeth," said Robbie.

"We only have one aunt." Sophia sighed and looked out the window, exasperated out of proportion with her brother in the usual manner of girls her age. I wondered if she was thinking about my mother, if she was being deliberately obtuse.

"Yes, Elizabeth."

"Did she come to the house?" Agatha asked from the back.

"Yes."

"She can't have children. There's something wrong with her."

"Agatha! That's none of our business," Sophia snapped.

"It's called infertile." This was Robbie, ever eager to put a name to things. It was his way of controlling his unpredictable world. "I bet it was before lunch."

"Why?" I asked, intrigued.

"What did she want?" I let Sophia change the subject but snuck a glance at her. She was staring out the window, too intently to be convincing.

"She came to talk about you children. To tell me what to do, that kind of thing. 'Dinner at six, bedtime at seven,' I think is what she said." My attempt at humour passed them by, so I continued. "I think she just wanted to check up on me, make sure your father had made the right choice."

"I hope you didn't listen."

"Why not, Sophia?"

"She doesn't have any children, and she has no idea about children. After the accident, she completely disappeared. Went out to that bloody island every day and didn't dare show her face."

"Oh. I'm sure she just didn't know what to do. Some people are like that, they don't know how to cope in bad times," I said, thinking of all the people I had lost in my life when my mum died. Even school friends I had known all my life suddenly stopped inviting me places, like having a sick mother was contagious, or a single father was dangerous.

"Sophia said bloody," Agatha chimed in.

"Mum says worse. She says f—"

"Robbie! That's enough!" I shouted, just in time,

nearly crashing the van into one of the bordering hedges.

"She says being married to our father is enough to make anyone say it."

As much as I wanted to hear more about Daphne and her profanities, we were approaching the house, and I had only limited time to capitalize on this out-pouring of information before Sophia bolted from the car and retreated to her room, as she did every night after school. "So you don't see very much of Eliza-beth?" I asked tentatively, very much wanting to get back to that subject but not wanting to alert Sophia to my interest.

"Not anymore. She used to be around all the time. Mum and Dad used to fight about it."

"Why?"

"Dad said she's a bad influence on Mum." This was Robbie, and judging by the look Sophia gave him, she wasn't happy he had shared this information. It seemed she was in charge of what I could and couldn't know. Robbie stopped talking.

Elizabeth had led me to believe that she and Daphne were not close, but here were the children telling me they were friends, more than friends, it seemed. Eliza-beth must have gotten over her initial unhappiness with Max's wife, but she hadn't included that in her story.

She hadn't included herself in the story at all, I realized now. "What does she do out on the island?" I could see it from where I stood, bleak and uninviting, the sort of place where there really wasn't much to do aside from acquire a serious case of windburn.

Sophia snorted. "What do old people do anywhere?"

"We don't know, they've never taken us out there," Robbie added, looking at me apologetically, as if I, along with Elizabeth and Daphne and Max and Mrs. Mins, was considered to be one of the "old people."

"Mum says it's too dangerous."

"Mum thinks everything around here is dangerous," Agatha said, her voice clouded in emotion.

"Well, she was right, wasn't she?" And that was that. Another topic of conversation swiftly dead-ended by Sophia.

We travelled the rest of the short distance in silence.

"Here we are," I said as we pulled around next to the back entrance. It had become our habit to pull up close to the house. It was difficult to bring Agatha all the way across the gravel drive in her wheelchair, and this way worked much better for us all. I went around to the back of the car and, meeting Sophia there, took my opportunity. "I got your letter," I said, in such a rush I could hardly elaborate.

"What letter?" Sophia looked at me disdainfully. Her face took me straight back to high school. I had to remind myself I was the adult.

"The letter," I said in a meaningful way, aware that Robbie was approaching and Agatha was still waiting in the car. "You can trust me."

"You're not—"

"Tessa. No. My mother died."

Her eyes popped, and I could see she understood. She was just about to say something when Robbie pushed past us, grabbing his schoolbag in a way that sent the wheelchair flying into Sophia's body. The moment was lost. "I don't know what you're talking about."

Robbie looked from Sophia to me in confusion, and Sophia took her chance to disappear into the house. We would not see her again until she made a surly appearance at dinner.

Once in the house, the children looked suspiciously at my burnt biscuits but were polite enough to try them. Even Agatha, for the first time since I arrived, ate something other than toast and Marmite.

Robbie ate three quite enthusiastically, but Agatha took a couple of bites and then returned hers to the plate. "It's quite hard," she said, "and it hurts my wobbly tooth."

"Do you have a wobbly tooth?" I asked, feeling the

space between us open up yet again. A mother wouldn't need to ask this question. My mother had seemed to have a personal inventory of everything inside my mouth, and knew almost before I did when a tooth was starting to come loose.

"Two," said Robbie, helpfully, reaching for another biscuit before I could stop him. "Possibly more after these biscuits."

"Can I wobble it?" I asked, and then regretted it. Agatha was just starting to talk to me; I wasn't sure she would be comfortable with me putting my hand in her mouth. But she nodded, and I gave the bottom tooth a little wobble. "Those ones always go first."

"Mine did," Robbie said, baring all his teeth, despite having a full mouth of crumbs. "Then these ones went next."

"Close your mouth while you're eating, Robbie," I said before turning my attention back to Agatha. "I'll have to make you some softer biscuits next time."

"Mum used to make soft biscuits."

"Did she?"

Agatha nodded. "They were sweet and flat, and had a funny name."

"Anzacs," I said.

Robbie's jaw dropped, once again revealing the inside of his mouth. "How did you know?"

"Just magic, I guess. So you better watch out, I know everything. And I also know you probably have some homework to do, so how about you get set up on the table while I make the dinner."

For once, Robbie did what I asked him straight-away, and I was just pushing Agatha through to the sit-ting room to watch some after-school television when I heard the back door slam. "Who in the bloody hell left that car on the driveway?" Max started shouting before he was even inside. Pointlessly, as no one else drove the little van.

I had not seen him all day. He seemed to exist on the periphery of life at Barnsley. He didn't eat with the children and spent most of his time in the study. At night, he disappeared for hours; whether to the local pub or to somewhere else, I hadn't quite worked out. Still, it suited me. I didn't fancy sitting watching television with him on the sofa.

"It was me," I said, coming back through the door, suddenly hyperaware of the remains of the biscuit dough, which were everywhere. I tried to hold eye con-tact with Max, mostly to prevent him from seeing the mess, but he wouldn't look at me.

"I know it was bloody well you," he roared. "Only an Australian would leave a car lying about like that, doors wide open as if it's been involved in a bank heist."

A glance out the window told me he was right; the front passenger door was wide open, the front seat getting wet in the light drizzle. It was Sophia's fault. A twelve-year-old should be expected to shut the car door after herself, but I could hardly blame her without looking like a petulant child myself. "I'm sorry," I said, "it's much easier to get Agatha into the house from there. The wheelchair gets stuck in the gravel."

"Mrs. Mins never had any trouble," Max said. I waited for him to say something about the state of the place while he was at it, but I was beginning to realize that Max suffered from an extreme case of domestic blindness. Anything on the other side of the hotel office was immaculate, while back here, in his private quarters, his standards were remarkably lower. It was almost as if this part of the house didn't exist to him. Not so the forecourt, evidently.

"Maybe Mrs. Mins was too frightened to say anything," I said. The scratching of Robbie's pencil stopped immediately, and I could feel him listening.

It took a long time for Max to answer.

"Maybe you're right," he said, flicking at the end of his nose as if there was something bothering him, "but the car is to go in the car park. I'm sure you'll work something out." He stormed out.

I let it go but resolved to continue parking the car

in the exact same place. The place where it best suited his children. Agatha had a hard enough time getting around without the added indignity of being dragged through acres of gravel at the end of the day. It was fine to have rules—my father certainly had enough of them—but to have rules for no reason was ridiculous.

I was still fuming when Max reappeared a minute or so later. He coughed, looking slightly sheepish. "Have you seen Daphne?"

22

Daphne's handbag was still in her bedroom, unused for weeks. Her car, a write-off from the accident, sat in the car park, undrivable. I didn't know enough about her belongings to make a judgment, but the children seemed convinced there was nothing missing.

The children and I searched the entire house and hotel, turning every single light on as we went and finding nothing. Mrs. Mins and Max searched the grounds, including the outbuildings.

Other people had disappeared from my life before. When I was eight, my mother died from lung cancer. My father's parents died young. After my fall from grace, friends had deserted me. But no one had ever left without a reason. Without me knowing where and why they had gone. It bothered me.

186 • JANE COCKRAM

But it didn't seem to bother the others.

"She does this from time to time," said Max. "It's nothing to worry about."

"She's gone on one of her benders," said Mrs. Mins, making sure Max was out of earshot.

The children said nothing.

By the time we gave up, it was close to midnight, and there was no trace of Daphne anywhere. Mrs. Mins left for her cottage, and Max was about to retreat to his study.

"Would you like me to phone Elizabeth?" I asked. If she and Daphne were as friendly as the children had reported, it seemed to me that Daphne might have gone there.

"Maybe tomorrow," Max replied, without looking back.

"What about the police?"

He stopped dead. Turned around quickly. "Absolutely not. I am not going to waste their time with my wife's theatrics."

I remembered Daphne's scared face, the urgent transfer of the key. Max had known her longer than I had. Perhaps she *was* prone to theatrics. But still, I was starting to second-guess my first instinct to hand the key over to Max.

I resolved to get back to the notebook as soon as I could. As soon as the children were in bed and asleep, which took some time, given their highly agitated state, I crept down the stairs, retrieved the notebook from the locked drawer, and stole back to my room. Back to my reading.

It was as if Max was speaking a foreign language at first. It took me a while to adjust, to understand that when he spoke of Barnsley House, he was speaking of his childhood home, and when he mentioned Nanny, he was not talking about his grandmother but rather a paid servant. For someone who had grown up on the Northern Beaches in Sydney, this was a big adjustment. My nanny had a perm and drove to bingo in a Corolla, but the woman

Max spoke of was younger and, by the sounds of it, quite attractive. (Hard to believe he was talking about Meryl, ha ha.)

You were just babies when your mother died, hovering around the edges of retaining memories. Max can't remember the night of the fire, but he says he gets flashbacks sometimes; you may have noticed he can't stand Bonfire Night, and he stays away from that bedroom in the east wing as much as possible. Your mother, Beatrice, was, as you know, thought to be very beautiful. It's funny, sometimes you hear of someone from previous generations being described as a beauty and then you see a photo, and think, Were they on drugs? Beatrice was gorgeous, though, even in the old photos. In fact, Sophia is starting to look a lot like her, heaven help us.

They featured Beatrice in the frontispiece of *Country Life*, which was unusual, as by that point she was married with children, but it must have been a quiet month for debutantes, I don't know. I'm sure you know more about that kind of thing than I do. Maximilian put her up to it (your father. What's with the repeating names? I find it endlessly confusing, and I forbade my Max from continuing the tradition with dear little Robbie).

Maximilian was feeling anxious

about the accomplishments of
some of the previous mistresses
of Barnsley—and this was even
before that wretched book!—and he
wanted to show off his wife as being
very much up to her predecessors.
If only by virtue of her looks!
Never mind she had two toddlers
and a baby at that point and
probably wasn't feeling her best.
They took her photo, and she was
included in the June 5, 1969, edition.
He showed me the magazine once.
There is a copy in the library—if
you haven't seen it, it's tucked
between some old Encyclopedia
Britannica volumes.

I made a note to hunt it down in the library.

Apart from her looks, which veered more towards Elizabeth Taylor territory than pastoral beauty, Beatrice's claim to fame among those who knew her was her parties. The house was always filled with people, and the parties would go on for days, all the rooms along the east wing corridor filled with guests who were literally eating and drinking your parents out of house and home. Max told me the wine cellar was completely full before your parents drank it dry. Shame we weren't around in those days! And that was even before they started the festival.

I flicked a couple of pages. It was nothing I hadn't read about in *The House of Brides*.

Beatrice had a full-time nanny, an older lady, but that wasn't enough. With the three of you, the nanny was swamped, and Beatrice was being called to the nursery too often for her liking. She asked a young girl from the village to come and help. You can see where this is headed.

Meryl started at Barnsley House in the summer of 1969. She was only fourteen, and Max was two. Meryl came from a troubled family. Her father was a fisherman, and her grandfather, and before that her grandfather's father. It was not an easy time to be a fisherman— small boats like Meryl's father's were becoming outclassed by larger vessels backed by massive conglomerates. He was losing money fast, and borrowed against his boat to feed his family, never quite making enough money to pay it back. They lived from week to week, but as you know, the coastline around here is perilous, and that January a storm struck that was worse than usual. Some people described it as a hurricane, others disagree—but anyway, it was nasty, and it caused destruction all along the coastline. The little boatshed down at the cove was ripped out to sea, the tennis court washed away, the garden on the island became a landslide (this was when most of the grapevines washed away, thank goodness).

Meryl's father lost his boat in the storm. He had no choice but to go to work on one of the large fishing trawlers, hoping to make enough money to feed his family and pay off a boat that lay in pieces at the bottom of the ocean. Taking his eldest son Michael with him, he was out at sea for months on end, leaving his wife at home with the other four children. Meryl was at school, but with three children younger than her, the burden of schoolwork plus helping her mother with her brothers and sisters became too much. Leonard was born years later, making the situation even more intense. If she was going to pursue her dream of studying politics at university, she

needed a job where she could make
money and study.

Obviously Barnsley wasn't quite
such a big employer in those days as
it had been in the past, but it was
still the first port of call for anyone
looking for domestic work or manual
labour.

Beatrice, your mother, snapped
Meryl up right away. She liked the
idea of a younger girl, someone she
could boss around—the older nanny
had been with the family for years,
and Beatrice was intimidated by
her. Nanny always knew best, and
Beatrice found her suffocating and
patronizing. Meryl made herself
indispensable almost immediately,
never leaving the children to cry

and doting on Max in particular. She loved living at Barnsley and could often be seen pushing the pram around, making the most of the grounds and house she had previously only been able to admire from afar. At night, she could study while the children slept. It was the perfect setup.

From what Max tells me, Meryl was every bit as gorgeous as his mother. Hard to believe, isn't it? Where Beatrice was dark and refined, Meryl was fair and ethereal; Beatrice wore well-cut expensive clothes, while Meryl wafted around in long bohemian dresses. It wasn't long before Maximilian started to pay Meryl extra attention. For the *first time, he was spotted outside his office frolicking on the lawn, and even taking Meryl out for days on his clipper. A perfect storm was brewing, and Beatrice didn't even notice. That summer she had other things on her mind. The photograph in Country Life had done more than make her husband proud, it had captured the attention of Peregrine Grenville, an admiral in the Second World War.*

My hands went to my neck, to the fob chain.

P.G.

Peregrine Grenville.

A token of illicit love, then, rather than a precious family heirloom. It was understandable that my mother had not mentioned his name. I was only a child. I wondered if she even knew about him.

He was much, much older than Beatrice, and a notorious womanizer, but something about the photo piqued his interest, and on the pretext of visiting friends nearby that summer, he sailed down the coast and moored in the little cove. The boathouse had been rebuilt in the spring, and on the very day Peregrine sailed in, Beatrice was hosting a party to celebrate its rebuilding.

Beatrice was bored. Shipped down to the remote Barnsley straight after a whirlwind romance and speedy engagement, she was only twenty-two, with three children and a distant husband. It was the late 1960s, and it felt like time had moved on everywhere except for Barnsley, where she remained simply a mother and a wife while all her friends were living glamorous lives in London.

Peregrine, with his blow-in charm and cavalier attitude towards tradition, shook things up a bit, and it wasn't long before he was fully ensconced in the Barnsley fold. After a couple of days of sleeping on his boat, he gave up any pretense of moving on to his friend's house and took up residence in one of the guest rooms. The friends were summoned to Barnsley and the party relocated, to be extended for weeks, all through a long hot summer. (I am always suspicious when your English summers are described as hot, but Max swears that's how it was described to him—in fact the heat is one of the reasons why everything unfolded as it did, according to him.)

Peregrine was one of those men made more attractive rather than less by his advancing years, and at an age when he should have been planning for retirement with a wife of a similar age and looking forward to grandchildren, he had not given up seduction. In fact, years of practice had made him very good at it. He had a keen eye for people's weaknesses, he knew how to exploit women, and he was very handsome, with a rugged tanned face and straight hair that falls forward over his eyes in photographs.

Peregrine, with his nose for mischief, sensed a familiarity between Maximilian and Meryl almost right away, and on the very first night at the boatshed, he suggested as much to Beatrice. (You can imagine the scene: a hot summer's night, the lights strung across the jetty and twinkling, music playing through the old stereo system. All those records your father had sent down from London that we still play in the restaurant.)

With Peregrine's words in her ears, watching the houseguests launch themselves fully clothed into the still, dark water that night,

Maximilian and Meryl among them, Beatrice felt a lifting of something. Commitment, maybe? Or loyalty to Max? In any case, after that night, her eyes were opened and her moral framework shifted. Peregrine suggested that she was trapped in an unfaithful marriage, and then he suggested how to escape it. Beatrice took his suggestion, and within days they had slept together. The boathouse was their special place, and the small anteroom off the main building—the one with the camp beds for the children— was where they secreted themselves for hours that summer, coming out now and then to bathe, and only returning to the house for dinner. It was a flagrant betrayal, and for some time everyone except for Maximilian was aware of it.

For the first time, I thought properly about the world my mother was born into. I had never considered her life independent of mine, had never thought of her as someone's daughter or as a younger sibling of Max and Elizabeth. She had grown up without a mother, with a father who was at best ambivalent, and—it dawned on me—with Mrs. Mins for a nanny. Who did she look up to when she was a girl? Someone must have encouraged her to pursue her writing, urged her on to great things, just as she had for me. But the Barnsley of the notebook seemed devoid of any likely candidates.

Meryl, however, was keeping a sharp eye on proceedings. You have to remember she was only fourteen at this point, and when she was not required in the nursery—which was often, considering that the children still napped during the day—she had the teenager's talent for skulking, moving unseen and unheard about the place, as languid and indiscernible as a cat.

At that point, Meryl still had plans to return to school in the autumn. She wanted to study politics and always had her nose in a book from the Barnsley library. Maximilian encouraged her interest, suggesting titles and telling her about his illustrious friends. Taking herself down to the cove one afternoon for a swim and a read, she was floating in the water where she could lie in wait for Beatrice and Peregrine undetected.

I tossed the notebook aside angrily. These old stories didn't help me a bit. The only interesting part was that

Mrs. Mins had lied about when she first came to Barnsley House, as if there was something in the past she wanted to forget. Something she wanted to hide.

It didn't tell me where Daphne was. It didn't tell me what had happened between Max and my mother. With those questions on my mind, I finally let myself succumb to sleep.

23

It was the second to last day of school before Christmas, and I slept in. I was dreaming about my father coming to Barnsley House, looking for me. He was angry, shouting about his credit card. In the dream, I wasn't surprised by his appearance. It seemed inevitable and real, and the anxiety it created only increased as I woke up to find Robbie hovering over me.

"Miss?" he said.

I had no idea where I was.

"Have you got our reindeer ears for the concert?"

The question only added to my discombobulation. "What?" My head throbbed mildly, my mind was woolly. The dream had thrown me back into the real world. My real world. The one in which I had stolen from my father and lied to him.

"For the concert. Tomorrow night?"

Finally, something connected in my brain. "The reindeer ears! Yes! I mean, no! I looked in the attic and couldn't find any."

Robbie's face fell.

"I'll find some today."

The smile, when it came, was not convincing. "Robbie?" He paused, on his way out the door. He was already fully dressed in his school uniform, his hair combed down as if he was from another era. "Is your mum back?"

Robbie shook his head sadly and shot out the door before I could ask any further questions.

After the children left for school, I tapped on the door of the study. With the children at school, I assumed my time was my own, but Max's outburst about the car made me loath to ignite his anger again.

"Come in." He was sitting at his desk, frowning at a piece of paper. As he looked up, he slipped it under the same red ledger I had seen the other morning.

"Hi. Hi, Mr. Summer," I stuttered.

"Hello, Miranda. You can call me Max." He looked towards a portrait of a rather stern-looking man on the wall opposite. "It's . . . easier." He was right, it *was* easier.

"I just wanted to let you know I'm walking into

the village to pick up some things for the children. A costume, actually. For the concert tomorrow."

Max looked at me vacantly. Waiting for the point. He had a lot on his mind, I supposed. "I won't be long. Maybe an hour? Or two. You would know better than me. How long does it take to walk into the village?"

"Which one?"

"South Bolton?" I tried to remember what the taxi driver had told me.

"Ha! You won't be walking there. I expect you mean Minton."

"Do I?"

"It's miles to South Bolton. You can drive there if you like but there's nothing there. The lanes are tricky for beginners, though. You have to watch for deer at dusk." His voice caught in his throat.

I looked out the window. Sun streamed through the glass. It seemed odd to be thinking about dusk at this time of the morning. "Maybe Minton, then."

"I think it's best. There's a coast path at the bottom of the garden. You'll need sensible shoes."

I was almost out the door when Max spoke again. "Why do you need to go to the village?"

"The children need reindeer ears. I looked in the attic and couldn't find any."

He looked even more confused, perhaps a little alarmed.

"For the concert."

"What concert?"

"The Christmas concert. Tomorrow."

"Yes. Yes." Max looked vaguely panicked.

"It starts at six thirty."

"Right. Yes. Good-o. And, Miranda?"

"Yes?"

"Don't mention anything in town, just yet. About Daphne." I nodded. I didn't know what else I could do.

It felt good to leave Barnsley. As I set off in the sunshine, looking for the coastal path Max had mentioned, I hoped Daphne, wherever she had gone, had felt the same as she left. When I saw her, she had been frail, sickly. Some time away from Barnsley would probably do her the world of good.

The air was brisk; even with my hat, coat, and scarf I would be cold. But thanks to the ongoing obsession people at Barnsley had with my footwear, I at least had sensible shoes on.

The path started by the tennis court and stepped down to beach level almost immediately, so that once you were on it, you were invisible to anyone who might be watching from the hotel. It was helpfully signposted with specially crafted Barnsley House signs, insignia and all: the one at the beginning of the path informed me it was a mile and three quarters to the village. My conversions from imperial to metric were a little rusty, but I calculated it to be almost four kilometres. A reasonably robust walk, when the return trip was taken into account. I thought guiltily of my activewear tucked in a drawer upstairs, unused, and felt pleased I was finally getting some exercise, however sedate. #wellness #active #freshair

The clear skies made the water of the ocean seem bluer than before; the notion of swimming in these waters in the warmer months became more possible, even appealing. Along the path on the land side, bushes of immense stature—azaleas and rhododendrons, by the look of it—awaited the magnificent flowering of summer. After a short time the path curved around into a little cove and became damp underfoot, bogged down with leaf matter. Another, smaller path ran from the main track, a Barnsley house signpost indicating that it was the way to the boathouse.

The description of the boathouse from the notebook was still fresh in my mind, and the weather was amenable. My curiosity piqued, I took the smaller path down to the water's edge. Perhaps Daphne had come down here to get away from the house's claustrophobic atmosphere. Max said he had checked it, but I wasn't convinced he'd checked properly; given the fear in Daphne's eyes, I thought she might be hiding from him.

A small weatherboard cottage clung to the edge of the rocks, and beyond it a handful of tin boats bobbed alongside the wooden jetty. In comparison to the rest of Barnsley, the boathouse and the jetty had been maintained to an immaculate standard; the timber of the jetty looked recently oiled, and each white wooden post on the jetty gleamed with fresh white paint.

A glimpse inside the sparkling windows revealed a nautically themed lounge with white slip-covered sofas and fairy lights. There was no sign of Daphne, but I could imagine Beatrice and Peregrine sitting up at the driftwood bar on a warm summer's night, sipping on cocktails, hidden away from the world among the old lifesaving rings and glass buoys.

A creak in the jetty behind me disturbed my reverie. "This is private property, missy."

A thick accent made the words almost incomprehensible, and I turned to see the source. The man towered above me, far taller even than Max, and a thick beard made his age difficult to guess.

He must have been up before the sun rose, as he was wearing clothes to suit far more inhospitable weather, full-length raincoat and trousers in waxy fabric and a rain hat, the type fishermen wear in picture books. The skin of his face was olive and weathered in the places where it was not covered by beard, his eyes sea-green and searching.

"I'm the new nanny. Up—up at the house," I stammered, feeling exposed. I'd just realized the extent of my vulnerability in this tucked-away location.

"Are you just? You're older than I thought." He sniffed and reached into his pocket, revealing a packet of tobacco and a sheaf of papers. Was I the only one around here who didn't smoke? "Meryl mentioned I might find you sniffing around."

I stood frozen as he tried to roll his cigarette. Despite his wet weather gear, the papers seemed to have grown damp, and he struggled to separate them with fingers made uncooperative by the cold. Finally he did it and lit the thing, taking a long inhale and turning to look out to sea, rather than at me. "It looks beautiful on a day like this." I nodded. "But they're not easy waters. The island is farther than it looks."

It was true. From this angle the island seemed farther away than it had from the house and was now partially obscured by the headland on which Barnsley House sat. I could only see the protruding tip, where the garden looked almost tropical, and I said so, not knowing how else to fill the silence with this enormous brooding man, and wondering how long I had to wait before I could make my getaway.

"It's more tropical down here than in any other part of England. We can get plants going that wouldn't make it anywhere else. Mr. Summer's great-great-grandfather planted that garden out there for his wife, as a wedding present. She couldn't travel, you see, and he wanted her to see the plants he saw when he was out on his boats, so he brought them back to her. Put them on the island so they wouldn't mess with his garden over here."

"That's romantic," I said, for want of anything else to say.

"Not romantic, no. Pragmatic. If it's romance you're after, the Summer men are not your best bet, I'd say."

"I'm not after . . . ," I started to say, but he turned his knowing gaze back to me, and I let the sentence hang, unfinished.

"It's a bloody nightmare anyway, that garden. I look after it as best I can, but those two don't help at all." He jerked his head towards the island. "The more you do, the more you do, my mother used to say, and those two do nothing at all. Nothing."

"Which two?"

"Elizabeth and Tom." Disdain was obvious in his voice. "I don't know what she sees in them all."

"What who sees?" Now was clearly not the time to make my connection to "them" known.

"Meryl. My sister. She thinks the sun shines out of their—" He stopped. Twitched.

Looked around as if someone might be watching. I followed his line of sight. A small camera, tucked under the eaves of the boatshed. Someone *was* watching.

"I'm Miranda." I thrust out my hand, hoping that for anyone watching, this would look like an innocent encounter. A chance meeting between two strangers. Which was exactly what it was.

He smiled and shook his head, took one last inhale of his cigarette. "I'm Leonard. Everyone around here calls me Mr. Mins." Ahh, the famous Mr. Mins.

He extinguished his cigarette on the sole of his heavy work boot and then, once every last ember was completely black, tucked it back in his coat pocket. "Max doesn't like them lying around," he said, by way of explanation, "and who can blame him? Filthy habit." He laughed, coughed, and then laughed again. "And we don't want to upset Max, do we?"

Finally he took my outstretched hand in his and squeezed it firmly, looking me in the eye the whole time. "I've really got to get going," I said, trying to edge away slowly. Something about this man was making me feel uncomfortable.

"You wouldn't think it now," he said, either not hearing me or choosing not to, "but in summer the tide goes out so far that on some days you can walk all the way out to the island." I looked at the water, tight up against the stones of the shore, lapping madly at the underside of the jetty although there was no wind at all. I couldn't imagine the cove empty of water, like the enormous sandbars on the beaches I played on as a child.

"No, I can't imagine that at all," I said. "I'll see you around—I'm just heading into the village."

"Not in the winter, though," he said, shaking his head. "She wouldn't have gone in the water."

"What do you mean? Do you know where Daphne is?"

Mr. Mins looked at me sharply. I immediately regretted saying anything. "It doesn't pay to gossip around here. You'll need to learn that quickly."

Even though his accent was strong, I understood every word he was saying. I turned and bolted back towards the main path, completely giving up on the idea of a civil farewell, and I didn't stop running until I reached the edge of the village. Lucky I was wearing my sensible shoes.

24

Minton was unexpectedly beautiful and strangely familiar. It must have been used as a location for the sort of television program my father and Fleur watched on a Sunday night, the kind I openly sneered at until realizing in the last year just how comforting escapist television could be. Surely I had watched a crotchety vet cycling through these streets, or a busty maiden bidding farewell to a seagoing suitor in that very town, but I couldn't quite place the memory.

Walking through the small cobbled streets, I had the sensation of being in an alternate universe. Colourful cottages opened right onto the streets, and little weather-beaten pubs looked as if they had been serving the same ale and pies for generations. It was quiet, only a few locals around the place, but the profusion of ice cream shops and postcard stands suggested that in summer it would be very busy indeed.

The kind of shop I was looking for was everywhere in Australia, in every suburban shopping strip and local mall. These sold everything from wrapping paper to dog beds, Halloween costumes to plastic baskets. I hoped these types of general goods stores were a universal concept, and I was pleased when turning into the street along the water's edge I saw the telltale sign: piles of plastic tubs outside a shopfront.

Reindeer ears in hand and mission accomplished, I wandered through the streets for a bit. A part of me hoped to come across a café like the ones I missed from home. Despite everything, I craved the kind of food I used to eat. Açai bowls. Green juices. Smashed avocado on seeded sprouting bread. Turmeric shots. There was nothing even remotely close, only closed-up fish and chip shops and some bakeries selling Cornish pasties. I settled for a block of chocolate from the Boots chemist to eat on the walk back to Barnsley. There was no one here to see me, after all.

As I headed back in the direction I had come, I thought about what to do next. I had come all this way—given up my job and thrown my already fragile relationship with my father into jeopardy—on the whim of a hysterical teenager. I needed to get Sophia alone so that I could really talk to her, but the slammed doors and teenage sulks were making this more difficult than I expected.

The truth—and I hadn't admitted it to myself until now—was that I hadn't really cared about Sophia when I got the letter. It was an easy out, a reason to escape. It was a chance to find out more about my mother, but really, it was a chance to find out more about me. In coming to Barnsley, I'd find out more about the woman I had idolized and why she left her family home. Maybe I'd find out why she'd been banished from her family. Maybe I'd find out what she'd done wrong.

Assuming she'd done something wrong.

From what I'd read in the notebook, the favour of the Summer men could turn on a dime. Maximilian, my mother's father, had worshipped his beautiful wife Beatrice, until one day he hadn't. Max, my uncle, loved Daphne but hadn't married her. Perhaps my mother's only real crime had been to tell the truth about the men in her family. She had put her head above the parapet, and had been swiftly knocked down. I knew the feeling.

All the little laneways looked the same, and none of them ran in a straight line. After I passed the same pink stucco cottage for the third time, I gave up on retracing my steps and instead headed towards the shimmering

water beckoning through the jammed-together buildings. It was much the same down at the waterfront, the
prime real estate in town seemingly divided between
food outlets and impressive-looking holiday homes
with curtains closed tight until the summer months,
but at least I could finally see the beginnings of the
coastal path farther along the sea wall.

My mother would have walked these same streets.
I imagined her passing the empty picnic tables and
chained-up sandwich boards, thinking about the dead
women who had gone before her—Elspeth and Gertrude and Sarah and Beatrice—like I was now. They
were crowding in on me too. Not only the women from
The House of Brides, but the more recently departed.
My mother. Daphne. There was something broken at
Barnsley, and I had to try and fix it. And to do that, I
needed to know what it was.

Stepping out towards the water, lost in my thoughts,
I was nearly sideswiped by a small bus. The horn
sounded immediately, deafening even through the
cacophony of the gulls. Heart racing, I leapt back on
the path. The Minton community bus roared off back
up the hill, grey-haired heads bobbing in the window,
seemingly unruffled by the near miss.

Deciding it was dangerous to stay any longer in a
town of rampaging senior citizens, I headed in the di-

rection of the path. The chocolate bar in my pocket weighed heavily on my mind. I was thinking about tearing back the wrapper and taking the first delicious bite when the sun glinted off a small bronze plaque on a low-lying pale blue building, taking my mind off the treat for a moment.

MINTON HISTORICAL SOCIETY

Stuck to the inside of a small window near the plaque was a sign with the name Jean Laidlaw and a phone number. "Closed for the winter," it read; "Please call for an appointment." There was a phone number underneath.

There was no time now. Looking at my watch, I could see that I would have to rush to make it back to Barnsley before lunch. I took out my useless phone, out of range and out of credit, and took a photo of the card. Another day.

As I straggled up the hill at Barnsley, relaxed after my walk and buzzing from a sugar high—my body was still unaccustomed to onslaughts of refined sugar—I saw Max coming across the lawn from the direction of the boathouse. He seemed uncomfortable, twitchy, constantly looking over his shoulder as if someone or something was watching him. I remembered the camera I had seen at the boathouse earlier. Maybe someone was. "Have you been looking for Daphne?" I asked. It seemed like a reasonable enough assumption.

"No. She'll turn up soon enough. It's only been a day or so."

The *only*, in my opinion, seemed an understatement. For Daphne, in her condition, to be missing a couple of hours might have been dangerous. "Has she done this before?"

"Not since the accident, no." Max looked around, as if someone might be listening. "But before, well, it was quite a common occurrence."

I must have looked doubtful, because Max stopped, forcing me to stop and look at him, head-on. "Listen, Miranda. You mustn't get too caught up in this. Daphne is prone to, ah, prone to—"

"Disappearing?"

"Drama."

We walked back towards the house together. In an unusual gesture of chivalry, Max relieved me of my shopping bag, and in an even more unusual gesture of interest, asked me what was in it. Was he trying to deflect my attention? Or worse, was he actually interested in me? "Presents for the children," I replied. "Reindeer ears." As if the felt horns with ringing bells knocking against his trouser leg were not obvious enough.

"Christmas," he said in a monotone. "Of course."

"Monday," I said helpfully, as if the date of Christmas might have changed this year. "I've been meaning to ask you, am I expected to work?"

"I haven't really thought about Christmas, to be honest," he said, rubbing at imaginary whiskers on his chin. "I haven't made any plans yet."

Understandable. "Maybe Elizabeth can take over," I said hopefully, "or Mrs. Mins." Please don't ask me to cook, I was thinking. My repertoire in the kitchen did not quite extend to turkey, or goose, or whatever the festive roast meat of choice was in this country.

At home, we would have seafood: dozens and dozens of prawns shelled by my father on Christmas Eve; crayfish ordered in from the fishmonger in advance, and oysters shucked Christmas morning. At nighttime we would stuff glazed ham in soft rolls, swinging our feet in the pool as we reflected on the day. That wouldn't quite work here, I suspected.

"There is something you could do for me," Max said, "that would help me greatly. Would you come into town with me to get Christmas presents for the children? You seem to have gotten to know them quite quickly, and I am sure you would have more ideas than I would about things they would like."

"But I've just been!" I said, struggling to put my conflicting emotions into words.

"You've been to the village. I propose we head into town. It's only forty minutes or so if you know the back roads."

"I need to be back to meet the children." The prospect of getting back to the notebook was slipping away.

"You'll have plenty of time. Might even be time for lunch in a pub, if we get going now."

"What about Daphne?"

"*Enough* about Daphne."

It seemed I had no choice in the matter.

25

We drove into town in an old army-green Land Rover Defender. It looked like a farm vehicle to me, so I said so.

Max agreed. "Barnsley is a working farm, you know. Back here, we have hundreds of Jacob sheep." He gestured to some of the paddocks we were passing. The size of the place shocked me; in my mind Barnsley stopped at the end of the driveway. "It's a very sensible car, and a real workhorse—it's never let me down."

For once, Thomas was absent, but he had left reminders of his presence; thousands of black dog hairs that quickly attached themselves to my clothing. I tried to brush them off, and Max, keeping one eye on the road, muttered, "I wouldn't bother if I were you. That's a battle you won't win. Next time wear black."

He stopped suddenly. So did my heart. "Why are we stopping?" The words came out all jerky.

The cliff on which we were perched looked back towards the village and over the bay.

I couldn't see the road from where I was sitting. Just water. Rough and choppy and menacing. I could swim, but it was a sheer drop. Daphne was gone, and now I was alone with Max. Would anyone even realize I was missing?

Max leaned across from the driver's seat so that his body was almost in front of mine. I held my breath, partly because up close his scent was overwhelming, but mostly because there was no denying his intent. But then he placed his left hand on the seat next to me and gestured towards the water. I exhaled. "In the summer, this bay is filled with fishing boats and families paddling." Max's eyes scanned up and down the coastline, searching—for what, I did not know. "It probably doesn't look like much of a beach to your Australian eyes"—the word *Australian* curled on his lips—"but in July, it's heaven on earth."

"Yes, sometimes white sand and azure water is overrated," I said. "Sunshine too." *Keep it light.*

Max ignored me. "It wasn't easy building this road. It came at great cost, and with extreme difficulty. The machinery caused mayhem on the roads around here, but Daphne insisted. She said this view reminded her of home."

This time it was me doing the scanning up and down the coastline. Even squinting and trying to conjure up a summer's day was no use; the outlook was bleak, and nothing like the beaches of my childhood.

At last Max drove on. He had all the windows open, which helped with the all-pervading doggy smell but made conversation quite difficult. I concentrated on watching the scenery and trying to get a sense of my bearings. It was useless. Every time I anticipated turning one way, we turned the other.

The land behind Barnsley House quickly turned rural, and we drove past farmhouses, down roads fenced by hedgerows, and past brambly pathways. Numerous times we stopped and reversed back into small cuttings to let farm vehicles past. In one there was a small wooden structure instead of a gate.

"Do you know what that is?" Max asked.

I swallowed nervously before I answered. "A kissing gate."

He raised his eyebrows and kept driving.

Max was not joking when he said we would take the back roads; dropping bread crumbs would be the only way I would ever find my way back to Barnsley. I tried to imagine Daphne out on these roads in the dark.

"Would she have taken a taxi, do you think?" I asked Max as we slowed down to come into town and it was possible to talk.

"Who?"

"Daphne. The taxi driver who dropped me off, the other night, he was very chatty. He'd probably be able to tell you where she went. She couldn't have gone far." I looked at Max, but he was resolutely focused on the road. "In her state," I added as we pulled up at traffic lights, the first I had seen in days.

Max looked at me intently. An uncomfortable silence persisted until finally the light went green and the car behind us honked. His flesh turned white on the gear stick as he shifted the car into first gear.

When he finally spoke, his words were forced. "I have a saying about Christmas shopping: Something they want, something they need . . ."

"Something to wear, something to read," I finished the sentence for him. "My mother used to say that too. Would you like me to ring the taxi company?"

He ignored me again. "Daphne never goes along with it. The piles of presents she buys the children. It's criminal."

Criminal. The word brought the conversation to a dead halt, and we both sat quietly again, me furiously thinking about Daphne, and Max's reluctance to do even the slightest bit of investigation into her disappearance, and Max, well, just looking furious. "Where to first?" I asked when we arrived in town amid a cluster of pedestrians and hanging Christmas decorations. It all looked merry and Christmassy, and I suddenly felt more festive, managing to put Daphne out of mind for a moment.

"The bookshop?" Max suggested, eyeing the clothing shops suspiciously. Music was blaring out, a cacophony of noise. He winced.

"Why don't we just get this over and done with?" I said. "Wait here."

I ducked into the first boutique, noticing that the mannequins in the window wore the tight jeans and strappy tops Sophia favoured. My days in retail had served me well, and I felt confident making quick decisions and estimating Sophia's clothing size. Once I had gathered up some items, I signaled for Max to come in and pay, and he did, producing a wallet stuffed with an array of credit cards. He hesitated before selecting one, seemingly at random, and I noticed that he didn't look the shop assistant in the eye until she had completed the transaction and the shopping was safely in my hands. "That wasn't so hard, was it?" I asked, relishing the chance to take the upper hand. For once I was in my comfort zone, and Max was far removed from his.

"Let's not get complacent. That's one present for one child. I have three, you know."

We continued the pattern in the next few stores, Max waiting outside while I selected the presents, and only coming inside to pay at the last minute. Even I was surprised by how much I had learned about the children in such a short time: I knew that Agatha needed some new pyjamas, and that ones with unicorns would be best; Sophia talked so often about her friend Jasmine's iPod that I convinced Max to buy her one, and Robbie would love anything in the colours of his beloved Southampton.

When we reached the bookshop at the other end of the street, I was surprised at how efficient we had been. "We're almost done," I said as Max held the heavy front door open for me and a gust of warm air flooded past me into the street. He put his hand on the small of my back as I passed by, and my body tensed. His touch was too high to be suggestive, too low to be familial. The smell of the bookshop was at odds with the discomfort I was feeling: safe, papery, and familiar.

Max idly picked up a Winston Churchill biography and another book I couldn't see properly from the nonfiction table and tucked them under his arm. We browsed silently for a few minutes, listening to the familiar notes of "Little Drummer Boy." I selected some books for Robbie, mainly historical ones on the grislier aspects of the Tudor period, and then got the assistant to find me a small guide to haunted houses in the area. Sophia was easy: I found some beautiful new editions of Jane Austen that would look nice by her bed even if she didn't read them. "About Agatha," I began, as "Little Drummer Boy" finished and "Let It Snow" took over.

"Yes," said Max, humming along facetiously. "What about her?" His mood seemed to have lifted with the music.

"I think we should buy her some books without absent parents in them."

"Lovely idea. Barnsley's in that." Max gestured to the small book I had in my hand for Robbie. "Some old duck is meant to stalk about in the east wing. Could give him nightmares."

"Oh." Some old duck? My grandmother. His mother. I swallowed my shock, convinced it was yet another test meant to trip me up. I forced myself to remember my mother—somehow Max had banished her to the other side of the world. He wouldn't get to me as well. "I'll put it back, then." I looked around to see where the girl had got it from so that I might discreetly replace it.

"I wouldn't worry about it. The living are of more concern at Barnsley than any old stories about ghosts.

Might do him good to get a sense of the history of the place."

"Are they?" I spun around, eager to take the conversation further, but Max had moved on. I slipped the book back into my pile, resolving to read it myself before deciding whether to put it under the Christmas tree or not. Before deciding what was more dangerous at Barnsley.

Time was ticking on. I chose a gorgeously illustrated story with hidden elements for the reader to spot, and some fairly innocuous chapter books about two girls and a pony. That would have to do, although I feared the books would be a disappointment to Agatha after the exciting adventures of Pippi Longstocking and Co.

"Is it time for lunch yet?" Max asked as we left the bookshop, in a voice that hovered near a whine. It could also have been interpreted as flirtatious if he wasn't my uncle and I liked that kind of thing. Which I didn't.

"I have one more idea for Robbie," I said, guiding him towards an electronics store I had spotted earlier. It was much busier than the bookstore had been, and we had to push through a crush of people crowding in on displays of tablets, laptops, and other electronic equipment. Most would be totally useless at Barnsley with the state of the internet connection.

An older couple stepped aside, shaking their heads in bafflement at the product before them, and we were able to move closer. "I thought this might be good for Robbie. It's a camera, and you can take it everywhere with you. You can even get a headband thingy and strap it to your head, so the camera sees what you see. It might come in handy for his ghost hunting."

I turned to Max, expecting to see a smile, particularly because I had delivered the last words in a deliberately vaudeville spooky voice, but he was not amused. In fact, he was already moving away. "No. Absolutely not," he said as he retreated.

"Why not?" I asked, not seeing the fury building on Max's face.

"Because I said so, and I am his father."

By this point we were back out on the pavement, and I was grateful for the cold air, which went some way to relieve the slow burn creeping across my cheeks. It was embarrassment making me blush, but it was tinged with anger. I was beginning to resent the way Max's moods swung from post to post, leaving me swivelling my head and wondering at his next move.

"It's just a camera."

"I do not want any more cameras in my life," he said. "They have caused enough trouble over the years."

I remembered the cameras I had seen around Barnsley: in the restaurant and at the boathouse. Who had they caused trouble for? Did the cameras hold the clue to Daphne's disappearance? It was another mystery to add to my growing list.

26

The car ride out of town was just as blustery as before, the scenery unfolding in the reverse direction. I tried to take note of the turns and roads we took until we were on a country lane that I was positive, despite my confusion, we had not travelled on that morning. Still waiting for Max to say anything, I kept quiet. At last we pulled into the car park of a small country pub. Set down by a river, it was no bigger than a house, and yet there were cars everywhere. We had arrived somewhere very popular.

"Shall we have lunch?" Max said. The look on his face suggested he knew he had behaved poorly, and that lunch might be a sufficient reparation.

"Are you paying?" I refused to let him intimidate me, even though fear and suspicion were beginning to nag at the darkest edges of my subconscious. Plus, a slight anxiety was niggling: Max was showing more interest in me than was strictly appropriate, given that I was an employee, and, well—even though he didn't seem to know it—his niece.

"You asked so nicely, I can't help but feel inclined. But one course only for you. And make it a starter." A small smile played at his lips, but it didn't carry to his eyes. There was something else there, but I couldn't put my finger on it. I jumped out of the car and slammed the door.

"The Stag's Head," read the sign hanging above the door, and below it, on a small brass plaque polished to sparkling, "Proprietor: M. Summer."

"Is there anything around here you don't own?" I asked, forcing myself to keep the atmosphere light as Max pulled back the door. It was easier to be relaxed in the cozy dining room with low-hanging beams and tables filled with diners, away from the claustrophobic confines of the car. For a lunchtime during the week it was very busy, and most of the diners noticed Max coming in, muttering to their dining companions while looking in his direction.

It seemed likely that someone in this small community might know something about Daphne's disappearance. Perhaps she was staying with one of them. Perhaps she had flagged down one of their cars. Perhaps she was here.

"It appears even the owner might struggle to get a seat at this time of the year," he said, oblivious to the attention, scanning the room for signs of an empty table or an imminently departing guest. "We might have to go through to the snug."

"I wouldn't bother," a voice said from behind us. "There's a whole pack of schoolteachers in there, celebrating the end of the year. What's the collective term for teachers, anyway?"

The voice was instantly recognizable, but Max waited until he had turned to face her before he spoke. "Elizabeth." They kissed on both cheeks, taking great care to minimize actual physical contact.

"Fancy seeing you here."

"Just supporting the family business." She held her cigarette packet in her hand, clearly on the way outside.

"Having a free lunch, you mean?"

Elizabeth ignored him. "Take our table. We were just leaving, weren't we, Tom?"

Before Tom had a chance to answer, Max said, "Won't you join us?"

"Don't be patronising, Max; it doesn't suit you. We've already eaten."

Judging by Elizabeth's slender frame, which was

highlighted that afternoon in a fitted tweed dress cinched in at the waist with a mustard-coloured belt, any eating had been moderate, in direct contrast to the large meal I was hoping to consume at Max's expense. I had been surviving on the cobbled-together suppers I made for the children: pasta with pesto from a jar; herby scrambled eggs courtesy of the Barnsley kitchen garden and henhouse, and, of course, Marmite on toast. I had grown to quite like Marmite, but I craved a proper meal: meat and vegetables, eaten with a knife and fork in adult company.

Elizabeth peered around me, looking for someone. "It's not like Daphne to miss a pub lunch," she said. Max ignored the comment.

"Who's driving?" he asked. Telltale wine fumes emanated from Elizabeth, and a candid demeanour that seemed to absolve her of responsibility.

"That's a fine question," she said, "coming from you." Neither of them seemed to notice that the pub had grown quiet around them, the diners having abandoned their careful nonchalance in favour of outright staring. "Nothing more sanctimonious than a reformed addict."

"I'm driving, Max, so it will be all right," Tom finally piped up. His desire to end the spectacle must have overcome his reluctance to speak in company.

"All right, Tom. Mind you take care if you go out to the island. It's calm now, but the radio said the wind will come up this afternoon."

"We've done it a thousand times, Max," said Elizabeth, not to be quieted for long. She seemed torn between wanting to go outside with her cigarettes and go in for the kill. "I'd say he knows the channels out to the island better than anyone."

Tom gripped Elizabeth tightly just above the elbow, her grimace and the white of his knuckles the only indication of the strength of the hold. She continued to talk while she was being guided out the door. "Our table's out the back, behind the fireplace. You don't need me to tell you that, though, do you?"

To my surprise, Max laughed. Once the door was safely closed behind his sister, he said in a voice that was louder than strictly necessary, "Well, we can always count on Elizabeth to put on a good show, can't we?" We walked through the restaurant, the eyes of the diners once again averted, apart from a few who rose slightly out of their seats and either nodded to Max or shook his hand. Max was friendly, greeting people by name, and even clapping a hand on one man's shoulder and asking him about the recent sale of some land. When the man asked after Daphne, though, Max quickly moved on, and by the time we got to the small table out the back, exhaustion had crept across his face.

"I'll sit here," he said, taking the corner position on the cozy bench seating. "I like to keep an eye on things. How about a drink?" Right on cue, a pint of what looked like soda water was placed in front of him, and a slightly rounded blond woman with a matching round red face said, "What would you like, love?"

As I made my decision, the waitress watched me carefully, taking in every detail. She seemed disappointed by my appearance; a sensible grey sweater with a checked shirt collar peeking out from underneath. Jeans and ankle boots. No cleavage, no tattoos, no noticeable cosmetic surgery.

"Um," I said, casting about for some sort of drinks list, a blackboard with wine on it, anything that might help me.

"She'll have a lager, thanks, Sue."

"You sure about that, love?" Sue looked at me, ignoring Max, as if I didn't know my own mind. I did.

"Yes," I said. "Please," I added to temper my steely expression. A beer might make a nice change, and in the small world around Barnsley, it didn't pay to get anyone offside. You never knew when they would turn up again.

Sue examined me again. It must have been some time since there had been a newcomer in the pub. "Daphne all right?" she finally asked, capping her pen and not looking at Max. "Been a while since we've seen her."

Max swallowed, the motion in his throat purposeful.

"She used to be in here all the—"

"She's still recovering from the accident, Sue. I'll pass on your regards."

"I'm sorry about Elizabeth," Max said when Sue was gone, even though Elizabeth was the last thing on my mind. "She tends to drink a lot. Always has. It's been worse lately, and she doesn't seem to be getting any better. It doesn't help that she and Tom are just knocking about on the island day in, day out with nothing to do."

"She doesn't bother me. I quite like her."

The front door slammed, and Max craned his neck to see who was at the door. "Careful. She seems fun, but she's calculating. Don't tell her anything you don't want used against you. She's convinced . . ." He tailed off as Sue reappeared with my lager, making a great show of adjusting the coaster just so underneath the glass and loitering as long as possible.

"She's convinced what?" I asked, the second Sue was out of earshot. I didn't want Max to lose the thread of the conversation, but it was too late.

"Tom just lets her walk all over him. He was a mate of mine, you know, from school. We used to be really close. That's how they met. Tom used to come home with me on school holidays because his own family was dysfunctional. Swapped one of those for another." He shook his head as he took another sip. "Anyway, how are you settling in? Ready to swap your dysfunctional family for ours?"

I hurriedly took an enormous sip of my beer. Gulped it down and then felt the bubbles fizz in my nose. My eyes watered from my attempt to contain the gas. Anything to avoid eye contact with Max.

He was waiting, though. He wanted an answer. I thought about what to say. The longer I stayed at Barnsley, the less I could imagine reentering my old world: a family life in which I scratched around in the margins, desperate to be included, desperate to be forgiven. Friends who avoided my calls and were moving on quickly into graduate jobs and beginning careers while I rustled up a full week's work with a retail job. Boys I had known all my life passing me over for younger or more interesting girls, girls with less history. At least here at Barnsley, I had an outsider's allure, a glamour of otherness that disguised my transcendent failures. It was intoxicating.

"I like it," I said. Not only did I like it, I felt needed.

The children needed me. And maybe even Daphne needed me.

"For now. Wait until after Christmas, when the cold really sets in. By February you'll be crying for your mother."

"My mother died, a long time ago."

Max eyed me carefully. "Did she?"

"When I was a child. I was the same age as Agatha, almost exactly."

"I'm sorry."

"Don't be. It's hard for children, though."

"And your father?"

"Remarried. A couple of years later. It was too soon, for me, but he was happy. My stepmother is nice, but she's not my mother, and she never pretended to be."

"That's a relief, I suppose."

I had never thought about it that way before. Most of my childhood I had wished to feel more included, more loved, by my stepmother, but at least she had relieved me of any obligation to love her. There was a moment of eye contact, and then Max looked away.

"Ah, Sue, there you are."

"Will you be having something to eat today? It's just that the kitchen is about to shut, and we wouldn't want you going hungry."

"It would be a shame, wouldn't it, in my own pub and all."

"A terrible shame, Mr. Summer."

"Could you suggest something from the menu that wouldn't trouble the chef too greatly to prepare?" He looked at me, smirking.

"The ploughman's is quick and easy. We just whack some cheese and bread and so forth on the plate, and out it comes."

"Thank you, Sue, I'll have the venison."

Sue looked baffled but took the order anyway, writing it carefully on her little spiral notebook and placing an asterisk alongside. I assumed this was to alert the chef to a "special" customer, which seemed redundant, considering the chef was leaning over the pass and peering into the dining area, making it very clear he was waiting on our order.

Once again, I searched around for a menu, but none seemed to be forthcoming, and Sue, ever the reluctant hostess, failed to produce one. Remembering the counter meals of my youth, I asked, "Do you have a chicken parmigiana?"

Sue looked blank.

"Roast of the day?"

"Not until Sunday."

"They do a lovely chicken pie here," Max said, finally coming to my aid.

"Right."

Sue noted this on her pad, no asterisk.

The window next to Max's head looked out onto the car park, and beyond that the lawn seemed to run down to a creek. The foliage was dense, and I could imagine Daphne and Max sitting out at one of the picnic tables in the summer, the children running in and out of the creek.

The children! The car park had emptied out. A look at my watch told me it was past three. Somehow I had lost track of the time. "Max. I need to get back for the children." I could see them waiting at the bus stop, Agatha patiently in her wheelchair, Robbie making lovely excuses for me, Sophia huffing. I realized I didn't want to let them down. Not when they already had enough upheaval in their lives.

"Is that the time already?"

I watched with relief as he signaled to Sue behind the bar, and she came rushing over. "Can we have another round of drinks, Sue? And would you ring the hotel, speak to Meryl, and ask her to meet the children at the bus?"

Sue looked very interested by this turn of events.

"I really should go. It's my job." I stood up.

"No, your job is to do as I say." Max put his hand on my arm, and I sat down. Was it my imagination, or did he leave it there slightly longer than was necessary?

For the second time that day, Max's words brought down a deadly silence. This time though, he moved to break it quickly. "I'm sorry for being so peculiar about the camera, earlier."

"Oh." I was struck by the random nature of Max's thought patterns. "That's okay. I just thought Robbie would like it."

"I think he would like it very much."

The food arrived. Sue settled our plates, brought salt and pepper, and delivered our new drinks. "The cameras are everywhere around the hotel, as I'm sure you know," Max said after she left.

I didn't know, but I didn't say anything, listening carefully as I lifted the pastry of my pie to let some cool air into the piping-hot ramekin. My appetite had disappeared.

"They're mainly there as a deterrent to guests. We have a lot of valuable furniture, antiques and the like, in the front part of the hotel. Do you know when we opened we lost all the silver pepper mills in the first week? I suspect it was the staff, but either way, the cameras stopped it. It seems to put people off stealing if they know they're being filmed."

I forced myself to swallow the food in my mouth quickly even though it threatened to scald my tongue, seizing the opportunity to say something about the cameras.

"Perhaps there's something on the video cameras to show where Daphne has gone? I mean, she didn't take a car, did she? So she must have left on foot. Or someone must have come to get her."

The look from earlier came back into his eyes. It lasted longer, and I recognized it this time.

Fear.

"Video cameras cause more trouble than they're worth, and I won't have Robbie sneaking around the hotel with one. End of story."

It wasn't. Not for me. Max kept sidestepping the issue of Daphne's disappearance. I put his lack of logic down to stress. For the moment. "Do you not drink?" I regretted the clumsy change of subject almost as soon as I said it, but I wanted Max to think that I had moved on. I also wanted him to talk so he wouldn't notice I wasn't eating.

"I quit a few years ago, out of solidarity with Daphne. The shame was, she didn't feel the same way." He shook his head, took another sip of his soda water. "I grew to quite like it, the not drinking. I slept better"—at this I raised my eyes, remembering the shouting on my first night—"and I was more productive during the day. It never ends well for my family, drinking."

"I'm not much of a drinker myself," I said, gesturing to the nearly empty beer in front of me. "Well, not really."

"You wouldn't last long in the Summer family, that's for sure." Max shook his head, the words vaguely threatening. He cut another tiny piece from his venison, the pink flesh delicately falling away from the whole. Fingers light on the fork, he gathered up morsels from around the plate, a scraping of mashed potato, a smearing of jus, an errant pea.

"What do Elizabeth and Tom do, out on the island?"

Max started humming. "I quite like this song. Reminds me of my youth."

I strained to hear the music. The din of the lunchtime crowd had subsided slightly, and I could only just hear the song if I sat still and didn't chew. The opening notes of "The Dance of the Sugarplum Fairy" were unmistakable.

We ate in silence for a little while, listening to the music. All the Christmas classics came on, but none prompted any further reactions from Max. Every time the door opened and shut, his head snapped up. Every time it wasn't who he was expecting, he returned to his lunch.

I forced myself to eat. The food was really delicious, and aside from some small approving noises from both of us, we concentrated on it purely. It was almost companionable. My beer was warm now, and flat. I finished it off anyway, feeling my anxiety subside a little, bolstered by the rare warmth that it had encouraged. A ruddy-faced man, cheeks pink from the cold, walked past and asked after Daphne. I waited until he had walked off again.

"You must know everyone in the area."

"Yes, pretty much." Max pushed his knife and fork slightly to the right, even though they were already perfectly positioned at twenty past four.

"You must have a lot of friends."

"Ha!" Max said. He looked around and made sure no one was nearby. Even as he did, a woman at the bar waved at him and then flushed as he smiled back.

Convinced she was out of earshot, he replied, "Knowing people and liking people are not the same thing. Especially in a small place like this."

This was something I could relate to. At the height of my popularity, I had almost a hundred thousand followers on Instagram. Every day, I got a great big hit of endorphins from all the love and approval they gave me. Now my oldest friends didn't even call me on my birthday. Knowing people and liking them—or being liked—was definitely not the same thing, despite the delusion social media created.

"The Summers mostly stick to themselves. We— Daphne, Elizabeth, Tom, and I—we used to do everything together. I miss those days. And Daphne, being Daphne, made hundreds of friends. They've all dropped off now. They think—" He stopped abruptly.

Visibly pulling himself together, he stood up. "This was a bad idea, coming here. Let's go."

I hadn't finished chewing, but I pushed back my chair and rushed after Max. Inside, I felt a small knot of fury and panic forming. It wasn't unfamiliar to me, this knot. I had felt it before after my mother died, and I hoped this time—in these circumstances—it would be temporary. That it wouldn't stay around for years, like it did then.

27

Mrs. Mins was waiting for us by the kitchen door in her jacket, clearly not impressed at being coat-hangered back into child-care duties. Thomas crashed through the door, his tail wagging madly, almost knocking her over. She shook her head at Max and then said something in a low voice. I couldn't hear what it was, but I could guess.

Daphne had not returned.

Chastened, Max said, "I'll just put the car away." He looked at me meaningfully.

Mrs. Mins headed towards a path that led inland away from the house and the sea. A small Barnsley House sign marked "Private" indicated that it wasn't part of the hotel. "And then you'll come to the cottage?" she asked Max.

"And then I'll come to the cottage," he replied, in a submissive voice I hadn't heard before. It seemed to placate Mrs. Mins, and she started to walk away.

"The cottage?" I asked.

"Hotel matters." He climbed back into the Defender and slammed the door.

Mrs. Mins had almost disappeared into the tree line when she turned and called back to me. "Your father rang for you on the hotel phone. He asked you to call him back."

I froze.

I shouldn't have underestimated my father and his lifelong career in journalism. This was a man who had uncovered both high-level corporate corruption and low-level celebrity scandal. It wouldn't have taken much for him to connect the dots between the letter, my missing passport, and the credit card charge. I knew he would eventually work out where I had gone, I just didn't think he would do it so quickly.

Mrs. Mins watched me carefully. "He seemed quite"—she groped around for the right word, enjoying my discomfort—"frantic."

I didn't dare to ask for details. *Frantic* summed it up. I thought about what he must have gone through the last few days. Me, missing. My passport, missing.

My phone, switched off, my emails unanswered. The charge on his credit card.

Acid rose in my throat and I shut my eyes, concentrated on swallowing it.

Mrs. Mins didn't move, so I ducked inside quickly before she could ask any questions and leaned against the other side of the door, grateful for the solidity of the oak and the sturdy brass bolt. Despite my guilt, one thought persisted. *Please don't let him have told them who I am. Please don't let him have told them who I am.*

When I first came here, Barnsley House had been a fairy tale, populated with characters rather than human beings. And now, just as I was getting to know my Barnsley family as real people, it seemed my lies were going to have consequences. Again. I needed to stop my father before he said anything.

I had my hand on the receiver when the children walked in, Robbie first and then Sophia, pushing Agatha. "Is it supper?" Robbie asked innocently.

I took a deep breath and withdrew my hand from the phone. "I suppose it is. Toast?"

The late lunch, the two glasses of beer, and my racing heart had rendered me incapable of anything more elaborate.

Agatha nodded happily, and Sophia sighed the deep

sigh of the disappointed adolescent as she skulked off to the snug to wait.

The dinner and bath rituals dragged on forever that night. With every minute that passed my father would be growing more furious, more likely to phone again and blow my cover. It was surprising he hadn't already.

At last the children were all in their beds, or at least their bedrooms. Agatha and Robbie were reading quietly, and Sophia was doing her homework. I went back down to the kitchen, enjoying the quiet. Compared to the other days I had spent at Barnsley, it had been busy, almost overwhelming. The meeting with Mr. Mins. The long walk to the village. The near miss with the community bus. The trip into town. The pub lunch. It all felt like a lifetime ago.

One of the children had left a kitchen chair by the Aga, so I sat myself down there and propped my sock feet up against the warm door, pressing the familiar numbers of my father's telephone number. I was hoping to convince him that my return phone call was a coincidence. That there had been some sort of mix-up when Mrs. Mins had taken the message for me. The time difference would help—his normally sharp journalistic brain would be addled by sleep, his reading glasses on the nightstand. The number from the private line in the kitchen should be just different enough from the one he dialed earlier for the office. Optimistic? Yes. Deluded? Maybe. But I didn't have another choice.

He answered at once. "Hello?" he said, and even through the overseas connection I could hear the bedsheets rustling, my stepmother muttering in the background. By my calculations, it would have been quite early, but he was always an early riser and had passed that predilection down to me.

"Dad, it's me."

"Poppet," he said, using the name for me that, despite a new marriage, two further daughters, and a series of misdemeanors on my part, he had thankfully never reassigned.

"I'm sorry it's taken me so long to phone you. It's been a bit hectic here." At least this wasn't a lie. "We went to Liberty today. Couldn't afford anything, god, no. But nice to pretend—"

He cut me off. "I know where you are."

"What?"

"It's a bad idea, Miranda."

"Denise and Terence's house is great, Dad. They have an apartment for me upstairs, so it's fine for me to stay a bit longer. We're going to head to France after Christmas and stay with friends. Skiing—we haven't done that for years, have we? Not since the year Ophelia broke her wrist on the first—"

"Miranda," Dad cut me off. *Too many details. Keep it simple, Miranda.* "I called you at Barnsley."

My mouth opened and closed silently. The excuses were thin earlier, but now totally implausible.

"You shouldn't be there." He paused, and I heard him reposition himself. He would be climbing out of bed, shaking his head at my stepmother, telling her don't worry, go back to sleep. I imagined him by the window, looking out over the neighbour's rooftops and towards the bay.

"Where? London?"

"Cut it out."

He was definitely moving through the house now; I could hear his breathing change as he crept past my sisters' bedrooms, the phone line silent for a moment. Then the sound of the coffee machine humming into life, and my father's voice again, at normal volume. "Barnsley House. There's a reason we never took you there, you know."

"What?"

"Miranda. Stop lying for once in your life. Can't you see the danger you're in?"

Danger? Mostly my father left the histrionics to the women in his life. Fleur. Ophelia and Juliet. Me. Always me. Dad was the sensible one. Pragmatic. Sometimes harsh, but mostly fair.

I laughed nervously.

"Why do you think your mother came to live on the other side of the world from her family? They're not . . . nice people, Miranda."

"They don't know who I am," I whispered, admitting defeat, glad Max was with Mrs. Mins, the children in bed. A floorboard cracked in the hall outside the kitchen. In the hotel. I told myself there was no one there.

"Why am I not surprised?" I felt my father's frustration, imagined him rubbing his eyes and shaking his head, just as he had been the morning it all came to a head last year. An early morning in winter. Photographers and journalists camped at the bottom of the front steps, me sitting crying at the bench. Dad making coffee, anything to restore some normality to the situation. Me taking the coffee, no longer pretending I didn't drink coffee or put toxins in my body.

"I was going to tell them . . . but then when I got here, they thought I was the nanny, so I let them believe—"

Dad cut me off. "For once in your life, you might have done the right thing."

I thought of the school sports days where I had won blue ribbons. My endless A-plus reports. Top of the class in year twelve. School prefect. Scholarship. I had endlessly strived not to be ordinary. And then I'd wiped out all the achievements with the disgrace I had brought on myself and my family.

So I agreed with my father. The best thing about being at Barnsley was the anonymity. And not just because it kept me safe. It was because I was giving myself a chance to be ordinary. He misinterpreted my silence as surrender.

"Now listen. I don't know what sort of half-baked story you've told them, but I want you out of there. I'm buying you a ticket home, and I'll email you the details. Can you get to London? I'll call Denise and let her know you're coming."

"I'm staying here, Dad." I didn't realise it until I said the words, but it was true. Barnsley House was mysterious, yes. It was creepy. But I wasn't ready to leave yet.

"No, Miranda. Just no. I don't care what they promise you. After what they did to your mother . . . No. I'll get Susie to book the flights today."

"What did they do to Mum?" Fear in my voice. He was gone.

The house was silent. And then, the sound of footsteps in the hallway. In the hotel. A light beneath the crack in the door disappearing. Someone had been in there, listening. It couldn't have been the children.

There was no way they could have gotten around that side without me seeing. Max and Mrs. Mins? I wasn't sure.

I thought about my conversation with Dad. My vehement denial of fear. I had lied again. I *was* afraid. As the days passed by, I'd become afraid of what had happened to Daphne. I was afraid I might have been the last person to see her. I was afraid something might happen to the children.

I was afraid something might happen to me.

28

"Nice ears."

Max's breath was hot in my own ear, his face close to mine. It took me a moment to register that he was talking about the children's reindeer ears, bobbing about onstage in front of us as the whole school belted out a rousing rendition of "Jingle Bells."

"Two quid," I said, feeling proud of myself for both my use of the local vernacular and my frugality.

"Bargain." He moved his face away, and I let myself breathe again.

We were all in a row, the happy family from Barnsley. Sophia, on the aisle, there under sufferance and only just managing to disguise her disdain; Mrs. Mins in a fawn shearling jacket that I felt sure she wouldn't have been able to afford on her wage, not if it was anything like mine, anyway; and Max, jolly and proud, and proving that you don't need your wife or alcohol to have fun. He oscillated between Mrs. Mins and myself, unable to keep still. We were all in a row. Everyone except for Daphne.

It was hot in the hall, and despite this, Max wore a large overcoat buttoned up to his neck, enormous boots sticking out underneath. Even with him rugged up like that, I could feel the approving gazes of many of the surrounding mothers; if he was trying to disguise himself, it wasn't working. I took my jacket off and jammed it under the seat, next to an enormous carryall Max had also insisted on bringing.

Mrs. Mins swatted him on the thigh with a rolled-up program, and I turned away, determined not to witness any more. I concentrated on the stage. Agatha, at one end, her wheelchair defiantly decorated in tinsel and stars cut out from foil. A little girl, not much taller than the wheelchair, stood behind her and clung protectively to the handles. She was taking her task very seriously. Farther down the row, and up a small bleacher, stood Robbie, wholeheartedly singing along and following the actions, despite the many boys around him who were doing neither.

"What else did you find when you were up in the attic?" I felt Max's words before I heard them. A strange sweetness in his breath. Deliberately timed during a rather raucous moment in proceedings, at a point where others around were unlikely to hear. I pretended not to, either.

He tried again soon after, repeating the question, placing his hand briefly on my arm to claim my attention. "Did you find anything interesting when you were in the attic?"

"Interesting" was an understatement. There had been all sorts of things in the attic. In fact, I had spent half a morning up there. Trunks of old fabric, seed catalogues, Daphne's cookbook collection, which, I was surprised to see, included plenty of the clean-living titles I used to find so inspiring. A great deal of time had been lost paging through them, remembering my days of bliss balls and açai bowls. There had been dozens of photographs of racehorses as well as a full jockey kit. Tubes of rolled-up plans, including some that seemed to detail the original layout of the garden. And large boxes, right by the door, filled with contemporary clothing. Also Daphne's, I presumed.

But anything that seemed relevant to this moment, to the children's Christmas concert, and urgent enough to necessitate an anxious whisper in the dark? I didn't think so. "No."

My answer stopped him in his tracks, and he leaned

back in his seat, drumming his program on his leg in agitation. I tried to concentrate on the children on the stage in front of me, but I could feel Mrs. Mins's eyes on me. Sweat pooled under my arms. I struggled to keep my face impassive, even though my mind was racing at a million miles an hour. I tried smiling at Mrs. Mins, but she set her eyes on a point beyond me, as if she had been looking there all along.

The children stopped singing, and applause filled the hall. I beamed at Agatha, hoping she could see me in the dark room, clapping like mad. Her eyes were searching until finally she saw us and blushed proudly. Max hooted beside me and placed his thumb and forefinger in his mouth, emitting an ear-splitting whistle. I couldn't help but laugh, and onstage Robbie and Agatha were laughing as well. Robbie shook his head in embarrassment, a token gesture; the smile on his face told another story.

For a moment, the clapping and cheering drowned out everything else. The headmistress stepped up to the lectern, and the hall went quiet. The headmistress started to speak, her tinsel earrings catching the light, giving her a luminous glow. A shout went up at the back of the room, and she stopped talking. Squinted into the stage lights. The children waited expectantly behind her.

For a moment, I thought it was Daphne.

"Max?" Then the voice was undeniable. Max's grasp tightened on the program, his knuckles translucent in the light. One by one, every head in the hall turned towards the rear.

Every head except Max's.

"Max?" The voice was coming closer, and the people around us had begun to murmur.

The joy on Agatha's and Robbie's faces was replaced by fear. I fixed my eyes on them, determined not to show my panic. Just in case they looked at me, instead of the man and woman crashing their way down the aisle. Max sighed deeply and stood up. "I'm here, Elizabeth."

"Oh, there you are!" She bustled down the aisle as if she were ten minutes early rather than never even expected. Max gestured for us all to squeeze along. "Those ears," she said as she crammed into the row, pulling a bewildered-looking Tom behind her, "suit Agatha." She put her hand up and gestured to the headmistress to indicate she was ready for the show to go on.

A small child appeared from the wings, carrying a rather large novelty cheque, and the headmistress took a deep breath before explaining to the school community the work that had gone into the year's fund-raising efforts.

"Snore." Elizabeth leaned forward and rolled her eyes at us. A waft of booze floated down the row. I bit the inside of my mouth to keep from laughing. Sophia took her aunt's hand and held it tight, in much the same way you might try to contain a toddler. Tom was no help; in his position at the very end of the row, it took all his attention not to fall off the side of the folding chairs.

"Shhh!" A woman's voice, exasperated.

I swiveled in my chair to see who was brave enough to silence Elizabeth. Mrs. Mins.

Next to me, Max closed his eyes. A man stepped up from the audience, accepted the cheque on behalf of the St. John's Family Mission, and spoke about the need for a compassionate community. It may have been my imagination, but it felt as if his eyes were drilling deep into our row. More applause, particularly from those sitting near us.

The band started up again, and my body relaxed. The children were singing along with the others, and Sophia kept a tight hold on her aunt, her gaze not moving from her brother and sister. Perhaps everything would be okay. The song continued.

We wish you a Merry Christmas, we wish you a Merry Christmas . . .

And then a voice in the darkness.

"Don't you shush me," Elizabeth hissed. Max's eye twitched slightly. "I've more right to be here than you." Max made a sharp intake of breath.

We wish you a Merry Christmas and a Happy New Year! Good tidings we bring to you and your kin . . .

Elizabeth leaned forward and looked at me meaningfully. My heart began to pound, and I turned my attention back to the stage. There was movement beside me, and the feeling of space opening up; someone behind us gasped. Mrs. Mins had gone. The eyes of everyone in the hall were on us and yet still the song continued. The conductor, her back to the audience and having no idea of the kerfuffle behind her, brought her arms out wide, and the children reached a rousing crescendo.

"Elizabeth, that was not necessary," Max said, and then opened his eyes. Where I expected to see anger, there was only pity. A deep sadness.

Elizabeth looked chastened, on the verge of tears herself. "It's a time for family, Max."

My thighs were on the verge of sticking to the seat, even through my jeans. The rest of the Summer family seemed oblivious to the spectacle they were causing, the endless material they were providing for later speculation in the Stag's Head or Minton.

"Family?" he hissed. "Meryl is more a part of this

family than you." I shifted uncomfortably in my seat as he continued. "Where have you been the last couple of months? When the children needed you? When I needed you? Out on that bloody island, doing god knows what. In the *bloody pub*."

The woman next to me snorted, then tried to disguise it as a cough. I turned my body away from her to build a shield for Max and Elizabeth. Trying to protect them.

Elizabeth was definitely crying now. Not in a hysterical way. In a deeply Elizabeth way, tears streaming down her cheeks in uninterrupted rivers. Silent tears. Her face composed. And then she leaned forward. Leaned back. Counted everyone off along the row, her face stricken as she realized.

"Where is Daphne?"

"Not now, Elizabeth." Max focused his attention on the stage. Uselessly. Elizabeth knew now, and she would not let it go. Even I could see that.

"WHERE IS SHE?"

"We'll talk about it at home," Max replied, his voice tense. "Not here."

Tom took Elizabeth's hand in his, hoping to calm her.

Up on the stage, the headmistress was speaking again, but in our row, apart from Sophia, who had sat frozen with her face resolutely facing the stage throughout, we were stuck in a complicated limbo. We needed to leave, but how to extricate the children from the stage without making even more of a fuss than we already had? Around us the hall had grown quiet again, but a different sort of quiet. There was an air of expectation. I looked around, wanting to know what was going on.

The first strains of another familiar song filled the air. "Shit," Max said, next to me. "Shit. Shit. Shit. Shit." He reached under the chair and dragged out the bag from underneath. "Shit. Shit. Shit." I looked at Elizabeth, but she had rested her head on Tom's shoulder, tired out from the emotion. Worn out from the booze. A small smile played at the edges of Sophia's lips, but she still didn't turn. That child had the composure of someone far older, and I had no idea where she got it from. Meanwhile, her father was losing it as he started to shed his clothes.

Underneath the giant overcoat was a full-blown Santa Claus costume. He reached into the bag and pulled out a hat and beard, and starting to ho-ho-ho, he stood up and waved a bell. He squeezed out past Elizabeth and Tom and Sophia, and as he went past, he bent down to place a kiss on both his sister's and daughter's heads. A sack dangled over his shoulder, and from within he pulled out toffees and flung them into the crowd. Delighted squeals followed him as he made his way to the stage, ho-ho-ho-ing and ringing his bell the whole time. By the time he made it up the stairs, he was surrounded by small children, all clutching at him and demanding sweets.

Daphne should have been there to see it, instead of wherever she was. This was the kind of memory a family should treasure—it wasn't right that she wasn't there. Nothing was more important than this. Not friends. Not alcohol. Not anything. There was no way Daphne would miss this by choice.

I forced myself to concentrate on the children again. Robbie, Agatha, and even Sophia watched Max with adoration in their eyes, laughing and whispering with their friends. Holding their hands out for sweets like all the others, even though I knew their hearts were heavy with the absence of their mother.

I knew I needed glasses. I knew I should have been wearing them. But even a blind person could see that Max had a better relationship with his children than I had thought. That, despite all their flaws and every-thing that had come between them, Max and Elizabeth cared deeply about each other. And that no one, not even Elizabeth, knew where Daphne was.

29

I was not the only person to notice.

Later, when we had returned to Barnsley and the children were tucked in—Max carried an already asleep Agatha, and I led a protesting Robbie—I was thinking about bed myself. Not a small Barnsley bed, but my queen-size bed at home, with its feather quilt and pillow-top mattress. Sheets warm and crispy from the summer sun. The window cracked open to let in the bay breeze. It was probably the thing I missed most about Australia.

Tossing and turning under the covers, I tried to convince myself I was back there. But something was playing on my mind, and wouldn't let me sleep. I wasn't short on worries, but as I ran through the usual ones—my relationship with my father, my past, my future—nothing flagged. It was something more recent. Something more Barnsley.

I sat upright. We had seen Agatha and Robbie into bed, but Sophia? No. She was old enough to look after herself. I had a sudden flashback of her sitting at the concert, staring at the stage, her face fixed and determined. As if she was trying to work something out. Or as if she had worked something out and was trying not to show it.

It wouldn't hurt to check on her. There was of course the risk of one of her withering looks or brutal dismissals. I could handle that possibility, though, if it meant I knew she was safe and sound in bed. I lay a moment longer, trying to piece together our movements when we got back to the house. We had all walked together from the car park—at Max's insistence—and Sophia had been at the rear. Max and I had headed straight upstairs with the children, and I had assumed she'd snuck into the snug to watch some television. I hadn't seen her, though. I pushed back the covers and grabbed the cardigan on the end of my bed. Just in case.

Sophia wasn't in her bed. The lights in her room were off, but the curtains were open, and by the silvery light of the moon I could see that her bedcovers were undisturbed. She hadn't been in there at all. I looked out the window, over the gardens. From there, they looked magical: bare-branched yews lit from under-neath, the garden lights still burning to guide us home from the concert. A frost had descended on the lawn, and it sparkled in places. Still, I didn't want to be out there. I wanted to be in bed.

There was no point in calling out to Max. He had disappeared to the cottage once the children were in bed, citing "hotel matters" again. It was up to me.

I couldn't think where she would be. I didn't know where there was. So I started with the Mins cottage, where perhaps she had gone in search of her father.

Adrenaline was shooting through my body, flushing out any last vestiges of tiredness as I dressed quickly and headed out into the cold night. The weather was with me. Great drifts of cloud parted as I stepped out-side, revealing the moon, which made it easier for me to progress across the lawn and towards the path where I estimated the Mins cottage to be. Not surprisingly, after the one marked "Private," there were no further helpful wooden signs.

Along the path in the pitch-black night, layers of sounds existed below the overwhelming roar of the sea and the ever-present wind. The darkness made my ears hypersensitive; each call of an owl or cry of a vixen startled me, stopping me in my tracks. I carried no torch, and it took some time for my eyes to adjust, the branches intertwining overhead to create a tunnel of darkness through which I ventured slowly.

At first I thought the crying was a wild animal. Soft and consistent, it was more like the whimper of a small creature separated from its mother than of a human being. It was coming from behind me. Not from the direction of the Mins cottage, but from the direction of the water. From down towards the boathouse.

I turned and ran, blood pounding in my ears, trying to stay upright on the unsteady ground. It was a relief to emerge on the lawn, and I gathered pace as I crossed the grass and found the path towards the cove, towards the boathouse.

She hadn't made it far down the path before she fell. It must have been the first or second tree root that had brought her down, and now she sat huddled under a dense bush, clutching at her ankle. Her eyes came up to meet mine, frightened. "Sophia!" I hissed. "What are you doing out here?"

The sound of my voice set her off, and the whimpers escalated into full-blown sobs, hysterical and guttural. I tried a different tack. "Are you okay?" I crouched down next to her. She shuffled ever so slightly away. "Have you hurt your ankle?" I reached out, and she flinched. I tried again, taking her ankle in my hand. She let me, but it was no use. In the dark, and through her jeans, there was nothing to see. "Let's get you home."

I thought she would protest, but she didn't. Whatever bravado had propelled her out here into the dark night had subsided, and fear had crept into its place. We hopped along a little way, her arm around my shoulder, my arm around her waist, the tears on her face glistening in the moonlight. I would have liked to carry her, but I knew that even if I was strong enough, Sophia's pride would get in the way. She was closer to being a woman than a child. "I thought Elizabeth knew where Mum was." The crying increased again. "I thought she must be with her."

In the dark, I nodded. I had thought so too. Hoped so. I didn't trust myself to speak. There was so much I wanted to say to her, but none of it seemed right at that moment. "Dad and Mrs. Mins said they searched the grounds. But they can't have. She must be here somewhere. She might be hurt." She stopped. "Like me. Maybe she fell down and needs help." Her face was close to mine, her eyes wide in revelation. Up close, she looked so much like Daphne. "Will you go down and look for me? At the boathouse?"

"The boathouse?"

Sophia looked at me meaningfully. "The boathouse."

Her eyes acknowledged mine; *Yes*, they said, *we know about the boathouse*. I swallowed. In front, I could see the lights of the garden, and the shadow of the house behind. I could almost feel the warmth of the upstairs corridor, the particular lavender smell of the bed linen.

And then I thought about Daphne as I had last seen her, pale and frail in the middle of the night. If she had ventured out in the dark, there was every chance she would have fallen down or tripped. If she was out here somewhere, she would be in a bad way. A couple of hours could be life or death. "Okay."

We pulled up at a garden bench, nestled under an old oak tree. In summer, I imagined it must be a pleasant place to sit, the lawn unfolding down to the sea. On a midwinter's night, it was barely hospitable. Sophia didn't seem to mind. "I'll wait here."

I ran. My heart raced the entire way. I was unfit, yes, but the rapidness of my breath owed more to fear than to respiratory issues. I was bloody terrified. It got darker and darker as the path twisted down to the boathouse, and I expected Mr. Mins to appear at any moment. Or worse. Finally, just when I was about to turn back, the path twisted one last time, and the water appeared, shimmering black in the moonlight.

There was nobody there.

I knocked on the windows loudly, not caring who heard me. I rattled the door handle, but it was locked tight, the blinds firmly drawn. Boats bobbed and banged against the jetty, but apart from that, there was not a sound. I stood still, trying to hear something—anything—over the beating of my heart. But there was nothing.

Daphne was not there.

As I gathered my breath for the return journey, I tried to imagine the cove as Daphne had described it in the notebook. The water warm enough to swim in. Music wafting through the warm air. The sound of people laughing, drinks being poured. A shriek of laughter, then a splash. Not deathly quiet as it was that night. It was almost impossible.

And then a voice came through the darkness.

My name.

It was not Sophia. It was Max.

I bolted towards the house.

When I finally made it to the edge of the lawn, where they were waiting, Max was wild, and I was so out of breath I couldn't speak. Which was probably a good thing. "Need I remind you that your sole responsibility here is to look after the children? Thanks to you, my daughter was seriously injured."

I nodded, trying to control my breathing and look sincere at the same time. "If it weren't so close to Christmas, I would be finding a replacement. Consider this your only warning."

Sophia said nothing, and we returned to the house, Max and I on either side, Sophia hobbling between us.

30

It was Christmas morning, and still Daphne had not returned. Elizabeth had not been seen since the concert, and the children had kept me busy. Max had barely spoken to me since the night of the boathouse incident. Sophia had told him that I had convinced her to go looking for Daphne. I hadn't denied it. The last thing Sophia needed was another adult bailing out on her.

The other two children were tired, and Sophia needed to rest her ankle, so the days between the concert and Christmas had been quiet; we filled our time with making shortbread and watching Christmas movies. *The Polar Express*, *Elf*, and, of course, *Home Alone*. I kept my head down and committed myself to what was, in Max's opinion, my sole responsibility.

Despite everything, there was a magical feel in the air when the children rose early on Christmas morning. I could hear rummaging in the corridor from before six in the morning, but the bed was so warm and the sky beyond the windows so dark, I waited until the noise had escalated to an unbearable point.

When I emerged from my room, a woolen cardigan pulled on over my pyjamas, Robbie was wedged between Agatha's bed and a bookshelf, clutching at his elbow. Despite this, he was in good spirits. Even Sophia, on the other side of the bed and clearly the antagonist, was smiling.

"Shhhh!" I said. "You'll wake your father."

"That's the point!" Agatha said, giggling. "If we don't make a racket, he'll never wake up."

"It's too late for that," came a low grumble from behind the door. "I'm up."

"Is Mum back?" Robbie asked hopefully. The giggling stopped. Sophia, in particular, looked on the verge of tears. My heart was breaking for them.

When Max emerged from behind the door, it was clear that he too was struggling with Daphne's absence. "She'll be away a little longer, I think," he said, his voice strangely strangled.

"She's not here for Christmas?" Agatha's voice was small.

"It's not like her. I don't care what you say," Sophia shouted, and ran off down the stairs, leaving the rest of us mute.

"Shall we go down, children?" Max was trying to put on a brave face, but his hands shook as he tied the cord of his dressing gown. He kissed the top of Robbie's head and then lifted Agatha out of her bed to carry her downstairs. She burrowed her face into the spot between the shawl of the dressing gown and his shoulder. I could tell she was crying by the movement of her shoulders.

I remembered my first Christmas without my mother. My father and I attempted to celebrate alone, but the day was fraught. By the next year my stepmother had arrived, and she managed to make it special again, in her own way. I was beginning to appreciate how hard she'd worked to make that happen.

Yet here at Barnsley there was no Christmas tree, no decorations aside from the paper chain we had made and strung up around the kitchen, no smell of Christmas baking. It could just as well have been any other day. I hadn't seen the Christmas presents since we snuck them back into the house after our furtive shopping trip; for days I had been expecting Max to ask me to wrap them. When he hadn't, I could only assume they would either be presented in their carrier bags or wrapped in some fashion by him.

I took my time down the stairs, peering out over the landscape for snow—no sign. By the time I got to the kitchen, they were all waiting for me. Even Sophia. There was no sign of any presents. What sort of a Christmas morning was this?

Robbie, however, seemed to have pepped up slightly. "Come on! Dad said we had to wait for you." He tugged at the door, the one that divided the kitchen from the rest of the house. Beyond that door lay the hotel.

This was unusual. The children were not allowed in the hotel part of the house, and apart from our search party the other evening, I had been very careful to ensure that this restriction be enforced.

But it seemed Christmas Day was an exception to the rule. Max helped Robbie with the door, and the children flew through. He and Agatha propped the door open for me, letting it close gently behind them once I had passed.

"Feels just like it did when I was a child," Max said with a pantomime shiver. "Lucky you."

No wonder my mother had escaped to Australia. I doubted I would last one night in this part of the house. I thought of the cozy kitchen just through the doors, the warm snug, the study with the open fire. Why couldn't we stay in there?

Robbie and Sophia skidded to a halt outside a set of double doors, looking to their father for permission to enter. When he gave it, they threw the doors open and made gasps of delight despite themselves. Max increased his pace to almost a jog, pushing the wheelchair up close so that Agatha wouldn't miss out.

It was the room I had peered into on that first morning: a large formal sitting room, framed at one end by the bay window I recognized, and at the other by an enormous fireplace, in which a roaring log fire was burning. The lamps were lit, and tea lights twinkled on all surfaces, but the real showstopper was the gigantic fir Christmas tree in the bay window, dressed from top to toe with lights and glass baubles. It was spectacular, and the mound of presents beneath it even more so. There were boxes of them, great piles of presents, far more than we had purchased. Max, or someone else, had evidently done a lot of Christmas shopping, so what was the purpose of our sudden and urgent mission only days earlier?

I pushed these thoughts aside and took a moment to enjoy the children's reactions to the spectacle. Even for an adult it was magical, Max had taken so much trouble to make Christmas special. My idea of Max was shifting before me, his character so fluid I could barely grasp it.

Hanging back, enjoying the warmth of the room but feeling superfluous, I wondered if there was a way I could back away without anyone noticing. The table was set for breakfast, and by my counting there was a place for me, but my presence felt conspicuous. I deliberately kept to the shadows while the children explored the piles of presents and unpacked stockings filled with chocolates, trinkets, and clementines.

"There's a present under there for you," Max said, catching me midstep as I edged farther and farther away. "More than one, I think."

"Oh. I have some things for the children. I'll go and get them," I replied, thinking I would take as long as possible, perhaps even run myself a bath and leave them to it.

"I think there's enough here for now. Come. Sit. Here, next to Aggie." It was the first time I had heard Max use the pet name. He shuffled her over, closer to him. Having no real reason to retreat, I gave in. I watched as the children opened their presents, tucking the small pile accumulating for me down one side of the sofa, so I could open them later in the privacy of my room.

The children were in raptures, tearing away the

wrapping from their gifts. Among them I recognised the things we had chosen on our shopping trip and saw that they were well received, if unnecessary in the deluge. Who had organized this for Max? In the shops with me he'd been uncomfortable and seemed to have little idea about his children's desires, and yet gift after gift was being unwrapped to shrieks of delight. There was no sign of Mrs. Mins, and yet I detected her hand; only she in this household possessed the twin skills of subterfuge and efficiency. I suspected that Elizabeth's comments at the concert were the reason she was missing her moment of glory.

Max gave nothing away, and of course I could not ask him, for the generous array before us was the work of Father Christmas. Who, though, had decorated the tree and adorned the room? What was the point of having such elaborate decorations and only revealing them on Christmas morning? Max brought me some coffee, and I sipped it tentatively, convincing myself I liked the taste as much as the smell. "It's been a tradition here since I was a boy," he explained, seeing my confusion. "The Christmas tree is not revealed until the day of Christmas. It's not unusual, actually—it's the way it was always done, once upon a time."

"Stuck in the past as usual," I remarked, meaning it as a joke but finding that the words sounded bitter on my lips. It was anger, I suppose, at his ability to so completely excise my mother from these memories. As if she had never even existed. Was he planning to do the same with Daphne? I wouldn't let him.

"Only with the things that matter." Max watched me carefully. I sipped my coffee again and turned towards the children.

"It's beautiful," I said, and it was true. The room, grand and imposing as it was, felt warm and welcoming, and so different from the day I had peeked through the window. The tree was one thing, but it was the excitement radiating from the children that made it special. The only thing missing was their mother.

As if he'd read my mind, Max said, "Daphne always loved it in here at Christmas." The decorations and the lights and the fire in the hearth had made the room come alive, but I felt Daphne's absence keenly. I couldn't imagine how the children were feeling.

"Loved?" I asked, the words bitter on my tongue, but Max had turned away.

"Open your presents!" I felt a tug on my sleeve, and it was Robbie.

"Go on, you've got a great pile." He was right; the stack next to me was threatening to tumble.

"Go on." Max nodded towards the gifts. Agatha and Sophie stopped what they were doing to watch.

There were three parcels, varying in size from large to book-shaped. I opened the largest first, a hangover from childhood I suppose, and discovered another box within, nestled in which was a pair of glossy red boots.

"Gumboots!" I exclaimed.

"Wellies," Agatha corrected me from her spot on the sofa. "What did you call them?"

"Gumboots."

"That's what Mum calls them too."

"That's right, she does too." Max looked mildly shaken. He fluctuated between speaking openly about his wife and bristling at the mention of her. It was as if it was simultaneously too difficult to talk about her and too difficult not to: I found it hard to determine any pattern in his behaviour.

"They're lovely. Perfect for the weather here. I'll be able to take you guys for long walks, now I have the right boots." Everyone went quiet, and I realised my mistake. Not looking at Agatha, I quickly added, "I love the red."

"We'll always be able to see where you are," Max said quietly, the slight threat in his voice at odds with his festive demeanour. He met my eye as I reached for the next present.

The paper was thick like parchment and heavily embossed with gold patterns; my hands were shaking, and my fingers fumbled at the silk ribbon, unable to loosen the knot.

"Here, let me." Max reached into his pocket and revealed a small folding knife with a bottle opener and a screwdriver, the type you might see in a hardware store. He put his hand on top of mine where I held the parcel, and it was warm. Applying a gentle pressure to my hand, he flicked at the ribbon, and it fell to the ground.

There was tissue paper inside, and then a waxed cotton jacket, a shorter version of the one I had seen on Mr. Mins down at the cove, lined with soft tartan cotton. I brought it out of the wrapping and held it up; I could tell by looking it would be the perfect size. It was not something I would wear in normal life, but that life seemed to be on hold, and this jacket was better suited to my new life here at Barnsley. My light down jacket had been no match for the relentless drizzle and cold winds. I was touched that Max had noticed—touched and a little worried.

I was contemplating opening my third present from Max when the door opened, and Mrs. Mins arrived. Her presence, combined with Daphne's absence, made me feel uneasy.

Mrs. Mins seemed uneasy as well, a contrast to her usual unruffled behaviour. "Merry Christmas, Summers!" she called out, jolly and festive. She was wearing yet another clinging wrap dress, this time in red velvet. Her cheeks were flushed, and although she was fully made up, her eyes were tired. She looked as if she had been up for some time. I thought guiltily of the way I had lounged in bed until the last possible moment.

"Merry Christmas, Mrs. Mins," the children replied, showing no inclination to get up and greet her.

Mrs. Mins disappeared out the door and returned pushing a trolley laden with silver-topped servers. She lifted them onto the sideboard one by one, resting them on special stands and placing matching serving spoons in front of each one. Once they were all in order, she came over to the sofas and kissed each of the children in turn. Agatha and Robbie smiled at her, but Sophia turned away slightly, the kiss landing somewhere closer to her hairline, a telltale smudge of red lipstick at her temple.

Giving Max a great eyeful of her cleavage, Mrs. Mins bent down to kiss him on the cheek. He remembered his manners at that moment and jumped up, grabbing her hand and almost butting her in the head before gathering himself and kissing her on both cheeks. "Merry Christmas, Meryl. Thank you for everything."

"It's nothing," she said, still hanging on to his hand, though every inch of the room we were in indicated a great deal of effort. "The goose is in the oven, and I've left instructions for when to pull it out. The vegetables are in the warmer—I know you like them soft—and the sauces are in the pantry. I've got breakfast here for you. Sue is coming in later to clear up, so you don't have to worry about that."

Great. Sue. The eavesdropping waitress from the pub. I made a mental note to make myself as scarce as I could later on in the day.

"Thanks, Meryl. You've thought of everything."

"Are you sure about the pudding, Max?"

"Yes, quite. The children would prefer ice cream anyway."

"I never liked pudding," I said, hoping to relieve the tension in the room. It was true: the rich boozy fruity sponge was my least favourite thing as a child, and I only ate it so I could move on to my chocolate coins.

"Is there anything you don't have a strong opinion about?" Max asked.

"I think I've been quite reserved in my opinions so far."

Max snorted. I felt Sophia's eyes on me. Cautious.

"Right, well, breakfast is ready," Mrs. Mins said. "There's scrambled eggs, smoked salmon, croissants, and pancakes for the children."

At the word *pancakes*, I made an involuntary but

audible sound of excitement. What had gotten into me? After years of avoiding refined sugar, I was becoming obsessed. It seemed there was no end to my cravings for food devoid of any nutritional value. "And for Miranda," Max said, raising his eyebrows at me.

Mrs. Mins looked at both of us in turn and then, lacking either the ability or the desire to decipher what was going on, turned and left the room. Max smiled at me, and made a gesture imploring me to serve myself. "Come on, kids. Leave those things be for a minute."

One by one they dragged themselves away from the presents, Sophie helping Agatha into her wheelchair and pushing her towards the table. Robbie stood up last, a small camera perched on his head.

"Robbie, what's that?" I asked. Max moved up beside me.

"It's a camera," he started to explain, "and it films whatever I see. So right now, it's filming you. And now"—he spun around—"it's filming Dad."

"Turn that off, Robbie," Max said. "I can't believe Father Christmas sometimes." And he winked at me over Robbie's head, not bothering whether the camera caught the moment or not.

31

Hot and cold. That was the nature of Max. At first I thought it was just me, until I saw that Max was the same with everyone, even his children. Once you became accustomed to it, it was easier to bear; if you were in his favour, the enjoyment was tempered by the knowledge you would soon be out of it, and vice versa. But it was no way for children to be brought up, the ground unsteady beneath their feet. Unconditional love was an unfamiliar concept to the Summer children. For them love was here and there, arbitrary and rarely predictable. Great demonstrations of love or generosity were followed by abrupt upheaval or criticism. Christmas was to be no exception.

Mrs. Mins had provided more than enough breakfast for the five of us, especially given that she had also left a full Christmas dinner in the kitchen, but we tried our best to make a dent in it. Max ate with gusto, as did Robbie. Sophia ate eggs and salmon but no toast, and Agatha made a special concession to the occasion and tried the pancakes. We were making progress.

"You didn't open your last present," Max said as we watched the children play with their presents. I was hoping he hadn't noticed, but there was no point pretending I hadn't.

"No. I didn't."

I hadn't bought him anything. Why would I?

The book-shaped present was covered in the same expensive-looking paper as the others, and I unwrapped it quickly, talking to the children as I did, anything to relieve the sense of tension I felt with Max's eyes on me. It was, not surprisingly, a book. The Winston Churchill biography I had seen Max select in the bookshop. An odd choice, and I was unable to disguise my confusion. I hadn't at any time expressed any interest in Winston Churchill, and I had very little knowledge of him, but still the gift gave me a little thrill of collusion. Perhaps Max saw something in me that I myself had not recognised? A latent but encourageable interest in bygone prime ministers?

"Oh Christ!" Max said. "She's wrapped up the wrong book. I wondered where that had gone." He snatched it from me. Unnecessarily, I thought. "I've got no idea where your other present is." He spoke as if the missing present was my fault, and I blinked, shocked.

"Maybe it's this one, Dad?" A small voice from beyond the table. Robbie. Timid. Waving another book-shaped gift.

"Well, bring it over, then." Max held out his hand and roughly took it from the boy, not seeing the worry on his face. He thrust it towards me. Aware now that I had four sets of eyes on me where before I had only had one, I unwrapped it, again, as quickly as possible. Part of me knew what it might be, and another part thought he wouldn't dare.

He did dare.

The familiar cover. A brand-new edition, with the title embossed in gold. The entire back cover a photograph of my mother in profile, smiling up to someone above her. "*The House of Brides*," I read, as if I was seeing it for the first time—I hoped.

"Have you heard of it? It's very famous," Max said. I shook my head and studied the cover intently. A stylized illustration, more Art Deco than previous editions, giving it a P. G. Wodehouse feel. Another lie. This was no comedy. "My sister wrote it."

"Oh?" I feigned surprise, thinking of the chapter

about Max's mother. About all the other family secrets laid bare. Why would he want me to read this?

"I thought you might be interested in the history of the house, of my family. Of course, you can't believe everything you read in there. She got a few bits wrong, here and there. But the nuts and bolts of it are right."

"Thank you."

"After we were in the bookshop the other day"—he cast a quick glance towards the children to see if they were listening; Agatha and Robbie were absorbed in Legos, but Sophia was staring a little too intently at the instruction booklet not to be paying attention—"I thought you seemed very interested . . ."

I looked up, panicking.

"Interested in the area. I just thought you might like it."

I tucked it under my arm. "Thank you," I said, backing towards the door. It was hard to walk backwards in the new red gumboots I had slipped on earlier at Agatha's request. "I might go and let you have some time to yourselves now. As a family. I mean . . ." I didn't know what I meant. Daphne's absence was glaring. Why hadn't he phoned the police? She had been gone for days now. Even if she was on a bender, she could be lying in a ditch now. Or worse.

"Before you go, I wonder if I might speak to you about something?" Max asked, looking nervously over towards the children. "Perhaps we'll step outside?" It could only be about one thing: Daphne. It was as if he could read my mind. Max guided me through the double doors and closed them gently, the Christmas carols only faintly audible in the cold air of the hallway.

"Was it really this cold? When you were growing up?" I asked. I thought of our warm house back in Australia. Radiators in every room. My father said my mother had been quite specific about that on the plans, even though she had never lived to see them fulfilled.

"No. Only if the boiler broke down, which it was prone to do from time to time. My grandfather modernised the house—heating and the rest—but my father remembers it like this, and he liked to remind us what it was like by keeping the heating turned right down low. Daphne couldn't believe the cold when she first came, but she soon took over and got all the radiators going at full bore. She's spoiled me—I can't bear the cold as much as I used to. But the bills!"

"Did you ever live in this part of the house? You and Daphne?" I wanted to bring her into the conversation. No one else seemed able to do it. I felt the intensity of Max's eyes on me.

"We thought we would," he eventually answered.

"We had a room at the front, just above us now. It overlooked the sea, and we had rooms alongside us for the children, all lined up in a row. The hotel became too popular, though, and we decided to move to the back of the house, leave those rooms for the paying guests. Everyone wanted the sea view. They still do."

"The Yellow Room?" I asked, surprised Max would take his new bride to the room in which his mother died.

"Yes. That's it." He seemed about to add something else but stopped himself. Physically put his hand to his mouth.

"What did Daphne think about that?" Daphne struck me as the type who would prefer the dramatic water views, but I also thought she might object to sleeping in the room where her mother-in-law had died.

"Oh, she's a businessperson, first and foremost. She wasn't like other English girls I brought here, all wound up in the self-importance of the place, and feeling put aside if we put them in an attic bedroom. She could see that that way of life was over, and we needed to do something new here."

"She was right," I said. From what I could tell, Daphne was just what this place needed. Her restaurant had made Barnsley House a tourist attraction, and a recognisable name, and even though she was on some sort of hiatus now, she had already left a legacy stronger than those of many of the Summer women immortalised in *The House of Brides*. Memories of Max frowning at the ledger and fishing through his wallet for a viable credit card came back to me. How much longer could Barnsley limp along without her?

"I have to go to London," Max said suddenly, keeping his eye on a spot above the doorway. There was a family crest there, carved into the wood, and he concentrated on it as if seeing it for the first time. "Tonight."

"Tonight?"

"Shh. Yes. Don't make a fuss." I must have made a noise, a squeak of disbelief. He added, "For the children's sake."

"But why? It's Christmas." For some reason, I was close to tears. He was not my father, but it was Christmas, and I knew what it was like to feel shaky at Christmas, and I remembered how much I needed my father on that day above any others. Agatha was finally eating something different, and Sophia had been so keen to show her father her presents. Robbie was dying to explain to Max how his camera worked and planned to go ghost hunting with him after dark.

"I know it's Christmas, for Christ's sake." He looked

upset, and justifiably so, but someone needed to stand up for these children. First their mother disappears, and then their father takes off on Christmas Day. "It's about Daphne."

"Is she in London?"

"I don't know!" Max snapped. He rubbed his eyes, his chin, his head. Slumped against the doorframe. "Her brother is. Daniel. He may know something."

"He may? That's a long bow. Why don't you just call the police? Like a normal person."

His head snapped up. "We are not calling the police."

"Do you have to go? The children will be so upset."

"Do you think I would go if I didn't have to? I'm not a complete arsehole."

"That's not what it looks like," I said, careful not to raise my voice, and aware the children could come looking for us at any moment. Aware that they were starting to trust me. I didn't want them to see me fighting with their father.

"What does it look like?"

"I heard shouting. On the night she disappeared. She was frightened, Max. Something bad could have happened to her." I didn't want to let on that I had seen her.

I moved in front of the door, wanting to block Max's

escape route before I asked my next question. "What happened, Max? What happened to Daphne?"

The tiniest smile played on his lips. So faint, and gone in an instant. In the silence, the opening notes of "Good King Wenceslas" were discernible. "Maybe you know something, Miranda? You were the last one to see her."

I swallowed nervously, but he continued, oblivious. "Sneaking around in the guest rooms. Daphne was visibly upset when I found you both. I had to put her to bed."

He came closer, and I could smell the coffee on his breath, the harsh odor overpowering all others. "What were you up to?" He leaned in. "Who are you?"

I tried not to breathe. His face was so close to mine, the proximity both menacing and intimate. I squeezed my nails into the flesh of my hand, willing him not to come any closer. Not sure of his intent.

"No one." It was a whisper.

"Good girl." Max raised his pointer finger and placed it on my lips. "Good girl."

Bile rose up, and I forced it down, trying not to move my lips. Trying not to give Max any encouragement. I stepped back, out of the doorway. His finger lingered in midair, a warning now.

Finally he lowered his hand to the brass handle of the door back into the drawing room. "I'm just asking you to keep an eye on the children. I'll go after they're in bed and be back as soon as possible." He paused. "We'll find her, Miranda." His voice cracked, but he was gone before I could see if there were any tears.

32

Max's departure was a wake-up call; once his hypnotising presence was removed, I became gripped by a strange mania. Driven not quite by fury but something similar, I resolved to make the most of his absence and get on with my investigations. This time I would not let technological obstacles or matters of decorum stall my progress. I would be ruthless in the pursuit of what I wanted to know.

I was going to find out what happened to Daphne. I was going to find out what Max had done to my mother. I was going to find out what Elizabeth knew. I was going to find out what it had to do with me.

Max's car had barely retreated down the driveway when I tapped at Sophia's door. It was still early, but there wasn't any light showing under her door; I wondered if I had left it too late. The twin pillars of Christmas, excitement and exhaustion, had made it a long day, but it was normally her habit to read late into the night. Agatha and Sophia escaped into their books, while Robbie overcompensated with friendliness and a zest for life. They all seemed to be young insomniacs.

After a moment's pause, she said "Yes?" in a worried voice. Her timidity surprised me. Headstrong and combative most of the time, after the events of the other night she seemed cowed by the darkness.

"It's only me," I said, and lowered the handle. A cloying teenage smell wafted out from within: scented deodorant mixed with cheap perfume and sticky lip gloss. It reminded me of school changing rooms and the emotions that ran high within them. I swallowed nervously, casting aside those memories, my sympathy rising towards Sophia for still being in the middle of those years. Despite the darkness under the door, a bedside lamp cast a small halo of light near her pillow. She was reading a tattered old paperback, not one of the books she had been given for Christmas, and looked so peaceful I felt bad for disturbing her. "What are you reading?" I asked, gathering up the courage to say why I was really there.

"It was one of Mum's favourites," she said, holding it up. "I took it from her bedside table after—" The words wouldn't come, so I interrupted her by reading aloud the title.

"*I Capture the Castle*. I don't know it."

"I think Elizabeth gave it to Mum when she moved here, just after they got married. She said it would explain a lot about the place, about the English. She said I could read it when I was a bit older."

"And you're a bit older now."

"Yes." I wasn't sure if it was appropriate, but it felt like it wasn't my place to come between a mother and her daughter in this way.

"Maybe I can borrow it when you're finished?"

"Okay." She closed the book and looked at the cover. "You've got a bit of reading to do already."

"*The House of Brides*?"

"Yes."

"Have you read it?" I was about the same age as Sophia when I read it for the first time. I'd skipped through most of it, especially the long descriptive passages about church architecture and the landscape. Mostly I was just disappointed it didn't hold more of the essence of my mother. And that there was nothing about me.

"Dad won't let me."

Not really an answer. I left it be. "How is your ankle?"

A flash of guilt crossed her face, and she reached instinctively to her foot. "It's much better, thanks."

I waited a moment for what I hoped was coming next.

Nothing.

"Did you have a good day?" I asked.

She thought for a moment, sitting up in her bed and leaning against the upholstered headboard, her long blond hair slightly tousled from the pillow. "It wasn't as bad as I expected," she said, slowly. "It was different without Mum—I knew that it would be, but it was also weird that Elizabeth and Tom didn't come. Christmas used to be such a big thing. We would go to carols in the village, and then Elizabeth and Tom would come back to the main house. Even when we were really little, we were allowed to stay up late, and the grown-ups would let us join in the games, and we would sing. One year I got a karaoke machine, and I could barely even get a turn—Mum and Elizabeth were on it the whole time, singing all these old songs while Dad and Tom rolled their eyes. It was fun."

"What was your mum like?" I asked. "Before the accident?"

"Mum was so much fun. Happy all the time. She used to let us help her in the kitchen. Podding broad beans. Snapping asparagus. She said the only way to learn was to get involved. And she never lost her temper, even one time when I tried to shuck oysters without her permission." Sophia paused, showed me the small half-moon scar on her palm. "She was always so encouraging. Like Robbie? And the ghosts?" I nodded, encouraging her to go on. "Dad used to roll his eyes, but Mum would drive Robbie all over to find ghosts. Even when she was dead tired from the restaurant. She said I would find my thing too. And that it didn't matter what it was, she would support me all the way."

"Still, being the child of a brilliant parent can be tough. It can put pressure on you."

Sophia looked puzzled. "Mum's not like that."

I had missed my mother so much growing up—but I missed her even more when I was an adult. Everything I had achieved was a result of her advice, every second of success I owed to her insistence that I do something special. There were times in my life when I had so much wanted her to be alive—the launch of my app, the weekend I was featured on the cover of the Sunday supplement magazine—and then all the times when I was so glad she wasn't there to see what I had become. I was so worried about making her proud of me. Perhaps Sophia would understand when she was older. "She sounds amazing. I can see why you miss her." I could too.

The quiet of the house was even more eerie now, in comparison to these memories. It was not yet ten o'clock, and already the house was almost completely dark. Sue had been and gone and taken all evidence of the Christmas dinner away with her. The tree, so resplendent at dawn, felt miles away from the tiny dormer room where we were now. By tomorrow morning I anticipated that there would be not one sign of Christmas anywhere in the house. "Did you like your present?" I asked. The wash bag I had bought her was sitting on the desk, alongside a mound of gifts. It was practical for sleepovers, somewhere for her to keep her endless bottles of body spray, and for if she went away to school, but now it just seemed a reminder of her possible departure. Looking at her now, safe in her wallpapered room, I could not imagine her away from the place. Would she need to go, if I stayed?

"It's lovely, thank you." Her manners surprised me, suggesting a violent sulk was not her default setting after all. Someone had attempted to bring her up well. Was it Daphne or Max, or had she learned manners by osmosis, surrounded by people who behaved well in public but concealed so many secrets?

There was a pause. For a moment we both listened to the sounds of the house. It was never silent in this house by the sea. The noise of the ocean was a con-

306 • JANE COCKRAM

stant, but when the wind blew through the bare winter branches, it was hard to tell the two apart. The original honeycomb glass dormer windows in this part of the house were beautiful but loud; someone had folded cardboard into the cracks to alleviate the rattling.

It was now or never. Dreading the idea of disturbing Sophia's sanctuary and wishing I could have caught her alone anywhere but there, I sat down on her bed. I straightened the cover with my hand, fiddled with a tassel, and drew a deep breath. Sophia looked at me expectantly. "Sophia?"

"Yes."

"Why did you lie about the letter?"

"I didn't lie. I didn't send you a letter."

Classic liar's obtuseness. I recognized the signs. "Why did you lie about sending my mother a letter?"

"Why did you lie about receiving it?"

I moved over. Sometimes telling the truth needed comfort and close quarters. "I didn't lie."

Sophia looked at me pointedly.

"I didn't. No one ever asked who I was." Apart from Max, earlier that day, in the corridor. But that was rhetorical. I think.

"I wasn't planning on lying. I was planning on coming here and seeing you, and checking everything was okay. I was planning on helping. Which is what you asked for in your letter," I reminded her.

"So why didn't you say right away who you were?" Sophia said, as she fiddled with a tassel on the end of her quilt.

"It was a bit weird when I got here, to be honest," I replied. Her eyes bulged, but I continued. "I could hardly turn up and ask to speak to you without saying who I was, so when the option of being the nanny presented itself, I thought it was a good temporary solution." I didn't mention my father's warnings. Or my own trepidation on arrival. The sense that something was just not right.

"Temporary," Sophia repeated.

"Yes, well . . ." We both kind of laughed. Slightly, anyway. "So now you know," I said.

"Now I know," Sophia agreed.

"It feels good, being out in the open," I said, truthfully. "And it makes it harder for me to leave now."

"Good." She smiled slightly. "I thought Dad was going to ask you to leave the other night, when I hurt my ankle."

"So did I, to be honest," I said.

"I'm sorry I said you made me go looking for Mum." Finally. The apology I had been waiting for.

Sophia continued slowly. "And I didn't mean to lie about the letter. I was just a bit, well, confused at first. And then you asked me in front of Robbie and Agatha, and I didn't want them to know. I'm glad you're here, though. Especially now that Mum has gone."

I seized the opportunity to learn more. "Has she done it before?" I asked. "Just disappeared?"

Sophia blushed, and I felt bad asking her to betray her mother. I would have defended mine to the ends of the earth.

"A couple of times. Once, she went to a rehab clinic. I didn't know that at the time, though. None of us did. We just thought she'd gone on holiday. I heard Dad and Elizabeth talking about it later. Another time she was gone for a week. Mostly though, it was a couple of days. After the lunch service on a Sunday, she'd have a few drinks, and we wouldn't see her until Monday or Tuesday."

I closed my eyes. No wonder no one seemed too fazed by the latest disappearance. They'd had to deal with it plenty of times over the years.

"This is different, though." The insistence in her voice made me open my eyes. "She'd never have left us at Christmas."

The room was quiet as her words sank in. "I know." It was all I could think to say.

"What's Dad doing in London?" Sophia asked suddenly. My allegiance swung from Max to the vulnerable child in front of me.

"He's gone to see your mother's brother." Max had asked me not to make a fuss about his departure. Even though I wasn't disposed to follow his instructions right now, Sophia's face made me immediately regret my indiscretion. I could see they had been in the children's best interests.

"Uncle Daniel?"

"I don't know. Your father didn't say."

"Does Uncle Daniel know where Mum is?"

"I guess maybe your Dad thinks he might."

Sophia yawned. It was late. I felt like there was no way I could sleep, but that I should leave her so she could. Something had been bothering me, though. "Why did you think my mother could help you?"

Sophia looked sheepish. Now I was here, I realized just what a difficult feat writing that letter would have been. She could hardly have tucked it into the outgoing post in the hotel office. She would have had to get an international stamp, find my mother's address, and after all that, go to the village to post it. It wasn't impossible, but for Sophia, a child who could barely summon the energy to converse most days, it seemed like an insurmountable task.

"It was just something my mum used to say about her sometimes. Mostly when she was drunk."

"What was that?" My heart raced at the prospect of hearing something about my mother. Something new. Something about her and Barnsley. "Mum used to say, 'I never knew Tessa, but she is the only Summer with any sense, getting out when she did.'"

33

The office was empty but bore the feeling of recent occupation. A slight warmth, an unidentifiable human scent. I checked the French doors. Unlocked. Looking out into the dark night, I realized that anyone out there could see me. Trying to look official, and reminding myself that Max had asked me to take care of things in his absence, I bolted the doors and pulled the curtains tight to shut out the dark night. To shut out Mrs. Mins. Who else could it have been?

The wallpaper on the computer screen was a shot of Barnsley. The lawn was covered with a dusting of snow, or frost, it was hard to tell. Either way, the beauty of the place stopped me in my tracks. The ethereal majesty of the pollarded willow and the cloud-cut box hedges hovering above the ground was otherworldly, and yet it was only metres from where I sat. I could hardly believe that anyone could leave here and never return. Despite all evidence to the contrary, I could hardly believe that someone could be miserable here. My mother. Daphne. I clicked on the icon for the search engine, hoping to find some answers.

First, and so I would have an alibi in case anyone came in, I logged in to my email. Messages started to load, hundreds of them. Most were junk, but many were from my father, with the subject lines in capital letters somehow managing to convey his increasing frustration. The sheer number of them threatened to overwhelm me with guilt and shame, so I ignored the earlier ones and opened the last, sent only hours earlier. The subject line was "Tessa." Or more accurately, "TESSA." Reluctantly I fished out my glasses from my coat pocket and began to read.

Miranda.

You're not responding to my emails. I'd like to think there's a good reason, but I suspect there isn't. The best I can hope is that you are reading them, even if you're not responding. Which in itself is quite rude, and I would hope we have brought you up better than that.

Eye roll.

I haven't been entirely honest with you.

The letter you read from Sophia was not the first time someone from Barnsley has been trying to contact you.

A sharp intake of breath that could only have come from me. I had a feeling what was going to come next.

Your aunt Elizabeth has been trying for some time.

Did Elizabeth know who I was? Why hadn't she said anything?

She will try and convince you that your mother carried out a grave injustice against her as a young woman. Elizabeth has never been able to prove this, and over time, her letters have become more hysterical, angry. I worry that she will take this anger out on you.

Please, Miranda, as much as these people are your family, they are not your friends. This sudden interest should be treated with caution. I only hope you can extricate yourself before they discover your true identity.

Dad

That was it. Just "Dad." No love, not even any warm regards. I had pissed him off again.

He had always had my back, even at the worst of times, and now it seemed I had finally tested the limits of our bond. I'd been so wrapped up in the lives of these people I barely knew that I had somehow managed to destroy the one true relationship in my life.

We were so close once. When it was just the two of us, and then still when Fleur and then Ophelia and Juliet came along. I thought he would be proud of me when I started to become successful, but that was when he first began to draw away from me. And then when everything happened, he seemed more upset than he should have been. He started to look at me as if he didn't recognise me. Or worse: as if he did.

I started to type out a reply to him but the words wouldn't fit together. They wouldn't say what I meant without sounding insincere or hysterical. With every word I typed, the ghost of another word would appear.

Fraud, con artist, liar

Liar liar

Frustrated, I closed the email. I would have to come back to it later. I would have to work out a way to properly apologise to my father. Opening another tab, I started to type things directly into Google as they came to me.

Barnsley House. Max Summer. Daphne Summer. The Summer House. Daniel.

All of the searches produced reams of information, endless pages of stories about the famous women who had lived at Barnsley House, the scandalous past that seemed to echo through into the current day. More serious articles were scattered in between, reports of the countless significant structures Sarah Summer had rescued from ruin or reviews of Gertrude's best-selling crime novels, all set, it seemed, in the local area, and some right here at Barnsley House.

I scanned numerous articles from *Country Life*. There was one from before Max's time, about his father, and his modernization of the house. Max's father had found it difficult to find staff after his wife died, it said, as rumours of a ghost persisted and scared many potential domestic helpers away. Eventually he closed down that section of the house and made do with less help.

There was another article outlining an auction that had taken place at Sotheby's of much of the house's paintings and valuables. A famous John Singer Sargent portrait of Max's grandmother had brought in the most money and now hung in a gallery in Chicago. A silver salver as big as a small car had once held almost one hundred bottles of champagne, and the author of the article speculated that it would be melted down and re-purposed.

A more recent article echoed the sentiment of the profile on Daphne. A love story, a derelict house transformed. "A Phoenix Rises from the Ashes," it was titled, and was accompanied by a photo of Daphne and Max I had not seen before, posing on the steps at the entrance, both in Wellington boots, with a young Thomas perched obediently in front of them. Next to that photo was another photo of a bedroom. The caption read "The famous Yellow Room overlooking the lawn sloping down to the Cornish sea where Gertrude Summer wrote her books is now available to hotel guests."

Something at the bottom corner of the screen caught my eye. A camera icon, the CCTV program. My heart started to race. Daphne was missing, and I was sure the answer could lie within the camera footage, despite Max's avoidance of the possibility. Did I dare? My hands started to sweat on the mouse. There was no one around; the children were sleeping. Max was far, far away. I clicked before I could convince myself not to. Immediately a box popped up, requesting a password.

Of course. Max wasn't that stupid. I wondered who had the password. Max, definitely. Mrs. Mins? Elizabeth? I didn't know. There were so many possible passwords. I tried "Barnsley." I tried "Daphne." And then the connection dropped out. It was true, then, about the dodgy internet. I rested my head on the desk to think.

Just for a minute. And then fell asleep.

I dreamt someone was calling my name. A woman. I couldn't see her face, but I recognised the voice. It seemed natural to me, in my half-conscious state, that the voice should be a mixture of my mother's and Daphne's, even though I could recall neither in waking hours. Death and humanity, nature and horror, seemed so closely linked in this house.

The door cracked open, then tiny footsteps. My name again, whispered now, in a child's tentative voice. Not a woman at all. A small boy.

"Robbie, you frightened me," I said carefully. "Can you please take that thing off?" I quickly shut the computer down.

He raised his hand towards the camera on his head. "What, this?"

"Yes. You need to ask people's permission to film them," I said, attempting to frame the situation as a moral dilemma and not a matter of deceitful conduct on my behalf.

"Why? Dad doesn't."

"That's different."

"It's not. Elizabeth said. You're meant to have signs up, at least."

"What else did Elizabeth say?" I asked. What other conversations had Robbie heard? Had I said anything around him?

"She said there must be something on the videos. She was very cross."

I bet she was. "When was this?"

"The day after the school concert."

Of course it was. "What did your dad say?"

"He said he had checked, and there was nothing."

It was too much. I felt like I had only been asleep for two minutes, and now my brain refused to catch up. "It's early, Robbie." Did no one in this house ever sleep?

"It's not that early, really. Just dark."

"I don't believe you."

He showed me his watch, a Christmas present. The numbers were initially fuzzy and shocking to my bleary eyes. I rubbed my eyes—they were less fuzzy but no less shocking. "Robbie!"

He grinned. "Come on, Miranda. It's no fun when it's light. Wouldn't you like to see some real English ghosts?"

I groaned. "I'd just like some sleep."

Robbie looked at me innocently. I sighed and stood

up. This was not turning out to be a nine-to-five job. Perhaps Grant and Farmer would have been a better fit after all. "Can you turn that off?" I asked. The red light was still glowing. I didn't need to be filmed at such an early hour, particularly after the little sleep I'd had the night before.

"Do I have to? I'm searching for ghosts. My new book says there is one in the east wing." Max had given him the book after all. I suspected I would be the one dealing with the fallout from that particular parenting decision. If only I had taken the time to read it first, as I had planned.

"What does your book say?" I asked. Robbie was not the only one with ghosts on his mind. I didn't want to validate his belief in ghosts, but I was starting to be less of a skeptic.

"I'll read it to you." He was wearing a type of utility vest, like a fisherman, with dozens of pockets and mesh inserts. Out of a particularly large pocket on his left side he produced the book Max had bought at the bookshop in town. Even though it was only a day old, it already bore the signs of intensive study; pages were dog-eared, sections highlighted in coloured pen, and sticky notes flagged chapters of interest.

"You've been busy," I commented.

"I don't sleep well."

"Perhaps you would sleep better if you read fewer ghost stories."

Robbie looked at me quizzically and began to read. " 'Barnsley House, on the West Country's rugged coastline, holds a spectacular position looking out across to the famous Minerva Island. Both are owned by the Summer family, and are said to be haunted by previous inhabitants. The ghost at Barnsley House is a relatively recent phenomenon, and unlike most of the other ghosts outlined in this book, did not emerge in the haunting hysteria that captivated early-nineteenth-century society. Instead, the ghost of Barnsley House was first sighted in the 1970s, and despite attempts by poltergeist experts to film it, has never been captured on film. Barnsley House is currently run as a boutique hotel, and guests report hearing shouting in corridors when there is no one present. In one particular room, the Yellow Room in the east wing, there have been numerous instances of the bath running in the night. The first appearance of the ghost was just after the death of Beatrice Summer, the mother of the current owner, Max Summer. Beatrice burnt to death in a house fire during a summer music festival.' "

Robbie stopped reading, his eyes wide and searching mine, waiting for me to make the connection.

"Grandma," he said in awe. "My grandmother is a ghost."

Mine too, I wanted to say. But instead I said, "Don't be ridiculous, ghosts aren't real." How was it possible that I was beginning to feel more fear than a small boy? "Give me that book." I turned it over to see who had written it: Hugo Whittal, a likely-looking type with horn-rimmed glasses and his shirt buttoned up all the way. "Hugo Whittal has no idea what he's talking about. I suspect he goes around old houses looking for people who have died and invents stories to match."

"Hugo Whittal is a very well known ghost hunter." Robbie snatched the book back. "Once Mum took me to see him talking at Exeter University. I'm going upstairs to see Grandma."

"Robbie. Wait. Are you sure you want to go up there alone?"

"I don't have a choice. I expect you're too scared to come with me. Even though ghosts aren't real."

Even though I was slightly scared, I could barely let him proceed alone. Expecting the girls to sleep for a little bit longer yet, I agreed to go with Robbie, on the proviso he switched off the camera for now and showed me where the light switches were. After much muttering and protesting he agreed, making me promise he could switch the camera back on and the lights off if we heard anything suspicious.

Robbie led the way up the wide wooden staircase, which turned at right angles to itself, a stained-glass window at the landing. The walls were bare, and now I knew why: all gone in the sale and never replaced. "This is the east wing," Robbie whispered.

Despite my refusal to believe in Hugo Whittal's ramblings, there was a peculiar sense of occupation about this wing, even from where we were standing. Again. My senses were on high alert. Something didn't feel right. "Is there a light?" I whispered back. For all my bravado, I couldn't talk at a regular volume.

"I'll see."

Robbie edged his way down the hallway, running his hand up and down the paneling as he went, his footsteps silenced by the plush carpet underfoot.

"What's that?" I asked. Music was playing. Classical. Low, but not so low it couldn't be heard through the heavy doors.

Robbie shrugged. He moved quickly through a fire door—obviously installed rather too late for Beatrice—and there it was, on the right at the end of the passage.

The Yellow Room.

The music grew louder as we stopped outside the door. Robbie looked at me, a question on his face. I nodded, and he pressed the small button on the side of his camera. The red light came on. In the glow, I saw his breath make shapes in the air. I let out the breath I was holding, and mine did the same.

Robbie put his hand on the handle. I waited for him to press down, expecting it to resist him and for us to retreat, perhaps with plans to find the key another day, or perhaps forgetting about the mission entirely. Either option seemed preferable to gaining entry and finding out what lay beyond. To my great surprise, the handle dropped and the door released from the frame.

Robbie looked at me and pointed inside. I nodded. We were having whole conversations in sign language. Robbie pushed on ahead, and I didn't stop him. The music was definitely coming from within. He stepped inside and froze, looked back at me in terror. I leaned forward, my feet stuck still, and heard it. Running water.

The door to the bathroom was closed, a small line of light underneath. The curtains had been pulled back to allow for dawn to creep in as it slowly approached. As far as I knew, no one had been in this part of the house since Daphne and I, days earlier. Had she been here the whole time?

Unsure what state she would be in, I grabbed Robbie's hand to pull him from the room. He snatched it back, pointing at the bed. It was unmade, and seemed recently slept in. A Roberts radio on the bedside table was set to a station, the music humming. The air of the room smelled different from the hallway as well, the damp air overtaken in here by a warm perfumed humidity. There was someone in the bathroom, too human to be ghostly.

Robbie grabbed my hand, and we turned to run. In that moment, Hugo Whittal's volume of nonsense slipped out of Robbie's pocket. It fell on the chest at the end of the bed, making a bang as it landed. The running water stopped. There was a pause, and then a voice called out. "Max, is that you?"

34

"It's Mrs. Mins."

Robbie was still white with terror as he whispered those words. A part of him was not convinced. It could yet be a ghost, and he wanted my reassurance.

I tried to hide the disappointment in my voice as I replied. The disappointment that it was not Daphne. "I think so, yes," I said, and the door opened.

"What on earth are you doing up here?" It was Mrs. Mins, and yet on that morning she looked so different from when I had last seen her, I doubted I could have identified her in a lineup. Despite the frigid air, she wore a lace-trimmed dressing gown that she was holding together tightly, which only succeeded in making it more rather than less revealing as it clung to every curve and betrayed her nakedness underneath. With-

326 · JANE COCKRAM

out makeup her face was pale, her features disappearing into nothing, her eyebrows and eyelashes almost completely gone. Her lips pursed in anger.

"Hello, Mrs. Mins. We thought you were a ghost."

"Don't hello me, Robbie. You know you're not meant to be up here," she said sharply, and Robbie looked taken aback. He wasn't used to being spoken to like that, not by her.

She turned to me and brought the brunt of her anger. "You should know better. This area is out of bounds to the children. And to you."

"I'm sorry. Robbie wanted to look for ghosts." The excuse was weak and my judgement was poor, but her reaction seemed out of proportion. It was not the middle of the night, it was almost breakfast time, and although technically we were in the hotel, it was, after all, Robbie's home. He had more right to be there than she did, as far as I could see.

"I'll have to tell Max about this."

It was the first time she had threatened me. "I beg your pardon?"

"I'll tell Max that you went against his orders and brought the children into the guest rooms. Ghosts! It's your job to be responsible, not encourage Robbie's little obsessions." She leaned over, and I saw the smooth skin of her chest, the swell of her ample bosom as she picked up the book. She didn't give it back.

"Max bought him the book, not me."

She ignored me and started to flick through it. Robbie gripped my hand tighter and looked at me pleadingly, clearly wanting to get out of there as soon as possible. "I thought you would have been sleeping in this morning, after your late night," she said, keeping her eyes on the book. I could see she had already found the Barnsley House page, but it was hard to tell if she was actually reading it or holding it open to taunt us.

"What do you mean?"

"You know what I mean. Sneaking about in the office. Using the staff computer. I wonder what Max would think about that? Don't you? Wonder?"

"I wasn't sneaking about. I was emailing my father." I felt like I was a schoolgirl again, though I had never had a teacher so menacing as Mrs. Mins was that morning.

"Why are you here?" she asked, her eyes flashing. Her temper, suspected but unseen, had surfaced.

"Why are *you* here?" I countered. Attack was the best form of defense, and her lies about Italy were fresh in my mind.

Robbie, either by design or by accident, came to my

rescue. The red light on his camera was still flashing. Mrs. Mins turned her attention towards him, her voice almost normal again. "Your father asked me to stay in the house to keep an eye on things while he is gone." She smiled matter-of-factly.

"Max didn't mention it to me."

"I think you'll find there's a lot of things Max hasn't mentioned to you."

She was right. "We should be getting back to the girls now," I started to say.

Mrs. Mins ignored me and began to read aloud from the book. " 'Barnsley House is currently run as a boutique hotel, and guests report hearing shouting in corridors when there is no one present. In one particular room, the Yellow Room in the east wing, there have been numerous instances of the bath running in the night. The first appearance of the ghost was just after the death of Beatrice Summer, the mother of the current owner, Max Summer. Beatrice burnt to death in a house fire during a summer music festival.' " She snorted. "Running water! I imagine you must have been terrified when you heard me running a bath."

"Oh. No . . . not really," I stammered, although I'm sure our ashen faces must have demonstrated otherwise.

"I've heard people say"—she leaned in and gave

Robbie back the book, making sure he was listening— "that old Mrs. Summer was running the bath to try and save herself. It's not true. I was there. I saw it all. She was running that bath to drown—"

"That's enough, Mrs. Mins." I dragged Robbie out of the room, pulling him across the carpet so that his feet barely touched the ground.

"That's my grandmother she was talking about," Robbie whispered in awe as we got to the bottom of the staircase and I had finally let him walk on his own again.

Mine too, I wanted to say. *Mine too.*

35

After that morning, I felt the presence of Mrs. Mins everywhere. Even if I could not always see her, she seemed always able to see me. I would have to fight her at her own game; if knowledge was power, I would arm myself against her. I felt positive she knew something about Daphne's disappearance. I felt positive she had something to hide.

It was more difficult for me to move about covertly: while she lurked in shadows and had keys to every lock, I had three children in tow; where she had access to the computers and knowledge of the family history, I was scraping around for morsels of information and studying old photographs. It was time for me to find an ally.

By chance, that very morning Elizabeth phoned from the island. I hadn't seen her since the concert, even though she must have been at the house at some point to have the conversation Robbie overheard. She was ringing, she said, to see how Christmas had gone, but I suspected she was really phoning about Daphne. I took the timing of her phone call as some sort of sign that she could be trusted. My father's email implied that she had known of my existence all along, and yet she hadn't worked out my identity. Despite my father's warnings, I couldn't see the danger in Elizabeth.

Robbie and I were back in the kitchen, eating our way through piles of hot buttered toast with plum jam, bottles of which I had found in the larder, labeled in Daphne's handwriting. There were piles of jars tucked away: quince preserves and cucumber pickles, pear jams and apple chutneys, and I was trying to encourage the children to eat them. In my mind, I was reinforcing a connection between them and Daphne, but on a more selfish level, I was looking for an excuse to eat them myself. They were absolutely delicious, and I was starting to see Daphne as more than the shell of a woman I had met in the restaurant.

"Hello, dear," Elizabeth said, and continued without giving me a chance to say anything. "Has Max really gone to London?" Nothing stayed quiet around here. I wondered how Elizabeth knew this.

"Yes, he left last night. Did you have a nice day?" The toaster sent four more slices slowly upwards. Its gradual mechanism was distracting, so different from the violent springing of toasters I had known previously. I gestured to Robbie to butter the toast and then watched as he dug the knife into the butter and made deep rifts in the bread with it.

"A nice day? Yes. Of course I did." Even through the poor phone connection, I could sense her puzzlement.

"Christmas."

"Was it? Oh yes, it was yesterday. No wonder Max has gone to London."

"Does he always go to London at Christmas?" Max's sudden and urgent trip to London was yet another mystery that had been overshadowed during the night's and morning's developments. I had also googled the name Daniel, but without a surname or any other detail that had proven rather pointless.

"No. Why would he go to London at Christmas?"

It was too early and I had not had enough sleep to deal with Elizabeth's circuitous style of conversation. "Would you like to speak to the children?" I said, changing tack and hoping she would follow.

She didn't. "Whatever for?"

"To wish them a happy Christmas?"

"Have you seen Daphne yet?" Her phrasing was peculiar. It was as if Daphne were sleeping in, or in the shower. I kept an eye on Robbie and said that I hadn't.

A deep sigh came down the line. "We might have to go back to plan A."

"Plan A?"

"We talked about it on the phone last time."

So much had happened in the intervening days, I could barely remember the last phone call, let alone plan A. It took me a couple of seconds to remember she had phoned to cancel our trip to the island. "The island?"

"Yes. I've changed my mind. I think it would be lovely if you came out here."

"To the island?"

Robbie looked up from his sourdough massacre and nodded furiously, clasping his palms together in a praying motion.

"Yes."

"It will be rather difficult, with just me and the children, especially Agatha."

"Oh no," she said, shrill and interrupting. "Don't

bring the children." I shook my head at Robbie and tried to turn away from him, my head tucked towards the dresser in a futile attempt at a private conversation.

"I have to, Max is away, and—"

"I'll talk to Meryl."

I could feel Robbie's eyes on my back, and felt I should at least try again, on his behalf. "Perhaps she could come with me? That way we might all be able to come?"

"No. Not a great idea. Just you. Tomorrow?"

"Um, okay." I shook my head at Robbie in what I hoped was a sympathetic manner. "If you can sort it out with Mrs. Mins."

Robbie sniffed in disappointment and took his plate of desiccated toast with him into the snug.

"Elizabeth?" I tilted my head back to make sure Robbie was definitely gone. Out of earshot.

"Hmm."

"Was Daphne really afraid of water?"

A pause. Noise from the television floated from the snug. "That's what she claimed."

"And that's why she never took the children out to the island."

"I suppose." Elizabeth was used to steering conversation; her discomfort was palpable.

"Why?"

"Why what?" Her voice was distant, as if she'd moved her face away from the receiver. It seemed certain she was doing something else. The click of the lighter and an inhale confirmed it.

"Why was she afraid of the water?"

"You young people—everything has to have a reason. Some things just are."

I waited.

"There was some nonsense about a catamaran incident in Sydney Harbour. I never quite understood the ins and outs of it. Besides, she didn't like to talk about it."

That made sense, I supposed. Made sense as much as any of Elizabeth's stories did. "Right. Good. Now listen to me. This is the important part. I've been thinking about Daphne a lot these last few days, and I think she would have left me something. A message, something. You're up and down, all over the place. Sticky-beaking in everything, I hear. I wondered, have you found anything?"

In a split second, I decided to trust Elizabeth. I had to trust someone. I quashed the niggly voice inside me, the one asking why Sophia hadn't gone to Elizabeth for help. Sophia was a child, incapable of making adult decisions. The children themselves had said how close Elizabeth and Daphne had been. I put aside my father's warnings. Something had happened to Daphne, I was sure of it, and Elizabeth could help me work it out. "I might have found a key I could try . . . ," I began, unsure of just how much to confess.

"Say no more. Bring whatever you find with you tomorrow. Go down to the jetty at ten, and Leonard will bring you across." She hung up.

36

Boxing Day, a day that always seems to stretch on forever. That day was no different, reminding me of the Boxing Days I had spent as a child when the adults seemed to spend the whole day napping and produced few interesting meals, and I longed for it to pass. Running on less than no sleep, I was raiding the children's Christmas stash and using their supply of sugar to stay awake. Much to Sophia's horror, I had already consumed almost half her tin of Quality Street, and despite my promises to replace it, she watched beadily as the pile of colored cellophane wrappers steadily grew.

If only my thousands of followers could see me now, existing on sugar and starch, my body crying out for some fibrous greens and my left eye constantly twitching from a lack of magnesium. I knew what my body needed, but for the first time in years I was ignoring it, piling on the pounds and ignoring the low-level anxiety accompanying them. It felt great.

The children had loads of things to keep them occupied—a small consolation, as most required either my participation or my guidance. After countless games of Twister with Agatha spinning while the three of us writhed on the mat, I had finally declared it time for a movie. We sat together and watched the Christmas movies repeating on television, some that I had seen and some more traditional ones that, much to the children's disgust, I had not. All the while the notebook called to me from the drawer upstairs. I had cast it aside in frustration, but after Elizabeth's phone call, I was certain there was something important in there. A clue to Daphne's disappearance.

We had just started on *The Sound of Music*—not a Christmas movie but voted for on grounds of family tradition—when Robbie spoke. "Dad used to watch this with us every year, usually in bed. We would spend the whole day in bed on Boxing Day. Mum would sleep, and Dad would pull the curtains shut and pass the chocolates around." I kept my eyes on Captain Von Trapp—no great hardship—to disguise my interest in this latest titbit about Daphne.

"Your mum would sleep all day?" I asked.

"She was usually tired after all the Christmas parties, and cooking for us at Christmas." There was no sadness in his voice, only acceptance.

"And the karaoke on Christmas Night," Sophia added drily.

We had leftovers for supper and kept an eye on the phone. Robbie brought the handset in and placed it on the coffee table, and without directly mentioning it, we all expected it to ring and for the caller to be Max. It didn't. Eventually, yawns overtook conversation, and even Sophia looked sleepy. The last couple of days had taken as much of a toll on the children as they had on me. "Time for bed, guys," I said, looking at my watch conspicuously. "It's late."

"It's not, really, not for holidays," Sophia said, and the other two joined her in a chorus of support.

"It's been a long day. I'm going to bed too." The prospect of what lay ahead energised me despite the onset of a post-sugar slump.

"Just a little bit longer?" Agatha raised her head from the cushion just long enough to mutter the words.

"No." I switched off the television and dragged myself off the sofa. The children reluctantly followed.

The wind started to bang at the window frames. It seemed to have a particular sense of timing; every night once the children were in their beds it would build from a rustle to a roar, sending the overhanging branches crashing into each other and scratching at the windows.

Mrs. Mins was on my mind that night. Every rush of wind in the trees disguised her approach; every stick cracking underfoot was her creeping between the gnarled trees. Even the owls and vixens seemed to be howling her name. She was everywhere: lurking in the kitchen garden at dawn; concealed outside the office window in the darkness; sleeping and bathing in the east wing. For someone whose main remit was to run the hotel, she seemed to be running much more. I felt sure she had something to do with Daphne's disappearance.

Robbie, in particular, was upset that night. Our early-morning adventure had affected him in ways he had adeptly concealed. These children were experts in camouflage, in hiding both themselves and their emotions. Even as I grew closer to them, I could sense them retreating.

It took some time to settle Robbie, not in the way you might settle a baby, through tenderness and human touch, but through distraction and common sense. I knew better than to openly mention the ghost walk that morning but instead drew his attention to other books in his Christmas pile; there was an adventure story and a graphic novel, and I hoped reading them would give his active mind some relief. Could a boy that young make the connection between the ghost story and what Mrs. Mins was saying—that his own grandmother had tried to drown his father? My anger at Mrs. Mins swirled, growing every moment I thought about it.

Finally they were all asleep; even Sophia had drifted off, *I Capture the Castle* open on the pillow next to her. I carefully placed the bookmark on her page and made sure to close all their doors firmly. I whistled softly to Thomas, and when he came, I moved his bed from Max's room onto the landing, right at the top of the stairs, so that anyone trying to get through would have the loyal Thomas to deal with.

Then I retrieved the notebook from its hiding place and settled into the comfortable chair in my room, set beside an unused fireplace so that it had a clear view of the door, which I'd left open so that I could hear the constant reassuring sound of Thomas snoring. Within seconds, despite the weather outside, I was back in the throes of those sultry summer days.

Years later Meryl, with no regard for the fact that Beatrice was Max's mother, described what she saw to him that afternoon in great detail. He was upset when he told me, and my hatred of Meryl began at that moment. I could see how she had manipulated my Max his whole life, and somehow gained enormous power over not only his emotions but also his psychological state.

Meryl was stuck in some sort of limbo between the two generations, and not being the obvious age match for either of them, eventually made a play for both. When it failed with Maximilian, she bided her time for a number of years and then moved on to my Max. In the absence of his mother, he was vulnerable, and she became everything to him.

Everything.

I don't think this will come as a shock to you.

It did to me.

Of course I had suspected this. I had watched as Max disappeared to the Mins cottage on "hotel business" night after night, leaving his fragile children in my care. I had felt the territorial gaze of Mrs. Mins upon me as I moved through the estate. But to think that the relationship had started when Max was barely an adult and under the care of Mrs. Mins was disturbing.

I turned back a few pages in the notebook. If Mrs. Mins was fourteen and Max was two when she came to Barnsley, then by the time Max was eighteen—and I really hoped he was eighteen—Mrs. Mins would have been thirty. I assumed the age difference was similar between Mrs. Mins and my grandfather. After our encounter with Mrs. Mins in the east wing when she had casually mentioned Robbie's grandmother's death in front of him, I suspected she had no scruples. Now I was sure.

There must have been some knock-on effect to my

mother and Elizabeth as well. Yet again, I felt sorry for my mother and the childhood she'd missed out on.

So that afternoon, the final afternoon of the festival, Meryl was bathing. She had told Max's father, Maximilian, of her plan and had anticipated him coming down to watch her. To my mind, this was a setup by Meryl—she knew what was going on, and she drew your father down to the cove. She wanted him to see what Beatrice was up to. My Max never agreed with me on this. Either he doesn't understand how manipulative teenage girls can be, or he underestimates Meryl.

Suddenly the door to the boathouse flung open. Beatrice and Peregrine emerged. Meryl did an elegant duck dive under the water and swam under cover so that she was partially concealed by the jetty. Meryl had never seen Beatrice looking so unkempt. Her hair, normally pinned up in a loose chignon at her neck, was messy, and she was pulling on a silk kimono with one hand, the bottle of champagne in the other making it difficult.

They were fighting, and Meryl listened carefully, wishing that the waves would stop pushing up against the jetty so loudly. She struggled to hear everything, but the gist of it was that Peregrine was going back to London, and Beatrice didn't want him to.

It was a summer fling for Peregrine, but for Beatrice it had been more. She saw him as her ticket back to London. He knew the right people, had a lovely little house in Chelsea, and most importantly, at his age, he didn't want any more children. Beatrice lived in terror of having another child.

Meryl watched as Beatrice tried everything in her power to make him stay. By this point, they were right above her and she could hear through the gaps in the boards. Their feet moved back and forwards. Peregrine was trying to climb aboard his boat, and Beatrice had hold of his arm.

"I don't love Maximilian. You know that." Her voice was pleading, and Peregrine's voice when he answered was calm and indifferent. Even the teenage Meryl could see that it was a losing battle and Beatrice was going about it the wrong way. Just let him go! she thought, even though every part of her was hoping Peregrine would give in and let Beatrice climb aboard with him, leaving Maximilian all for her. She hoped he was still up on the hill, watching this.

"You're married. You're gorgeous—" There was a pause as he kissed her, and the sunlight coming through the gaps diminished as they came together in an embrace. "But we've had our time. I really can't take advantage of Maximilian's hospitality any longer."

"I'm not married!" Beatrice shouted. "Not anymore!"

Meryl felt sure Maximilian would have heard. There was silence, and then something small whizzed past Meryl's head, landing in the water with a delicate splash. Instinctively she reached out and caught the object, so tiny it seemed a miracle her fingers had wrapped around it at all. The ring. Meryl had admired it on Beatrice, the sapphire so large in comparison to her tiny fingers, and she wedged it quickly on her own pudgy ring finger, forcing it down, worried that an ill-timed wave would wash it away at the moment when it had finally become hers. For it was hers now, she could see that immediately. Maximilian could never take Beatrice back after what he had seen that afternoon, and he would finally be hers. That she had rescued the precious family sapphire would be icing on the cake.

At that moment, Maximilian, horrified to see his family heirloom disappearing into the waters, and unable to take another second of his wife humiliating herself—and by extension, him—let out an almighty shout. He came charging through the shrubbery, emerging onto the rocks like a crazed warrior.

"Beatrice!" he called, in a stern voice. "Don't you dare get on that boat."

Beatrice protested, of course, but the combined force of Maximilian and Peregrine was too much for her. They were in cahoots, and she was powerless to take either of them on. Peregrine took advantage of the confusion to cast away from the jetty, farewelling Maximilian with sympathy in his voice, as if they had just had a rather competitive game of tennis, and one of them had to be the loser.

Beatrice ran off in the direction of the house, where the festival was in full swing, refusing to look at Max, her kimono flapping open behind, her sobs audible even after she had disappeared up the path. Meryl saw her chance and emerged from the water, aware that she was fully naked but not caring, not now that she would be the mistress of Barnsley. She climbed up the ladder, and Maximilian, who had been watching Peregrine's boat recede into the distance, was shocked to see her. He had forgotten she was even there.

I have taken the liberty of inventing most of the conversations reported in this notebook, going by what Meryl told Max and what my Max has told me, but this next conversation is quoted exactly. My Max said Meryl was quite adamant about it, as she has never forgotten the words spoken to her on the pier that day. Perhaps if she had, things might have turned out differently, but Max's words that afternoon cut her deeply, searing into her soul and changing her forever. (I'm assuming she wasn't born a psychopath!) "Maximilian," she said, "I'm sorry."

He didn't reply. Instead he shook his head slightly, as if trying to deter a pesky fly. His face was red, his eyes wild, and he turned his body away in disgust at Meryl's nudity.

Meryl came up behind him, and, careful not to reveal the ring on her finger, not yet, she wrapped her arms around him, pressing her body against his, feeling the heat of him through his shirt and hoping he could feel the coolness of her body in the same way. There had been moments during that summer when she had snuck into his dressing room, smelled the shirts he had discarded on a chair, spritzed his aftershave on her own wrists, but nothing compared to this; the familiar fragrance heightened by sweat, by warmth, by a living, breathing human. She inhaled deeply, buried her face in his back, waited for him to relax into the embrace.

"What are you doing, you silly

child?" The rejection was abrupt, and she almost fell on the splintered boards.

"Don't worry about her now," she said. "She's gone. We can be together."

Maximilian turned around, his eyes cold. Meryl felt them travel up and down her body, coolly assessing what they saw, lingering on her full breasts, his lip lifting in disgust.

"Put some clothes on," he sneered.

Meryl panicked. The power she had held over him was shriveling away, and she became the same woman Beatrice was, in the exact same place, only moments before. "I love you, Maximilian," she cried. And she did, she really loved him.

My Max denies it, but a woman knows. The love you feel for someone as a teenager is no less powerful than what you feel as an adult; in fact, in most cases it is stronger. I think her love for Maximilian was at the root of everything that came later. You know what I'm talking about.

"I don't love you. You're making a fool of yourself." He turned to walk off, the shape of her body imprinted damply on his back, a reminder of how close they had seemed only moments before.

"But Beatrice—" Meryl was crying now, wondering how this had all gone so wrong.

Maximilian turned around

sharply, looking about him to see if there was anyone watching. "Beatrice what?" he asked coolly. "Beatrice is an adult. Which means she'll be back at the house getting ready for the final dinner tonight. She'll come down and entertain our guests, and she will sit at the dinner table as if nothing has happened. We will have wine, and when the meal is over, she'll wink at me in recognition of another evening having gone well, and later I'll bring her down here myself, if she likes it so much. If you have any sense, you'll make yourself scarce."

Poor Meryl was never the same after that day.

37

"Mum! Mumma!"
    The shout cut through the still night air,
and I panicked for a moment, the words so foreign
and unheard in these parts that heat spread through
my body, my heart quickening. A ghost? was my first
thought, partly brought on by what I was reading, and
partly by Robbie's ghost hunt the day before. And then
the child called out again, and this time the voice was
recognizable. Robbie.

I pushed the notebook down the edge of the armchair, loath to leave it for even a minute, knowing that
every moment I spent away from it was a chance for
Mrs. Mins—or Meryl, as she was known in the notebook—to make her move. Having second thoughts, I
went back and concealed it with another cushion, even

though I doubted all the cushions in the world would stop Mrs. Mins. There was nothing in the notebook to implicate her or Max. Of course she would lie about her past at Barnsley House if the early days had been so humiliating for her. But I couldn't quite put my finger on why Daphne would feel so strongly about this story from the past.

Robbie was sitting up in his bed, feverish.

"Mum?" he called as I came through the door, the sound of the word on his lips making my heart ache for him.

"No, it's just me, Robbie," I said, and switched on the desk lamp, the room coming into life as I did. The covers had come off again, and his pyjamas were soaked through with sweat. "Miranda."

"I don't feel very well," he said, tears coming into his eyes. "I want my mum."

He looked so distraught at that moment, I would have done anything to conjure up Daphne for him. He needed his mother. Having just spent the last hour with her voice inside my head, I could sympathize, I wanted her back as well.

There was nothing I could say, so I went to his wardrobe and selected a new set of pyjamas for him, a short cotton pair to replace the thick winter ones he was wearing. "Here," I said, "I'll get a wet washer.

You change into these." He seemed so wretched and vulnerable, I wanted to stay and help him, but I knew he would be embarrassed. When I came back with the wet washer and some fresh sheets, it was starting to rain, the drops on the window quickly escalating from isolated splats to furious streams. "Looks like tomorrow will be a good day to stay in bed," I said, making up the bed as efficiently as I could and removing the quilt. As I said it, I remembered Elizabeth's request that I come out to the island. I couldn't see myself in a boat in this sort of weather, but I doubted she would let me postpone.

"My throat hurts," Robbie said as he lay back down. "Could I have some paracetamol?" His voice was croaky with the effort of talking.

"I'll get you some now." I paused, reluctant to ask, but having no idea where I might find it.

There wasn't a medicine cabinet in my small bathroom, and I hadn't seen it in the children's bathroom either. For all Max and Daphne's faults as parents, it seemed they at least paid heed to the pharmaceutical companies' advice to keep medicines out of reach of children. As if Robbie sensed my hesitation, he croaked, "In Mum's bathroom. Not the pills—I can't take them. The ones you put in water, please."

Max and Daphne's bathroom opened off their bedroom at the end of the hall. Its door was always tightly shut; whatever lay beyond was mysterious and impenetrable to me. Just to go beyond the door seemed like a major transgression, but I really had no choice. Instead of being worried, I felt my anger at Max for leaving his children at Christmas rise in a fresh wave.

The storm was building up momentum around the house, and through the hallway window I saw a light flashing on a faraway point, warning off ships and other vessels. There was peril at sea tonight. I hoped Daphne was somewhere warm. And dry.

I crept down the corridor and past Thomas, who, sensing my intent, rose from his cushion and followed me, ever loyal, to his master's room. It was cold beyond Max's door. He must have switched off the radiator, trying to emulate the austere conditions of his childhood. The curtains were open. Max and Daphne's room was the only place in the private quarters from which you could see the sea. The view opened up in the opposite direction to the hotel grounds, over the private driveway and beyond that to the open sea. The bed was positioned to take in that aspect, and I imagined Max and Daphne lying in each other's arms while they looked out at the waves thrashing against the distant rocks.

Aware that Robbie was waiting, and feeling the

questioning presence of Thomas, I moved into the small bathroom. The smell of Max was everywhere about me as I opened the door. I flicked the lights on and saw that, unlike the rest of the house, the bathroom was completely modern, tiled from ceiling to floor in dark marble and fitted with sleek black tapware. I couldn't imagine Daphne, from what little I knew of her, in a bathroom like this.

The little basket of pills and potions was easy to find: it was in the cabinet under the sink, not out of reach of the children after all, and it was overflowing with bottles and foil-wrapped tablets. Searching through for the paracetamol, I found bottles with Daphne's name on them, and my heart sank. I wished I knew more about prescription drugs.

But Daphne wasn't my main concern at that moment. Or she was, but in a different way. I was concerned about what her absence meant for Robbie. The poor boy was lying feverish and distraught, and he just wanted her. At that moment, no one else would do. Not me. Not Mrs. Mins. I knew how he felt. But thanks to Fleur, I knew that a little bit of care and attention could go a long way to making him miss his mother less.

Pushing Daphne's pills aside, I reached for the paracetamol box. It was curiously heavy when I picked it up, and the bottom dropped out, overburdened by the weight it had been asked to carry. Sheets of pills slipped out and then a small object hit the bathroom floor with a soft thump. Thomas let out an anxious yelp. "Shhh, boy, it's okay," I murmured, trying not to let him sense my unease. It was a small ring box, covered in burgundy felt, worn in some places, the hinges rusted. Knowing that I should not open it, that it was none of my business, I eased it open slowly, and gasped. Inside was a ring. The ring. Even though I knew nothing about jewels, I recognised it from the description in the notebook. Meryl must have returned it to the family.

Unable to resist, I took the ring out of the box and slid it easily onto my finger. The oval blue jewel in the center—the sapphire—was flanked by two triangular diamonds, and even in the muted light of the bathroom, the entire thing sparkled in a magical way. It was beautiful, and I took it off reluctantly, wondering if there would be a time in the future when I might own such a ring. If there was, I would never take it off. I wondered why Daphne had.

Robbie groaned in his bed. Remembering my mission, I returned the ring to its box and grabbed the paracetamol from the floor. At the last moment, I took the ring box and put it in my pocket, some sudden instinct telling me it was the right thing to do. Despite my rational mind telling me it was not, I went with my instinct.

Mrs. Mins was waiting outside the door. I gasped when I saw her, and a small smile played on her lips. I thought of the door I had carefully bolted downstairs, earlier. "I saw the lights on," she said. "Is everything all right?" She had me trapped between the door to Max's room and the hallway, the ring box in my pocket causing an obvious protrusion in my jeans. Jeans I should have changed out of long ago; even the fact that I was fully dressed was suspicious. If she looked at me too closely, she would see the ring box for sure, and she *was* looking at me closely, scanning the room behind me and then my face for evidence of misdeeds.

"R-robbie is ill—I had to get him some paracetamol," I said, hating the stammer in my voice, wishing I could calm my nerves.

"It will be his tonsillitis again, poor love. It's always playing up in the winter." Her words were kind, but the delivery was cold. Her hair, wet from the rain, was plastered against her cheeks, giving her a slightly manic look, and her cheeks were flushed from either the change in temperature or the excitement of finding me trespassing.

"How did you get in?" I was trying to take control, but anyone could have heard the fear in my voice. "I locked the doors. With Max away, I thought—"

"I came in through the hotel, dear." She jingled the keys at the end of the lanyard around her neck. "Max pays me to keep an eye on things."

Mrs. Mins was outfoxing me. She was running on the same amount of sleep as me, and she was older, yet she was agile where I was slow, ruthless where I was cautious. I could see that unless I changed gears, she would end up with exactly what she wanted. I just hadn't worked out what that was yet.

The notebook was poorly concealed between the cushions of the armchair and easy for her to spot. Safely hidden away by Daphne, discovered after only a couple of days in my possession. The weight of disappointment crashed through my terror; I had let Daphne down, after all she had endured.

I held up the paracetamol, my hand shaking. "I really should—"

"I'll take care of this," she replied firmly. "You must be tired after all this creeping around. First the office computer, then the east wing. Your light on at all hours. I wonder when you will learn it's best to leave sleeping dogs lie."

Mrs. Mins guided me back into my room and told

me to go to bed and rest. That things would be better in the morning. She waited as I undressed in the bathroom and was still there when I reemerged.

Letting her think I was meekly obliging, I climbed into bed and mimed a yawn. She pulled the quilt right up to my neck, tucking me in tight, her body low and heavy across me as she did, her tongue making an odd clicking sound. Her hand rested on my shoulder, so close I could smell her breath and the noxious scent of her stale perfume. I *was* bone tired, and despite the notebook calling to me from the armchair, I could feel my body relax into the mattress, my eyes heavy.

"I'll sit with Robbie. Don't you worry. I'll be right next door," she whispered. From anyone else, those words would have been a comfort.

38

I woke early and jumped out of bed. Sleep was not my friend at Barnsley House. It came when I least wanted it and eluded me in times of exhaustion. On that morning, though, I was grateful for my inability to sleep in; I needed to get back to the notebook.

The more I read, the more I felt sorry for Mrs. Mins. I felt like I could relate to her, in much the same way I had felt drawn to Daphne. She, like me, had been seduced by the romance of Barnsley House; she, like me, had felt drawn to the house and the people in it, despite their differences in age and background. I could see shades of his father in Max's behaviour towards me: charismatic and engaged one moment, aloof and dismissive the next. I wondered if Daphne had felt the same. There were still some pages to go, pages filled with the familiar scrawl before the words once again turned to lists and recipes. Time was against me, I felt as if the children would stir soon, and I wanted to finish before then.

Too late.

There was a light tap on the door, followed immediately by a twist of the doorknob before I even had a chance to reply. Mrs. Mins. Who else?

After admonishing me for not yet being dressed and reminding me of my duties, Mrs. Mins told me that Robbie had woken in a much worse state. His fever had grown, and the thermometer reading was high enough for concern. I knew the basics of fever management, and I interrupted, telling her I was able to manage the situation on my own.

"You look after the girls," Mrs. Mins said, her voice softly menacing, "and I'll take care of things up here."

I had no choice. Agatha and Sophia needed breakfast, and even though I could trust Sophia to make some toast and Marmite, I still felt uneasy about asking her to carry Agatha on the stairs. I looked in on Robbie and promised him I would be right back.

With Mrs. Mins safely ensconced upstairs playing nursemaid, I took the opportunity to ring Elizabeth. Every part of me wanted to get rid of the notebook; the details of what I had read the night before and in the early hours of the morning were swirling around in my head, and the dark images would not leave me. Fire and betrayal, hatred and revenge. I felt like I had stumbled into a horrible new world, a gruesome and tainted arena in which I had no business. The halcyon lawns of Barnsley no longer seemed so magical. The idea of handing the notebook over to Elizabeth and forgetting all of it was beginning to seem tempting.

Elizabeth answered straightaway. As soon as I spoke, she said, "I thought it would be you."

Every conversation I had had since arriving at Barnsley had been overheard, either with or without my knowledge, and this one was no different. I tried to communicate as obliquely as possible, aware of the two girls watching me carefully as they munched their toast.

"I can't bring the . . . thing," I started, turning towards the wall, praying Elizabeth wouldn't ask me to repeat myself.

"You've found something? A notebook?" she asked. Sharply.

"Yes. But I can't come to the island today. Robbie's sick. And the weather . . ." I trailed off, waiting for the agreement that I felt certain would be forthcoming.

"The weather?" Elizabeth laughed, shrill in her disbelief. "Oh, dear, this is only just getting started. Wait until February before you start using the weather as an excuse."

"Well, Robbie—" A hand grasped me on the shoulder, and I jumped. I turned around, expecting to see one of the girls, and gasped. It was Mrs. Mins, and she was gesturing madly. "Hang on," I said into the phone. "Mrs. Mins wants to say something."

I could hear Elizabeth muttering as I covered the receiver. My heart was racing, and I tried to replay my end of the conversation quickly in my mind. Had I said anything too revealing? Something about the look in Mrs. Mins's eyes told me I had.

"I need you to go and collect some medicine for Robbie from the village," she said.

"What's she saying?" Elizabeth was squawking, but I ignored her.

"The weather . . . ," I started to say. "It's pretty bad." Pretty bad was an understatement. I wanted to shout at these people and tell them to look out the window at the teeming rain, the wind blowing the trees almost horizontal to the ground. There were some in the far reaches of the garden that were permanently in that shape, and I could see now how they had become that way.

"Dear girl, Leonard will take you to the island if you need to go," Mrs. Mins said in the background, making a show of brushing toast crumbs from the counter with her veiny hands. "Just not today."

"Are you coming?" Elizabeth's voice came down the line, entitled and insistent.

It was hard to ignore Elizabeth, and I felt the pressure from both of them, for different reasons. I knew why Elizabeth wanted me out there. The discovery of the notebook had marked a turnaround in her attitude towards me; for the first time I had something she wanted, and she barely disguised her desperation. I too desperately wanted to see what Elizabeth could decipher from the notebook. The clock was ticking for Daphne with every day that passed.

But my loyalties lay with the children. After all, I was here as their guardian. More than that, I was family. Sophia and I were bonding. Robbie was sick, and Agatha needed my assistance. It actually felt good to be needed. As much as I wanted to get back to the notebook, it would have to wait. "I'll have to come tomorrow. If the weather improves."

"You'll be fine. There's a little shelter on Leonard's boat, and you've got that spiffy wear Max gave you for Christmas," Elizabeth said, resigned to the new plan. I had given up on wondering how people at Barnsley knew things about me seemingly before even I did.

"Tomorrow, then," I told Elizabeth, who was quiet for a moment before she responded.

"Only Meryl would be able to rally the pharmacist at this time of year," she said in a mischievous tone, laughing.

"Hmmm . . . ," I replied, hyperaware of Meryl's proximity. "Mrs. Mins is going to get Mr. Mins to bring me out."

"You lucky thing. I'd go out in a storm with Leonard any day. Can you bring some eggs with you?"

And once again, she hung up without saying goodbye. It was only later I realized I had never actually told her that what I had found in the drawer was a notebook. She had somehow worked that out for herself.

39

My second walk into the village was remarkably different from the first. Only days had passed, and yet the path that had seemed so magical and lush on that first walk now seemed ominous, overgrown. Despite the canopy of trees above, the rain was breaking through, landing on me in heavy droplets. In a rush, I had decided to pull on the wellies Max had given me, but only metres down the track they felt cumbersome, rubbing at my ankles and making each step arduous. It was going to be a long, slow walk.

I was cursing my decision, wondering whether I should turn back, when Mr. Mins appeared at the top of the path to the cove. Just like his sister, he had the lurking thing down pat. Even in bad weather it seemed there was no escaping the Mins family. Did Max pay them extra for their unnatural vigilance, or was it something they took on of their own accord?

"You again?" I tried to gain the advantage by speaking first.

"Lovely weather for a walk," he replied, standing aside to let me pass.

"It wasn't my idea." I gave him as wide a berth as possible, which necessitated a near impalement on a fallen branch.

"Oh?"

I wasn't stopping to chat. Not today. "It was your sister's suggestion."

He flinched. "I'm sure she has good reason to be sending you out in this." There was sadness in his eyes, deep under the brim of his hat.

"Robbie's sick."

"Not again." He sighed. "Poor little man."

I nodded. The empathy in his voice made my eyes water, as if I was about to start crying. Not trusting myself to say any more, I nodded and continued in the direction of town. Barnsley had brought all my emotions to a knife edge—I seemed to oscillate wildly between anxiety and exhilaration, fear and nostalgia.

Getting away from the place—from the people who

374 • JANE COCKRAM

lived there—for a little bit would be good for me, but even without looking around, I knew that Mr. Mins hadn't moved. I could still sense his presence.

"Miranda." It wasn't a question. He spoke my name in a rush, as if his mouth had opened without his brain's consent.

I stopped. Waited. But he said nothing. I took a deep breath and walked on.

By the time I came down past the little chapel of St. John's—where Sarah Summer had started her distinguished career—and through the graveyard into town, the threat of tears had passed. Physical exertion had worked its magic; a slight elevation of my heart rate had brought the sweet relief of endorphins. It was nothing like the rush I used to get from a morning run and a dynamic Pilates session, but my body still welcomed it like an old and trusted friend. Exercise. I needed it to keep me sane. No wonder I was going so crazy.

The streets in Minton were quiet, hardly surprising so soon after Christmas. Most people were still celebrating with family, eating turkey sandwiches and counting down the days until they had to return to work. I was half expecting the pharmacy to be closed as well, but Mrs. Mins had taken care of that. A short man with a ruddy face and hastily combed hair stood at the front door with a small paper bag. "You must be Miranda," the pharmacist said. He waited for me to nod before he handed over the parcel, as if there might be an untold number of young women wandering the streets with the view of obtaining illicit pharmaceuticals. "Simon Pale."

"Thank you. It's very kind of you to come in on a day like this."

We both looked over the small cobbled road towards the harbor; Christmas bunting swayed madly in the wind, and strong waves crashed against the stone wall. It was the most picturesquely located pharmacy I had ever seen. "It must be very beautiful here in summer," I said, parroting what everyone kept telling me, as Simon seemed to be keen for conversation and in no hurry. Perhaps he was escaping relatives at home or felt uncomfortable about handing the medicine to a stranger. Either way, he showed no signs of moving on, despite the sea spray being carried towards us by the wind, leaving wet blotches on the paper bag in my hand.

"Oh, it is," he replied eagerly, as if it was the first time he had heard such an idea. "How long are you planning to stay?"

"I'm not sure."

He scratched his hair, leaving it askew. Perhaps it hadn't been hastily combed at all. Perhaps that was just how it looked.

"It will be good for Daphne. To have some help." He picked up a solitary plastic shopping bag that had come sailing past, flattened it out, and tied it in a knot.

"So I gather."

"I told Meryl I'd drive it out, you know. This is no weather to be out walking."

At the edge of my vision I saw movement, a vehicle. I concentrated on it, read the number plate.

HV 323 THF

My father and I used to play a game on long trips with number plates. The aim was to come up with a nonsense sentence, using the letters—the sillier, the better. The prize was one of my father's rare and intoxicating belly laughs.

THIRSTY HUNTING FOX

TIRED HUNGRY FRIEND

THAT'S HER FANTA

Sometimes I didn't even realize I was playing; it was like second nature. My brain just took over. Like now. I tried to focus, to comprehend what the windswept pharmacist was telling me.

THE HURTFUL FEMALE

I shook my head. "What did you say?"

"I said I would bring it out to Barnsley. It's no trouble, practically on my way home." He laughed to diffuse the look of confusion on my face.

"What did Mrs. Mins say?"

"She said . . ." He looked uncomfortable. The penny had dropped.

I nodded ever so slowly, encouraging him to continue.

"She said you had nothing better to do."

"Oh." My mind flashed back to the kitchen, the phone call with Elizabeth. Mrs. Mins had definitely heard. She knew I had plans to go to the island. Why did she want to stop me so badly?

"Oh, there's Jean Laidlaw."

I snapped my head around, thoughts of Mrs. Mins vanishing. Jean Laidlaw!

There was relief in his voice, a thrill at the change in conversation. "Hello, Jean! Merry Christmas! Did you have a lovely one?"

"Oh yes, terrific! Won't eat for days." They continued their conversation at a great distance, arms gesticulating, the noise of the wind and waves no match for their cheerful banter. Then it was over, as quickly as it had begun. The pharmacist gave me a cursory wave before ducking inside his shop and snibbing the door behind him, pleased to have dodged a tricky conversation.

It seemed like a good idea to go and talk to Jean Laidlaw, even though I knew I should be rushing home with Robbie's medicine. As I headed across the uneven surface towards the historical society, the number plate on the van beckoned to me once more.

HV 323 THF

TEMPTING HER FATE

40

"Hello, Jean!" I said, trying to emulate Simon's chummy friendliness. Jean looked at me blankly. I could hardly blame her. Then recognition sparked.

"You're Lisa. From the church. They told me you were coming down to help." She gestured towards the van. Up close, I could see it was filled with plastic chairs, the kind you might hire for a party. "Where's Tony? I thought there were going to be two of you?"

She wrenched open the door of the van. Despite her age—she must have been close to seventy—she was agile. Her hair was still dark and cut in a pageboy. Not one hair moved as she bounced up the steps. I hesitated. Could I pretend to be Lisa from the church? My heart started to race in anticipation of an unexpected subterfuge. But what if Tony turned up? What if Lisa turned up?

"I'm Miranda," I said finally, feeling the adrenaline retreat sadly. "I'm working up at Barnsley House."

"Ha!" Jean Laidlaw turned and looked at me closely. "I bet you wish you were Lisa from the church then! That place . . ." She shook her head. "Well, there's no sign of Lisa and Tony, so you'll have to do. I expect they got held up by a fallen tree or Christmas."

"I wanted to ask you a few questions, actually." I slipped the medicine into my coat pocket. Robbie could wait a moment longer. Daphne could wait as well. I wanted to know about my mother.

"I bet you do." Jean's small frame disappeared farther into the van, and then a towering pile of chairs was pushed towards me by an invisible force. "Talk and work, dear, talk and work."

"What's all this for?" I asked as I pulled the chairs towards me, the top few threatening to topple the whole pile. "Where do I put them?"

Jean gestured towards the open door of the historical society. "Our New Year's Eve do. I'm not surprised you don't know about it. None of the Summers have been for years."

"A party?"

"Well, it's a historical society, so we use the word

'party' loosely, Miranda." She smiled out the door. "We do a reenactment of local history. Simon over there, from the pharmacy, is very active, always happy to take on a big role. Smugglers. Pirates. Something in town if the weather is really bad. Like today. And then we all come back for wine and crackers."

Jean picked up on my lack of interest and stopped talking for a moment as she climbed down from the van, slamming the door behind her. "So what do you want to know?" She gestured towards the open door, and we went inside. It was barely warmer inside than out.

"A little bit of the history of the house, I guess. And the family." And then, to show I was serious: "I've read *The House of Brides.*"

Jean snorted. "That's unusual." Busying herself in the tiny kitchenette, she plugged in a small kettle. "Tea?"

"Yes, please. What's unusual?" Jean picked two mugs out of the sink, tipped out the murky water within them, and put a tea bag in each. The mugs didn't look as if they had been washed properly. Ever.

"A girl like you, come down to see me. How long have you been there?"

"A week. Or so." Jean looked at me suspiciously, and I cursed my newfound truthfulness.

"And you've read that book already?"

This time I was ready. "There's not much to do up there, of an evening. Max gave it to me for Christmas." I thought of my dog-eared copy, hidden away again in my rucksack.

"Max? Sounds like you're very friendly with Mr. Summer already."

The kettle boiled, more of an eruption than a whistle. Steam billowed out, and the front of the cabinets immediately became damp. Jean poured the water, jangled the bags hurriedly, and splashed in some milk from a crusty-looking carton.

"Do you know much about the author?" I asked. "The other sister? Do you know what really happened? No one talks about it at Barnsley."

"I'm not surprised. It was a big mess." We went into a small room on the other side of the kitchenette. It was lined floor to ceiling with books, the only gap between the shelves a murky window looking out over the harbour, which hadn't been cleaned for some time. The only seating was two plastic chairs, the kind you might take camping or to a barbecue. Jean Laidlaw sat down and took a folder from the shelf behind her. It looked the same as all the others on the shelf to me, but she paid scarce attention to the others, as if she knew exactly the one she needed. "Those poor girls," she said, flicking through what looked to be aged and yellowing newspaper articles.

"Sophia and Agatha?" I asked.

"Therese and Elizabeth."

The mug wobbled ever so slightly in my hand. I took a sip to stop the movement, and the tea was as bad as I had anticipated, the milk slightly sour. "Did you—do you—know Therese and Elizabeth?"

"I was the headmistress at Balcombe House." Jean must have sensed my confusion. "It was a small prep school on the other side of the moor. Long gone now. All those little schools are. The house was sold and made into apartments for baby boomers." She kept flicking through the articles.

"And were they at the school?"

"Were they? Yes. Of course, their father sent them off to far smarter establishments when they got older, but in the early days they were mine. 'Give me a child until he is seven and I'll show you the man,' Aristotle said. He was right, and not just about boys. I could have told you what was going to happen with those girls on the first day I ever took them in. I can't find it."

Jean slammed the book shut and stood up, her mug empty. The break was over. "I hope this Tony and Lisa turn up soon. We've got a lot to get through."

"What were you saying? About Elizabeth?"

"Elizabeth? I thought you wanted to know about Therese?"

"Oh, I'm interested in them all, really."

"That book. People say it did great things for the area. Created an interest. There was talk of making a film here for a while. You can imagine what Simon over here was like! He thought it was going to be his big break! It all fizzled out, thank god. I don't care what people say, that book has done nothing but cause trouble from the very first day it was published. Before that, even."

"What do you mean?"

Jean sighed. She looked down in front of her, and seemed to draw strength from whatever it was she saw. "Those girls. Therese and Elizabeth. They couldn't have been more different. Therese, oh, she was sharp. Sharp as a tack, we used to say in those days. And the charm on her. She could get away with murder, just by flashing that smile of hers."

That fit with what I remembered of my mother, but it was nice to hear it from a stranger. I smiled and nodded despite myself, feeling tears in my eyes again. What was wrong with me? It must have been all the processed food I was eating.

Jean looked at me oddly but continued. "Elizabeth

had all the brains, all the brains for the three of them, really. I never taught Max, but he got by on his looks and his name, and it was lucky he had them, because he didn't have much else. Oh, she was smart. She could write like an angel, but she gave it away after what happened with Therese. I asked her to help me with the newsletter once in the pub and the look she gave me! I thought she'd be glad of something to do. Anyway, that's in the past."

There were voices outside. Against the noise of the wind and the ever-present calls of the circling gulls, the sound of humans was distinctive. Jean got up, the meeting over. "But you're the historical society! The past is what you do!" I cried.

I wanted more. This woman had known my mother! It had been so long since anyone had talked about her, and now she was just going to walk out and stack chairs?

The old headmistress reared her head; Jean drew her shoulders back, raised up her chin, and seemed suddenly taller than she had before. I felt a strange affinity with my mother; had she too cowered before this imposing woman? "Why are you so interested?" Outside, the van door slid open with a screech. Tony and Lisa, though late, had arrived ready to work. "What did you say your name was?"

"Miranda," I squeaked. "Miranda Courtenay." I was

suddenly grateful that my mother had never used this surname, preferring to call herself Therese Summer even after her marriage. Relief at my mother's decision to keep her maiden name surged through my body.

"Miranda."

Jean didn't flinch, just turned back to her shelving. Assuming it was the end of the conversation, I took my tea, tipped it down the sink quickly while Jean wasn't looking, and called out goodbye. When I turned around to leave, Jean was behind me. Holding another ledger. It was almost as big as her tiny frame, and yet she seemed to have had no trouble carrying it. When she spoke, her voice was calm and unhurried, her small wrinkled finger tapping on a newspaper article.

The story was headlined "Balcombe House Production of *The Tempest* Takes the Area by Storm!" The people in the old photograph that accompanied it were wearing costumes, and some of them had their faces obscured by wispy beards and bedraggled wigs, but one girl, at the center of the photograph, was magnetic, her eyes looking directly at the camera and an expression of pure triumph on her face. It was my mother.

Looking up at Jean, I felt pride and excitement, like I was forging a connection to my mother by being there, in the place where she grew up. It was like I was meant to be there, as if I had been drawn to Jean for a reason. I smiled at her, thrilled at what she knew about my mother and wondering what other treasures she might unearth for me. But Jean's face was stony, her placid mouth twisted in anger. "You're just like her. It's not just your looks. It's something else as well." She examined me, and I felt my back stiffen. Mum had always been a stickler for good posture. "Your self-entitlement. And your name. It's just like Therese to name you after that role. Her shining hour."

I gasped, the ferocity of her assessment taking me by surprise.

"You have a real nerve, coming in here after what your mother did. If I were you, I'd be very careful around here. And I wouldn't tell anyone—anyone— who you are." She snapped the ledger shut, so hard that a gust of air pushed my hair back from my face.

I ran. I ran all the way back to Barnsley, the brown paper package bouncing up and down in my pocket and chafing at my chest. By the time I got back to the house I could barely breathe, and my feet were lacerated by the rubber of the gumboots. Mrs. Mins took one look at my pale and sweaty face, saw something in my panicked eyes, and ran me a bath, relieving me of my duties for the rest of the day.

41

I needed to sleep. It was all too much for me. Or perhaps I was coming down with what Robbie had. Either way, when Mrs. Mins stuck her head around the
door and told me that Robbie, dosed up on paracetamol
and antibiotics, was sleeping soundly and that the girls
had gone to bed easily as well, I was too tired to argue.
Too exhausted to care. Tucking the ring box into my
pyjama pocket and the notebook under my pillow, I
switched out the light.

And lay there. For hours. And hours. Eventually I
relented and took the notebook out from its hiding place.
Daphne's voice carried me back in time immediately.

*You couldn't blame her, though,
could you? I know what my Max*

is like, and going by what he has told me, his father was one hundred times worse. I mean, I get upset if my Max asks me to put another log on the fire. There's just something about his tone, sometimes. You know what I'm talking about. The old Summer charm—when it's on, it's very, very good, and when it's not, it's lethal. Literally.

Anyway. Meryl was furious about what happened that day, but she didn't blame Maximilian, like a normal person would. No, she blamed Beatrice. There were two reasons for this: one, because Beatrice had made a fool out of her beloved Maximilian, betraying him and not appreciating him or their precious children; and two, because she hadn't jumped on Peregrine's boat and sailed off into the distance. That would have solved all Meryl's problems, in her opinion.

You've probably worked out by now that this is where it gets murky, where there's a chasm between what Meryl told my Max about the night Beatrice died, and what my Max thinks really did happen.

My Max and Meryl slept together for years—he told me that the very first night we met. And he's regretted telling me ever since, I think.

That was all ahead of him, though, when he was growing up. All he knew was that Meryl loved him, and as he grew into a teenager, that love seemed to change into something more sensual. You have to remember that even though we think she is old now, she was only twelve years older than Max. So when he was seventeen, which was the year it first happened, she was twenty-nine, and she looked amazing.

Seventeen!

I might not have been 100 percent accurate about the ages, but I was right about the no scruples part. I don't care how amazing Mrs. Mins looked—Max wasn't even an adult!

Can I just reiterate that? Amazing. My Max has shown me photos—well, okay, I found them in his sock drawer—and she was banging. Banging. They're still in there, if you can come up with a legitimate excuse to have a poke around in his sock drawer.

It went on for some time. Max would come home from boarding school and creep down the corridor to her room. In those days, the rooms we live in now were the servants' quarters, and Meryl lived there, in the end room with the tiny bathroom.

My room. I looked around me nervously, suddenly feeling Mrs. Mins's presence strongly. Don't be ridiculous, I told myself, and kept reading.

My Max was over in the east wing, a couple of doors down from Beatrice's old bedroom. Maximilian had taken over the library downstairs as his bedroom, saying he couldn't handle the stairs, but my Max knew it was because he couldn't bear to be close to where it had all happened. Anyway, it went on for years, the pair of them sneaking around, Meryl never letting on about her feelings for Maximilian. She only told him about that first fateful summer years later.

The relationship between Max and Meryl went on all through my Max's university years and right up until Maximilian died, which was when it came to a head. My Max had feelings for Meryl. He says now it wasn't love, but I think he is trying to spare my feelings, and also himself from ridicule. There hadn't been anyone else before me, only Meryl, and when we met he was in his early thirties. Something was holding him back from finding a proper girlfriend, and that something was Meryl, no matter what he says. In fact, one of my conditions on coming down to Barnsley was that Meryl had to go. She had missed out on university to stay and wait for Max, and by the time she worked out that Max wouldn't marry her, it was too late. Max found her a job at a small family-run hotel in Capri, owned by a friend of his father's. She became quite senior, well respected within the industry. After a couple of disastrous seasons and problems with staff, Max convinced me to travel to Capri with him and bring Meryl back to help out. I wonder now if that had been his plan all along.

Anyway, this is getting ahead of things, and I want to go back to what happened that summer, the summer they lost Beatrice.

Maximilian was right; that night after the scene at the cove, Beatrice came down to dinner as usual. And as usual she had taken the edge off her misery with a number of pre-dinner gins. Everyone was there, all their close friends gathered together for the last night of the festival. Beatrice sloshed her way through dinner, constantly lifting her glass for refills of wine, barely touching any of the food on her plate, and chain-smoking. (That's where you get it from obviously, Elizabeth.)

Meryl, coming in with the children to say good night, only saw part of the display, but she said Beatrice was slurring her words and holding her head up with one hand, her elbow resting on the table, sprinkling ash everywhere as she gesticulated wildly. The guests that night were a combination of stragglers from the summer parties and new arrivals for the festival. There was one noticeably empty chair, which Beatrice still seemed to be directing all her attention towards: Peregrine's.

Meryl came across Beatrice

again, staggering along the upstairs corridor, not long after the children were in bed. She helped her along, and saw her to her room. She said she didn't enter the room at that point—that even though Beatrice was drunk, she didn't feel it was appropriate. This might be true. Maybe.

I'm sorry, I know this is your mother, and this will be hard for you to read, but a lot of it is in that bloody book anyway. As much as you and Max hate it, I'm sure you must have read it. Max says Tessa's problem was that she didn't care about anyone else when she wrote that book. That she's a narcissist. But he's just as tied up with the mythology of Barnsley and the House of Brides as she was.

I mean, I think I have Tessa to thank for my marriage. I'm sure that bloody book was the reason he couldn't bring himself to marry Meryl. A member of staff. Not exactly House of Brides material.

Anyway.

Sometime later, maybe an hour or two, Meryl came up to the east wing to check on the children. She heard shouts coming from the main bedroom, but thought nothing of it, especially after the events of the afternoon.

It was only when she got to my Max's room, and his bed was empty, that she started to worry.

Racing back along the hallway, she smelled the smoke for the first time. The old walls in that part of the house are solid and three feet thick in some parts, the doors made from the heaviest of oak and almost as impenetrable, so the smoke was mostly contained until Meryl got back to the door. Not bothering to knock this time, she pushed the door open. The smoke was so thick, it was difficult to see, and there was no sign of anyone at first.

The flames had already taken over the thick drapes, and as she walked in, the pelmet crashed to the ground and the fire leapt across the carpet.

They were in the bathroom— Beatrice lying on the bath mat,

the water from the bath overflowing around her, and little Max crying over the top of her motionless body. Meryl grabbed Max but left Beatrice behind. She said she couldn't shift her, but did she even try?

Back then, Meryl was hailed as a hero. She rescued Max, and she raised the alarm about the fire, saving Barnsley House from being completely engulfed by the flames. Maximilian was distraught, and he desperately missed his wife. If Meryl thought the death of Beatrice would create an opening, she was wrong. It just made her workload heavier, for the full-time nanny quit in disgust at the scandal, leaving Meryl with full care of the children.

Maximilian would disappear for months on end, escaping the bad memories of Barnsley in favour of overseas holidays and friends' houses.

I suppose you know your father was never around—you don't need me to tell you that. You also know that he died when Max was twenty, after the affair between Meryl and my Max began. Gossip started in the village soon enough. You know what it's like. But I'm not sure if it ever reached your father's ears. In any case, he never said anything to Max.

Max—a young adult now—and Meryl were cooped up in that house together. And then Meryl's younger brother Leonard, who had been out at sea with his father, suffered a nasty accident on a trawler. A hook caught him in the face and sent him flying across the deck, breaking his legs in the process. Coming home to recuperate, he was a further burden on his mother.

Leonard came to live at Barnsley, and his presence took the pressure off the others for a bit. You were away at school and university during these years, but between the three of them they kept Barnsley just in the black, and stopped it going the way of many other country houses at the time. Unusually for someone so young, Leonard had a strong agricultural instinct, and before long he was advising my Max on most of the farm matters, as well as running maintenance around the place. There's no problem with Leonard, never has been. In fact, it was something he said, after Agatha's accident, that got me wondering. That made me realize that my Max and Meryl were sleeping together again.

Max won't listen to me. Every time I bring something up about Meryl, he thinks it's the jealousy talking, or that I'm trying to blame her for the accident. I know the accident was my fault. But I don't think she'll wait around forever. She made her move after the accident, and it worked for her.

She won't let him go again. She's dangerous, and I need your help.

That was where it ended. I flicked furiously through the rest of the pages, my eyes racing across every line in case some code was embedded, some clue hidden, but there was nothing. Nothing but fear and desperation. The same fear and desperation I was starting to feel.

42

The urge to leave was sudden and unstoppable. Daphne's last words in the notebook were unambiguous. I was in over my head. The place felt rotten to the core, and I could see why my mother had fled. I was sure my presence, anonymous or not, was stirring up trouble. Sooner or later, Max or Mrs. Mins would realize that I had the notebook, that Daphne had trusted me. Sooner or later they would realize who I was. I was flesh and blood, yes, but I was bad blood. And Barnsley would be a safer place for everyone without me.

But would it really be safer for the children without me? The thought persisted as I grabbed my rucksack and jammed in as many of my belongings as I could reach. The only thing I really cared about was my battered old copy of *The House of Brides*. I made sure to leave the one Max had given me on the bedside stand, resolutely unopened. At the last moment, I took the notebook and placed it under the pillow. I was sick of the notebook and the secrets, sick of it all. It wasn't my story to protect.

Inside, the house was silent. I paused outside each child's bedroom, offering up not quite a silent prayer but a wish, a hope that with my leaving, peace would be restored to Barnsley. That Daphne would come back. That there would not be yet another generation of Barnsley children who found themselves floundering and motherless. An apology as well, that I wasn't up to the job.

But outside, the wind was howling, pushing at Barnsley's solid walls, finding resistance and pushing harder again. Thomas looked up at me as I passed, the inside of his eyes red and heavy. He closed his eyes again, not sorry to see me go. I buttoned up my jacket and thought about scratching him behind the ear. But instead I carried on. Before I could change my mind.

There was nothing at Barnsley for me. I'd be no one here, once they found out who I was. At least in Australia, I was my own person. Not a very popular one, but still. I'd always be Tessa's daughter here, and I hadn't realized until I came here what that would mean. Just

as my mother was Beatrice's daughter, I would be forever in the shadow of my mother. I had seen the disgust
in Jean Laidlaw's face—better to deserve that disgust
than inherit it.

The van was not in the forecourt. Someone had put
it away. And perhaps after the night I'd gone down to
the boathouse for Sophia the garden lights had been
switched off. The rain started again as I trudged in the
darkness towards the car park, taking care not to let
the gravel crunch under my feet, sticking to the edges
of the forecourt, where the overhanging branches gave
me some shelter. Ignoring Daphne's banged-up Volks-
wagen with its shattered windscreen, I climbed into
the van, silently thanking my lucky stars when the engine started first go. The noise seemed immense and
I waited for lights to go on in the house but there was
only the soft, steady glow of Agatha's night-light in the
window upstairs.

In the manner of Beatrice, and my mother, I had
tried to run away from my problems. Beatrice had
unsuccessfully tried to escape on Peregrine's boat; my
mother had boarded an airplane and never looked back.
Yet their problems had still found them. Beatrice had
died a lonely, grisly death, and my mother had never
reunited with her family. All at once I could see what I

had back home: a father who loved and supported me, a family who had protected me from the worst year of my life. A job. A *real* fresh start.

I hadn't driven myself beyond the gate of Barnsley House before, but I hoped I would be able to find my way. There would be signs, I reckoned, to South Bolton. I could wait there until morning and catch the first bus to London. Denise would be pleased to see me, and maybe, just maybe, I could patch things up with my dad. Find a job, pay him back. Little by little. Max would find the van eventually.

It wasn't really stealing. Just like using my dad's credit card to buy my airline ticket wasn't really stealing. But this was different. This was the last time. I would write a letter to Max explaining everything once I was back home. Once I was safely out of there.

The drive was pitch-black too, but I didn't dare turn on the headlights until I was away from the house, in the part of the drive thickly lined by trees. The car inched along, and I leaned forward, somehow finding the wipers. The squeal was deafening in the quiet of the car.

Daphne had left in the dead of the night as well. Perhaps even just after I had seen her in the upstairs corridor. She had looked frightened, yes, but there was something else in her eyes I hadn't been able to put my finger on. A slight indication of the woman she had been before the accident. The image of her shaking head returned to me, as it had so many times over the preceding days. The finger to her lips, her eyes steely.

Determination.

That was it.

I was feeling a similar resolve myself. I was leaving Barnsley on my own terms. And I had a feeling that whatever had happened to Daphne that night had sprung from a like awakening of latent determination. The same determination that had pushed her cookbooks into the best-seller lists and earned her a Michelin star. The same determination that had built up the Summer House and turned around the fortunes of Barnsley.

Keeping one eye on the rearview mirror for signs of life at the house, I squinted hard to see the driveway in front of me. I caught a glimpse of movement in the trees and swerved, thinking of Daphne's cracked windscreen, anticipating a deer, a person. But it was only a rabbit. I watched it hop away, reminding myself to breathe, and looked back at the road in front of me.

I almost didn't see the tree. I flicked on the headlights just in time. It was enormous, blocking the entire road. I hit the brakes. The van skidded along the gravel road and fishtailed out slowly. I clung to the wheel, afraid it wouldn't stop in time. Afraid that the noise would wake up the whole house. The van was parallel to the tree by the time it came to a stop, the trunk right up next to my window, dark and gnarly. If the windows were down, I could have reached out and touched it. In better weather, I might have been able to climb it. To clamber to safety.

But then where?

There was nowhere to go.

I rested my head on the steering wheel for a moment, my heart beating fast. The rain was coming down hard, the van sinking into mud that was growing softer by the second.

I had to move right away. My only hope now was that I could get the van back to the car park before anyone realised I had taken it. Before it got bogged in the mud. Before they found me.

I shifted into reverse, but the wheels spun hopelessly. I pushed the accelerator down more gently a second time, and the van eased forward slightly. Sank again. I closed my eyes, took a deep breath. Tried again. The van finally moved backwards, out of the swampy mud. I took my time, put it into drive, and pulled it around so it was facing Barnsley House again.

The house looked even darker. I told myself it was

my imagination. As I inched back along the driveway, there was definitely something different. Where before there had been the warm light from Agatha's room, now there was nothing but black. My skin prickled. I started to shiver in my damp clothing.

I parked the van and felt my way across the dark car park. By the time I got back to the vestibule, I was certain. The house was in total darkness, and as I slipped through the door into the kitchen, I felt the difference immediately. The room was still warm from the heat of the Aga, but there was no steady hum of the fridge or soft glow of fairy lights. No light anywhere. Even though I was certain, I flicked the light switch beside me to be sure. Nothing.

The power was out.

It took me a long time to find my way back to my room. Arms in front of me, taking careful steps, I felt my way along the cold, uneven walls until I reached the heavy door at the bottom of the stairwell. Once I had pushed through into the stairwell it was easier, each step guiding me to the relative sanctuary of my bed.

"Miranda?"

The call was quiet, tentative. If I had been asleep, I doubt I would have heard it. I wasn't even sure I *had* heard it until Thomas whimpered softly in response.

"Miranda?" It came again.

Agatha.

I paused on the stairs, wishing I could strip out of my wet clothes. Take a shower. Bunker down in my flannel pyjamas. "I'm coming," I replied. Her cries were different from Robbie's. Less urgent. They didn't tear through my heart like his did, but the genuine need in her voice made me move more quickly down the dark corridor. "Agatha."

My eyes had grown accustomed to the dark, and I could see straightaway that she was sitting up in bed, her eyes shining in the dark. "My night-light! You turned off my night-light." She pointed to the side table, where her night-light stood useless. Shaped like a goose and charming when illuminated, it looked slightly off-putting as a shadow. I tried not to look at it.

"No, Agatha. It's all right." I sat down next to her and patted her hair. Felt her forehead with the back of my hand. It was instinct. Something learned from my mother and never forgotten. The movement stirred up something else, though. Something that *had* been forgotten. Before I could snatch at the memory and pin it down, Agatha spoke, and it escaped.

"I thought you turned it off."

"No, Agatha, I wouldn't do that. The power has gone out. Lie down and try to get some sleep."

She looked at me as if I had suggested that she swim to the moon. "I can't sleep without my night-light."

"Yes. Right. That makes sense." I thought for a moment. A little bit about my bed, but mostly about how frightened she must be. First her mum gone, then her dad. Then to wake up in a dark room. How long had she been awake? "How about if I stay right here?"

She nodded and curled back down under her covers. There was an old eiderdown at the end of her bed, so I pulled that over my shoulders and wrapped into a ball, ignoring the sticky wet denim of my jeans as best as I could. A radiator ran down the wall, and I placed my feet on it, hoping for some warmth, but it was stone cold.

And then a warm hand appeared from under the covers, found mine, and grabbed tight. I squeezed it back, finding comfort in the skin-to-skin contact, and a tiny smile formed on Agatha's lips. I closed my eyes.

The memory from earlier reappeared, fully formed. The dark bedroom of my childhood, a feverish night. It had always been my father who came in the night when I was ill: mopping up vomit, administering paracetamol, fetching lost stuffed toys, and changing wet sheets. But this time my father had been out to dinner, and my mother had come.

The door had flung open, light from the hallway flooding in. My mother abhorred weakness, and from an early age I had been trained to sleep in complete darkness, with the door shut. Just like she was brought up, she used to tell me. "What is it? What is this incessant caterwauling?" she asked.

I swallowed nervously as she marched over to my bed and pushed the back of her hand against my forehead. Suddenly my throat didn't seem too sore, my head not aching at all. "Nothing."

Her hand remained on my forehead, and I waited for her verdict. She sighed deeply and finally removed it. "You're right. You're barely tepid."

She stood up to go, and then stopped. "You know I have an important meeting tomorrow. I told you I needed a good night's sleep."

It did ring a bell. But my mother needed a good night's sleep every night. She thought *everything* she did was important. A dinner party would require a month-long preparation schedule of frantic cleaning and planning, only for her to laugh and smile when guests complimented her "effortless entertaining." She would lock herself in her study for days in advance of a two-minute radio segment.

It wasn't worth defending myself. I pretended to

fall back to sleep, and when she slammed the door, I squeezed my eyes shut tighter to keep the tears in. The next morning my father had taken me to see the family doctor, who had immediately prescribed antibiotics for a virulent infection, and I missed a week of school.

I drifted off to sleep on Agatha's bed after forcing that memory from my mind. It felt disloyal—I was sure my mother would have an explanation, were she here to defend herself.

After what seemed like only moments, I heard Mrs. Mins knocking on my door down the hallway. "It's seven o'clock!" she called, rapping sharply. "Rise and shine!"

Agatha's hand was still in mine, and when I opened one eye to see if she was awake, I was surprised to see Sophia in the bed as well. She was awake and looked pleased to see me.

"Thanks," she mouthed.

"That's okay," I whispered back.

"I *am* awake, you know." Agatha's voice was muffled but spritely. "Sophia, do you know the power went out?"

"I gathered that." Sophia stretched her long legs outside the covers, pointing her toes to the ceiling. The swelling on her ankle seemed to have gone down. "The generators will kick in this morning. Mrs. Mins will sort it out."

"A tree came down on the drive," I said. "I expect that had something to do with it." Sophia looked at me curiously. "We're all stuck here together," I joked. The girls didn't laugh.

I remembered the notebook left under my pillow and jumped up, but Mrs. Mins was already in Agatha's doorway, her hands by her sides and empty. Her mouth was tight with disapproval at the sleeping arrangements. It struck me again that my mother had grown up with Mrs. Mins; the strict upbringing she described had come from her hand. It made me resent her even more.

Mrs. Mins.

Not my mother.

Not then. But something was starting to shift. "Elizabeth has been on the phone again," Mrs. Mins said after I had dragged myself out of bed—fully if slightly damply dressed, one benefit of yet another late-night excursion—and we were headed down to Robbie's bedroom. Mrs. Mins wasn't looking her usual pulled-together self either—her hair slightly greasy at the roots, the skin under her eyes dark and shiny. She was starting to look every year of her age.

"Oh?"

"She has arranged for Mr. Mins to take you to the island today."

"The weather . . ."

"Leonard is able. You'll be safe with him." Mrs. Mins wouldn't look at me.

I took a surreptitious sniff under my arm and hoped there would be plenty of fresh air on the boat.

"How is Robbie?" The door to his room was closed, and when we opened it, cold air rushed out.

"I'm fine." Robbie was awake and smiled weakly at me. "I thought maybe we could download the footage today from the other morning."

"Of me in my nightgown? Now that would be terrifying," Mrs. Mins said, and turned away to open the curtains. It wasn't like Mrs. Mins to joke and I couldn't see if she was smiling or not. Robbie raised his eyebrows at me. It was good to see a little bit of animation in his face after the wan torpor of the day before.

"It's freezing in here," I said, pulling my cardigan together.

"I turned the radiators off last night. He was burning up." Mrs. Mins bent down to touch the panel. "I can't get it back on again."

"Get back under the covers, Robbie." I leaned down beside her and tried to turn the knob. She was right—it was stuck firm.

"What did you do to this?" It came out much more accusatory than I had meant.

"Old plumbing, Miranda. There's nothing you can do."

I'd had enough of her defeatist attitude. There *was* something we could do. Every one of the rooms along the upstairs corridor had a lovely corner fireplace, some of them far bigger than the rooms deserved. If we got the fire going in Robbie's room, it would warm up in no time. "There is."

I crouched down on the hearth and craned my neck up the chimney. It looked clear. Even though parts of Barnsley were well maintained, I wasn't sure the care extended to fireplaces and chimneys. In a house like this, the chimneys should be constantly cleared; otherwise, there could be bird's nests, bats. My father had the chimneys cleared out at the start of every winter, even the ones we didn't use. Surely Max or Mrs. Mins did the same. There was a pile of firewood by the back door for the fire in the snug; I could get a fire going in no time.

"No, Miranda." Mrs. Mins gripped at my arm as I went out the door. "It's not safe."

For once, I wasn't going to let her intimidate me. Not she of the closed bedroom doors and stiff upper lip. These children needed to feel loved and secure. That was the most important thing. They needed to know that I was going to look out for them. I was not going to let Robbie freeze. I shrugged off her arm and pushed past her.

43

"The eggs!"

Mr. Mins somehow heard me through the driving rain, the tearing wind. He cupped his hand to his ear, though, thinking he had misheard. "Elizabeth wanted me to bring her some eggs."

Mr. Mins shrugged. We can only do so much, his shoulders said.

"Please?"

"I might have some up at the cottage." He sighed and looked up from the rope he was untying. "Come on."

We walked up the hill, side by side but not talking. I had rescued the notebook from where it lay undisturbed under my pillow and tucked it inside my jacket, safe from the weather. Even though I was committed to taking it out to Elizabeth, I felt certain there was nothing in there that could help us. Daphne had given me the key as if it would unlock something important, and it had offered nothing but another sordid Summer tale. There was nothing to tell us where she was.

Mr. Mins seemed deep in thought. We were almost to the cottage when he dragged me under the canopy of a yew tree. The rain lashed at us and the wind was roaring through the trees. He had to shout to be heard. "What are you doing here?"

Blood rushed into my ears. My heart raced. "I'm taking care of the children."

His eyes traveled deep into mine. Expecting to see hostility, I was surprised to find only concern. "It's not safe for someone like you." Concern, yes. But also tenderness. It had been a long time since someone was concerned for my well-being.

"Someone like me?" We were shouting, and yet it felt intimate.

"A rival. That's all you are to her."

I tried not to stare at his scar as he spoke. Now that I knew its origins, I wondered how he could bear to be on a boat ever again.

"To who?" But I knew. I wanted to see how deep his

disloyalty ran. I wanted to see if he would tell me the truth. He couldn't bring himself to say her name.

"Wouldn't you be better off working for a nice normal family?"

"Does such a thing exist?"

"Not around here." He grimaced, looked around once more. The rain had finally stopped, but wind had moved into the void it left. He dragged me farther under the tree, where we were almost protected from the weather. Even though my body wanted to respond, I forced myself to stay still. I didn't want to fall into his trap. He was Mrs. Mins's brother, after all. "What's really going on here?" he asked. "What's with the sudden trip to the island in the middle of a cyclone?"

"I thought this was just a passing shower."

He shook his head. Rubbed his chin, as though he had stubble.

"I don't know if Elizabeth will be able to help you."

"Maybe I'm helping her."

"Maybe you are. But you're in more danger than she is. There are already enough missing people around here." He muttered something else, but I didn't quite catch it. Whatever it was sent a crimson shadow across his cheeks. Or was it the cold air?

"I've got nowhere else to go." It was true, and I could have pretended otherwise, but the time of concealment and ego had passed between us. Trust was moving into its place.

"You're not in love with him as well, are you?" His head turned towards mine, his eyes watching me carefully.

We sat for a moment. Alone. For the first time since I'd come to Barnsley, I was unwatched. Unfollowed. It made me brave.

"Max is my uncle."

Mr. Mins said nothing, only whistled. A long, slow, incredulous whistle. And then: "Does he know?"

"No. I don't think so."

"Does anyone know?"

"Elizabeth, I think. And Jean Laidlaw."

"Another bloody Summer secret," Leonard said, shaking his head at the thought.

The words struck something in my mind. The niggling thought that there was something in the notebook I had overlooked.

The Summer secret pudding recipe.

"Mr. Mins!" I shouted. "Have you got internet at the cottage?"

44

"Thanks, Mr. Mins." I pressed against him, made playful by a new sensation. Hope. It felt better than a hundred likes. Better than a thousand likes.

"Call me Leonard."

"Thanks, Leonard." I smiled at him, and he smiled back, a little warily but enough to make his lip pucker slightly and his eyes twinkle. Enough for me.

We were sitting on Leonard's sofa, in a small and cozy space tucked away in the eaves of the cottage. More a self-contained flat than a bedroom, it had a living area and a kitchenette and, beyond that, what I imagined was a small bedroom. The whole room smelled like Leonard and was warm in a way I had forgotten existed since I had been at Barnsley. The laptop on my lap meant we were sitting so close together that our sock feet were touching.

An unfamiliar movement in my pocket made me jump. My phone. For the first time in days, I had stumbled into some Wi-Fi. Tentatively I pulled it out, angling the screen so Leonard couldn't see it. Texts. Alerts. Notifications. The trembling was unending, and at the sight of all the updates a familiar anxiety returned, sudden and insistent. Leonard was watching me, curious. I took a deep breath and turned the phone off. I felt instantly better.

We returned our attention to the notebook lying open on the sofa next to me. The heading at the top of the page read "Secret Summer Christmas Pudding Recipe," and beneath was a list of ingredients. Nothing unusual, and certainly nothing I would consider highly secretive, but having never been a big fan of pudding, I could hardly call myself a connoisseur. Dried fruit. Bread crumbs. Brandy. I wasn't surprised I didn't like it.

Written in grey-lead pencil under the ingredients in tiny letters was a word consisting of a mix of upper and lower case. Now I knew what I was looking for, it seemed obvious, and I wondered at how I had overlooked it previously. "Hang on," I said, reaching into my jacket pocket and self-consciously pulling out my glasses.

The letters and numbers pulled themselves into line:

ThOmAs
1732

Leonard watched as I plugged the word into the CCTV password prompt. The small rainbow circle whirled, and the program opened. "I should have guessed 'Thomas' would be the password."

"Never underestimate the love between an Englishman and his dog." Leonard pressed one sock against mine again. It was thick and woolly, like someone had knitted it. Bright red. The other one was brown.

"What's with the 1732?"

"It's the year Barnsley was built. Older than your Australia."

"So are those socks, by the looks of things." I paused. "And you."

"Is that your way of asking how old I am?"

"I don't think I want to know."

"I'm around forty," he said, smiling. And for a moment I forgot about Daphne missing. The foul weather, the boat that was waiting to take me across treacherous waters to the island. Elizabeth waiting for me. The secret notebook. My mother. It was all gone. I was just sitting in a warm room with a good-looking guy who wasn't really that old and, judging by the footsies, kind of liked me too.

It had been so long since I let myself feel something for someone. I'd had plenty of boyfriends at school, but once I got to university, I was afraid of getting serious with anyone. Afraid someone would fall in love with me. Afraid he would ask me to move in with him. Afraid he would slow me down.

My mother had written *The House of Brides*, and then, nothing. She told me that getting married had changed everything for her. And that a baby had been the final nail in the coffin of her creativity. Every time I disturbed her at her desk, she would shake her head and mutter "A pram in the hallway . . ." before instructing me to close the door on the way out.

And now here was Leonard. Making me doubt everything I had believed. As if he'd read my thoughts, or perhaps misinterpreted them as trepidation over the task at hand, he squeezed my hand and we continued.

The videos were arranged in folders by dates and locations. There was footage from the restaurant, the hotel lobby, the guest wing corridor, the front entrance of the hotel, the boathouse, the car park, the tennis court, and the swimming pool. The swimming pool!

I hadn't even realized there was one. There were no cameras in the private section of the house.

I counted back on my fingers to work out the date Daphne went missing. It was only six days before, but it seemed like a lifetime. A lot could happen in six days. Not for the first time, I hoped she was in London with mates or back in rehab or even, as this is how desperate I was getting, in a bar somewhere. "Where should we start?" Leonard asked.

"The car park?" It was a long shot, but perhaps she had gone out through that entrance.

"No. Her car is still there. It's banged up from the accident, but it's there all right."

"The front of the hotel?" I clicked on it even as we were deciding. "She must have left somewhere between midnight and dawn." I fast-forwarded through the hours.

"Nothing good happens after midnight," Leonard said, and we settled in to watch the empty hotel entrance.

"What made you come to Barnsley?" I knew what I had read in the notebook, but I couldn't believe a man like Leonard would do something unless he really wanted to.

"I went to sea with my father when I was very young. I didn't have a choice, not really. It was a rough life, but I had no other choice. I couldn't come home and be a burden to my mother, and especially so after my accident. Meryl said that Max would pay for my surgeries, and there were a lot of them, and it was a lot of money, and he would pay for my rehab."

There was nothing on the footage from the first camera.

"Boathouse?" Leonard asked.

I clicked on the folder. Leonard moved his foot away and coughed. "There was something. The day after Daphne went missing. I thought nothing of it at the time."

"Oh?" I was concentrating on the screen.

"A boat. It wasn't tied up properly. Got a bit smashed up on the rocks."

I took my eyes from the screen, looked at him carefully. "You thought nothing of it?"

"Daphne is afraid of the water. She wouldn't go out in a boat."

At that moment there was movement on the screen, and I paused it, then wound it back and played it again. A shadow, and then two figures appeared. We watched without talking. I held my breath, watching their backs, waiting for the figures to turn. They were holding hands, a man and a woman. A dog. Thomas.

The man let go to unlock the door, and the woman

rubbed her hands together, flicked her hair back. Her
gold hoops shone in the light. The man turned around
and looked up at the camera before he pulled the door
shut behind him, leaving Thomas outside. It was Mrs.
Mins and Max. Even though I was expecting to see
them, I gasped. The blinds went down, and then nothing. For a long time. Leonard and I waited. I moved
onto the floor, needing some space. There was movement on the screen.

"Leonard, look!" He came and sat with me. A figure stumbled across the bottom of the picture—a tiny
woman, dressed in a slip of a dress despite the time
of year. Daphne. She stumbled, fell down on the jetty,
dropped what she was holding. The dog ran to her. She
let him lick her hand, rubbed behind his ears.

"Daphne."

I nodded sadly. Leonard reached for my hand again,
and I let him take it.

The woman picked herself up, inspected her knee
for a moment. Dusted it off and bent down to collect
what she had dropped. A bottle. She brought it up to
her mouth, drank deeply, and then chucked it into the
water. Raised her arm up into the air, pleased with the
way it had landed. Then she turned to face the boathouse. "Oh no," I said.

Daphne tried the door handle first. When it wouldn't budge, she started banging on the door. Thumping like crazy. Thomas frisked behind her, thinking it was a game. There was no way whoever was within could not have heard her. There was no way Max and Mrs. Mins could not have heard her. "Come on, Meryl," Leonard said under his breath. I recognised his shame. "Open up."

They didn't open up. After a few minutes Daphne stopped banging and tried to peer through the windows. When they didn't give up their secrets, she sat down on the jetty and looked out to sea. The minutes ticked past.

And then a movement at the window. The unmistakable shift of the blinds as someone peeked out. Then nothing. Daphne sat for a bit longer, until something beyond the camera piqued her interest. She rolled forward to her hands and pushed herself up, staggering slightly as she went. "Don't do it, Daphne." I couldn't help myself. She couldn't hear me, and I couldn't hear her, but I knew what she was thinking. That Max and Mrs. Mins had gone out to the island.

The next couple of minutes were unbearable as we watched her untie the rope on a small wooden speedboat. Leonard sighed, and I felt sure he recognised it as the one smashed on the rocks. She pulled back the chain and fell back. Tried again and got the boat going. And then Daphne was gone.

Leonard's phone began to ring. "She'll want to know where I am," he said, the phone trembling slightly in his large hands. "I told her I would take you out there first thing."

"Who?" I asked. The fearful look in his eyes made me nervous. Only a sister could make someone look like that.

I pictured Mrs. Mins watching from Barnsley, waiting for us to land on the jetty at the island, becoming more anxious as we were delayed. Was she watching from the east wing window, or had she become so desperate she had moved outside, weathering the storm just so she could keep vigil?

The weather had eased slightly while we were inside, but now it was brutal once more. Leonard looked out the window at the sky, his fingers where they held the phone white with tension, or effort, or both. "We better get going. I don't want her to get suspicious."

We were on the boat halfway between the mainland and the island, still hidden by the tip of the cove, when Leonard spoke. I was huddled in the small shelter, uselessly trying to stay dry and not think about Daphne.

The footage kept repeating in my head. "I googled you, you know."

Despite the ferocious headwind, my head spun to look at him.

"Miranda Courtenay." The sound of my name on his lips felt good.

"How did you know my surname?"

"I checked your luggage. You're not the only snoop around here." He must have been the one who had taken it to my room. I waited for the shame to descend at the thought of Leonard finding me online. There was nothing. The truth felt strangely comfortable. "A modern-day charlatan . . . another wellness hoax."

"You found me," I sighed, and Leonard nodded. "My dad paid a company a lot of money to bury my old profile—it didn't work. I'm meant to be building a new online presence to help speed up the task, but it's a bit hard here."

"Yes, it was all there."

For some reason, I found this comforting. I wanted him to know the magnitude of what I had done. If it was left for me to explain, I might be tempted to soften the blow. "I can see why you might have wanted to run away," he said. It wasn't a joke, though his strong accent made it sound like one.

434 • JANE COCKRAM

"Yes."

"But I couldn't see why you would have come here."

"And now you know."

"And now I know."

I picked at my fingernails, pulled back some loose skin. Anything not to look Leonard in the eye.

"How old were you, Mother Miranda?"

I counted back in my head. "I was twenty-four."

Leonard groaned. "Did you ask a doctor?"

"I didn't ask anyone. I was so sure about the nutritional benefits of my diet, I didn't think I had to. I had so many people telling me how my cleanses had changed their lives. I thought I was invincible." It was true. I had.

"It's not like you actually promised anything, though? Just a vague suggestion."

"Um . . ."

"Oh, Miranda. And someone called you out on it." Sympathy. There was definitely sympathy in his voice. It gave me hope.

"They certainly did." Her name was etched on my mind forever.

45

There was no one waiting on the jetty. The boat launched towards the pier, and Leonard shot out a foot, stopping it from crashing with a sure and steady push. He tossed out the rope and jumped out after it. "I have to leave you," he said as he looked up and down the length of the rocky shoreline. "Meryl needs me at the house. A tree's come down on the drive."

My cheeks burned. Leonard mistook the flush for anger.

"I'll be back to get you, though. Say, an hour? Two?" He looked at me reassuringly.

I had no idea. The terrain looked inhospitable, and two hours out there seemed an eternity. Still, with Elizabeth there, I felt like we could make some progress. I wanted to tell her what we had seen on the footage. I wanted her to come with me to the police. "I'll be fine." It wasn't one of my better lies, and Leonard didn't look convinced.

"Okay." He helped me onto the jetty and gave my hand a little squeeze before he let go.

My heart pulsated in response, and I gave him a shy smile. "I really will be." I tried harder this time to make him believe me. I knew Elizabeth would look after me. She knew this island inside out. I had faith she would appear at any moment. After all, I had her eggs.

Leonard saluted me and set off back into the wind. I rushed off, looking for cover.

Looking for Elizabeth. At the end of the jetty was a rusty old gate with a solitary lantern above it. From what I knew of the deep darkness in this part of the world, at best the light from it would be ineffectual; the way things ran around here, it probably didn't work at all. Beyond the gate the land rose steeply, and a set of vertiginous stairs snaked up the hill through dense foliage.

And at the top stood Mrs. Mins.

"Elizabeth couldn't make it after all," she called out as she started to descend the stairs.

I turned around to run back to the jetty, but Leonard's boat was far away, pushing around the headland. I froze. There was nowhere to go.

Mrs. Mins was fit despite her age, and she was down the stairs in no time. She threw her arm through mine in a jaunty fashion, as if we were about to set off on a jolly adventure. I wasn't fooled. Her elbow was too sharp, her grip too forceful. But there was no way of extracting myself without making a fuss. Whatever I did, wherever I went, I was still alone on an island with Mrs. Mins. "I've got something to show you, dear," she said, pulling me up the stairs. "And I think you have something for me."

I had to draw on all the inspirational memes I had ever reposted to move my legs one after the other and follow Mrs. Mins up the hill. *Do something that frightens you every day. Feel the fear and do it anyway. From great risk comes great reward.*

I wasn't sure if it was because of the absence of the accompanying polar bear graphics, but in the face of real danger they weren't quite so effective as I had once believed them to be. Once again I felt ashamed of my own insincerity. My past insincerity.

As I climbed that hill, panting and fretting and sus-pecting, I knew I would never be that person again. The person who would do things without thinking of others. The person who would do something just to look good.

"I'm sure you know the history of the island," Mrs.

Mins shouted as we climbed. "All that late-night computing! It's so easy these days to find out people's histories. Of course, what you find online is never the full story, is it?"

Despite the severity of the incline and her age, there was barely a puff in her voice. Meanwhile I, decades younger, was struggling. It took all my effort to keep up with her, and had it not been for her still-strong grasp on my arm, I would have fallen behind. "Wikipedia. That one. There's plenty on there, I should think. But did you know, anyone can get on that website and tinker around. Add a tidbit here and there. Change a name, change a date. It's quite easy if you know what you're doing." She was definitely crackers. I looked back, and far below I could see Leonard's boat struggling back to the mainland, the hull cracking against the gathering waves. He was gone, then. "It's just like life. The truth is what you make it: add a little here and there, take away what you need. It's a work in progress. You of all people know what I mean by that, don't you?"

Heat raced through my body. Panic. Did she mean what I thought she meant?

We weren't completely up the hill when she stopped and pulled me aside. I hadn't noticed it as we were climbing, but the path forked ahead of us, and a narrow track veered ever so slightly to the right.

It was overgrown, like so many paths around Barnsley, but here the plants growing along the track were subtropical—this time it was ferns and not brambles blocking my way.

The package under my jacket was pressing against my skin. I hoped Mrs. Mins wouldn't notice. The canopy of tree fern fronds protected us from the worst of the weather, but all of a sudden the silence seemed ominous. Scary. I imagined Daphne arriving out here in the middle of the night. In the pitch-black. She was the only thing keeping me going. The thought of her, out here, all this time.

I had no choice but to follow Mrs. Mins farther down the path, deeper into the greenery. It seemed unlikely anyone had passed through recently; the path underfoot was boggy and almost impassable. "Where are we going?"

"It was a special place of Max's great-great-grandmother's. You'll see when we get there. It's hard to explain."

"Would we be better off heading back?"

"The English weather too much for you?"

"It's hardly an outdoors sort of a day, is it?"

"Lucky we're heading for shelter, then."

Daphne, I thought, hold on. I'm coming.

The path curved around more lush foliage. On one

side plants with fronds the size of small cars towered over us, alien in their dominance.

"Gunnera."

"Pardon?"

"The plants. *Gunnera manicata.* Some people call them dinosaur food. Sound friendly, don't they?" She stopped, turned to face me. "They're not. Look underneath, and there's thousands of tiny spikes." I reached out to feel the foliage, mesmerized by the size of the leaves. They must have been at least six feet wide.

We climbed again. Mrs. Mins said something I couldn't quite hear. I asked her to repeat it, and she laughed and told me we were nearly there. The leaves cleared, revealing a small building on the very edge of a cliff face. I stopped myself just in time, and Mrs. Mins smirked. It was the structure I had glimpsed from the study on my very first morning at Barnsley House. "It's a shell house. Max's great-great-grandfather built it for his wife. They were all the rage back then. I can't think what they would have gotten up to in here. Or I can, if I know anything about what the men in the family are like."

Moments before, I had felt hot and sweaty from the trek up the hill. Now the moisture on my neck turned cold, the warmth evaporating. She carried on without looking at me or without any sign of recognition. I told myself to calm down. I tried not to think of my father's warnings. Everything was fine.

Mrs. Mins had called it a house, but it really looked like a small fortress to me. It was hexagonal in shape, its six walls rising to a pitched stone ceiling, wired at some point in history to train more well-behaved climbers than the ones that now engulfed them. A small oak door, built for people of a smaller generation, was partially covered in vines. Mrs. Mins shifted them carefully to the side. No sound came from within. "Daphne!" I shouted. "I'm here."

Mrs. Mins snorted and blocked me. "Don't be stupid."

I leaned against the wall, trying to gain some shelter under the small overhang of the eave.

"Family bolt-hole," Mrs. Mins said, still standing out in the rain like a true psychopath. "Some families have a villa in the Algarve. He has this. The Summer family have always been self-flagellating. Generations of Summer men have hidden out here when the going got tough. Not Max, though." She snorted. "He seeks refuge on the Med. Money is no object."

She twitched and looked through the window. It was grimy with years of dirt, and I doubted she could see much. I hoped Daphne could hear us.

From this spot, we had a clear view of Barnsley. If

Daphne *was* here, she would have been able to keep a watch on the place. At night, I imagined she could track the occupants of the house by the lights in the rooms, and by day, it was close enough to see figures on the lawn, if not make out their identities completely. No boat could pass the narrow entrance in the cove to Barnsley without passing by this watch point.

"Do you have the notebook?" she asked, without looking at me.

I was certain I had not mentioned a notebook to Mrs. Mins. Panic sluiced through my body, turning my limbs liquid. "What notebook?"

Mrs. Mins laughed and shook her head. "Daphne was always writing in her notebook. Recipes, lists, menu plans. Her life was in that notebook. And now it's gone."

I clenched my lips together and shook my head.

Mrs. Mins leaned in towards me. "It went missing right about the time you arrived."

"I don't know anything about a notebook." My lie sounded quite convincing. Years of experience had paid off. Mrs. Mins stepped back for a moment.

I thought about running. But the path we had come along was slippery; one misstep, and I would be lost to the cliffs below. If by some chance I made it down the path without falling, where to then? Mrs. Mins must have a boat somewhere, but I hadn't seen it. Beyond the shell house, in the other direction, the island lay wild and unknown. She knew I was trapped. *I* knew I was trapped. Sophia had come to me for help. Daphne had asked me for help. I had let everyone down.

"Max said you were quite cozy with Daphne before she went missing. Tucked away in the guest rooms. Chatting!" Mrs. Mins was calm. She knew she held all the aces. "I'm not letting you go until you tell me where it is. No one will miss you. No one misses Daphne." A small but triumphant laugh.

"Leonard knows I'm here."

"Oh yes, Leonard. What's that old saying?"

I knew what she was getting at. "Blood's thicker than water."

"Precisely."

46

At first I thought I was hallucinating. The events of the morning had turned me upside down and inside out, and it seemed certain that my brain was playing tricks, taking images from *The House of Brides* and making them real in front of me. I thought I was dreaming, finally succumbing to the nightmares that enveloped the rest of the family. But even after I squeezed my eyes shut and opened them again, and shook my head to be sure, the flames were still there. Distant, but there.

Oh my god.

The fire.

Smoke plumes billowed from an upstairs window of Barnsley House, and flames chased the smoke in flashes. It was the flashes that had caught my eye; the brief jolts of red and orange in an otherwise colorless English sky.

Robbie.

I had been so sure I was right. Guilt flooded through my body, turning my limbs to liquid. I had been so sure I was doing the right thing for Robbie that I hadn't listened to Mrs. Mins's warnings. Just like I hadn't listened to my father when he warned me that I was heading down a dangerous path with Mother Miranda. "Mrs. Mins," I said, quietly at first, aware that she was waiting for my answer to her question. "Meryl." This was no time for pleasantries.

"What do you know about the notebook?" she repeated, coming in closer still.

"Mrs. Mins! There's a fire."

"Ha! If you think I'm going to fall for that . . ."

Mrs. Mins didn't want to turn around. She didn't want to take her eyes off me, but she could see the panic in my face. She had no choice. Her shoulders dropped from around her ears, and her head cocked slightly, as if she was trying to decipher something foreign. And only after that did it begin to move from side to side in denial.

"Is it the east wing?" I said hopefully. I knew it wasn't, though. I wanted to blame the supernatural; I wanted it to be like the ghost stories I had heard. A phantom fire. A talisman from the past. An omen for the living. I knew it wouldn't be. It was real. And it was my fault.

"It doesn't look like it. It's hard to tell."

I was scarcely able to see anything past Mrs. Mins. I wanted to run, but I couldn't. The inhospitable landscape and the threat of more storms. The odds were stacked against me.

"I told you not to set the fire! Stupid girl!" For a second I thought she was going to slap me, and then she stepped back. I almost wished she had.

"The nursery wing?" My voice wobbled. More than anything, I wanted her to be wrong.

"Yes." She started talking to herself. A jumble of names. *Robbie. Agatha. Max.*

"Robbie. He'll still be in bed." I could barely get the words out. "Who did you leave him there with?"

It wasn't just Robbie, though; there was a chance they were all up there. Sophia, like most teenagers, spent a lot of time in her room, and Agatha, if she was up there alone . . . It didn't bear thinking about.

Mrs. Mins made a sound unrelated to the rest of her. A rush of air, a crush of sound, an uncontrollable cry. The animalistic sound of a mother whose offspring are under threat. Once, and then again and again.

And then just one word. "Max." I shook my head. Max wasn't even there. "He asked me to look after the children."

"Leonard is over there. They'll be fine," I cried, even though I didn't believe it.

"I have to go." Mrs. Mins started moving away from the shell house. I ran after her.

"I'm coming!"

"No!" She pushed me back, and I reached out for her, pulled at her sleeve. The sound of fabric tearing. She lurched away, her arms pushed out behind her. Tilting forward, barely upright.

"Mrs. Mins!" I shouted. "I'm coming." I ran after her again, slipping in the mud. "I'm coming," I said. "The children . . ."

"The children?" she asked. Behind her, I could see Barnsley. Flames licked up the outside wall, and yet the house looked strangely quiet. There should be people on the front lawn by now, raising the alarm. I should be able to see Leonard, or the children, or the fire brigade. But the tree was down, and it would be difficult for the fire brigade to get through. My heart was racing at the thought of what might be. "The children are no business of yours."

"But Agatha—" I stopped. The name felt clunky

on my lips, like a nickname I wasn't familiar enough to use.

Mrs. Mins looked around and then opened the door to the shell house. "Go inside." The scorn was clear on her face, the dark below her eyes hollowed deeper with every minute. She was thinking.

One minute, two minutes. I felt a tug on my arm and was being pulled towards the shell house. Mrs. Mins pushed me inside, and I lost my footing, tumbling over the rug on the floor. The door slammed, and I heard a key turn. And then her voice came through the keyhole. "You didn't think I'd really let you go, did you, Miranda?"

47

There was no doubt then that I was really a prisoner. I screamed in frustration. I screamed for Mrs. Mins. I screamed Leonard's name. In desperation, I called for Elizabeth. I banged on the wooden door until the skin on my hands was shredded and splintered. No one came.

And then, defeated, I slumped down, my back to the door, and looked around me. There was no sign of Daphne. I sniffed the air through my tears, but there was nothing. Not the slightest smell of a woman. Only the smell of the nearby sea and dampness. Once upon a time, someone had covered every inch of the interior wall with seashells; some large, some small, some more like flint than shells, some more exotic species from foreign beaches. It must have been conceived as a summer house, as the temperature inside, in the middle of winter, was bitter. The rug on the floor, ancient and worn in places, did little to stop the cold from rising from the damp ground below, let alone the wind from whistling in under the door.

There were three windows, placed equidistant around the walls, and all were so overgrown with foliage that they were impenetrable, apart from one. It looked out to sea, and under it someone had placed a small desk—a writing desk, because on it sat a typewriter and other signs of a writing life: notebooks, an old soup can filled with pencils, piles of paper bound with rubber bands, and books cracked open at the spine, the edges of their covers curled up with damp. The low bookshelves running all the way around the room were also filled with books. Some I recognized, many I didn't. A writer's den. But who was the writer?

Behind me, a camp bed was made up. It looked as if someone had slept there recently; the pillow was still dented with the shape of someone's head. It had to be Daphne. Maybe she had been here, and I'd missed her.

The thought of this filled me with rage yet again, and I grabbed the blankets and threw them across the room in frustration. Then I picked them up and tried to rip them in half; with my hands, with my teeth. It was no good. They were made in a different era, in a time when things were made to last. Every inch of the scabrous wool resisted my attempts to tear it apart. There was no way I could get out; the windows were too small, and the door was solid.

The image of Robbie in the fire wouldn't leave my mind, not for an instant. The feeling of shame came back, and I succumbed to it, surrendered completely to the familiar destructive guilt. Mrs. Mins had told me not to light the fire, and I hadn't listened. I thought I knew best. Again. I was wrong. Again.

Screaming was not getting me anywhere. I let my eyes run over the spines of the books. *Brideshead Revisited. Cold Comfort Farm. Rebecca.* No surprises there, but nothing to help me. An entire shelf of Agatha Christie. Reference books: *The Dictionary of Art, A Medical Dictionary, Debrett's.* Cookbooks: *Larousse,* Elizabeth David, Anna Del Conte. And then there it was, almost hidden, over by a pile of old *Country Life* magazines: *The House of Brides.*

I let my fingers run over the name on the spine, following the letters in and out of the groove and summoning up her memory with each. The book fell open easily; it was a hardcover, a first edition, by the look of it. I turned to the cover page, expecting to see my mother's handwriting, a meaningful inscription to her only sister, but there was nothing.

There was nothing on the next page either.

I flicked through, looking for a card, a note, something personal from my mother. An envelope fell out. A thick parchment envelope, the gum dried out and yellow with age. The envelope opened with only the slightest touch. Newspaper clippings. I pulled them out, one by one, looking for a note I was sure would be hidden within. I wanted some clue of the relationship between my mother and Elizabeth. I wanted to know what she called her, what turn of phrase she used; whether they had nicknames for each other, a sisterly shorthand.

At home, in a small red case at my father's house, I had saved all the cards my mother had given me for my birthdays. From my first year until my eighth year I had one for every birthday, each filled with her large, loopy print: a funny message, an anecdote about something cute I had done that year, why she had chosen that particular gift for my birthday. Altogether, I had no more than four hundred words from my mother. But those four hundred words told me almost everything I knew about her. I was desperate for more.

There was nothing apart from the clippings. Only reviews of her book from the time of its publication. There was nothing here I didn't know. I chucked the clippings on the bed and went back to the window. The weather had come in low again, making it difficult to see the house; there was a faint glow in the distance, but I couldn't see actual flames, like I had earlier. It didn't seem possible that a fire could burn on in the rain. I hoped it was under control and someone would notice I was missing. I hoped Leonard would remember I was out here, in all the confusion.

Idly I picked up the clippings, flicked through. There was nothing there I hadn't read before; the headlines were similar to the ones that still surfaced from time to time in nostalgic articles about a particular moment in time.

"A HISTORY OF A HOUSE,
AND A FAMILY."

"BARNSLEY HOUSE:
THE BIRTH OF A FEMINIST MOVEMENT."

"THE HOUSE OF BRIDES:
THE STORY OF A HOUSE TOLD
THROUGH FOUR FORMIDABLE WOMEN
WHO LIVED THERE."

"A HOUSE OF BRIDES,
AND IT TOOK A DAUGHTER TO
PULL IT TOGETHER."

I picked one at random and began to read.

The astonishing story of the women who
lived at Barnsley House could only be told by
someone close to the family. Someone who
had access to documents in the vast family
archives; someone who could gather together
what must be hundreds of photographs from
the time and pull out only the most evocative.
Someone who knew where all the skeletons
were hidden and who was not afraid to unlock
the cupboard and let them all tumble around
on the floor, exposed. It takes a brave soul to
do all this. There was only one woman for
the job.

One woman for the job. My mother. She always said
she had to leave the country after she wrote the book,
that she could never stick around after it was published.
Her family was furious, humiliated. Fancy bringing
the family secrets out into the open like that! No wonder she went to Australia and never came back again. I
could see it more clearly now.

I picked up another article. This one dwelt less on
the historical aspect and more on the prose.

Therese Summer writes like an angel, which is hardly surprising, given her family lineage. Summer was brought up in the halcyon surrounds of Barnsley House and treading the same boards as Gertrude Summer and Sarah Summer, so it seems inevitable that their creative urge and delivery should seep into her bones through some sort of mystical osmosis. Every word is well judged, every well-judged word precise. It would read like fiction, if it were not too fantastical to be believed.

My mother never wrote again, after she finished *The House of Brides.*

In public, she said she had done what she set out to achieve: she had written her life's work, and she had nothing left to write about. But I remembered her sitting at her desk, angry when the words wouldn't come. Sobbing with frustration. Making excuses. And doing anything to avoid admitting failure.

As I sat in the shell house, surrounded by the signs of a writing life, something stirred in my brain. Certain phrases began to repeat themselves.

Things began to stack and restack. People. Stories. Fact. Fiction.

The birthday cards: fun and frothy, but vague and verbose. Nothing like *The House of Brides*. What did Elizabeth say, the first time I met her? "Lots of promise, never amounted to much." Was there bitterness in her voice then that I didn't recognise?

The astonishing story . . . could only be told by someone close to the family . . . Could only be told by one woman . . . but what if there was another woman who could have told it? No. It couldn't be. *You're just like your mother . . .*

Elizabeth was a real storyteller. The stories about the past she recounted were so real, so dynamic with detail, that sometimes even she got confused between fact and fiction. The books she wrote for Daphne. The signs right here in front of me that she was writing still.

I returned to the bookshelf, pulled down a book I had passed by earlier. A copy of Daphne's most famous cookbook, *The Summer House*. There had to be a clue in Elizabeth's writing. I read the introduction. It was Daphne's voice, as I knew it via the notebook.

Friendly, familiar, passionate. Everything Elizabeth was not. I couldn't detect her hand.

I flicked through the book one more time, hungrily searching the photographs for insight into Daphne and her family. There were no photographs of Elizabeth and Tom, only the children and Max. I had almost given up when the book fell open to the title page. There had been no dedication in *The House of Brides*, but Daphne had made one in *The Summer House*.

For Elizabeth, the real writer in the family xx

48

"MERYL! MERYL! MERYL?"
Silence.

I was just about to shout again when a beady little eye appeared at the keyhole. "Miranda, is that you?"

A man's voice. And then a face at the window, gnomic and worried.

"Can you see the fire? Has it stopped?" My voice was desperate, and it frightened me when he didn't answer. The key turned in the lock, and there he was—drenched, his wet clothes emphasizing his small frame.

He registered the surprise on my face. "I trained as a jockey once." He shook his head. "You should never have come here."

I pushed past him. "Why does everyone keep saying that?"

I started to run, and Tom followed. I kept running, afraid he might change his mind and force me back into the shell house. Deep under the cover of the greenery again, I couldn't see what was happening on the mainland, and I had no strategy other than getting back there as soon as I could.

"Slow down!" Tom called. "You'll fall."

"The fire! I need to get back to the children."

"Leonard is there." It wasn't enough to slow me down. I knew Leonard was capable, but I needed to see them for myself. Touch them. To convince myself that human life wasn't dispensable. Which made me think of my mother. And what I was beginning to suspect was the truth behind her departure from Barnsley.

"Why do Max and Elizabeth never talk about Tessa?" Silence again. This was off script, and without Elizabeth he was uncertain. "Tom?"

"Tessa?" It wasn't the question he'd been expecting.

"Tessa. My mother." The truth came easily. It felt good. I felt something in me unfold, loosen.

Tom was quiet for a moment. "Elizabeth said it was so, and I didn't believe her."

"Why do they hate her?"

"For god's sake, woman, I'm thinking."

"I don't know what happened between them."

"How could you not?"

"I was still very young when she died." I had already started puffing. Tom chased after, sounding even worse. "Was it something to do with the book? *The House of Brides*?" My voice wavered.

"Did your father never say anything?"

"No," I said, firmly. "I don't think so." Less firm. I thought about Fleur. My dad had always deeply appreciated her creative achievements. He took visitors on tours of our garden, and pulled the car over so she could admire gardens whenever she asked. He adored her, *and* he respected her work.

He loved my mother, but the battered copy of *The House of Brides* had been hidden away in my room since I was old enough to read. He had never once come looking for it. "It's not something we talked about."

With every breath, the cold air rushed in, and I was struggling to stay calm. In, out. In, out. Panic loomed. It was even harder going down the hill than coming up; every time I placed my foot in the mud, it ended up much farther down the hill than I'd intended, so that I was half sliding and half lurching towards the bottom. Tree roots lay just below the sludge and threatened to trip me at every moment.

"I hate to think of people laughing at Elizabeth behind her back," Tom said.

"Why didn't she do something? If that's what she thought?"

"Your mother was very clever. She took all the notebooks, all Elizabeth's notes, with her when she left."

"Max would have known, if Elizabeth was telling the truth. Max would have said something." There was a fire burning across the sea, but as the minutes passed, I felt less certain I would be able to do anything to help. The clock was ticking. I was no closer to the children. I was no closer to finding Daphne.

"No. He didn't believe Elizabeth. She had a history of hysterics," he puffed. "Plus, she liked a drink, even then. Didn't we all! Max thought it was another of Elizabeth's delusions. He didn't know she was out here writing, day and night. The house and its history were her obsessions. Max thought she was just jealous."

Max knew Elizabeth better than any of us, and he didn't believe her. It had to be nonsense. My disbelief turned to anger. I turned to look at Tom and hit a tree root. My knees hit the ground first, and I wasn't quick enough to use my hands to break my fall. The pain barely registered.

"My mother wouldn't do that!" I knew she wouldn't. The mud was spectacular; it covered the lower half of my body almost instantly. Getting up seemed impossible. Everything seemed impossible. Realization was crushing down on me.

Tom reached out a hand. Up close I could see the open pores on his nose, the sweat forming in his moustache. He smelled like Elizabeth. I wrenched my arm out of the bog and let him help me up. "It was a terrible time," he said. "The countryside was in turmoil. She had failed, spectacularly, and lost a lot of money. Caused a lot of problems for Barnsley, and other farmers in the area."

I couldn't see how my mother, with her long silk separates and oversize spectacles, could cause problems for farmers. We started to hobble down the hill, moving more slowly, more carefully now.

Tom sensed my confusion. "Do you not know anything about those times?" he asked. "Your mother poured a lot of money into a rare breed of sheep. She had fancies of becoming a shepherdess. Can you not see where I'm going with this?"

"No." Once again my spectacular lack of interest in current affairs was evident.

"There was a virus. It was years before the foot-and-mouth outbreak, but it was almost as bad. Not only was the flock she brought in from Yorkshire completely infected, but it got into the existing Barnsley flock as well. Shut the farm down for months. The lot of them had to be burned. And those in the surrounding farms. She wasn't a popular lady around here. Elizabeth and Max were heartbroken. She hadn't consulted them at all. Some bloke from Yorkshire had talked her into it."

This flight of fancy, this disregard for other people's feelings, sounded more like the mother I remembered. If I didn't want to go to swimming lessons as a child, then—poof—they were cancelled. School—optional. On a sunny day, we went to the beach or the park, whatever other commitments we might have had scheduled. From a child's perspective, it was delightful; but now, from an adult's, I could see how little respect she had for other people and their emotions and how quickly it could become tiresome. "So she ran away to Australia," I guessed.

Tom's face was sad. "And she took my Elizabeth's book with her."

49

Elizabeth was waiting at the jetty, the motor running. I took a flying leap at the boat, moving as fast as my banged-up knees would allow. "Steady on, or you'll fall in." She took my arm as I came aboard. Tom stopped under the lantern, bent double. He gestured for us to go on.

"Elizabeth." I pulled the fob chain out from under my jacket, about to explain myself.

Elizabeth nodded curtly. The thing in me, the lie that had loosened earlier, unspooled itself more. "You're bigger than your mother," she said, tugging on the cord.

"When you say things like that, I'm not surprised my mother ran away from here."

Elizabeth laughed out loud, a rare rich melodic song, and the engine thrummed into life.

"Where were you? I thought you were going to come to the island to meet me." The release of nervous energy and the emotion of the conversation with Tom had gotten the better of me, and I started to cry. "I thought Daphne might have been on the island."

There was sympathy on Elizabeth's face, and also the slightest look of distaste at my emotional state. "Meryl phoned me and said Leonard refused to make the crossing in the bad weather. Leonard! He would never do such a thing. I should have known right away she was lying." Elizabeth shook her head, shocked at her own gullibility.

The boat was smaller than the one I had come out in. No shelter, no awning. I had fished in a similar boat at Wilsons Prom when I was a child. We called them tinnies, and the only difference between this one and them was the small, tattered Union Jack attached to a slight metal post at the rear. The endless rocking didn't seem to bother Elizabeth, her small body just as agile on water as on land.

As I got my breath back, I looked towards the house. The cover of the storm made it difficult to see clearly, but it looked as if the fire had subsided. Where before bright orange flames had pulsed through the cloud, now there were only dense pockets of grey. *Please let the children be safe.* There was no one on the lawn. They must be behind the house. I hoped they were behind the house. I kept repeating my mantra: *Please let the children be safe.* There was a flash of movement across the grass, and I leaned farther from the jetty, trying to make out the figure.

Elizabeth followed my line of vision. "Leonard has the children."

Relief flooded through me. The children at least were safe.

We were heading away from the island, but not in the direction of the cove with the boathouse and the jetty. Rather, the boat was circling around the headland and up the coast, towards the spot where Max had pulled the car over on the day of our shopping trip.

"Where are we going?" I asked.

"I want to show you something," Elizabeth replied.

It was freezing. The mud was starting to dry in great cold chunks, and every inch of my clothing was saturated. I tried to let go of my worry for a moment.

"Elizabeth. I know what you think my mother did." I could barely talk, my teeth were chattering so fiercely.

She didn't seem surprised. "Bloody Tom. Doesn't

talk to anyone for ten years, and then opens his mouth when it's least required." Her mouth tightened around the words.

"I worked it out myself." *And Tom confirmed it.* "When did you work out who I was?"

Elizabeth ignored me. "We were very close, Tessa and I, once upon a time. I think that's why I was so willing to accept Daphne when she arrived. I missed the sister dynamic. And Daphne was so, well, Daphne. I could have hated her, but I could hate anyone if I put my mind to it, I suppose. She was so fresh and uncomplicated; she had nothing to do with what had come before. I liked that about her. The Summers had been making a mess of the place—and themselves—for generations, and she wasn't caught up in it all." Her face clouded over, and she seemed to remember something. She stopped the motor, and we bobbed in the choppy sea. I could no longer see the island, or Barnsley.

"Why did you think Daphne was on the island?" she asked.

I said another silent apology to Daphne as I unzipped my jacket slightly to retrieve the notebook. Elizabeth shook her head, showed no signs of reaching out for it. "So you're not going to read it?" I asked, incredulous.

All the trouble she had taken to get her hands on the stinking notebook, putting my life—and Leonard's—at risk so I could bring it to her, and she didn't even look at it. It didn't make any sense.

"Read it?" Elizabeth laughed. A puzzled look settled on her face. "Just give me the gist. Where is she? Did you find a password for the cameras?"

"But Daphne—"

"If I know Daphne, it will be a lot of waffle about Max and Meryl and the past. A lot of excitement and fluff. Most of the time Daphne couldn't string two words together."

I didn't agree. Reading the notebook had given me a sense not only of who Daphne really was but also of the story behind *The House of Brides*. The truth behind the mythology. Plus, it didn't add up. Daphne had built a mini empire based on food: cooking it, serving it, but mostly, writing about it.

"What about her cookbooks?"

Elizabeth spun around. Her hair, normally so perfect, had come loose on one side. "Her cookbooks? I wrote every word of those. She could cook like an angel, but could she write? No."

It was too much for me to take in. I couldn't understand what she was saying. Daphne's voice from the notebook was so similar to the friendly tones of her cookbook. *So* Daphne. Elizabeth must have been one talented writer. I remembered the inscription:

For Elizabeth, the real writer in the family.

"How does it feel to have been duped?" Elizabeth's eyes, which had been darting about, fixed on mine. "Hmmm?"

I was lost for words for a moment. Elizabeth was meant to be my ally. The person at Barnsley I could trust. The world tilted slightly, and I hung on to the side of the boat, thinking for a moment it had something to do with the water. She continued. "And how is it different from what you did? Or what your mother did? I'd say fraud is quite the family business."

Elizabeth sighed and flicked her cigarette into a corner, where it joined an already substantial pile of soggy butts. "I worked it out straightaway. But you seemed so convinced no one knew who you were. Even if I hadn't, I would have worked it out soon enough. First there was your name. *Miranda!* Of course Tessa named you after Miranda. She was insufferable during that production of *The Tempest*, wafting around the house, reciting her lines."

I found myself nodding involuntarily. That sounded like something my mother would have done.

"The nanny agency rang the morning we were in Max's study and said they were having trouble finding a candidate so close to Christmas. You're lucky I took that call. And I saw your fob chain," she added.

My hand went to my throat, grabbed hold of the necklace, fearful suddenly that Elizabeth might snatch it from my neck.

"I could go on."

I shook my head. She had made her point.

"You look just like her, once you know. I kept on thinking Max would notice, but he didn't. Too distracted by your behind to even look at your face. Same as always. He doesn't take all the staff to lunch at the Stag's Head, you know." Her head tilted. "Actually, he would probably take Meryl. And Leonard. But there was something off about him taking you."

I blushed and felt grateful she hadn't been there in the bookstore. At the concert. On Christmas morning.

Then a memory flickered across her face. "Where are the eggs?"

Just like her brother, she was prone to erratic conversation.

"The eggs?"

"I asked you to bring the eggs."

I had no idea where I had left the eggs in all the commotion. Or why they were so important. "I don't know," I said.

"Of course you don't know. You're just like her. Only care about yourself. I didn't care about you either, to begin with. I've never been very interested in children, let alone hers. I'd look you up from time to time, make sure you weren't anywhere near Barnsley. Facebook is wonderful for checking you people out. And then you started carrying on with the healthy living nonsense and all the photos." Her voice was heavy with disdain. "The recipes. Smashed avocado. Green goddess omelettes."

I lowered my head in shame. It had never left me, but I had been less burdened by it while I was at Barnsley. Leonard's reaction had been so kind, I had forgotten the vitriol other people felt towards me. And now it came crashing back.

"The photos of food were all right, I suppose. Some of them were quite attractive. You're not bad with the camera. Unless of course someone else took the photos? That would be par for the course." She looked at me suspiciously.

"I took the photos." It was the truth. It wasn't hard to take a good photo; I'd done courses. There were plenty of them around. How to maximize your Instagram profile. How to sell on Instagram. Flat lays. I spent a lot of money on things like that, once upon a time, but I couldn't imagine explaining that to Elizabeth.

"But then you started spouting off about all the benefits of all your food. Making promises about what eating your recipes could do for people. Immune system. Fertility. Acne. You were telling women you could cure their infertility."

She was right. I had only done it once—but I regretted it immediately. I'd taken it down almost straightaway, and thankfully not too many people had seen it. Elizabeth had, though. People always say that your online footprint lasts forever, and I hadn't really understood. I did now. All those claims I made without anyone questioning me, and then one day, someone did. She posted it on Facebook, and then it got reposted, and then a network current affair program picked it up. It wasn't my father's program, not at first. He held on for as long as he could, but in the end the story became too big, and he gave in.

People came out of the woodwork, saying I had made claims on my app about fertility and weight loss and aging and inflammation. They said there was no truth in any of it. Some of my claims were exaggerated, I admit, but some, I thought, were true at the time. Some, though, the smallest, tiniest number, I knew were lies as I wrote them. "I was trying to help."

"Pfffff." Elizabeth narrowed her eyes. In the harsh light of day, she looked older than ever. In my old life, I would have recommended turmeric shots for inflammation and aging. Green juice with kale, carrot, pineapple, and cucumber. I would have told her to quit the booze and get rid of the cigarettes; she had the drawn face of a drinker and feather wrinkles around her mouth from too many inhalations. "Did you really think you were helping? I did some research about your app. You made a lot of money from your lies, didn't you?"

"It's all gone now." It was. All gone. The publisher sued me when it had to pulp the entire print run of my cookbook, and the rest had gone to lawyers. I had one copy hidden away for a time in the future when I might be able to look at it without feeling a wave of nausea. *A Bountiful Life*, by Miranda Courtenay. Even the thought of it brought a familiar wrench in my stomach.

"All those people, conned by you. Feeding your lies with their money. I had to stop you." She paused and looked at me. "You're just like her."

"Stop saying that!" I shouted. Saliva sprayed out of my mouth, the words hurting my throat as they came out. "Stop it."

Elizabeth straightened up. "Anyway, I sorted *that* out." Rain had started up again, smashing down on us, making it hard to hear Elizabeth. She began to shout above the noise.

"What?"

"I put a stop to your lies. I was too late for your mother, but I could do something about you. So I did."

50

"I thought you might have worked it out by now."

I shook my head, blindly. If anything, I was more bewildered than ever. The more I heard from Elizabeth, the less I knew. The truth was floating around me, but I could only snatch at it helplessly, never quite knowing if I had grasped the right bit of information.

Elizabeth. Daphne. Mrs. Mins. The children.

My mother.

It was all too much for me. I wished I had made it out of Barnsley the night before. I wished the tree hadn't come down. By now I could have been sitting in Denise's kitchen, drinking tea and sharing stories about my mother with someone who remembered her fondly. Instead here I was, stuck on a boat with Elizabeth.

Oceans and moors lay between me and home. Oceans and moors lay between me and the nearest bus stop. I could scarcely believe I had been so naive as to trust her. What did she mean, she had put a stop to my lies? The internet had put a stop to my lies. The vicious network that had helped me become someone important had whipped its head around and attacked me. The people who had been my champions, reposting my photos and sharing my links, following me and liking me and commenting and collaborating, had been just as quick to snatch me down from my cyber pedestal. Unless.

She half smiled, proud of her handiwork. "The internet is a real hoot for people like me."

Rage rose inside me. My aunt. My mother's sister. Ruining my life for sport. The dark days following the current affair story were among the worst of my life. Even worse than losing my mother, because this time I was to blame. I'd let my father down. I'd let all my followers down.

And didn't they let me know it! The trolls descended immediately. Some I had known and conversed with online. Others I hadn't. One in particular led the charge. Lizzie Winter. Her name had haunted me, and I spiraled down the internet for days, trying to find her true identity. Now I knew.

Lizzie Winter. Elizabeth Summer.

"I've been following you all these years, wondering if the apple falls far from the tree. It doesn't." She frowned, as if remembering something nasty. "What was in the notebook?"

I swallowed. There was no way I was telling her what I'd seen on the video. After what she'd done to me.

I stared out to sea. The anger had made me mute. Numb. All my life I had wanted attention from my mother's family at Barnsley. More than that, I had wanted love. And yet what Elizabeth had delivered was revenge. Coldhearted and bitter.

"I'll take you back," Elizabeth said, oblivious. Misinterpreting my silence. "Although I'm sure Leonard has the situation under control."

She pushed the handle full throttle, with a renewed focus on the horizon. It shifted and bobbed in the distance, mostly obscured by the rolling ocean. Nausea rose in my belly, and my head throbbed.

The numbness inside me was transformed into something else, a tidal wave of emotion. Childhood loneliness. Resentment at losing my mother. Shame at how my life had turned out. And it manifested into pure, physical rage. A violent alchemy of blame. Hatred of the woman in front of me.

I wanted to hurt her. A cry escaped my mouth, raw and murderous, and I lunged at Elizabeth, the shock flashing on her face as she realized my intent. She moved aside, and the boat tipped. The momentum was too great. I heard Elizabeth cry out as I flew towards the water. The cold was immediate, leaving me stunned. Not knowing where I was. Not knowing I had gone overboard.

Not realizing I was sinking.

51

I t was quiet. .
   So quiet.

For a moment, maybe even longer, I was still, the water swirling in silent bubbles around me. The transition from above water to below had been so sudden, so brutal, that for a few beats I couldn't even comprehend it. And then I started to thrash. I moved my legs and arms so wildly that I was going around in circles, unsure which way was up or down, whether I was going deeper or rising to the surface.

I had been dumped plenty of times in Australia. Big, powerful ocean waves had left me breathless. One time the water had pushed me right down to the sand, leaving my face scraped and bloody. I had always found my way to the surface, though. The bright light of the summer sun had shown me the way, and in one particularly rough episode, a young surfer had pulled me onto his board and paddled me back to the shallows.

Not this time, though. The water around me was dark. My heavy winter clothes dragged me down, negating any natural buoyancy. And the water was cold. Colder than I could have ever imagined.

Panic set in, and I moved my arms and legs harder, my body pulsing in useless circles. I stopped. Then swam towards what I thought was the surface, trying not to consider the possibility that it wasn't. Trying not to think about what had happened to Daphne. That these waters had form.

My chest started to hurt. I closed my eyes, hoping that would somehow reorient me. Something nudged against my shoulder, hard and insistent. Adrenaline, already rushing and strident, pulsed again. I tried not to think about sharks. It nudged again. I opened my eyes and saw dark wood. Coming from above.

I grabbed hold, and pulled. And then it pulled back. In seconds I was at the surface, the water choppy and ferocious but no match for the great mass of air above it. I swallowed, great greedy gasps that were part seawater, part oxygen. My hands stayed tight on the oar, and I swiveled to see Elizabeth, steady and strong on her feet despite the rolling ocean.

"Miranda!" she called, her voice already different. It had lost its edge, its sureness, and in their place was uncertainty and fear. I nodded to show her I was all right. It was as much as I could do.

Years of water safety training came back to me as I treaded water, waiting for Elizabeth to pull me towards the boat. To pull me back to safety. It didn't occur to me until later that she might not have.

But she did.

She pulled me to the boat with a strength that came from years of horse riding, of rowing out to the island when boat engines failed, of climbing up the goat track to the shell house when she got there. But her power was more than physical. It was a strength that came from within—from a series of disappointments I was only just beginning to understand.

Elizabeth took off her thick woolen jacket, put it over my shoulders, and propped me at the stern. Keeping an eye on me, she started the motor and dipped her head slightly, as if trying to see something in the distance. My teeth started to chatter. Soon after, the left side of my body was twitching. It was completely out of my control.

"It's the shock," she said. "It will wear off soon." Her words were comforting. "Daphne shook for an hour after she gave birth. Every time. Check the inside pocket."

I found a small flask in the pocket of Elizabeth's jacket.

"Medicinal." She nodded. "Shame they wouldn't let me give it to Daphne in the birth suite. Would have sorted her out straightaway." My hands were shaking so much I couldn't unfasten the lid. Taking it from me, Elizabeth quickly opened it and handed it back.

The liquid burned in my throat, but the effect was steadying. I coughed. Coughed again. A noxious mix of seawater and brandy came rushing up, and I wasn't quick enough. It spewed up from deep within me, running down Elizabeth's jacket and onto the floor of the boat below, where it sloshed against my boots.

"There now," Elizabeth said. "Better out than in." But she was looking at something else. Hoping to see Barnsley, or another boat, I turned to see what had diverted her attention from my hideous retching. A sheer rock face loomed up out of the ocean in front of me, a wall of impenetrable stone.

"It's pretty conclusive, isn't it?" Elizabeth said softly, turning back to me.

"What? What do you mean?"

"I don't think anyone throws themselves off the edge

of that and expects to live, do you? It's where Gertrude died."

Gertrude Summer. The writer. The American heiress, and my great-grandmother. "It's hard to imagine being that desperate, isn't it?" Elizabeth asked, her eyes searching the rock face as if it might reveal its secrets. "Even in my darkest days, I've never been tempted by that sort of thing. Have you?"

I shook my head, the shakes elsewhere in my body starting to subside. It was true. I just hadn't been. I took a cautious sip of the brandy. My stomach protested slightly, but I registered a softening of the rough edges of my shock. Another small sip, to make sure.

"I don't think Daphne was desperate. She had her problems, just like us. But she had things to look forward to. And that is what makes the difference, isn't it?"

My eyes flicked nervously between the cliff and the boat. Elizabeth. I knew something Elizabeth didn't.

"What do you think happened to Daphne?" The edges of my mouth were dry, threatening to crack in the cold. Licking them only made it worse, and besides, my mouth was just as parched. After all I had just been through, I needed water. Elizabeth laughed, but not the same way she had earlier. This time it was sad, slightly bitter.

"I don't know, but I know she wouldn't have killed herself. And certainly not at sea! That's why I liked her. No complaining. She was almost like one of us." She cast a look towards me—soaking wet and half drowned—and nodded, including me in the family resilience. I nodded back. Hating myself, because despite everything, I somehow still wanted Elizabeth to like me.

"Let's get you home," she said, starting the boat.

52

Elizabeth started talking and didn't stop. It was only later that I realized she did it to keep me awake. That I was at very real risk of slipping into hypothermia and unconsciousness. She knew enough about the women of our family to know that a good story would keep me awake. That we were all storytellers, deep down.

"Agatha hasn't always been in a wheelchair. I suppose you know about the accident. Did you know about Daphne and her Catholicism? It's a dirty secret around here. My father would have dropped dead if he had known Max married a Catholic. He was dead already, though. Luckily." Elizabeth looked twitchy, her brow furrowed as her eyes darted between me and the water in front of us.

I didn't say she had already told me what happened with Agatha, back on my very first morning at Barnsley. Besides, I figured the story would be different this time.

"Daphne came in and out of it. Mostly she liked the look of herself in the mantilla she wore to church when she got the urge. She never passed on an opportunity to try something new if it meant a new outfit. Hunting. Tennis. Sailing. She lasted about five minutes at all of them, but she always looked the part. I think her favourite part of setting up the restaurant was designing the uniforms for the wait staff. She went with some sort of deconstructed Scandinavian smocks in the end. Not my style at all."

My eyes were starting to close, but I felt a little smile form on my lips. Elizabeth was just so . . . Elizabeth.

"So, church. On a Sunday morning you would always hear her car start up nice and early, and she would head to the first service. Repent her sins. The children used to go with her, until Max let them off the hook. Only Agatha, sweet little Agatha, still went along with her. She didn't like to upset anyone. She doesn't like to rock the boat, does she?"

I nodded. I wanted to make a joke about rocking the boat but couldn't find the words. Or the energy to form them. We had no choice but to sit in the relentless rain.

My wet hair was like icicles around my face, but it was still flushed, like I'd been out all day in the sun. My throat ached. My head throbbed.

"Daphne shouldn't have been driving. She was just back from a fresh stint at rehab, and she is always at her worst just after she gets back home. It was early. She liked to go to the early service so she could get back in time to prep for Sunday lunch. It was the biggest sitting of the week for the restaurant.

"Early November, it was. Daphne and I had been up drinking late. Talking about a new cookbook she had plans for. I left her around midnight to go out to the island. It's my favourite time out there, the dead of night. It was calm, so the crossing was easy—it's not always easy in the middle of the night with a skinful of booze. I was in the shell house, working, and I could see that the lights in the restaurant hadn't gone out, so I knew she'd found someone else to party with. There were always transient workers in the restaurant. Lots of Aussies—we put them up in the farm cottages so they'd have somewhere to live. It was cheap labour, and they got experience with a Michelin chef, so it worked out for everyone.

"Problem was, they always brought drugs with them when they came down from London, and Daphne couldn't say no to anything. She liked trying new things, but mostly she didn't want these young cooks to think she was an old fuddy-duddy. She wanted them to think she was like them. She liked to forget about the three children upstairs."

I think I nodded off for a moment, the rocking of the boat and the brandy carrying me to sleep. Elizabeth's hand on my shoulder woke me, and I opened my eyes, hoping to see Barnsley, or the little jetty at the boathouse, but there was nothing. Nothing but water, and her worried face. Talking. Still talking.

"I had a breakthrough that night. The booze does that sometimes; get the amount just right, and it's like creative nirvana. Too little and you fall asleep, too much and you're a waffling lunatic. I hit the sweet spot that night, and I came up with the introduction for the new cookbook. It was framed around the seasons, you see . . ."

I closed my eyes again, remembering that feeling of creativity. I had it the night I came up with the idea for my app. The buzz I got from the idea, the certainty it was the right thing to do, and the energy it created in me. Like I could do anything. That was the feeling I missed the most, the creative buzz. Perhaps Elizabeth and I were more similar than I thought.

"That morning, after very little sleep, Daphne got up. After a big night, she had a lot to confess. The others were all still sleeping when she and Agatha left the house. They were still sleeping when the police knocked on the door a little bit later. There had been a deer on the road. They're culling them now. Too little, too late, I say. Can you imagine, waking up to that kind of news? Max didn't even know they had gone."

My eyes snapped open. It was too horrible to imagine.

Behind her, there was a speck of movement on the water. A boat, perhaps, though I doubted anyone else would be crazy enough to be out in this weather. I shook my head, convinced I must be hallucinating.

"Daphne never forgave herself. The police did tests at the crash site, but she was just under the limit. It was all the other stuff, though, the things they can't test for. Perhaps if she'd had a good night's sleep, she would have been quicker to react, that kind of thing."

"And you still don't think she would have killed herself?" My voice sounded slurred, even to my ears. Like I was still underwater. I tried to think about what I'd seen on the CCTV footage. Of what I'd read in the notebook. My thoughts were foggy, but despite my confusion I remembered that Daphne was scared of Mrs. Mins.

But fear didn't prove anything. And the CCTV footage didn't prove that Daphne *hadn't* killed herself;

it just proved that Daphne went out on the water, and Max and Mrs. Mins could have stopped her. It was too much for me.

"No. She was getting better. She really was. We were finishing the new cookbook, and it was coming along well. It was a culmination of a life's work. A guide to cooking by the seasons. But they will pull the pin on it—without her it's not worth anything. All my work, gone. Again."

We roared along, the waves slightly less ferocious but the wind just as bitter. I thought of the children, hoping they were okay. The urgency to see them pushed through my exhaustion. I needed to see them.

As if reading my thoughts, Elizabeth spoke. Shouted, over the noise of the engine. "Max found a new surgeon in London, someone who thinks they can help Agatha. It's only a matter of a couple more operations, and she might be able to walk again. Despite what the local surgeons said. Daphne will be so pleased when she comes back." For the first time, the smile on Elizabeth's face was genuine, her eyes filled with love. They reminded me of my mother. The way she looked at me.

Their faces blurred together. I saw her, finally, as my mother's sister. I saw she was capable of love, despite everything. I started to understand the losses stacked up in her corner. Her mother. Her sister. Her fertility. Daphne. Maybe even *The House of Brides*. I, more than anyone else, understood that people make mistakes. I, more than anyone else, understood the meaning of forgiveness.

"Elizabeth. I want to tell you something. About Daphne." The words were woolly in my mouth.

Her smile disappeared. She took the boat around a bend, and we pulled into a little cove. We were so close to Barnsley now. By my amateur reckoning, the cove with the boathouse lay just around the next bend. But what I had to say couldn't wait any longer. I had to force myself into lucidity. I pushed Elizabeth's jacket from my shoulders and felt lighter.

The cove was protected from the worst of the weather. Even the colour of the water was different, an azure blue, so bright it seemed almost unnatural after the washed-out ocean. I edged cautiously towards Elizabeth and took her hand, mostly to steady myself. It was as small as a child's, delicate and vulnerable. At the thought of the task ahead, I felt a tightness come back into my body, into my hand on hers.

I told her what Leonard and I had seen on the footage. She gasped and tried to snatch her hand away. Even as the boat rocked steadily, she kept her eyes firmly on one spot on the horizon. Her cheeks were sucked in, and her nostrils flared as if she was making a great effort to control herself. It was only when I put my head on her shoulder that the tears began to roll down her face. I was crying too. But where Elizabeth cried like a movie star, I was a sobbing, heaving mess. The anger and the fear were leaving my body.

"So Max is not a criminal," she said, finally. "I had thought . . ." She stopped. "He's weak and he's damaged, but he's not a criminal." There was relief in her voice.

"He's just a man in a family full of really strong women," I said. Elizabeth snorted. I thought she was crying again, but when I looked, she was laughing. Even with her blotchy eyes and nose red from the cold, she looked more alive than I had ever seen her. I felt a rush of love for her. It took me by surprise, this sudden and urgent rush of affection for someone who moments before I had hated deeply.

There was movement in the corner of my eye. I hadn't been hallucinating after all. It was sailing towards us, at a clip, heading for the same safe harbour we had pulled up in. "There's a boat."

Elizabeth spun around quickly, nearly tipping overboard as she did so. Her eyes squinted for just a second, and then she sighed deeply.

"Jean Laidlaw and the bloody historical society."

53

"Everything all right here, Elizabeth?" Jean shouted from a distance, an ability to project her voice clearly left over from her teaching days.

"All right, Jean." Elizabeth waved. As if what we were doing was normal. As if I wasn't borderline hypothermic. As if both of our faces weren't blotchy from crying. Well, mine anyway. Elizabeth's had two elegant tear tracks.

The boat came closer still, and I could see Jean's face clearly. Worry was etched in the already deep grooves of her face. Strangely, she was dressed like a pirate—or possibly a smuggler. Either way, both she and the man she was with were wearing long johns. Elizabeth didn't comment, just dipped her head slightly to hide her red eyes.

"You didn't tip her out, did you, Elizabeth?" There was a moment's silence. "Because I wouldn't blame you." A sharp look in my direction. Disapproval. It wasn't just the teacher in her either, it was deeper, more like revulsion. "She doesn't look like her mother, does she?"

"No, she doesn't. Not to start with. There's signs of her, though, as you get to know her. She laughs the same. Has similar hands." Elizabeth was comparing me in a *positive* way to my mother. It felt good. Even still, I wanted to get back to Barnsley. I *needed* to get back to Barnsley. I felt an almost visceral pull towards the children, and we weren't getting any closer.

"Jean," I asked gingerly, "could I possibly hop in your boat?" It was bigger, and sturdier. It had a cabin. They all ignored me.

"What are you doing out on a day like this?" Elizabeth asked.

"Rehearsal."

"Nothing stops you, does it?"

"It didn't stop the smugglers either."

"Quite right." They nodded in agreement.

"It's mostly cleared, anyway," Jean said, looking towards the sky. She was right; while Elizabeth and I were distracted, the rain had stopped. There was even a small patch of blue sky between the storm clouds.

"Jean," I repeated, my voice no longer quite so calm, "could you please take me back to Barnsley House? There's been a fire. I'm worried about the children."

"It's over. I heard it on the radio." She spoke to Elizabeth. "The house will be fine. Only minimal damage to the plaster, apparently. The drapes will need to be replaced."

"What about the children?"

"All fine." Jean and Elizabeth exchanged a look.

"Leonard?"

"Fine."

"Huge relief."

"Yes."

The breath left my body, the anxiety floating away. Leonard had saved the day, it seemed. I doubted I would get any more information.

"What are you doing out here, Elizabeth?" Jean asked. "Nothing good can come in this weather. If it's about the girl, we can sort it out on dry land."

"Sort what out? The story about the book?" I snapped, my desperation to get back making me edgy.

"The story?" Jean said as she brought her boat closer; the sea was calmer, and she was able to come right alongside us. The man behind her came into focus. It was Simon the chemist, looking apprehensive. I didn't blame him. He'd signed up for a light smuggling reenactment, not a showdown at sea. "Miranda, you have a chance to put your mother's wrong to right."

"You can't prove anything." My voice wasn't as confident now.

"Elizabeth can't, but you can," Jean said softly.

"She's lying." I said as I looked at Elizabeth, but she wouldn't look at me. Her eyes followed the water sloshing up and down the bottom of the boat.

"I taught both of the girls, Miranda," Jean said. "As a teacher, you know who has brains and who has a certain something that will take them much further than brains ever will. I'm sure you know who was who in your family. There's no way your mother could have written that book."

"Why didn't you do something earlier?"

"It was too late when I found out, and Elizabeth wouldn't talk about it, to begin with."

"My mother *was* a writer." Her whole life had centered around having written *The House of Brides*. Radio interviews, the local go-to expert on British social history, cover quotes on other people's books. And yet she had never published another word.

"Your mother was a fraud, dear."

It made sense. Shocking, brutal sense.

Just like me. We were cut from the same cloth, my mother and I. I had deceived thousands of people, and so had she. I had deceived those closest to me, and so had she. I had come to Barnsley seeking a connection with my mother, and I had found one. It was not something to be proud of.

Elizabeth finally spoke. "At first I was angry. I blamed everyone else. I blamed your mother for taking my book. I blamed Max for not believing me. I blamed myself for writing the bloody book in the first place and unleashing all the demons. I blamed Tom, because I didn't know if he was telling me the whole truth. Your mother did me a favour by stealing that book. She had to deal with the fallout. And she could never come back. I could never have left Barnsley like she did."

"She couldn't come back because of the sheep, not the book."

Elizabeth raised an eyebrow. "And who told you that—Tom?"

I nodded.

"Tessa wouldn't worry about a thing like sheep. She was in love with Tom."

I snorted. Nearly laughed.

"It might be hard for you to believe, but Tom was quite the catch in his youth." On the other boat, Jean nodded in agreement. Simon, at least, had the good sense to look surprised. "Tom spent a lot of time with our family, when we were growing up. Max, Tom, and

I were as thick as thieves. Tessa was the little sister. She mistook his kindliness for affection."

"She hadn't seen a lot of it," Jean added.

Elizabeth looked at Jean sharply.

"We thought she had just run off for a couple of days. She'd done that before, run away from school, run away on holidays. After a couple of days, I discovered that my disk was missing. Then Tom admitted that there had been a moment between them, and he had rebuffed her advances."

"And then there was the postcard from Australia," Jean shouted from the other boat. I looked at Elizabeth.

"And that was that," she said.

"And that was that," I whispered to myself. I believed her. The missing pieces of my mother's life were floating around me, threatening to fall into place like part of a monstrous and unfamiliar picture. Other pieces circled, still not seeming to fit anywhere.

"Then Daphne came," Elizabeth said, "and I thought it was all going to be all right. I thought Max had given up on Meryl, that the house-of-brides tradition would continue. Remarkable women marrying into the Summer family."

"But he hadn't." I was beginning to see where this was going.

"No. Not really. He had given up on marrying her,

but he had never stopped loving her. He loved Daphne, but she never stood a chance against Meryl. Against all that history. Not in the end."

"Could we go to the caves now?" Simon called out from his side of the boat.

Jean looked at him sharply. "We won't be missing this, Simon," she hissed. "Elizabeth has waited too long to tell her side of the story. We'll be reenacting this one day, you mark my words."

"What do you want, though?" I threw my arms as wide as I could muster, to indicate the boat trip, the cliff face, Barnsley. Me. Everything.

Elizabeth sat down. She slumped slightly, her narrow shoulders not rigorously held back for once. "I thought I wanted revenge. I thought I wanted credit for the book. I thought I wanted you to know what it felt like, to have your passion taken away from you."

"And now?" I asked quietly, sensing that something had changed. Finally understanding what had made her do what she had done to me. Seeing that she was telling the truth.

"Now, I just want that book to stop hurting people."

"Well, that's sorted, then," Jean said. She motioned to Simon to come closer. "If it's all right with you, Elizabeth, I'll take Miranda back to the house. She's looking a bit peaky." Feeling light-headed, I held out my hand to Jean, ready to leap across towards her. Towards warmth. And then I looked back at Elizabeth. My mother's sister.

She nodded. We were so close to home now.

"It's all right, Jean," I said, pulling my hand back. "Elizabeth will take me."

Jean looked at both of us, and smiled. Ever so slightly. It would have been barely noticeable if her face had not been so stern before.

Elizabeth's voice cut through my thoughts. "Jean, we're looking for Daphne. She's been missing for days." Elizabeth explained that Daphne had gone missing from Barnsley over a week before. That we thought she had gone to a friend's, to the village, to London. She hadn't come back though, and we were fearing the worst.

"Over Christmas?" Jean raised her eyebrows.

"You know Daphne."

Jean Laidlaw nodded grimly but could barely conceal her excitement at the prospect of crisis management. She immediately barked directions at Simon and headed towards the cabin and the radio. "Don't you worry," she called over her shoulder. "We'll get a search party together in no time."

I waited until Jean and Simon had sailed off towards town. With the weak English sunshine poking through the clouds above us, Elizabeth and I sat quietly, side by side. Every part of me was desperate for a hot shower, a cup of tea. Sleep. I took her hand, pretended I didn't feel uncomfortable. Pretended I didn't feel her recoil. I placed my other hand on top. I tried to do what I thought Daphne might have done, tried to channel her warmth and vitality. The good parts. "We'll find her," I said, and Elizabeth smiled sadly.

54

Some places get into your blood. Barnsley is in mine, now. It's one of the things that my mother handed down to me, alongside an aversion to the truth and an impulsive nature. I'm working on the last two, but I'm happy to keep the Barnsley connection strong, for as long as they all let me.

My friends would call it a #happyplace. It's more than that, though. It's a deep contentment, a sense of belonging. A breathing out and a relaxing of the shoulders. When I first arrived, it felt full of tension and sadness, but just like everything else humans throw at it, Barnsley cast off the melancholy. Now I know how warm the golden stone of the house feels in the summer sunshine. I hear the calling of the gulls and the splashing of the sea. I see the vast green of the lawn, the gardens in full bloom. Summer at Barnsley is heaven. Just like everybody said.

They found Daphne's body the afternoon of the fire. After the storm. Washed up in a nearby cove. The police came and questioned us all. They watched the CCTV and read the notebook. There was a full autopsy. Daphne's toxicology was off the charts. Accidental death by drowning was the verdict. She was killed by the thing she most feared, and it wasn't Mrs. Mins.

Elizabeth and I talked about everything after the fire, after the incident on the boat. I had come down with the flu quite badly, but Elizabeth insisted on taking me out to the shell house again once I was feeling a bit better. She told me she wanted to explain herself. She tucked me into the camp bed with blankets and a hot water bottle, and it didn't smell as bad as I remembered. As I lay there, she pulled out paper after paper, flicked through books, read letters aloud to me. It was a catharsis a lifetime in the making.

It turned out that Elizabeth had written every day since my mother left. She had saved reams of paper, all painstakingly written out by hand and then retyped on an old manual typewriter. There were novels, amendments to *The House of Brides*, the beginnings of a memoir. One of her half-finished manuscripts was called *Hereditary Sin*, and from what I could tell, it was loosely based on me. She snatched that one away quickly, with an apologetic smile.

And there was a file jammed with papers. Hundreds of rejection letters. All ending differently but saying the same thing.

We are sorry to say that your book does not suit our list at this time.

Sadly, we are not taking on any new clients unless we are completely passionate about their work.

You write very well, but not well enough, I'm afraid.

Perhaps you would like to resubmit in the future.

Some of them had been annotated by Elizabeth: white-hot pulses of rage scrawled in lead pencil. I didn't blame her for her anger. Why should her sister have all the literary success, while day after day Elizabeth slogged away, somehow unable to get a break, even though she could write as well as anyone else?

Every morning, she told me, she would fortify with a strong nip and then head over water and land, making the long trek to the post office to collect the mail. Every day anticipating good news, or perhaps just some encouragement, and every day returning home again via the pub, despondent and then just plain drunk. Eventually the rejections came by email, and she could start drinking straightaway, in the comfort of her own home. The only light in her life was Daphne and the cookbooks she wrote with her. Without any recognition. It's no wonder she got angry. I forgive her now.

The children are looking stronger with every day. Their skin is less sallow, their hair shiny and fair from the sun. They spend hours playing on the sand and in the swimming pool. Sophia seems to have regressed years, and is playing like a child; Robbie films everything with his GoPro. Boarding school is off the agenda for now. Agatha's surgery at Easter went well, and she is moving around with only a crutch. In time, even that will go.

It's not the day to do this, but I have been waiting all week for the right time, and it never arrives. I want to do it before tonight, before the first guests arrive and a new chapter at Barnsley House begins. I find Max in the garden of the cottage, where he lives with Mrs. Mins. I still can't call her Meryl.

"Max." He looks up, alarmed. Direct conversation is something we have mostly avoided since I revealed my identity to him. We have communicated in abstracts or through the children. His embarrassment floats off him in subtle waves. "I have something for you."

Embarrassment is replaced by fear. His Adam's apple moves in his throat, betraying his discomfort. The children's voices carry up from the pool below, and I wish I was with them. They are in good hands with

Juliet and Ophelia, though. I wish I were anywhere but alone in this garden, with Max. In desperation, I reach for my bag. My hands find the velvet box immediately; after days of checking, my fingers hardly need to be told. Max instantly recognizes it; before he can stop himself, his hands dart out to touch it. I fumble. The ring box, small and unmistakable, is revealed. "Why do you have this? Where did you get this?" His voice is firm, the vowels clipped. Formal.

Of all the things he could have asked, this, to me, is the least important. "I found it. In your bathroom."

"I thought the ring was lost forever," is what he says when he finally speaks.

"I found it in a pill packet in your bathroom when I was looking for medicine for Robbie."

"Meryl found that ring once before," he says, ignoring me. His skin is pale now, under his tan.

"I thought you might want the ring, for . . ." I can't bring myself to say her name.

"My mother threw it in the ocean, down in the cove. Meryl was swimming and found it." It's an abridged version, but still, it matches up with Daphne's story.

"We thought you might like it . . . for Meryl." There. I had said it. It felt stiff, foreign.

"We?"

"Elizabeth and I."

"The consolation prize?" he asked. There was sadness in his voice, but not the bitterness I was expecting. It had been tough for him, to relinquish control of Barnsley to Elizabeth and myself. He didn't really have a choice, though, not once we all saw the CCTV footage. Not once we all had a chance to go over the accounts.

"I think the Stag's Head was the consolation prize."

Max allowed himself to smile a little. "Elizabeth would probably say it was Meryl."

The sun was behind him, so I couldn't see his face, only feel the intensity of his gaze. "Elizabeth never liked Mrs. Mins," I agreed.

Max shook his head, laughed sadly. "No, that's wrong. She hated Meryl."

"Yes." It was true. Elizabeth had said as much.

"It started before that." Max took the ring box in his hand. Opened it, and stared at the ring inside. "Elizabeth was terrified I was going to marry Meryl long before Daphne came on the scene. She didn't think Meryl was good enough. She didn't think Meryl had what it took to be a Summer wife. Elizabeth talked me out of asking Meryl to marry me. She told me to find someone new. I was too young to know my own mind." It *was* impossible to disagree with Elizabeth; I had learned that lately as we argued over menu plans, room rates, and public relations strategies.

"When I brought Daphne home, Elizabeth loved her straightaway. She would have loved anyone who wasn't Meryl, I think. From the first, they were in each other's pockets. I thought she would die of happiness when Daphne asked for help with her recipes. They loved the same things: Barnsley, cooking, booze. I couldn't get a look in most of the time."

"So that's why—"

"Yes," he said sadly. "I didn't go back to Meryl until after Agatha's accident. Until there was no chance of saving my marriage."

I had one more question I hadn't asked Max. I hadn't had the nerve.

"What happened between you and my mother?" It was the final piece of the puzzle for me, really. The last obstacle between my old life and a new life at Barnsley.

"At first, I was angry about the sheep."

I sighed, much more loudly than I had intended. Possibly even rolled my eyes.

"I know, I know. It doesn't seem like much, but there was a lot of bad blood in the village about it."

"And then?"

"And then the book came out. And after what she

wrote about my mother—our mother—the sheep just paled in comparison."

I didn't say anything. It wasn't up to me to reveal Elizabeth's secrets. She had tried to tell him, once upon a time, and he hadn't believed her. Maybe that really was for the best.

The past was past, as my father said. As he had reminded me on the phone, when I told him I was going to stay on for a bit.

Dad had sounded contemplative then. I worried that I had upset him, just when we were starting to repair our relationship. But later that night he emailed me an A. D. Hope poem, "The Death of the Bird," though with the internet situation, I hadn't discovered it until days later. The poem had brought my mother solace during her dying days, he wrote, and as I read the second verse, I felt the same comfort.

Year after year a speck on the map, divided
By a whole hemisphere, summons her to come;
Season after season, sure and safely guided,
Going away she is also coming home.

With the poem, Dad had given me the gift of my mother's blessing, and his own, to move on with my life, reassuring me that making a home for myself at

Barnsley would not come at the cost of the one I already had.

Max was waiting for me to respond.

"That seems fair," I said finally. I touched my necklace, remembering how it felt on my mother's neck when she cuddled me. Holding on to the good memories.

Max played with the ring, holding it up to the sunshine, as if to see if it was real.

"I knew she wouldn't have thrown it away. For all her faults, Daphne wasn't cruel." His voice cracked, and he stopped talking, his fingers absently stroking the worn felt of the ring box. "Daphne had her problems, but she was a genius with food. I adored her. She deserves her place in that book."

"She had her own books."

Max looked shocked, and then he nodded. "You're right. She had her own books."

"It's better that way," I said. Max's eyes mirrored my feelings of relief and sadness.

I left him sitting in the sunshine and returned to the main house. Elizabeth and Leonard were setting up great long tables under the shade of the wisteria. There were overflowing buckets of big, blousy dahlias everywhere, ready to be arranged by Fleur. She and Dad would be down any minute. The view from the terrace made me stop, even though I saw it every day. Even though it was home to me now.

"It's going to be so beautiful." I sighed.

Elizabeth raised an eyebrow. "There's a lot to do before it's beautiful, Miranda. Here, Leonard, get on the other end of this. Hurry up, we haven't got all day." She picked up the end of a table before Leonard even had a chance to get to the end. He smiled and winked at me.

"I saw Max," I said, grabbing a linen tablecloth from the pile and shaking it over the table. "I gave him the ring."

"Good riddance," Elizabeth snapped. "That ring's been nothing but trouble." Her own thin gold band flashed in the sunshine.

"I think it's quite beautiful," I said, remembering how I felt when I first found it. I'd never seen a stone like it before.

"Well, you won't be getting a ring like that if you keep carrying on with him." She gestured in Leonard's direction.

Leonard shook his head, unable to contain a laugh. "She's right, you know."

I picked up two bottles of chilled mineral water from the ice boxes, went to Elizabeth, and threw my arms around her.

"Let's not talk about rings and brides anymore. Tonight's about us. The Summer women." We had worked hard, it was true. All through the spring we had painted and cleaned and dusted and gardened, Leonard and Elizabeth and Tom and I.

We had planned a new menu for the restaurant, respectful to Daphne but with a nod towards my passions. To healthy eating and wellness. To plants and fruit and raw ingredients. We had the dodgy internet fixed, and I dipped my toe back into social media, tentatively at first, and then with great gusto. It didn't control me anymore, though; once my work was done for the day, I simply logged off and forgot about it.

Tonight's opening was going to tip us over the edge in terms of followers. The place was going to be filled with influencers and Instagrammers, bloggers and journalists. I was happy to let them do their thing, and I'd do mine.

Finally Elizabeth put her arms around my waist. She was getting better at physical contact, I had to say. "To Daphne," Elizabeth said, raising her glass bottle.

I raised mine in response. "The last of the brides."

We clinked the necks of the bottles together, a sister and a daughter standing together on the lawn at Barnsley, remembering the women who had come before us, imagining the women we would become.

Acknowledgements

Firstly, I am hugely grateful to my agent, Rob Weisbach. Thank you for agreeing to read my manuscript, for offering such insightful and transformative advice, and for guiding me on every step of this amazing journey.

A massive thank-you to Sara Nelson for embracing my book with such gusto. Your enthusiasm and perceptive comments have been incredible, and it is an honour to work with you.

Having a background in publishing, I am well aware of the tireless work that goes on behind the scenes in sales and marketing and I thank everyone at Harper-Collins for every single time you read, support, and recommend my book. Special mention to Mary Gaule for holding my hand through the process of being a debut author, and to Miranda Ottewell for a precise eye and unequivocal comments during the copy-editing process.

Closer to home, I'd like to thank Kate Daniel for reading an early manuscript and giving me very handy feedback at a time when I most needed it, and Olivia Buxton for her calm and practical advice.

Thank you to my writing gang, Lisa Ireland, Vanessa Carnevale, Anna George, and Kirsty Manning, who have provided writerly chat, endless laughs, and ongoing encouragement. Special thanks to Sally Hepworth for repeated readings of manuscripts and never-ending generosity. It really is my treat.

Many dear friends and family have encouraged me through the long gestation of this book, but I'd especially like to thank the Chisholm and Cockram families. My parents, Rosanne and Robert Chisholm, and my brothers, Jack and Sam, have supported my writing from the early days of *Boscobel News*, and my sister, Anna, inspires me every day.

Very special thanks to my beloved Alice and Ed, who wished on so many dandelions for me.

Finally, and mostly, to Wally—who continues to believe in me and always, always encourages me to follow my dreams. I could not have written this book without you. I hope you like it.

About the Author

JANE COCKRAM was born and educated in Australia, where she studied journalism at the Royal Melbourne Institute of Technology, majoring in literature. After postgraduate studies in publishing and communication at the University of Melbourne, she worked in sales for Pan Macmillan and then as a fiction buyer at Borders, fulfilling a childhood dream of reading for a living. Cockram spent a year living in the West Country of England, where *The House of Brides* is set, and still daydreams about returning. In the meantime, she resides in Melbourne with her husband and two children. *The House of Brides* is her debut novel.

THE NEW LUXURY IN READING

We hope you enjoyed reading
our new, comfortable print size and found it
an experience you would like to repeat.

Well – you're in luck!

HarperLuxe offers the finest in fiction and
nonfiction books in this same larger print size and
paperback format. Light and easy to read, HarperLuxe
paperbacks are for book lovers who want to see
what they are reading without the strain.

For a full listing of titles and
new releases to come, please visit our website:
www.HarperLuxe.com